The four of them stared down at the skeleton for a moment before the photographer slipped out. Siobhán could hear him coughing in the dairy barn, as if trying to expel the images from his body.

Her gaze fell to the branches and brambles that had been used to fill in the pit. "Shine the light on the branches for me once more, will ya?" James swiveled the torch back to the branches. The top ones all sported bright green leaves and new buds. "Someone has recently been tending this pit," she said, pointing to the fresh leaves. "Covering it up."

"Tending a grave," Macdara said.

"Who would do such a thing?" the photographer said. He had returned without warning, making them all jump.

"A killer," Siobhán said. "A killer would do such a thing . . ."

Books by Carlene O'Connor

Irish Village Mysteries

MURDER IN AN IRISH VILLAGE

MURDER AT AN IRISH WEDDING

MURDER IN AN IRISH CHURCHYARD

MURDER IN AN IRISH PUB

MURDER IN AN IRISH COTTAGE

MURDER AT AN IRISH CHRISTMAS

MURDER IN AN IRISH BOOKSHOP

MURDER ON AN IRISH FARM

CHRISTMAS COCOA MURDER
(with Maddie Day and Alex Erickson)

CHRISTMAS SCARF MURDER
(with Maddie Day and Peggy Ehrhart)

A Home to Ireland Mystery

MURDER IN GALWAY

MURDER IN CONNEMARA

A Country Kerry Mystery

NO STRANGERS HERE

Published by Kensington Publishing Corp.

Murder on an Irish Farm

CARLENE O'CONNOR

Kensington Publishing Corp.
www.kensingtonbooks.com

To farmers and falconers, what fascinating worlds!

Acknowledgments

Thank you to my editor, John Scognamiglio, and my agent, Evan Marshall, for the continued support they offer with each book. Thank you to all the staff at Kensington Publishing; shout-out to Larissa Ackerman and Michelle Addo for all the fabulous events and publicity opportunities they offer us. From the copy editors to the cover designers, it takes a village, and this is indeed a special one. Thank you to Kevin Collins for indulging all my slurry-pit conversations and adding insight. And thank you to my mother, Pat, who always gives me little gems to add to the story. Thank you, Caroline Lennon, for bringing my stories to life through your award-winning audio narrations. And thank you, readers. I couldn't continue this without you.

Chapter 1

The big day was here, June 16 at half nine in the morning, in the village of Kilbane, County Cork, Ireland, where it seemed the entire town had flocked to Saint Mary's, the gorgeous collegiate church with the five-light windows, to witness and celebrate the marriage of Detective Sergeant Macdara Flannery and Garda Siobhán O'Sullivan. And what a grand day it was: the sun was shining down on them, and the forecast was more of the same. Given their reception was going to be held outdoors at the remains of the Dominican priory, or "the abbey," as most folks in Kilbane called it, Siobhán couldn't have asked for a better day. A day that took ages planning, and loads of money, would pass in the blink of an eye, but would be remembered and celebrated for the rest of their lives. *I do.* He would say it; she would say it. Siobhán O'Sullivan and Macdara Flannery would be wed. in less than an hour. The Mister and Missus, Herself and Himself, the wedded bliss, the old ball and chain. Then why did it not feel real?

"Hold still," Gráinne said, jerking Siobhán's head back and tightening her grip on Siobhán's auburn locks. Siobhán would have regretted allowing Gráinne to fix her up, but even the regret was futile; saying "no" would have meant years of resentment from her younger, stylish sister. The dressing room in Saint Mary's was suffocating, and Gráinne had every inch crammed with sprays, brushes, gels, tweezers, perfumes, patches, and pins. It was a full-on beauty assault.

The emerald tiara given to Siobhán by her siblings was on top of her head and secured with so many pins Siobhán was half expecting to receive incoming messages from alien spacecrafts. She was probably going to have a mad headache before the day was done, but it was a stunning addition to her attire, and although the emeralds in the tiara were not real, the one in her engagement ring was, and so were the studs shining from her ears. They had belonged to her mam, Naomi O'Sullivan. *Something borrowed*. And tucked into her bodice was a blue pin her father, Liam, had worn as a member of his hobby club collecting and trading model trains. *Something blue*. This way her parents were with her in spirit, and she knew they were looking down from heaven, and surely, they were thrilled with the union. Siobhán O'Sullivan had made a lot of mistakes in her young life, and would continue to do so, but Macdara Flannery would never be one of them.

"It doesn't feel real."

She felt a sharp pinch on the back of her arm and yelped. Gráinne laughed. "How's it feel now, pet?"

Siobhán shook her head and stared at herself in the mirror, feeling beautiful but wondering if the cosmetics were a little *too much.* She was terrified to ask her sister to ease up. She couldn't afford to get into a row. "Make sure he still recognizes me when you're done." She smiled to soften the message in case Gráinne took the comment as a first strike.

"You'll look so good, he'll marry you anyway," Gráinne replied. "Now sit still."

Siobhán sighed, looked at her eyes illuminated by dark lashes and eyeliner and shadow. They did look stunning, even if they belonged to someone else, someone with an affinity for glamour. Gráinne was trying to turn Siobhán into a version of herself. Siobhán's hair was in curls and piled on top her head, with tendrils hanging down. She wasn't even wearing her wedding dress yet, and already the corset and tights alone were cutting into her skin. Perhaps they should have eloped after all. A short ceremony in a comfortable dress, with a stop at the chipper, and she would have been happy out.

"Woah," said Ann, the youngest O'Sullivan girl, as she careened into the tiny room, her emerald dress swirling around her heels as she came to an abrupt stop. "Would you look at dat." Siobhán was thinking the same thing about Ann as they studied each other in the mirror through their heavily made-up eyes. Three beautiful women. Ann with her stylish blond bob, Gráinne with dark, shiny locks fashionably straightened, and Siobhán the redhead—although technically, her hair was auburn. But it was Ann that Siobhán couldn't look away from. She looked way too beautiful and womanly for a girl just shy of sixteen. Siobhán had an irrational urge to take a wet cloth and wipe away all the make-up on Ann's young face. But if she did, there would be war.

"You look lovely," Siobhán said to Ann instead.

"You look . . . woah," Ann replied.

"You're both gorgeous," Gráinne said: "You're welcome."

Siobhán turned to Ann. "Was that a good 'woah' or a bad 'woah'?"

Ann shrugged. "I dunno." She crossed her eyes and stuck out her tongue. "Just messin'. You look gorgeous. I don't even recognize ya!"

Siobhán closed her eyes and imagined what life would be like without siblings. *Bliss.* Gráinne pinched Siobhán again until she opened her eyes, then Gráinne tilted her sister's head back as she loomed over her. "Do you think you need a touch more eye shadow?"

"No," Siobhán and Ann said in unison. Noise filtered in from the church, the murmurs of friends and family. Maria and Aisling, her maid of honor and bridesmaid (along with Gráinne and Ann), were dressed and in the church, helping to usher people in. The bridesmaid dresses were a lovely shade of emerald green, and the groomsmen—Macdara had asked her brothers to do the honor—would all have matching bowties.

Siobhán's stomach tingled, and a smile broke out on her face. It spread to Gráinne and Ann.

Siobhán held out a hand to each sister, and soon all hands were clasped, squeezing and bonding. It was a mental snapshot Siobhán knew she'd remember the rest of her life, the three O'Sullivan lasses grinning like eejits in the mirror. Ann stuck out her tongue again, and tears welled in Siobhán's eyes.

"Don't you dare start the waterworks," Gráinne said. "You'll ruin my artistry."

"Right, so." Siobhán took a deep breath and thought about non-sentimental things. Who was at the garda station right now? Their newest member, Garda Aretta Dabiri, would look after things. It was astounding how quickly she was turning out to be a valuable member of the garda family. Aretta planned on popping in at some point during the ceremony to share in the good wishes and enjoy some food and drink from the reception. Why did it feel like there was someone they'd forgotten to invite? This time when Siobhán's stomach tightened, it was from worry.

"Let's get you into that dress," Gráinne said. "It's nearly showtime."

It did feel a bit like a show, one where Siobhán was worried she was going to flub her lines. Siobhán stood as Gráinne and Ann reached for the dress. It had been a special order, a creamy satin dress that had come close to Siobhán's liking, then had been transformed by their dear friend Bridie into something out of a fairy tale. She had removed the sleeves so it wrapped around Siobhán's shoulders, revealing more cleavage than Siobhán usually flashed, but nothing that would incite chins to wag. The bodice was framed in tiny white pearls, and the bottom of the dress flared out in a tulle skirt. A lovely emerald satin ribbon would cinch her at the waist. As she prepared to step into it, Siobhán felt the moment in her bones, the absolute joy of the here and now. She could hear her da's voice, feel his hug: *I love the bones of ya.*

I love you too, Da. I know you're with me. . . .

"I swear on me grave, I'll box you in the ears if you start the waterworks," Gráinne said.

Siobhán bit her lip and nodded.

"You can cry all you like after the photos are taken."

Photos. The photographer. She'd nearly forgotten all about him. "Has he arrived?" she asked.

"I'll check," Ann said.

"Help me squeeze her into the dress first," Gráinne said.

"Squeeze me?" Siobhán said. "There's no need to be squeezing me." She'd stayed away from curried chips and sugar for an entire month. Her sisters each held a side, and Siobhán stepped into the dress. They gracefully pulled it up and zipped it up, and as she'd attested, there was no squeezing to be done. They twirled her around, and for a moment even Gráinne was speechless. Gráinne reached for the long veil that would attach to the back of the tiara. Siobhán was nearly giddy with adrenaline as it was securely attached. Gráinne and Ann spread the veil behind her, then stepped away to have a look.

"Gorgeous," they all three said in unison.

Ann whirled around and zipped out of the

room. Siobhán bit her lip and thought of *horrible, horrible* things to keep her eyewater from leaking. She turned and picked up the bouquet of wild-flowers sourced by the local shop and dressed up with white roses and baby's breath with an emerald ribbon. They were sublime. Everything was absolutely picture-perfect.

"I'm ready," Siobhán said with a nod to Gráinne and with more confidence than she felt. "Tell everyone I'm ready."

A few minutes later, Ann skidded back into the room and looked everywhere but directly at Siobhán.

"What?" Siobhán said as her heart fluttered with a tinge of worry. "Is it the photographer?"

"No, he's here," Ann said. "He wants to know if you want some shots of you getting ready."

"I'm ready," she said. "I'm already ready."

"I could start all over," Gráinne said with boundless enthusiasm.

Siobhán shook her head. They were acting squirrely. "What is going on?"

"It's James," Ann said.

"James? What about James?" The eldest of the O'Sullivan Six. He'd been a bit mopey lately, since breaking up with his fiancée, Elise, and moving back from Waterford. He'd thrown himself into a new job, working as an apprentice with a few lads who restored old homes. It sounded like a fascinating job, and she was dying to hear more about it, but he'd been impossible to pin down for a chat.

"He's probably on his way," Gráinne said.

"On his way?" Siobhán could hear the panic in

her voice. "He's not here?" She did not want to be browned off on her wedding day, especially with her older brother.

Gráinne held up her mobile. "I've left a million messages."

Nervous looks were exchanged among the sisters. James was a recovering alcoholic. But he'd been sober for years. He wouldn't choose Siobhán's wedding day to relapse, would he? Not that addiction was a choice. And he'd suffered a breakup. Now he was supposed to celebrate love. Was that why he'd made himself scarce lately? What if he wasn't working at all? Had he been drinking for days, and Siobhán hadn't been paying attention?

"Father Kearney is pacing," Ann said. "He said to remind you he's on a tight schedule."

"I see." Father Kearney had warned them he had a busy summer. There had been quite a bit of back-and-forth about the wedding date, and when this slot had finally opened up, he had let them know in no uncertain terms that they would be on a tight schedule. A baptism was scheduled as soon as the ceremony was finished. And they had assured him they would respect that. She could not start her marriage off by breaking a promise to the parish priest. Siobhán gathered her dress and headed for the door.

"What are you doing?" Gráinne said, literally throwing herself in front of Siobhán.

"I'm going out there."

"You can't see Macdara before the walk up the aisle."

Siobhán stopped. "Don't be silly. We make our own luck. And it's nearly time for the ceremony."

Just then the door flew open, and her brother Eoin stepped in, looking handsome in his tux. Behind him the youngest O'Sullivan, Ciarán, clad in an adorable tux of his own—he was getting so tall—was clutching a violin and sweating profusely. He was going to play a song for the wedding. Siobhán wasn't thrilled about it; the last time she had heard him play, it had sounded like cats falling from trees.

Eoin looked at Siobhán and gave a nod. "Not the worst-looking bride I've ever seen," he said with a wink.

"Thank you," she said, giving him a gentle shove.

"James isn't here, Father Kearney is ready to bolt, and Macdara wants to know what you want to do." Eoin's words came out in a rush; unlike Gráinne's and Ann's hemming and hawing, he seemed to believe that bad news should be delivered in a single breath.

Siobhán gathered her dress. "Let's start the wedding."

"Without James?" her siblings asked in unison.

Siobhán stared at the faces of her brood, feeling the pressure to make the right decision. "I take it everyone has been trying to reach him?"

"We've all called him," Gráinne said. "And texted. He's not answering."

"We've given him long enough." She had no control over this. It was not her fault, and maybe it wasn't his fault either, but there was nothing to be done. Later they would drink champagne, clink glasses, and laugh about how James had missed one of the biggest days of her life. "It's grand. It's grand, it's grand, it's grand."

"The more you say that, the less I believe it," Gráinne said.

Eoin stepped forward. "I can walk you down the aisle."

As the oldest male, James had agreed to walk Siobhán down the aisle. A flicker of doubt gnawed at her. He wouldn't miss this. He wouldn't.

"I'll tell the organist to start." Eoin whirled around and tapped Ciarán on the shoulder. "Are you ready?"

Ciarán nodded, swallowed, then looked at Siobhán. "You look really beautiful," he said.

Gráinne poked her in the side. "Do. Not. Cry."

Siobhán took a deep breath, then bit the side of her lip. *Showtime.*

Chapter 2

Siobhán stood at the end of the aisle and gazed at Macdara, who, hands clasped nervously in front of him, stood next to Father Kearney. The husband and wife-to-be locked eyes. He was stunningly handsome in his tuxedo, his sky-blue eyes pinned on her, his usually messy hair carefully combed, his lopsided smile doing double time, making her heart dance in her chest, infusing her insides with bliss. He grinned, and she grinned back. *Gorgeous*, he mouthed, sending more pinpricks of joy rolling through her. Nearby she could hear the photographer clicking and flashing away. The pews were decorated with lovely white and emerald ribbons, and an emerald runner dotted with white rose petals lined the path. The organ began with a hymn, joined by the violin. All heads turned as Ciarán played. This time, it did not sound like cats falling from trees. He must have been practicing for ages.

It was pitch perfect. Hands found their way to hearts as white tissues popped out of handbags and the sniffling began in earnest. Siobhán bit down hard on the inside of her cheek. She wished Gráinne were here to pinch her. Before she knew it, the waterworks broke through, and wetness rolled down the sides of Siobhán's face.

Stop it, stop it, stop it. No more crying. Please stop crying. Think horrible thoughts again. Droughts. Misfortunes. Missing brothers.

She felt Eoin's arm tighten in hers. "Hold it together, luv."

"Should I have waited for James?" she whispered. How could they do this without him? Why wasn't he here?

From down the aisle, Macdara's smile faltered. He looked worried. About James? Her bridesmaids finished their procession, and they took their places up front. The melodic wedding march began, and as Siobhán and Eoin proceeded up the aisle, Siobhán took in all the friendly faces. Bridie gave her a bright smile; Annmarie waved. Mike Granger from the fruit and veg shop gave her a nod and a wink. Macdara's mammy, Nancy Flannery, sat in the front row, looking only at her son. Siobhán nearly laughed out loud. The golden boy. Hopefully, Nancy Flannery wouldn't object to the wedding. When Siobhán reached Macdara, she handed her bouquet to Gráinne. Eoin kissed Siobhán on the cheek and stepped to the side of Macdara; then Ciarán slipped in next to Eoin. On the other side, Maria, Aisling, Gráinne, and Ann outnumbered the groomsmen, but no one was counting. The music stopped, and Father Kearney cleared his throat. Macdara smiled, took Siobhán's hands and squeezed them. The tears in Macdara's eyes made her waterworks threaten to start all over again.

She leaned in. "Think of horrible, horrible things. That's all I've been doing all morning." Macdara's laugh rumbled out of him and warmed her insides.

"I'll take any horrible thing that comes my way," Macdara whispered in her ear. "As long as you're by my side."

"That does it for the vows, then," Siobhán whispered.

Macdara laughed again, until a look from Father Kearney silenced the pair.

Once they were settled, Father Kearney began with greetings and the opening prayer, and then everyone joined in another hymn. Siobhán's eyes continuously landed on the doors to the church, willing James to enter. Before she knew it, they were nearly to the good bit. "Friends and family, we are gathered here today for this most joyous and holy occasion, the matrimony of Macdara Anthony Flannery to Siobhán O'Sullivan." A sob erupted, and Siobhán didn't have to turn to know it was Nancy Flannery. Father Kearney's voice continued, and Siobhán tried to listen, but there were too many thoughts clouding up her head, and she heard nothing else until Macdara squeezed her hands, which was when she registered the question "Do you have the rings?"

"I do," Eoin and Gráinne said in unison.

Macdara turned his cheeky face to the crowd. "That's what we're supposed to say."

Siobhán laughed first, and then the congregation followed. The laughter continued to roll until the church doors burst open. Silence descended, pews creaked as everyone shifted, and all heads snapped to the intrusion. James stood frozen in the entry, wearing denim overalls and a dirty white shirt. He was covered head to toe in dirt. His eyes were wild, but alert. He didn't appear to be drunk. He looked terrified.

"Sorry, sorry," he said, holding up a dirty hand and taking a step back. "Carry on."

"Wait," Siobhán said.

"Finish what you're doing," James said, his voice wavering. "I'll wait out here." The doors clicked shut behind him, echoing through the church, louder than any sound Siobhán had ever heard.

"Shall I continue?" Father Kearney asked after a moment of stunned silence, throwing a harried glance at the doors along with the rest of the guests.

Siobhán was torn. She wanted to bolt after James, and yet she couldn't bring herself to do that to Macdara.

"I'm afraid we'll have to postpone," Macdara said.

"No," Siobhán said. "Let's get this over with."

Macdara laughed. He leaned in, his voice low and intimate. "I might be a tad sentimental," he said. "But I'm not marrying you in a get-it-over-with kind of way."

She bit her lip and looked to Father Kearney. "Perhaps you could do the baptism first, and then we could all return and carry on with our wedding?"

Father Kearney shook his head. "I'm afraid that's

out of the question. It's either now or we'll have to reschedule entirely."

"Reschedule," Macdara said. And before Siobhán could respond, he took her hand and led her down the aisle.

"Gráinne," Siobhán yelled.

Gráinne ran to her side. "Yes?"

"Help organize everyone. Bring them to the abbey. Enjoy the reception."

Gráinne clasped Siobhán's hands. "Are you sure?"

Siobhán nodded. "We can't just send everyone home. It's a gorgeous day. The abbey is decorated. Food and drink are arriving—not to mention the trad band—and if someone doesn't enjoy it, it will all go to waste."

"I'm on it," Gráinne said. "I'll see to it everyone has a cracking good time whether they like it or not."

"Good woman." Siobhán turned to the crowd. "I'm so sorry. Go to the abbey. It might not be as romantic as we'd planned, but it's sure to be great craic. We'll do this again soon. Promise."

James paced the footpath in front of the cathedral. "Congratulations," he said when Siobhán and Macdara approached. He looked down at his dirty hands. "Sorry I don't have any rice or confetti to throw at ye."

"Birdseed," Siobhán corrected. "And we postponed."

James crossed his arms and shoved his dirty hands under his armpits. "Because of me?"

"The state of ya," Siobhán said. "What on earth is going on?"

"I'm so very sorry," James said, looking at Macdara. "I need to speak with you in private."

Macdara took a step toward James, and Siobhán grabbed his arm. "Not on your life," she said. "What you have to say to him, you'll say in front of me."

Macdara and James exchanged a look.

"Macdara?" she said.

Her nearly husband cleared his throat. "I think this might have something to do with a surprise I had planned for my *wife*."

For a second Siobhán was startled. *His wife? What wife?* And then she realized he was talking about her. "Your wife." A nervous laugh escaped her. Macdara cocked his head and gave her a funny look. She touched her tiara. "It's so tight I think it's melting me brain."

"Macdara is right," James said. "I'd rather speak to him in private. Otherwise I'll have ruined not only your wedding but the big surprise as well."

"Unless you've been spending all your time constructing a time machine, I'm afraid it's too late," Siobhán said. "You're going to have to ruin it."

James threw a pleading glance to Macdara.

"The lady has spoken," Macdara said with a nod. "Perhaps we can still save some of the secret." He turned to Siobhán. "James has been working on a special project for me. A surprise."

Siobhán stared at James, covered in muck. "Congratulations. You could knock me over with a feather."

Macdara shook his head, then turned to James. "I see you've been working away."

James nodded. "I planned on just doing a little more this morning, with plenty of time to get ready for the wedding."

"I believe you miscalculated," Siobhán said.

"I blame myself," Macdara said. "It was too big a project to be completed by today."

"It was my choice," James said. He swallowed. "But when I started clearing some debris in the dairy . . . in the outbuilding . . . I found . . . a skeleton at the bottom of the slurry pit."

"Dairy? Slurry pit?" Siobhán said. "Outbuilding? Skeleton?" She was aware she was spitting out words without comprehending them, yet she couldn't bring herself to stop.

James continued as if she hadn't spoken. "I thought it was a large stone. It was all black, covered in who knows how many years of muck. It wasn't until I touched it, and realized it didn't feel like a stone, and then I turned it over and saw the eye sockets . . ." His own eyes were wide as he relived the trauma. "A skull. A human skull! I went cold, so I did. My entire body went ice cold. I swear to ye, I placed it back exactly the way I found it. Then I looked closer and saw tattered pieces of clothing. Strange. It looked like he was wearing a suit. And I saw more blackened bones, his finger bones, something that looked like an arm bone, more tattered clothing—and his shoes. A man's dress shoes. I think he was tall. If the distance between the skull and the shoes are any measure, he was tall. Can ye imagine? The poor yoke facedown in a slurry pit? I climbed out—and me phone slipped out of me pocket and into the pit. I didn't even root around for it, because if it's a crime scene, I was terrified to touch anything else. The neighbors didn't answer their door, and the rest of the lads weren't due to arrive until this afternoon, when we were supposed to remove the pit. I drove into town and stopped at the station to alert the guards. But, of course, they said that the only guards who could handle such a request were . . . occupied . . ."

"Us," Siobhán said.

"I shouldn't have burst into the church, but I didn't realize ye had started without me, and don't forget I dropped me phone into the slurry pit!"

Siobhán turned to Macdara. "Your surprise is a slurry pit?" Nothing about this moment made sense. Slurry pits. Concrete tombs where cows from days of yore had done their business. *Cow patties.* "The first anniversary is paper," she said. "I'm fine waiting a year for paper."

Macdara laughed. They weren't being cruel; humor was a common way to deal with the unimaginable. "Go big or go home."

Perhaps it was good the wedding had been postponed. Did she know this man at all? Why was a slurry pit part of a surprise?

Like floodgates set loose, words continued to spill out of James. "I knew you'd be freaking out that I wasn't there, and my tux was in the church dressing room, and I thought I could sneak in and not disrupt the wedding, because I can tell you one thing, that skeleton has been lying there for a long, long time, so I figured he—from the shoes and the remains of a suit, I think it's a he—could wait just a little longer." He stopped suddenly and took in Siobhán's dress. "I'm sorry I ruined your wedding, and by the by, you're the most beautiful bride I've ever seen."

"You are," Macdara said. "I meant to say that meself."

Perhaps this was a dream. A pre-wedding nightmare. Siobhán looked around. "Where's the wedding photographer?"

"You want to do our wedding photos now?" Macdara said.

"No," Siobhán said. "I want to bring him with us to whatever this is, this dairy, this outbuilding, this slurry pit."

"This wasn't what I had in mind for our honeymoon," Macdara said. "Or our wedding, for that matter."

"Well, it's a good thing we postponed," Siobhán said, hiking up her dress once more. "Give us two shakes to change."

They stood in front of the property, a sprawling old dairy farm just outside of town that had been abandoned for as long as Siobhán had been alive. Decades ago, it had been a bustling family business, but for ages now it had been used for agricultural grazing. The hilly green landscape was dotted with sheep and horses and cows. Siobhán knew the neighbors: Gladys and Benji Burns, an adorable older couple who mostly kept to themselves. Siobhán was still trying to process everything Macdara had told her on the way here as she took in the stone fence hugging the property. In the distance sat a large stone cottage, and behind it, an enormous white dairy barn falling to ruin. "You bought us an old dairy farm," she said, not believing the words even as they tumbled out of her gob.

"It was supposed to be a surprise."

"Fair play to you, I'm shocked to me core."

"It needs a bit of work," James said. "But it has character." He looked to the sky, as if searching for something. "I saw a hawk circling and swooping about earlier."

"A hawk," Macdara said. "That's a good sign."

"Could have been a falcon," James said. "I wasn't sure."

"Still a good sign," Macdara said confidently.

"Is it?" Siobhán said. "Birds of prey circling above me head sound like the opposite of a good sign to me."

"It is," Macdara insisted. "It's a good sign."

"What about a skeleton facedown in a slurry pit? What kind of sign is that?" Siobhán couldn't help but say. Macdara just gave her a look.

"The hawk seemed a bit stressed," James said. He glanced at Macdara. "Not to diminish your positive outlook."

"Stressed?" Macdara said, his confidence faltering.

"He kept swooping over the dairy barn with a loud cry," James said. "To be honest, it's what made me go back for a look. Otherwise you'd be married by now."

"Perhaps not such a good sign after all," Macdara grumbled.

"Take us to it," Siobhán said.

They were now dressed much like James, in denims and Wellies, including a pair for the photographer. Siobhán's hair was still dolled up on top of her head, and she'd kept the tiara on, mostly because taking it off would require a million pins to be let loose, and she had had neither the time nor energy for the task. She could only imagine what a sight she was. Wellies and tiaras weren't your everyday combination, and the wedding photographer seemed equally thrilled as he was horrified. Soon he was snapping away, the camera mainly fixated on Siobhán. "Save it for the skeleton," she said and couldn't help but smile when he shuddered.

"Photographing crime scenes is not what I do," the photographer repeated. He was a bit wide in the belly and most likely had been looking forward to the reception at the abbey.

"It is today." They were paying him well, and since he'd already announced he was booked after today and they'd have to find a new photographer (stressing that there were no refunds), she was determined to get her money's worth. "But after you're done here, you should pop into the reception at our abbey for a feed."

He didn't answer, but at least he continued to follow them. Their boots sank into the soft ground as they walked. Siobhán took Macdara's hand so she could speak privately with him as James took the lead. If this turned out to be a real skeleton, they would have to call in an official crime scene photographer, but first the coroner would have to arrive, and then he would be tasked with calling in the state pathologist, but this photographer was getting paid, and early pictures might help speed things up. There was no use calling in the cavalry until they had a look. For all they knew, someone had stolen a skeleton from a primary school and there was no need for an investigation. This could be pure shenanigans. An abandoned dairy barn was probably too tempting for lads out for a bit of misguided fun.

"Listen," Macdara said. "I'm not forcing us to move into this place. I got a good deal on it. With a little help from Mam."

"Your mam?" Siobhán said. This was unexpected. Perhaps Nancy Flannery approved of their union after all. Or perhaps she simply wanted Siobhán to freak out over a dairy farm. Either scenario was likely.

Macdara nodded. "It's a great investment, and if you want nothing to do with it, we'll spruce it up—that's where your brother comes in handy—and we'll either rent it out or sell it for a bit of a nest egg."

"The inside of the house still needs some work," James said. "All these older stone homes do. But I'm telling ye, nothing beats the charm. And you'll probably want to take the dairy barn down, but you'd be insane not to keep this property. Mam and Da always talked about buying it."

"They did?" Siobhán said.

"Don't you remember every time we drove this way, they'd start talking about it?"

"No," Siobhán said.

"They did," James said. "They talked about expanding the bistro into a restaurant. Believe me, they'd be thrilled." It struck Siobhán how all the siblings had had such different experiences of their parents. Ann and Ciarán had the least memories of them, which was why Siobhán tried to fill them in as much as she could. Knowing that her parents had liked this farm, had even thought of buying it, made the prospect shine a little brighter.

"I assure you the Realtor made no mention of a skeleton in the slurry pit," Macdara said.

Slurry pit. *Lovely.* If they stayed, they were definitely getting rid of that pit. Siobhán's eyes landed on their new house, for she realized "cottage" wasn't an apt description. It was a house. An impressive two-story stone structure that looked both charming and daunting. The wooden shutters framing the windows had been scraped clean of ancient paint, along with a heavy wooden door.

Macdara leaned in. "James was going to paint them, but I thought you might like to pick out the colors."

"Me?" Siobhán said. She was finding it impossible to believe that this was hers. *Theirs.* "I'll have a think on it." *Emerald green, to match the fields and commemorate their wedding.* Or maybe the same robin's-egg blue they had painted the sign to Naomi's Bistro. A cheerful yellow, or red. Red doors were good luck in Chinese culture. Should they borrow some luck? Perhaps he should have let James paint the shutters after all.

The Burnses' house was close enough to run over to if there was ever an emergency, but far enough away that neighbors couldn't be peeking in on them. "You don't expect us to buy cows, do you?" She had her hands full with her siblings, a bistro, and Trigger, their Jack Russell terrier. Come to think of it, Trigger would love to roam these fields.

"Definitely not," Macdara said. He stopped. "Why? Do you want cows?"

"Don't be an eejit." She gave him a gentle shove. "Although we wouldn't have far to go for a pint of milk."

"At the very least you'll want a few chickens," James said from up ahead. "If you did have a few cows for milk and planted a vegetable garden, think of the money we'd save at the bistro. And you should continue to let farm animals graze. You'll get a bit of income, and it will be much easier to keep up with the fields." He came to an abrupt stop and tilted his head to the sky. They were nearing the old dairy barn now. It was a long rectangular white building with bits hanging off the roof and sides. Siobhán and Macdara stopped behind James, and because it was nearly impossible not to look at the sky when someone else was looking at the sky, they all tilted their heads up.

"Is this a cloud game?" Siobhán said. So much for a day of sun. She pointed to a fat cloud forming off to the right. "I see the price tag for this little wedding do-over." Laughter rumbled from Macdara, and she grinned.

"Just checking for the hawk," James said. "Given you look like you have a small animal perched on top of your head."

"An animal?" Siobhán demanded as she patted her hair. It *was* piled awfully high. She whirled around and stared at Macdara. "Does it look like I have a small animal perched on top of me head?"

He stared and blinked.

"Tell the truth!"

He swallowed. "No. Absolutely not. No."

"Macdara. If we're going to be husband and wife, we have to tell each other the truth when we ask for it."

Macdara swallowed hard. "If you did—and I'm not saying you do. Because you don't. You really don't. Honest. But if you did, it would be . . . a lovely wee fox."

"A lovely wee fox?" She could hear the rage in her voice and clenched her fists. The photographer snapped a photo.

"A lovely, lovely wee fox," Macdara said, leaning in for a kiss.

Perhaps the truth had no place in a marriage after all. "That would make you the hound," Siobhán said, gently pushing his face away, before changing her mind and planting a kiss on him. The photographer snapped away.

James leaned into the barn doors, and after some tugging, they slid open with a loud groan. A miasma of odors wafted out. Old straw, decayed wood, earth, and something Siobhán could only surmise was ancient muck. "I figured you two would want to take this old barn down, so I've been cleaning it out to make the process go a little smoother, and the last bit I needed to do was clean out this old slurry pit. I was shocked it wasn't decommissioned, and thank God there's still a working lightbulb hanging above it. I tell ye I almost fell into it."

They followed James through the barn—and to his credit, it was stripped down to the framing,

empty stalls lining both sides of the massive space.
It was easy to imagine it had once been filled with
cows and machinery and milk pails. James crossed
to the back, where a faint line shone through a
doorframe without a door.

"That's the entrance to the slatted shed," James
said. "The pit and yer man are just through there."

"Slatted shed?" Siobhán was out of her depth.

"Do you know much about slurry pits?" James
asked before they stepped any farther.

"Pretend I don't," Siobhán said.

"Because she doesn't," Macdara said.

James entered through the door, and the group
followed, huddling close to the walls as to not fall
into the pit. Gray light filtered in between the uni-
formed slats in the walls, allowing for airflow. A
single lightbulb situated above the right-hand corner of the pit illuminated that corner, but the rest
of the space was shrouded in darkness. Despite the
airflow, the smell was stronger here—moldy earth
and muck. James pointed over the mass of darkness. "Concrete slabs would have been laid over
the pit when it was in use, they would usher the
cows in, and there was just enough room for the
waste to drop below. Slurry, in this instance cow
manure and water, is a natural fertilizer for farms.
The side walls are slatted to allow in fresh air."

"Airflow," Siobhán said. "I knew it."

"Once manure is mixed with water, it creates a
dangerous gas. Odorless, poisonous, and flamma-
ble. Too many stories had been told about farmers
and children losing their lives to slurry pit acci-
dents. Drowning and asphyxiation."

"That bulb isn't doing much for me," Siobhán said. "I can't see a thing."

"Hold on. I have a torch here somewhere," James said. "You'll also want to see this." They heard James rustling around and then a click as he turned on the torch he'd found. He maneuvered the circle of light to the right-hand side of the shed, illuminating an enormous pile of branches, some with bright green leaves. "I was surprised to see this stash covering in the pit," he said. "Took me ages to clear them out—otherwise I would not have seen the skeleton, and I wouldn't have found myself in the middle of a crime scene."

"Shine the light in the pit," Macdara said, getting a touch impatient.

James swiveled the light over the dark mass in front of them. Siobhán and Macdara inched forward to stare into the abyss. It was at least ten feet deep and ten feet long, like an enormous concrete bathtub. It was covered in layers of dried muck. James's torch shone on an iron ladder welded to one side of the pit.

"Back in the day the lads would have had to climb down into the pit to stir the slurry."

"Do you mind handing me the torch?" Macdara asked.

James handed it over, and soon the light shone on the gruesome discovery below. The skull indeed looked like a large black rock. The light traveled down, and next they saw what appeared to be a series of black sticks. *Finger bones.* Tattered bits of dark clothing could be seen, and toward the end of the pit, a pair of shoes. Siobhán's eye traveled back to the skull, and she was trying to locate the eye sockets when she remembered they were staring at the back of the poor man's head. He must have fallen into the slurry pit face-first.

There, but for the grace of God, go I. Siobhán shuddered, then crossed herself, and quickly Macdara and James repeated the gesture.

"I see why this gave you quite the fright," Siobhán said.

James nodded. "I had to lie on my stomach in front of this beast to remove the last of the branches. And shock is right." James produced a second torch and aimed the light at the left-hand corner of the pit. "Me phone is there."

Macdara exhaled. "You're lucky you didn't fall in yourself."

"I'd say we're all luckier than that poor soul."

The four of them stared down at the skeleton for a moment before the photographer slipped out. She could hear him coughing in the dairy barn, as if trying to expel the images from his body. Perhaps she'd been foolish to bring him; given how dark it was, the pictures would be of no use anyway.

"We're here now," Siobhán said to the skeleton. "We're going to look after you." Her gaze fell to the pile of branches and brambles that had been used to fill in the pit. "Shine the light on the branches for me once more, will ya?" James swiveled the torch back to the branches. The top ones all sported bright green leaves and new buds. "Someone has recently been tending this pit," she said, pointing out the fresh leaves. "Covering it up."

"Tending a grave," Macdara said. "Someone knew yer one was in there."

They all stared at the bones. A trickle of sweat ran down the side of Siobhán's face, and she shivered.

"Who would do such a thing?" the photographer said. He had returned without warning, making them all jump.

"A killer," Siobhán said. "A killer would do such a thing."

Chapter 3

A killer. Siobhán had floated the words to see if Macdara and James agreed, but as soon as she'd said them, she'd known she was right. It was the only logical explanation. Why else would someone cover this pit up with fresh branches? Dead men couldn't hide their own corpses.

"Someone's been covering up the skeleton, alright," Macdara said. "But let's not jump to conclusions about a cause of death."

"Say nothing until you hear more," Siobhán said. "But given he's wearing a suit, and someone is visiting him after all these years, I'm pretty confident in my statement."

"We've a long ways to go yet," Macdara said.

"I believe he's already waited a long time for justice," Siobhán said. She wasn't trying to start a row, but she couldn't shake the feeling that the man had been murdered. Murdered and hidden in muck for who knows how many years. It made her blood boil.

"How long does it take for a body to become a skeleton?" James asked.

"It depends on the conditions," Macdara said. "Mummified bodies have been found in bogs still intact. Remember Cashel Man, who was found in County Laois? He dates to two thousand BCE."

"Ours isn't exactly a mummy," James said.

"And Clonycavan Man in County Meath," Macdara continued. "He is 392 to 201 BCE."

"But our man is a skeleton," James said. "How long did that take?"

"It can take several weeks to several years," Siobhán said. "Depending on the conditions." And skeletons, she knew, could last hundreds of years in neutral soil. Given this concrete pit was like a tomb, who knew how long he had been languishing here.

"We'll need a forensic pathologist to determine the truth, but I'd say this one has been here a long, long time," Macdara said.

"When was this last a working dairy farm?" Siobhán asked.

"Not in our lifetime," James said. "I remember when Mam and Da talked about the property, they referred to it as an abandoned dairy farm."

"I think the house has been rented out more recently," Macdara said. "And the animals have always been grazing the fields. But the barn hasn't been in use in my lifetime either."

"And yet someone is still visiting," Siobhán repeated. She took the torch from Macdara and lay down as close as she could get to the skeleton. She ran the length of the torch over the pit, from the top of the darkened skull to his shoes. "That doesn't look like your typical farm wear."

"I told you," James said. "He's wearing a suit."

Weddings or funerals, that was when Irishmen wore suits.

Behind them, the photographer came alive with clicks and flashes. He'd apparently gotten over his disgust and was energized about the turn his assignment had taken.

"Take all you want. Just don't get any closer," Siobhán said.

Macdara nodded at James to back up as they slipped on the gloves and booties they had brought with them. They knelt next to the pit.

"If he's a wedding guest, he certainly wasn't one of ours," Macdara quipped.

"Wedding guest?" A female voice floated through the barn, somewhere behind them.

Siobhán and Macdara whirled around, along with James and the photographer. James had turned with the torch in his hand, and it was shining directly in the face of an old lady. She threw her hands up.

"Sorry about that." James diverted the light.

It took a few minutes for the colorful spots to disappear in front of Siobhán's eyes, but when they did, she saw the newcomer was petite, with a mass of gray and white hair piled on top of her head. Inquisitive eyes peered from behind thick, black-framed glasses. She wore a pink housedress and black Wellies, and she was wielding a rolling pin, as if she had run out of her house mid-baking.

"Is that your car parked out front? The one that says 'Just Married'?"

"We'll have to change it to 'Nearly,'" Macdara said.

The old woman stepped closer. "Now, here's the lovely couple. When we heard you'd be our new neighbors, we were chuffed to bits, so we were."

"How ya, Gladys?" Siobhán said. She felt foolish she hadn't recognized her sooner. Gladys and Benji Burns mostly kept to themselves, but they were still known and liked about town. "We couldn't ask for better neighbors."

"Aren't you a dear," Gladys said, brightening up. Her eyes traveled up to Siobhán's tiara, and she stared. "We so wanted to attend the wedding, but I suppose you can't invite everyone."

Guilt clutched at Siobhán. "You're invited to the next one," she said brightly.

Gladys tilted her head in confusion.

"We had to postpone the wedding," Macdara added. "Unless she means the husband after me."

Siobhán wished she was close enough to elbow him in the side, but the photographer was wedged between them. Gladys's gaze fell to the gloves on Macdara's and Siobhán's hands. They quickly removed them so they could not only greet their new neighbor but also nudge her out of the barn. The last thing they needed was the grapevine to kick up with rumors of slurry and skeletons.

"Postponed the wedding?" Gladys said. "Why would you do that?"

"We had a slight emergency to attend to—just a minor delay," Siobhán said. They had moved toward her en masse, herding her toward the entrance to the barn, and Gladys had no choice but to step outside. Back in the day this property was probably filled with sheepdogs, who could have done a much better job. Once outside, James slid the doors to the barn shut. Siobhán was relieved to be out in the fresh air, away from the horror in the pit.

"Apart from me brother and the lads working with him, when was the last time anyone was in this barn?" Siobhán asked Gladys.

"Nobody has used this dairy barn for ages," Gladys said. She cupped her hand over her eyes to block out the sun. "I thought maybe you'd found Charlie in the barn."

"Charlie?" the group chorused.

"Rose's hawk," Gladys said, tilting her head to the sky. The rolling pin bobbed in the old woman's hand, and now that they were in full daylight, Siobhán could see a splash of bright red at the end of the pin. Was that blood? "Rose Burns," Gladys continued. "She works at the Kilbane Wildlife Center and is always bringing her creatures out here for a change of scenery."

"Rose Burns?" Macdara asked. "Is she a relative?"

"My husband's first wife," Gladys said. "She lives in Charlesville, but her birds like it here. Plenty of room to soar."

"Your husband's first wife?" Macdara said. Back in the day divorce was rare in Ireland. Couples would live apart and stop speaking to each other, but marriage was forever in the eyes of the Catholic Church.

"Is Charlie a hawk or a falcon?" James asked, still scanning the sky.

"He's a Harris hawk, young man," Gladys answered. "Or so I've been schooled." She rolled her eyes, as if she hadn't appreciated the lesson. "Yes, Rose is my husband's first wife. They married young, and it was a mistake. We've been wed nearly fifty years now."

"Congratulations," Macdara said. "What's your secret?"

"Give each other a bit of space," Gladys said. "You'll have plenty of it out here."

Before the elderly neighbor could dole out any more advice, Siobhán quickly slipped her protective gloves back on and reached for the rolling pin. "May I see that?"

Gladys flinched, bringing the pin to her chest. "Why?"

"Blood," the photographer said loudly, pointing to the pin. He snapped a picture.

Great. She should have never brought him along. She was going to end up paying for this in more ways than one.

"Blood?" Gladys said. Startled, she looked down at her rolling pin. "No, no," she said. "I'm making cherry tarts." Before Siobhán could say another word, Gladys stuck the entire end of the rolling pin into her mouth and then took it out and presented it with a flourish. "See?"

Before anyone could reply, a piercing cry rang out, followed by a swoosh. Heads snapped to the sky, where a hawk with an enormous wingspan soared above them. The sight was something to behold. The purposeful glide, his wings spread out in all his glory. *Prehistoric.* Siobhán felt goose bumps as she kept her eyes on the majestic creature.

"That's Charlie, alright," Gladys said. "He's been well trained."

"By your husband's first wife?" the photographer asked. "And she regularly visits with her birds of prey?"

Siobhán turned to give him a look. Was he a reporter now? "You're free to go," she said. "Thank you for your help."

The photographer ignored Siobhán and turned to Gladys. "Is he trained to land on her fist?"

"Yes, indeed he is," Gladys said. "Rose is a falconer."

The photographer's eyes lit up. "Do you think she'd let me get a photo of him up close?"

"I don't see why not," Gladys said. "But I don't think she's here right now. That's why it's so odd that Charlie is flying around all by his lonesome."

"You really don't need to stay," Siobhán said to the photographer. "And we'll need you to leave us the film from your camera." She couldn't have him running off with their crime scene photos, even if none of them turned out to be helpful. On the other hand, she didn't want Gladys to cop on to the fact that there was a skeleton in the barn.

"It's digital," he said, giving her a look. "There isn't any film in me camera."

"Then we'll have to take possession of the entire camera until we've taken what we need from it," Siobhán said.

He began flicking through the photos. "Give me

your e-mail. I'll send them to you right now and delete them. You're not touching this camera."

Siobhán felt Macdara's hand on her arm, which was the only thing that prevented her from snatching it out of his hands.

Macdara handed him a business card. "You can use this e-mail."

The photographer stared at the card, then at his camera. "I'll need to go back home and hook it up to me laptop."

"Then you'll be leaving the camera with us," Siobhán said.

This time it was Gladys who touched Siobhán's arm. "I'd say that's *his* camera, dear, and Rose must be here somewhere. She wouldn't leave Charlie on his own." She turned to the photographer. "I'm sure Rose wouldn't mind if you took a few photos of Charlie. He loves the attention."

"You said she often trains Charlie on our property?" Macdara asked.

"It is your property as of only a few days ago, so I hope you aren't complaining."

"Not at all," Siobhán said. "We're just trying to get a picture." *Of a possible killer.* Should she demand entry into Gladys's house to see whether or not there were cherry tarts in the cooker? There were so many things they had never taught Siobhán at garda college.

"Something must have come up with Rose if she just left Charlie here. Benji saw him flying about earlier and said he looked spooked," Gladys said. "I'll give her a bell so she can get back here and get him under control."

The photographer shoved his camera at Siobhán and pulled another from his bag. "I expect that back as soon as you have your skeleton pictures."

"Skeleton pictures?" Gladys asked, her previously cheerful voice raised in alarm.

Inwardly Siobhán groaned, but she waved her hand, as if it meant nothing. "Just a photography term. Just pictures that . . . you know . . . are a bit blurry and white—like a skeleton."

"What utter hogwash," the photographer said as he took off across the field in search of the hawk.

The sound of tires on gravel caught their attention. In the distance a garda car was pulling in.

"That will be Garda Dabiri," Macdara said. "I gave her a heads-up about our situation."

Gladys squinted and once again tried to see into the barn. "Situation?" She took a step forward.

Siobhán blocked her path. "We can't let anyone in there."

Macdara took Gladys's arm. "Why don't I escort you back home?"

They turned to see Aretta had broken into a run. She stopped short when she saw them. She had a short but strong body, gorgeous dark skin, and inquisitive eyes. She was their first garda from Africa; her family immigrated to Ireland when she was a wee lassie. She was by the book and eager to learn, while still projecting confidence. Her uniform was pressed; the gold shield on her hat gleamed underneath the sun.

"I hear there's a skeleton in the slurry pit," Aretta said excitedly. "Dressed in a suit."

Before anyone could respond, Gladys Burns

dropped her rolling pin and let out a wail. She whirled around and raced straight for the dairy barn. Although the older woman couldn't outrun a single one of them, they mistakenly ran for the barn doors. Instead, Gladys dashed for the back of the barn. By the time the others caught up, Siobhán saw a door at the back standing wide open, another entry into the barn right near the slurry shed. They hurried in and ran across the cavernous space to find Gladys at the edge of the slurry pit. She had James's torch clutched in her hands and was shining it into the pit.

"No, no, no. No, no, no, no."

"Mrs. Barns, we need you to step out," Macdara said. "Or I'll have to put my hands on you and haul you out."

"Tommy," Gladys said, ignoring the warning. "My Tommy." She looked as if she was seconds away from crawling into the pit. Gladys and Benji did not have children of their own. Who was Tommy?

Macdara and Siobhán each grabbed ahold of Gladys, who struggled to get out of their grip. "You can't be in here, luv," Siobhán said. "It's a possible crime scene, and we have to protect it."

"I am so sorry," Aretta squeaked from behind them.

"You didn't know," Macdara said. "It's not your fault."

"It's my Tommy. It's my Tommy. It's my Tommy."

It took considerable skills to wrestle Gladys out of the dairy barn and back to her own property, while a still apologizing Aretta stayed behind to cordon off the scene and make sure no other civilians could get close. By the time they deposited

Gladys on her front porch, she was crying and babbling. The front door swung open, and an old man that Siobhán recognized as Benji Burns stepped out. He was a short man with a full head of soft white curls and kind blue eyes. He wore green overalls and a yellow shirt, as if he were a walking sunflower.

"Gladys," he said. "Whatever you've got in the cooker, it's burning!"

"Are your fingers broken?" Gladys asked. "Turn it off."

He stopped short when he saw the group gathered on his porch, and his concern turned to his wife. "Are you alright?"

Gladys shook her head, her hand over her mouth, tears spilling out of her eyes.

"She's had a scare," Siobhán said. "Why don't you turn off your cooker, and we'll explain everything."

When he didn't move, Gladys barked at him. "Do you want the house to burn down around us?"

He flinched, then shuffled back inside, shaking his head.

When the door swung open again, Siobhán knew it was too soon for Benji's return, but she still found it slow to process that another man had stepped out. He appeared to be in his early fifties, and given he wasn't wearing a shirt, it was impossible not to notice his muscular physique and one of those six-pack stomachs she heretofore thought was just an urban myth. *Silver fox* was the phrase that came to mind. He stared at Siobhán, and she stared back, wondering about the expression on his face, before she remembered she was wearing a tiara on top of her head. And possibly a wee red fox.

Behind her, Macdara cleared his throat. "Given you have the photographer's camera, why don't you just take a picture?" Macdara teased.

Siobhán elbowed him.

"Gladys?" the man said. "What is going on?" His eye traveled to the fields. "Where's my mam? Did she get Charlie under control?"

"Gladys has had a shock," Siobhán said. "Who are you?"

An amused look of defiance came into his eyes. "Who are you?"

"I'm Detective Sergeant Flannery, and this is Garda O'Sullivan," Macdara interjected. He was using his alpha voice. "Would you mind putting a shirt on?"

The amused look turned dark. "In my own home?"

"Technically, this isn't your home," Gladys said. "This is my stepson," she said to Siobhán. "Joseph is a potter, and he lives in Charlesville with his mam."

"I am indeed a potter, and I live in Charlesville, and my mam lives in Charlesville, but to be clear, we each live in our own humble abode." He winked at Siobhán. "Wicked," he said, turning to Gladys with a grin. "What are guards doing here?"

"Wicked?" Siobhán asked, trying to look anywhere but at the man's muscular arms and stomach.

Gladys laughed, a surprising but welcome sound. "It's always been Joseph's nickname for me. Wicked stepmother."

Joseph grinned. "Sometimes I call her Step Monster. Just to shake things up." He wiggled his eyebrows and flexed his pectoral muscles.

"How very mature of you," Macdara said.

Benji returned, sweating and breathing heavily. "Cooker is off. Your apple tarts are a disaster." He threw a look to his son. "Would you put a shirt on? We've got company."

Apple tarts? Didn't Gladys say they were cherry? Had that been blood on the rolling pin? If so, it was too late now; the old woman had licked the evidence clean, and the rolling pin was still lying in the grass near the dairy barn. And even if it had been blood, it certainly didn't come from their skeleton. But why had she lied and stuck it in her mouth? It was certainly odd behavior.

"Someone please tell me what has me wife in hysterics," Benji continued, pushing past his son. "Shirt on now," he growled before tending to his wife.

"Not a bother, Da," Joseph said before entering the house and letting the door slam shut behind him. Not surprisingly, he had well-formed back muscles to match the front. How many hours in a gym did that take?

Macdara sidled up to Siobhán. "See something you liked?" he teased.

"I only have eyes for you."

"Right, so." He patted his stomach. "I suppose we could lighten up on the curried chips."

"We?"

"Once we're husband and wife, you'd give them up too if I was forced to do so for me health, wouldn't you?"

"Don't make me choose between you and cur-ried chips."

"Detective Sergeant?" Benji pleaded.

Macdara straightened up and nodded. "This morning my brother-in-law-to-be uncovered a skeleton in the slurry pit. Your wife seems to think it's a man named Tommy."

"Tommy? Tommy Caffrey?" Benji stiffened. His gaze traveled to the dairy barn. "That can't be. It can't be."

"It's him!" Gladys said. "It's Tommy. I know it is."

Benji slapped his hands over his mouth, then caught sight of Siobhán's tiara and dropped them, as he tried to work out what he was seeing. "You've just come from your wedding?"

"Our nearly wedding," Siobhán said before Macdara could beat her to it. "It seems we've had a wedding crasher, and his name is possibly Tommy Caffrey."

Benji rubbed his hand over his eyes. "The irony," he said. "I was thinking that when I read about your wedding. It was fifty years ago today." He turned to his wife.

She nodded vigorously and clutched his hands. "It was," she said. "Fifty years ago, to the day." She turned to Siobhán and rose from her seat. "Wait a minute. That has to mean something. Doesn't it?"

"How can it?" Benji said. "Don't worry yourself to death. It's an odd coincidence, I'll tell ye that. But that's all it is. That's all it can be."

"What was fifty years ago today?" Macdara asked.

"*My* wedding day," Gladys said. "Fifty years ago today, I was supposed to marry Tommy Caffrey."

Chapter 4

"Today was your wedding day?" Siobhán repeated. "This exact date?"

"Yes," Gladys said. "I see you understand. This has to mean something." They had all gravitated off the porch and were standing close to the drive. Everyone stared at the dairy barn in the distance.

"That explains the suit," James said under his breath.

The tattered remains of what appeared to be a suit at the bottom of the slurry pit rose into Siobhán's mind. Another nearly wedding? If so, what an eerie coincidence. Siobhán didn't like coincidences, not one bit. "How is this possible?"

Gladys lifted her chin, as if she was being forced to defend herself. "He left me standing at the altar. Or that's what I thought."

"That's what everyone thought," Benji said. He

laid his hand gently on his wife's shoulder. She brushed it away. Had she always been averse to his touch? Did he notice it? Would Siobhán do the same to Macdara after five decades of marriage?

"I shouldn't have listened to them," Gladys said. "Has he been lying next door in that pit for fifty years? Is that what you're telling me?"

"We don't know anything yet," Siobhán said. "Including the name of our victim."

"We're not complete fools," Benji said. "Who else would it be?"

"Alan!" Gladys said. "He accused Tommy of stealing money from that partner of his. What was his name?"

"Howard Dunn," Benji said.

Gladys frowned, her hazel eyes looking slightly clouded and confused. "Howard Dunn, that's right."

"Who is Alan?" Macdara asked. "Are you saying our victim could be this Alan?"

"No," Gladys said. "Alan O'Leary is me brother. He's very much alive. But he may soon wish he wasn't. *He* was the one who found the note in me dressing room of the church. It was tucked into the corner of the mirror. Does that mean Tommy didn't write that note?"

"What note?" Macdara was getting frustrated as the older married couple ran away with the conversation.

"Tommy left her a note saying sorry and goodbye," Benji said.

Siobhán nudged forward. "What exactly did it say?"

"'Sorry. Goodbye,'" Benji said, enunciating slowly and clearly, as if Siobhán and Macdara were a pair of eejits.

"That's it?" Macdara asked.

"Tommy would talk your ear off in person," Benji said. "But he wasn't much of a scribbler."

"Do you still have this note?" Siobhán asked.

"Of course she does," Benji said. "She's one stack of magazines away from being on one of those hoarder shows on telly. If I go missing, you'll probably find me buried underneath a pile of junk."

"You're one to talk, with your tools," Gladys said. "Why on earth you need fourteen wrenches but can't find a single one when you need it is a mystery to me."

"I would like to see this note," Siobhán said. She didn't need to witness the kind of bickering earned through fifty years of marriage. Was this where she and Dara were headed?

Gladys huffed. "Despite what my husband thinks, I haven't seen that note in ages. I wouldn't know where to even look."

"The kitchen," Benji said. "She stashes everything in there." He locked eyes with Siobhán and mouthed, *Hoarder.*

The front door opened, and Joseph returned, this time with a shirt. He took a seat on the porch swing and settled in to listen.

"You also mentioned Howard Dunn," Siobhán said, removing a notebook from the pocket of her garda jacket. She needed to jot all of this down while the group was talking freely. Once they understood they were all suspects, they would clam up or start altering their stories. She was aware of Howard Dunn. He was an old-timer who would hang out in a pub only if it had a pool table, and he was a familiar face in the betting shops, but he wasn't a frequent visitor at the bistro, so she didn't know him on a personal level.

Benji nodded. "He was Tommy's business partner. Tommy wasn't the only thing that went missing that morning."

"The only thing that matters," Gladys said. "That's all anyone talked about at the time. The money. Not Tommy. The money."

"Money went missing?" Macdara asked.

Benji nodded, his facial expression conveying what a big deal the missing money had been. "Howard carried around a leather satchel in those days. Just before Tommy disappeared, it was stuffed with cash. Thirty thousand quid. They were going to use the money to start a snooker club."

"That's right," Joseph said. "I remember that." He sounded jubilant until all eyes turned to him. "Sorry," he said. "But it's bringing back a lot of memories."

Just then Aretta Dabiri returned from the barn and joined the group. She came to a stop just behind Macdara.

"Uncle Tommy taught me how to play snooker," Joseph said. "He said I was a natural." Gladys rolled her eyes; Benji frowned. Joseph grinned and continued to swing.

"Uncle Tommy?" Macdara said, focusing his gaze on Joseph. From the tone of his voice, he didn't like the man. Or the muscles.

"That's what I called him."

"My fault," Benji said. "Rose and I wanted him

to feel he had a big family, so every friend was uncle this or aunt this. One big happy Irish family."

Joseph nodded. "They saved me."

"Saved you?" Aretta asked.

"Rose and Benji adopted me," he said. "Spent my early years in a home for orphaned lads, and I'd always wanted a family."

"Did you know Tommy long?" Siobhán asked.

"Only about a year," Joseph said.

"You were his little shadow," Benji said. "They got along like a house on fire."

"He was larger than life," Joseph said.

"He was," Gladys said. "Everyone gravitated to my Tommy."

"Including trouble," Benji said. "Trouble gravitated to *your* Tommy. And it all exploded when that money went missing."

"Thirty thousand is a large sum even for today," Macdara said. "I'd like the phone number for Howard Dunn if you have it, as well as for your brother Alan." He directed the last bit to Gladys.

"If you're rounding up suspects, you might as well throw in my sister Linda," Gladys said. "She was the one among us who loathed Tommy."

"*Loathe* is a strong word," Benji said.

Gladys nodded. "Linda threatened to never speak to me again if I married Tommy."

Benji looked shocked. "You never told me that."

"You're my husband, not my priest," Gladys said. She turned to Siobhán. "Secrets are good for a marriage. Don't let anyone tell you different."

Macdara caught Siobhán's eyes and shook his head. She busied herself by writing in her notebook *Alan. Brother. Gave Gladys the note. Linda. Sister. Hated Tommy.* She snuck in one last note, knowing no one ever nosed around in her private notebook. *Secrets are good for a marriage . . . ?* She added the question mark, as longevity seemed to be the only thing Gladys and Benji had working for them. Shouldn't marriage aim for higher than that? She certainly wanted more for herself and Macdara.

"Did Howard ever open a snooker club?" Macdara asked.

"Not after Tommy ran off, no," Benji said. "His life dream down the drain."

Life dream? A snooker club? There were so many things Siobhán would do with thirty thousand euro. A snooker club would never have entered her mind. Balls and sticks. Why were men so obsessed with balls and sticks?

"But now we know it was a lie," Gladys said. "Tommy didn't steal that money."

"He still could have done," Benji said. He turned to Macdara. "Did you find a leather satchel in the pit with him?"

"We haven't had a chance to thoroughly examine the pit," Macdara said. "Even though it's been fifty years, we still have to do this by the book."

If there was a leather satchel in the pit, it had to be buried beneath the body. But Siobhán doubted that was where a satchel full of cash ended up. But she didn't like this new information. Just the rumor that there may be a satchel full of cash in the slurry pit could be enough to make troublemakers flock to the scene. That was the last thing they needed.

"Did Howard do it?" Gladys asked. "Did he kill my Tommy and then blame him for taking his money?"

"Joseph never liked Howard," Benji said suddenly. He eyed his son. "Isn't that right?"

Joseph tilted his head up as he considered it. "I know I liked Tommy, but I honestly don't remember much interaction with Howard. I know I liked playing snooker and running around the pub."

"You definitely did not like Howard." Benji turned to his wife. "Do you remember?"

She shook her head. "How would I know? I wasn't married to you then."

Benji looked as if her words had physically hurt him. He pushed it away and turned to Macdara. "This one time, Joseph spent the afternoon with Tommy and Howard. He came back, and he was literally shaking. All he would say is, 'Howard is mean.'"

Everyone looked at Joseph, who shrugged. "I believe you, Da."

"That's it, then," Gladys said. "You need to arrest Howard."

"We'll be looking into every possibility," Siobhán said. "But until we know for sure, it's not healthy to accuse anyone of anything."

"What are you waiting for?" Gladys said, pointing across the field to the dairy barn. "I want him out of there."

"I know you do," Siobhán said. "But first, we have to call the coroner, and after he pays a visit, he's going to call the state pathologist, and she's going to declare it a crime scene and call a forensic pathologist, and then the tech team will have to figure out the safest way to remove the bones, so they can be studied." She said it all in one breath, which left her exhausted.

Gladys stared and blinked, no doubt wishing she was still gripping her rolling pin.

A woman rounded the corner, whistling a cheery tune. All heads turned to look. She was tall, with thick black hair streaked with white that fell to her waist. Her outstretched arm was sheathed in a large leather glove, and perched on top of it was a hawk. It was a large creature, with regal posture and piercing eyes. Seeing it up close gave Siobhán goose bumps.

"There she is," Joseph said.

The woman came to an abrupt stop. "Me?" She glanced at the hawk, as if waiting for it to answer, then scanned the crowd. "Were you looking for me?" Now that she was closer, Siobhán could see she was an older woman—early seventies, if Siobhán had to guess—but she was definitely well preserved. The hawk swiveled its head as they spoke, taking in every little detail around him. It dawned on Siobhán that that was where the saying came from. *Watch you like a hawk.* This must be Charlie, and he was magnificent.

"All sorted, Mam?" Joseph asked.

"Charlie's been a bad boy today," she said playfully. "Did you call the guards about my runaway hawk? I'm sorry to trouble you. As you can see, Charlie is safe and sound now." Charlie cocked his head and set an eye on Siobhán. He seemed to be focused on her tiara. Or the wee fox on top of her head . . .

"This is Rose," Benji said. "My first wife."

"Rose Burns," the woman said. "I'd shake your

hand, but I'm a bit occupied." She nodded to Charlie. Her eyes fell to her son. "How's the scratch?"

"Scratch?" Siobhán asked.

"He tried to help me catch Charlie, but the poor thing was so upset, he accidentally scraped Joseph."

"Got to watch those talons," Joseph said, holding out his arm. An angry red scratch ran from his wrist to his elbow. "I don't know where I put me glove."

"Gladys has asked you to stop leaving that thing around," Benji said. "It's bad enough you got blood on her rolling pin."

Siobhán treated Gladys to a laser stare. "I knew that was blood on your rolling pin."

"Whoops," Gladys said.

"Why did you tell us it was from a cherry tart?" Siobhán said.

Gladys's face turned a bright pink. "I didn't want you to think we were the violent sort. Especially since you'll be our new neighbors."

"Does this mean there are no cherry tarts in the oven?" Macdara sounded disappointed.

Siobhán couldn't take her eyes off the hawk. She looked to see if Aretta was equally fascinated, but the newest garda was nowhere to be seen. When did she take off, and where did she go? Siobhán scanned the area and found her back at the squad car. She must have left shortly after Rose joined the group.

"They found Tommy," Gladys said. "He's in the slurry pit."

Rose took a step back. "What did you say?"

"He didn't do a runner," Gladys said. "Why is he in there?" Her voice was shrill and panicked.

"When you say you found Tommy, you don't mean . . . ?"

"He's dead, Mam," Joseph said. "They found his remains in the slurry pit next door."

Macdara held up his hands. "Please. We have no formal identification of the skeletal remains."

"I can't believe it," Rose said. "Give me two shakes to get this guy into his cage. The wildlife center will be so relieved to have him back." She turned and headed toward a bright yellow lorry parked in the drive. Black letters splashed across the lorry spelled out KILBANE WILDLIFE CENTER. She had fled so quickly after hearing the news about Tommy. And there had been a catch in her voice. Did she really need to return the hawk this instant, or was she wanting to take in the news on her own?

"Mam works at the wildlife center," Joseph said, noticing Siobhán's gaze. "But sometimes we bring Charlie here to train."

"Why is everyone chin-wagging when we should be focused on finding my Tommy's killer?" Gladys asked.

"We don't know anything for sure," Macdara said. "Including whether or not our skeleton is your Tommy. I promise you, we intend to find out. But you mustn't disturb the crime scene."

"You saw him," Gladys said. "He's still wearing his tux."

"We saw black material that could be a tux," Macdara said. "But there's too much muck, and it will be a long while before we know anything for sure."

"His tux," Gladys repeated, as if Macdara's words held no sway. "He planned on being at the church. He planned on marrying me."

Rose and Benji exchanged a look; then both looked away, as if they'd been caught doing something they shouldn't.

"Alan said he ran off. Why would Alan say that? Why did he make us all believe that?" Gladys whirled around and pointed at her husband. "Is Alan in the house?"

"No," Benji said. "I heard him leave early this morning."

"You did?" Gladys sounded shocked. "Where did he get off to?"

"How would I know?" Benji said. "I didn't grill the man as he was on his way out the door."

"Alan never gets up early."

"He did this morning. Had a measuring tape in his hand. I thought he was going to buy a snooker table."

"Snooker table?" Gladys said. "What do you mean?"

"I heard Alan on the phone, heard him mention 'snooker' several times. Then next thing you know, he's setting off with his measuring tape."

"Where in the world did he think he was going to put a snooker table?" Gladys sounded outraged.

"He's your brother. How am I supposed to know what's going on in that big head of his?"

"We don't have room for a Snooker table," Gladys said. "Where would we have put it?"

"I have no idea," Benji said. "I'm only telling you what I know."

"Men!" Gladys turned to Siobhán. "Are we done here?"

"For now," Siobhán said before Macdara could disagree. She, for one, needed to get this tiara and fox den off her poor head before the hawk made it his new home.

"I'm going to find Alan." Gladys hurried away from the group, still talking, her voice echoing across the fields. "I'm going to find him, and then I'm going to kill him!"

Chapter 5

Downtown Kilbane was in full summer bloom. Flowers sprang from window boxes and gardens, the grass around the abbey was bright and shiny, and birds soared and chirped underneath a clear blue sky. The sun was expected to make appearances all week, and not one soul intended on wasting it. The new bookshop in town, Turn the Page, had set up shelves on the footpath in front of the shop, stocked with all variety of books to draw in the townsfolk. When they first opened, they'd sold only literary fiction, but after an outcry from the villagers, they had quickly expanded their repertoire. Siobhán still wanted to read the books on Oran and Padraig McCarthy's must-read list, and she intended on working her way through it, but she was also thrilled to have her options expanded. A trip to the bookshop was now a monthly highlight, and multiple book groups were springing up in town, complete with cocktails and conversation.

But even that would have to wait—Siobhán wanted to concentrate on this case so they could reschedule the wedding. What were the chances of finding the skeleton fifty years to the date of another interrupted wedding? It was a worrisome thought, which was why, as soon as they left the farm, Siobhán dashed into the bistro for the solace of a cappuccino. Aretta, who did not drink cappuccinos, or eat much of anything, from what Siobhán could tell, accompanied her and took notes as Siobhán went through everything they knew about the case so far.

The sight of their sign, NAOMI'S BISTRO, in robin's egg blue, along with the sound of the little bell that dinged as they entered the hallway leading into the bistro filled Siobhán with joy. The bistro, named after her late mam, Naomi O'Sullivan, was both the home and business of the O'Sullivans. Their bedrooms were upstairs, and the downstairs functioned as a work space for breakfast and lunch, but they closed at suppertime, because that was family time. And if anyone was feeling claustrophobic, they could slip out to the back garden, where they would be accompanied and followed around by their Jack Russell, Trigger, who had to sniff everything anyone touched.

Siobhán stood in the main dining room now, surveying the place with nostalgia. She loved it. She loved their commercial kitchen with two large ovens; she loved the fireplace, which was usually roaring, even on a summer evening; and she loved the windows overlooking Sarsfield Street. Did she really want to leave this place and move into an old stone house? Could she see herself standing in front of the house with a mug of tea, watching as Ciarán and Ann tore across the fields? Would Grannie, Eoin, and James move in as well? Despite living above this bistro her entire life, they did not own the building. Wouldn't it feel nice to have some security? An investment? They didn't have to keep running a bistro, unless Eoin wanted to keep it going—not because they were depending on it, but because it was his passion. Was this meant to be? Was it time to move on? Or would it be too many changes too quickly for Ann and Ciarán?

Normally, the bistro would be jammers at this time of day, but today they were closed due to the wedding. She imagined that at this very moment the guests were in full throttle, enjoying the reception at the abbey. What a grand day to be out in the ruins of their gorgeous Dominican priory. Siobhán wanted them to enjoy it, but the thought of their interrupted nuptials was still so strange and shocking that she put it out of her mind. What were the chances they'd get another sunny day to celebrate outdoors? Siobhán headed straight to the cappuccino maker behind the counter to make a large one to go. As the machine whirred, Aretta spoke over the noise.

"I've been meaning to ask you. What did you think of the house?"

"What house?"

Aretta frowned. "Your new farmhouse."

"Oh." *Oh.* "I haven't seen the inside yet." She

turned to Aretta. She seemed to be wrestling with something. "Wait. Have you?"

She nodded. "I think it's lovely."

"Something to look forward to, then," Siobhán said. She handed Aretta a mug of herbal tea and grabbed them ham and cheese toasties from the case. She had a feeling that all meals today would be consumed on the go. Aretta turned down the sandwich, thanking her but saying that she'd brought her own lunch. Siobhán resisted the urge to demand proof—Aretta's birdlike eating habits were none of her business. She couldn't imagine getting through a day without delightful some-things to eat.

"I want to speak to the Realtor who sold Mac-dara the property and see what we can learn about any previous rentals," Siobhán said.

Aretta held up her mobile phone and jiggled it. "Why don't I pop out and give them a bell now?"

"Good idea. I want to know the last time they vis-ited the property, and we'll need the name of the caretaker."

Aretta nodded, then looked as if she wasn't sure where to go to place the call.

"The garden is nice, and you can get a clear sig-nal by the rosebushes."

"You read my mind." Aretta headed for the back garden.

Siobhán did not think they would learn any-thing relevant about previous renters. Their killer was someone who had never left. Someone still vis-iting the concrete tomb. No. *Tending it*. Fresh branches on top of the slurry pit may not seem like much of a clue, but it said something to Siobhán about the killer. He or she was showing a certain outlook with the choice of coverage. *Affection?* Flowers would have been too obvious, but most people would probably overlook branches. Had the killer loved the victim and felt guilty about Tommy's demise? Could the death have been an accident?

It would be a compounded tragedy if that were the case. Hiding a body was a crime.

And what would this person do once there was no grave to visit? If only they could assign a guard to trail each of their suspects. One of them had been tending a grave for fifty years. But recently, there had been a change—a big one. The sale of the property. The killer—assuming the victim was this Tommy and he had been murdered—knew the property had been sold. To a detective sergeant and his garda wife . . .

That was why he or she had been forced to take action. Either move the old bones or . . . *let someone find them . . .*

Why hadn't the killer removed Tommy's remains? Was it possible he or she had just assumed no one would clean out the old slurry pit? By the time they saw James working in the barn, had it been too late? Knowing her brother James, once he got started on that barn, he was probably hanging around most days. Even though he didn't drink anymore, he still had an addict's personality. She could imagine him working morning until night, day after day. Had the killer wanted to sneak in, but James had made it difficult? What if the killer had planned on removing the body during the wedding? James had even worked on the barn that very morning. His very life could have been in danger. He had been right there. Close enough to the pit to drop his phone into the depths. He'd started to leave for the wedding when suddenly he spotted a hawk in seeming distress, swooping around the barn. . . .

Had Charlie been set loose on purpose? Had the killer been trying to draw James out of the barn?

Then why hadn't the killer removed the skeleton the minute James took off? Perhaps he or she hadn't figured out where to put it. Or he or she had been interrupted before the skeleton could be moved. This was the challenge of a murder probe. The beginning of a case offered an endless array of possibilities. A garda's job was to whittle away the possible until it was left with the probable.

Aretta returned from the garden. "Mr. and Mrs. Tealy," she said. "I spoke to the missus. She says they haven't been to the property in ten years. The caretaker . . . Are you ready for this? Benji Burns."

"Interesting." It made sense to pay a neighbor to watch over the property, but Siobhán was disappointed. All the suspects lived in his orbit, so if he saw them hanging around, he wouldn't think anything of it, and chances were good even if he had seen one of them hanging around the dairy barn on a regular basis, he would keep that information to himself. And of course, he could be the killer, in which case he was definitely keeping that information to himself. "We'll have to ask Mr. Burns for a list of the farmers who used the property to let their animals graze. Maybe one of them can shed some light on the situation."

Aretta made a note of it. "What else?"

"We need to circle back to Rose Burns and find out exactly how her hawk got loose this morning."

Aretta laughed. "Circle back. Just like Charlie."

"Indeed," Siobhán said. "I find that very interesting."

"What are you thinking?"

"I'm thinking it was meant to draw James out of the barn. I'm wondering why our killer didn't get rid of the bones. It's almost as if the killer decided today was the day." Siobhán didn't realize she was pacing the bistro until she noticed Aretta tracking her moves. "The anniversary, if you will."

"I like watching your process," Aretta said. "It's like watching a chess master."

Siobhán laughed. "I'll take the compliment, but I'm not feeling at the top of my game just yet." She needed to speak with James and carefully go over everything about his work on the property, including any other lads who had been involved. "We need to pinpoint the last person to see Tommy alive."

Aretta blinked. "From fifty years ago?"

Siobhán nodded. "We have to try." At least all their suspects were still here fifty years later. That was a saving grace.

"Will we be scheduling official interviews?"

Aretta still had that eager-to-learn aura about her, and Siobhán was buoyed by it. It took years before the job started to wear on a person. Siobhán wasn't completely jaded, but she no longer got butterflies at the prospect of interviewing suspects. Macdara, on the other hand, still gave her butterflies. She'd certainly had them at her wedding. The thought of Gladys standing there, left humiliated and alone at the altar, sent waves of empathy crashing through Siobhán. It almost felt personal. It was personal, wasn't it? The killer had interrupted her wedding this time. . . .

"We will schedule official interviews, of course, once we have an official cause of death, not to mention a positive identification on our victim. For now, the goal is to have casual conversations with anyone who knew Tommy Caffrey. We can play hardball after the examination of the bones."

"I am fascinated by the study of old bones," Aretta said. "I read once that examiners could tell a man was a pipe smoker because of the way in which his teeth had turned in. Only a few teeth left in his poor head, but those two teeth gave away his pipe-smoking habit."

"It is a fascinating subject." Siobhán knew they could tell sex, age, habits, diseases and, in some cases, how the person might have died. Once more she thought of her father's familiar saying: *I love the bones of ya.* Tommy could no longer speak. But his bones could. One of their only tools, given the fact that fifty years had passed. The killer had gotten away with it for fifty years. Did this make him or her feel invincible? If so, they would make mistakes. They needed to watch their suspects carefully. *Like a hawk.* Siobhán turned to Aretta. "I need a favor, and it's not very professional."

"I'm intrigued," Aretta said, sounding somewhat worried.

Siobhán pointed to the tiara cemented to her poor head. "It's really stuck in there."

Aretta laughed. "I can help with that."

Siobhán sat down, and Aretta gently began removing the pins from the tiara until she could safely pull it loose. Siobhán's auburn hair spilled down in a mess of waves. The pressure that had been bearing down on her suddenly lifted. Siobhán massaged her head. The things women put themselves through. . . .

"Thank heavens. Maybe now my headache will go away."

They headed out of the bistro, and Siobhán threw a glance in the direction of the ruined abbey as they began the walk back to the garda station. Were her guests still there? Had they drunk all the champagne? Had they cut the cake? She sighed. *Let them eat cake.* They had a killer to catch.

Chapter 6

The Kilbane Garda Station was abuzz with activity as Macdara took over the wall in the main room to begin brainstorming the case. He approached the whiteboard and wrote *skeleton*. Underneath it, *Tommy?* and finally, *slurry pit*.

"We need to get a photo of Tommy," Siobhán said. She wanted to replace the image of that skull and bones with flesh and blood.

"I agree. Once Dr. Brady confirms his identity."

Dr. Jeanie Brady was good at her job. Siobhán had a feeling she'd be very intrigued by this case and up to the challenge. She handed Macdara the ham and cheese toastie, still warm from the microwave.

He gave her a cheeky look. "Thank you. You'll make a great wife."

He ducked just as she tried to elbow him and

laughed. "How did we pick our wedding date?" Siobhán asked.

Macdara cocked his head. "What do you mean?"

She approached the whiteboard, grabbed a marker, and wrote *Gladys and Tommy—wedding anniversary.*

"Is it an anniversary if the wedding never took place?" Macdara asked.

"It could also be a murder anniversary," Siobhán said.

"Dark."

"Their wedding date is our exact wedding date."

"Fifty years apart? You really think there's a connection?"

"I do not like coincidences."

Macdara rubbed his chin. "We conferred with Father Kearney. Didn't he pick the date?"

"We looked at the calendar together. I remember that." She wrote and underlined *wedding date* on the board. "But did he mention the sixteenth of June, or did we?"

"We wanted a Saturday in June. We looked at all the Saturdays. That's all I can remember."

Saturdays were a popular day for a wedding, and untold number of weddings probably happened on the same date all the time with no foul play being involved, but this one she just couldn't shake. "We need to speak with Father Kearney right away."

"What are you getting at?"

"I'm just wondering if the killer somehow . . . Is it too far-fetched to think the killer somehow nudged us to choose this date?"

Macdara frowned. "I don't see how that would be possible. We can certainly ask Father Kearney how he keeps his appointments, but I'm afraid this is just a very odd coincidence."

"I do not like coincidences," Siobhán said again. Macdara stuck the ham and cheese toastie in his piehole, the perfect excuse for Siobhán to keep talking. "The killer knew today was the fiftieth anniversary of the wedding that never was. I think he or she used the diversion of the hawk to get James out of the barn so he or she could move the bones."

Macdara gestured at the board with his ham and cheese toastie, sending crumbs flying. "So why didn't he or she move the bones?"

"That's what we have to find out."

"How? There isn't going to be any CCTV footage of the dairy barn."

"Old-fashioned detective work, I suppose." She sighed. "There's another possibility."

"Lay it on me."

"What if the killer had no intention of moving the bones? What if he or she decided it was time for Tommy to be discovered? And he or she chose this exact date. Gladys and Tommy's wedding day. *Our* wedding day."

Macdara sighed. "I just don't know how that would even be possible."

"That's why we need to speak with Father Kearney." She picked up a marker underneath the whiteboard. "There's yet another angle."

"Go on." Macdara leaned against a desk.

"Someone else, not the killer, has known about

Tommy's secret burial place. And it was this person who decided today was the day to reveal his whereabouts."

"You're not saying this is personal, are you?"

"Personal?"

"Our wedding. Was someone trying to stop our wedding?"

Siobhán frowned. "I don't know. Who would want to do that?" She gasped. "Do you think it was someone who wasn't invited?"

"Sorry I mentioned it. I thought we were just saying anything that came to our minds."

Siobhán jotted it down anyway. It was good to shake it all out, sift through the possibilities.

"I don't like the type of person we seem to be describing. A control freak. It makes us all look like puppets whose strings are being yanked." Macdara went to the window and stared out at the town square, as if the answer were out there waiting, just out of reach.

"Exactly," Siobhán said.

"I don't like having me strings pulled."

"I don't either, Pinocchio. But you know what else I don't like?"

"Coincidences," Macdara said before turning around and shoving the last bite of toastie into his gob.

"Coincidences," Siobhán said. "I do not like coincidences."

The day passed quickly, and by the end of the evening, just as the sun was dipping below the horizon, Macdara and Siobhán were back at the farmhouse. Given they were supposed to be on their honeymoon, Ciarán and Ann had already arranged sleepovers with friends. Siobhán and Macdara had picked up supper from the chipper, and once at the property Macdara pulled out a bottle of champagne. They sat in a pair of folding chairs near the house and toasted as the sun began to set, painting the sky in glorious shades of red and orange. The meal from the chipper hit the spot, and they stayed as the skies turned pitch black. Unlike the streetlights near the bistro, which muted the stars, here they were showcased in their glory, an overhead dome of twinkling gems. If Siobhán could, she'd lock this night up in a bottle like a message to herself. *Enjoy the small moments, because in the end they turn out to be the big ones.* She took Dara's hand, wanting to imprint the evening in her mind.

"Are you sure you don't want to go inside?" Macdara asked as they tidied up and prepared to return to Macdara's flat. Was he going to keep it if they moved into the farmhouse? Given its location right next to the garda station, it was probably worth hanging on to. It could also serve as a guest flat if they ever needed one.

"I can't decide," she said. "Part of me wants to wait until we're married."

"I feel the same," Macdara said. "Or we could pop in real quick before we change our minds."

They studied the house, as if expecting it to cast a vote. It remained neutral. "Let's wait," Siobhán said. "It will help motivate us to solve the case." The truth was there was part of her afraid to open that door. As if once she did, her future would be chosen and set—this time not just in stone but in a stone house. If she fell in love with the house, this was not the time to start interior decorating. If she didn't love it, now was not the time to break the news to Macdara. It would be a better experience if they waited until the case was solved.

"This case interrupted our wedding," Macdara said. "I'm extremely motivated to solve it." He pulled her in for a kiss that reminded her that no matter what future doors lay ahead of them, they would enter them together.

Before leaving, they walked around the outside of the house to make sure nothing had been disturbed, but the doors were all locked, and everything seemed in order. The house was far enough away from the dairy barn that it wasn't technically a crime scene, but Macdara posted a guard nearby just to keep an eye out.

"Let's have dessert at the bistro," Siobhán said. "It's not often we have it all to ourselves." Eoin, James, and Gráinne had also planned on staying elsewhere for the week. Given Siobhán and Macdara couldn't take time off for a proper honeymoon, they had planned on a few romantic days to themselves.

"You don't have to ask me twice."

They returned to the bistro, where Siobhán lit a fire and discovered Bridie had been a dear and left them a large chunk of wedding cake. It had been a three-tiered white cake dotted with emerald shamrocks and topped with a porcelain claddagh symbol inside a Celtic knot. *Gorgeous.* She intended on ordering the exact same one for the do-over.

Macdara stood in front of it with a large knife. "Are you sure this isn't bad luck?"

"Who are you kidding? You were about to dive into it face-first."

He grinned. "Not if you disapprove."

"Not at all. It's good luck."

"It's good luck to eat cake from a wedding that never was?"

"It will be, and it's not like the cake is going to last—not to mention there will be another cake at our future wedding, and we'll be saving part of that for our first anniversary."

"Anniversary," he said. "I like the sound of that."

"I'll fetch the tea—and make sure you save a slice for my face too."

After the most delicious vanilla cake with raspberry filling and real cream frosting, they stayed up half the night, conversation alternating between the case and their daydreams of the farmhouse. Soon the topic circled back to choosing the date for their wedding, and that was when Siobhán remembered something.

"Father Kearney's appointment book. He always writes everything down in that book, and anyone who ever attended Mass knows that he keeps it front and center on his desk."

"Okay," Macdara said. "And?"

"Maybe someone went through it. Maybe they penciled in engagements on other Saturdays, thus forcing our wedding to be at a precise date and time?"

"How did the killer know we were looking at a Saturday in June?"

"We've been talking about it for ages. They could have overheard me in the bistro, or one of us at work or at the chipper—anywhere we ran our mouths!"

"But . . . why?" He shook his head. "I don't think I'm with you on this one."

Siobhán was still mulling it over when the downstairs clock chimed three times. Siobhán groaned. "It's three o'clock in the morning."

"How is that possible?" Macdara said, stretching and rubbing his eyes. If they didn't get some shut-eye now, they might as well stay up the rest of the night. And even though it was a Sunday, Siobhán knew they were still going to be working the case. Murderers did not take weekends off. But sleepy minds would be no match for this one. They agreed to go up to bed.

Upstairs, Macdara gave her one of his looks. "This would have been our wedding night," he said.

Siobhán laughed. "It isn't anything we haven't already done," she said as she approached him for a kiss.

"True," he said with a half growl as he nuzzled her neck. "But not as husband and wife."

"We might as well practice, then," Siobhán said.

"As much as it takes," Macdara said. "I'm a slow learner. Now, where is that tiara?"

A few hours of sleep later and it was time to start the day. Macdara made a full Irish breakfast for them, and afterward Siobhán gave Father Kearney a bell and left a message requesting a meeting. They could have gone to Mass, but they both felt the urgency of solving this case. Siobhán had just reached a nearby slurry pit and was talking to the owner when Macdara rushed up to her.

"Hang up," he said.

She dropped the phone and gasped as she continued to stare at it. "He was mid-sentence," she said. "I can't believe I just did that."

"He'll get over it," Macdara said. "We have to go back out to the farm."

A knot formed in Siobhán's stomach. "What now?"

Macdara held up his mobile. "Benji just left me a message—something about an emergency. And now he won't answer his phone. I tried Gladys, and she's not picking up either."

"Have you called the guards posted at the dairy barn?"

"No," Macdara said. "If they're slacking on the job, I'd rather take them by surprise."

They headed out to the car, which thankfully they'd parked in front of the bistro. "A sneak attack on the guards posted at the barn," Siobhán said. "Noted."

"Do I hear something in your tone?" Macdara asked as they climbed in, and he started the car.

"I can only hope the sneak attack applies only to the folks at work," Siobhán said. "Because I, for one, do not like sneak attacks."

Macdara laughed. "Coincidences and sneak attacks," he said. "The things Siobhán O'Sullivan does not like."

"And sarcasm," she said. "As long as you're making a list."

*   *   *

The excitement of pulling up to their property was diminished by the small crowd gathered on the Burnses' front porch. Siobhán groaned. "Who are all those people? We asked them to keep this quiet."

"Yes, but did we really think they would?"

Siobhán made sure to slam the car door extra loud so they'd know how she felt about their impromptu lawn party. She began to count the participants. In addition to Ben and Gladys, there was Rose, another older woman that she did not recognize, Joseph, and an older man. Siobhán assumed the two newcomers were Gladys's siblings, Alan and Linda O'Leary. Everyone was gathered around Gladys, and when they stepped back, Siobhán saw why. Gladys was holding court dressed in a wedding gown. Siobhán knew her mouth had dropped open, and she could hear her mam's voice teasing her about collecting flies, but the sight of Gladys in a wedding gown was so unexpected that it took Siobhán a few minutes to collect herself.

"Is that why we're here?" Macdara leaned in and whispered. "Do you think she's lost the plot?"

"She's at least torn out a few pages," Siobhán said. "And they say you never wear it again."

"Should we call the medics?" Macdara pulled out his mobile and stared down at it, as if calling the medics for an octogenarian pretend bride wasn't on his Sunday to-do list.

"I keep putting myself in her place," Siobhán said. "It's unimaginable."

"It's unimaginable because you wouldn't be in her place," Macdara said. "You'd never believe for a moment that I'd leave you at the altar. And if you thought I did—heaven help me, you'd be on me tail."

Siobhán gave him a gentle shove. "I will have to face it one day. Your demise."

Macdara frowned. "Unless you go first."

"Men die first when all things are even, and you're nine years older. You're definitely going first."

"Thank goodness we're not writing our own vows."

As they drew close, Gladys stepped forward, fat tears running down her face. "I swear to ye it wasn't me."

"What wasn't you, luv?" Siobhán felt a squeeze of pity for Gladys. She gestured to the wedding dress, trying to keep her voice bright. "I see it still fits. Well done you."

Instead of laughing or even smiling at the compliment, Gladys stared as if Siobhán were the one that had lost the plot. "You don't know, do you?" Gladys whipped her head around and zeroed in on her husband. "I thought you told them."

"I just told them to come straightaway," Benji said. He jittered beside her, and sweat ran down the side of his face. He looked terrified.

Siobhán frowned. This wasn't about Gladys losing the plot. Something else was going on. Before Siobhán could come out and ask, Gladys stepped forward and pointed to the guards stationed in front of the dairy barn. Cigarette smoke curled into the air above them, and their voices rang with laughter. Were they being called out there because the guards were being disrespectful?

"We only went in to pay our respects," Gladys said.

"Went in?" Siobhán took a step forward. They didn't mean . . . They wouldn't have. . . . They *couldn't* have. . . . "Went in?"

"It's been fifty years," Gladys said, the pitch of her voice rising. "How can we ruin evidence when he's been out there for fifty years?"

Siobhán had that sinking feeling in her gut. "What did you do?"

Gladys looked down at her dress. "I wanted to show him. He's in his tux. I only thought it right. To wear my dress. He never got to see it." She gestured to the group behind her. "They should have all gone in. To apologize." Her comment ended in a shout.

"Tell her now," Benji said. "Or they're going to think you're guilty."

"Are you saying that you entered our crime scene again?" Macdara asked.

Gladys wouldn't make eye contact with him, but she nodded.

"Tell me you didn't touch anything."

"I ran out the minute I saw him." Gladys slapped her hand over her mouth, slammed into her husband's chest, and buried her face in his shoulder.

"Do you understand what's going on?" Macdara whispered to Siobhán.

"I'm still missing a piece of the puzzle," Siobhán said. "How did you get past our guards?" She directed the latter to the back of Gladys's sobbing head.

"She snuck in through the back door," Benji said.

"Snuck in?" Siobhán said. How in the world could an old woman in a wedding dress sneak past the guards?

"When the guards took a break," Benji said.

"Took a break?" Macdara stepped forward. "It's half ten in the morning. Who needs a break at half ten in the morning?"

"They drove off for a bit. I don't know why."

Siobhán and Macdara turned their gaze to the guards, who were now standing straighter, faces serious, cigarettes snubbed out. Apparently, Siobhán wasn't the only one who didn't like sneak attacks.

"I feel bad for them," Benji said. "They haven't a clue."

Siobhán didn't think she had a clue either.

"What are we missing?" Macdara said. "You called us out to confess that you entered our crime scene in a wedding dress or to let us know our guards are taking breaks?"

"No," Gladys said. "You don't understand." She buried her face in her hands and began to sob.

The woman whom Siobhán did not recognize stepped forward. Her hair was the same mixture of gray and white as Gladys's, but hers was cut in a bob. She was dressed in a pink suit with a pillbox hat, as if she had come straight from Mass. She held a matching pink handkerchief, and her eyes were puffy and red. "I'm Linda," she said. "Gladys's sister. It's my brother Alan."

Siobhán frowned and glanced at the other man in the group. He was tall and beefy, with a bald head. He wore a tan suit, as if he too had just come from the morning Mass. Siobhán nodded to the man. "Are you Alan?"

"No," Linda said, shaking her head. "You don't understand."

"My name is Howard Dunn," the man said with a slight bow. "I was Tommy's business partner back in the day."

Siobhán hadn't recognized him; then again, he wasn't in her regular circle of folk.

"The missing money," Macdara said.

"Yes," Howard said. "And I know you haven't processed the scene yet, and it's been fifty years. But if the money is still there . . ."

"We'll keep all that in mind," Macdara said.

Siobhán turned back to Linda. This was the sister who had apparently hated Tommy and had tried to talk Gladys out of marrying him. Linda lifted a small white handbag and removed a pair of baby booties. They were light blue. She handed them to Siobhán. "These are for you."

"For me?" Siobhán couldn't possibly have heard correctly. Were both sisters having a mental breakdown at the same time?

"You're getting married. Moving into the big house next door." Linda O'Leary pointed to the booties. "The baby will be next."

"Apparently, we're having a boy," Macdara said. Siobhán wanted to elbow him more than she'd ever wanted to in her life, but he was a safe distance away.

"Sorry," Siobhán said, turning to Linda once again. "What about your brother, Alan?" *A baby. This is what people are going to do to us. Pressure us to have a baby.*

"He's gone," Linda wailed. "Our dear brother is gone."

Siobhán was still lost. "He went somewhere gone or . . . ?"

Gladys stepped forward. "He's dead. Our brother Alan is dead."

"What happened?" Macdara asked. He pointed to the house. "Is he in there?"

"No," Linda said, pointing to the dairy barn. "He's in the slurry pit."

This time both Siobhán's and Macdara's mouths dropped open.

"You're saying it's not Tommy in the slurry pit? It's your brother Alan?" Siobhán asked, grasping at straws. That didn't make sense either. Siobhán needed her headache tablets.

Macdara started for the dairy barn. "I have half a mind to arrest all of you for trespassing."

"Gladys is the one who trespassed," Rose said. "The rest of us had no choice but to run in when she screamed."

A cold spot formed in the nape of Siobhán's neck as she watched Macdara stride for the barn, and the pieces fell into place. Gladys had donned her wedding dress. She'd planned on sneaking into the dairy barn to "show" Tommy. When she arrived at the slurry pit, she'd screamed loud enough to bring everyone else running. Siobhán took in their shocked faces, their grief, and she had enough pieces to make a picture.

Alan O'Leary, Gladys and Linda's brother, was indeed dead, but he wasn't in the house. Tommy was no longer lying in that dark pit all alone. There was *another* body at their crime scene. Not just blackened bones, this one had flesh and blood. A saying floated through Siobhán's mind even as she ran after Macdara and tried to convince herself that this could not be happening. Her mam used to love reading the American writer Erma Bombeck, and Siobhán could only imagine if corpses could talk, she could guess what the victims might say: *If life is a bowl of cherries, what are we doing in the pits?*

Chapter 7

Siobhán O'Sullivan had been many things in life. Sister. Mother figure. Lover. Fiancée. Friend. Bistro owner. Garda. Chocolate-and-crisp eater, jogger, brown-bread baker, scooter rider. But she'd very rarely been speechless. It seemed impossible to believe the sight in front of them, yet there he was, ten feet down, a large older man in gray trousers and a white shirt, lying faceup in the slurry pit. Beneath his bulk, Siobhán could see what appeared to be spiky black sticks poking out, but she knew what they really were. Hand bones. The dead body was crushing what remained of Tommy's skeleton. What little hair he had left on his head formed the letter *U* around a bald patch. His left temple was slightly caved in, with blood pooled around it and running down his left side. His right eye was wide open. Another patch of blood coated the back left corner of the slurry pit. It seemed apparent that the blow had probably killed him. Had he tripped, or had he been pushed?

"He would have fallen in facedown," Siobhán said, pointing to his head wound and then to the blood on the back left corner of the pit. "It appears he struck his temple on the back left-hand corner of the pit." *Just like Tommy?*

"He was facedown when I found him," a female voice from behind informed them. They whirled around to find Gladys right behind them. She certainly had a way of sneaking up on people, even in that wedding dress.

"You turned him over?" Siobhán wasn't surprised that Gladys would want to turn him over. After all, she had to see if he was alive and in need of help. The surprise was that this tiny woman had managed on her own.

"We had to turn him over. We had to see if he was alive," Gladys said.

"Who is 'we'?" Siobhán asked. The slurry pit had an iron ladder attached to one side, allowing farmhands easy access in and out. She quickly scanned the wedding gown, but there was no muck to be seen on it.

Gladys swallowed and shook her head. "I didn't even realize that I was screaming. They all came running." She lifted her eyes to Macdara. "Everyone but your guards, that is."

Macdara's face flashed red. He gave a curt nod. Siobhán could tell from the look on his face that the guards were going to be sacked. And rightly so. "Exactly who touched the body?" Macdara asked.

"It was Benji and Howard who turned him over." She began to sob.

Siobhán couldn't take it. This elderly woman was standing in front of a pit that contained her fiancé and her brother. She went over to Gladys and gave her hand a squeeze.

"Benji and Howard," Macdara said, easing up on his tone. "I don't suppose they wore gloves."

"Why would they wear gloves?" Gladys sniffed and blinked.

"Why don't we get you back to the house for a cup of tea?" Siobhán said. She was just about to guide Gladys out of the barn when she flashed back to a few minutes ago, when she was standing in front of the O'Leary house, staring at Benji and Howard. "I didn't see muck on their clothing either."

"Pardon?" Gladys said. The teary voice was gone, and this time Gladys was the one who sounded harsh.

"If Benji and Howard crawled down here and rolled this body over, why didn't I see muck on their clothing?" Yes, the pit was nearly dried up, but there would have been plenty of bits sticking to them, and she hadn't seen or smelled a thing.

Gladys stared at Siobhán, then at the floor, then looked away. "They showered and changed," she said. "Their clothes are in the wash."

Macdara groaned.

Gladys turned to them. "What on earth is the matter?"

"Do you think your brother hurled himself into the pit?" Siobhán asked. "Those clothes could be evidence."

"Evidence?" Gladys said. "Of what?"

"Foul play," Macdara said.

Gladys frowned. "I assumed he had a heart attack."

"And on the way down happened to conk his head?" Macdara placed his hand on Siobhán's shoulder. She was getting too worked up.

"Are you saying someone murdered me brother, just like they did my Tommy?"

"We aren't saying anything yet," Macdara said. "There will be a thorough investigation."

"No one would want to kill my brother. Who would want to kill my brother?"

Siobhán hesitated. Was now a good or a bad time to bring up the last words she'd heard Gladys utter on their previous visit? *I'm going to kill him.* Had she spoken to him? Siobhán was about to ask when Macdara cut in.

"I'm going to escort you home and get someone to make you a cup of tea," Macdara said. He turned to Siobhán. "I'll call in the team and be right back."

She nodded. A minute after they left, Siobhán spotted something underneath Alan's right hip. It looked like a piece of leather. She knelt to see if she could get a closer look. It was a glove. Tassels hung off the end. She'd seen something like this before. An image of Rose Burns's outstretched arm flashed before her, the gorgeous hawk perched like royalty on her fist. *A falconer's glove.*

When Macdara returned, she pointed it out. "The last time we were here, Rose was wearing one just like it."

"Interesting," Macdara said. "And it definitely wasn't there before."

Had Alan brought it out to the pit? If so, why? "I

wonder what else is on him or underneath him," Siobhán mused. She was dying to touch. Lift the bodies out of the slurry pit and scour them for more evidence. It was the worst bit about this job. The endless waiting. She understood the reasons for such protocol, but she dreamed of cases where she could just dive in and begin sifting through clues. Luckily, until Jeanie Brady arrived, there was plenty they could do, starting with interrogating their suspects.

Siobhán was standing in the middle of the field— *her* field, she had to remind herself—with her mobile phone poised to dial Dr. Jeanie Brady, when an unpleasant realization clamped down on her. "Oh, no," she said. "I can't call Dr. Brady."

Macdara, who was standing a few feet away, preparing to make his own phone calls, turned and raised an eyebrow. "Afraid she's going to flip out about our two-for-one murder scene?"

"She's the one I forgot."

"I'm not following."

"I forgot to invite Jeanie Brady to our wedding!"

Macdara exhaled, as if he'd been bracing for much worse news. "She won't hold it against you. She probably won't even mention it." His eyes gave off a sparkle of mischief. "Good thing you left your tiara at home this time."

"Very funny," Siobhán said, giving him a slug to the shoulder. "We'll invite her to the next one."

"The next one with me in it or the one you plan on having after I die?"

"As long as she's invited to one or the other, I'm sure she'll be happy out."

When Siobhán finished her phone call, she found Macdara and Aretta waiting for her in a patch of field between their house and the O'Learys'. Siobhán couldn't get over the fresh smell in the air. She imagined it had been quite different when the place was an active dairy farm.

"All sorted?" Macdara asked.

"Dr. Brady said they'll be here as soon as they can. And she was thrilled with the wedding invite."

"How did you invite her? We don't have a date set."

"I just told her we would be setting a date and she would be invited."

"Are we heading back to the station now?" Aretta asked.

Siobhán glanced next door, where the guests were still gathered on the front porch, with the exception of Rose, who was pacing in front of the house. This time she did not have a bird of prey on her arm, which meant she also did not have a falconer's glove on her arm. Was it the one lying in the slurry pit? How many falconer's gloves could be lying around Kilbane? Hadn't Joseph mentioned that he'd lost a glove? The falcon had scratched him, he'd bled, and the blood had got on Gladys's rolling pin. The one that Gladys had then pretended had juice from a cherry tart on it and had stuck in her mouth. For no apparent reason, other than she didn't want the guards to think they were the violent sort. "I think we should do some on-the-spot interviewing before our suspects can collaborate on a story."

"And while the events of last night and this morning are still fresh in their minds," Macdara added.

Aretta let out a laugh. Siobhán and Macdara turned in unison. "Your personalities are very different but complementary," she said, still laughing to herself.

"How do you mean?" Siobhán asked.

"You are the pessimist, and Macdara is the optimist."

"You're joking me." Siobhán was stunned. *She* was the pessimist?

"You are worried about suspects making up stories—*lying*—and Macdara is focused on using their memories to get us to the truth."

Macdara was looking anywhere but at Siobhán. Garda Dabiri had a blunt way of speaking, and although it could be somewhat irksome, it was also devoid of any malice. She offered irrefutable facts, but Siobhán often found they all supported a negative view of her. Macdara had told her that she was paranoid that Aretta didn't like her as much as she liked him, while also pointing out that guards didn't have to be friends. They simply had to trust each other enough to work as a team.

But Siobhán wanted a friendship. *Was* she a pessimist? "Every case has someone who lies," Siobhán said. "A single lie can break a case wide open."

Aretta nodded. "I will learn a great deal from both the pessimistic and the optimistic approaches."

Macdara cut in before Siobhán could reply. "I'm also going to keep an eye on the dairy barn until the replacement guards arrive. The others will be on desk duty until we have a serious chat about today's breach." Serious indeed. They had left the job while another murder was committed. That was a career killer.

Siobhán and Macdara pulled notebooks and Biros from their pockets in stereo, and Aretta laughed. She produced a third notebook and Biro with a flourish.

"Great minds," Macdara said.

They approached the Burnses' porch. Heads turned to them, and nervous glances were thrown to the notebooks as they waited.

"We have a few questions for everyone," Macdara said. "And some instructions."

"Instructions?" Benji said. He had the look of a schoolchild who had just learned today was a test day.

"I'm asking you not to discuss the case even amongst yourselves," Macdara began. "Don't leave town, and expect to be called into the station for a formal interview. In the meantime, we're going to have a quick chat with each of you right now."

"Shall we go inside?" Gladys said. "I can arrange some chairs, but I don't think I have this many." She began to point at each person, silently mouthing the count.

"We're going to talk to you individually, as opposed to in a group," Siobhán said.

Nervous glances were exchanged, as if they were silently checking in with each other about whether or not they should comply. Or maybe they were all worried about the others spreading their secrets around like fairy dust.

"Would you allow me to go first?" Gladys said. "I

need to change out of this dress and then get a cup of tea and some headache tablets."

"I'll fix you a cuppa," Linda said quickly. "It will be waiting for you." Linda turned and scrambled into the house.

Was there a reason she was in such a hurry? Why she wouldn't make eye contact? *She's hiding something.* Siobhán wanted to follow her in and question her first.

"Thank you," Gladys called after her.

"I can speak with Gladys inside," Siobhán said. "Let her have her tea."

"Be my guest." Macdara gave Siobhán a nod, and they hoisted their notebooks at each other. They could cover more ground and then share findings.

Gladys and Benji's kitchen was cozy. It was tidy but slightly cluttered and definitely lived in. Figurines and vases were arranged on top of yellow cupboards. Cross-stitch sayings of Irish blessings were framed and hung on the wall. It was a large enough area for a rectangular table with six unforgiving wooden chairs. The table was piled with books and pills and newspapers and a bowl of soft, rotting fruit. Another cupboard was stuffed with teacups, and Gladys shuffled over, removed two, and flipped the kettle on.

Siobhán's suspicions about Linda had been correct: it didn't appear as if she'd come inside to make a cup of tea. "May I see a picture of Tommy?" Siobhán asked. She wanted to be able to picture him.

"Of course," Gladys said. She hurried out of the

room, and moments later she returned with an album in hand. She held it out to Siobhán. "Most of these are photographs of my Tommy."

Siobhán opened it gingerly, as the pages were sticking together. A handsome young man with thick dark hair, piercing eyes, and a big grin stared back at her. It struck Siobhán that he would go from being a young man to being a skeleton with nothing in between. When victims died young, the tragedy was compounded. The killer had swiped his future out from beneath his feet, like a magician pulling out a tablecloth. A surge of anger accompanied her feelings of sadness. "He could have been a movie star," she said. You could see the charm in him, even from an old photograph.

"Everyone said so," Gladys agreed with a soft smile. "He was a charmer."

Siobhán flipped through the pages. There were many of him and a much younger Gladys, and if pictures didn't lie, then anyone could see the pair had been madly in love. "I'd like to keep one picture of Tommy," Siobhán said. "Not forever, of course, but I'd like our guards to relate to him as he was in life." It was already a challenge to get the image of those blackened bones out of her mind, that skull covered in fifty years of muck.

"I know just the one." Gladys gently took the album back and began to leaf through. "Here." She pulled out a picture. Three men stood in front of a pub, grinning. Gladys pointed to the men from left to right. "Alan, Tommy, and Howard with little Joseph." There he was, Tommy, with those same piercing eyes and carefree grin, leaning against the wall. The child, Joseph, with a dirty face and wild hair sat at his feet. His little hands were cupped, as if he was holding something precious. He appeared to be around six or seven years of age. Howard looked roughly the same age as Tommy, but he was shorter and bald, without a trace of a smile.

"Why this picture?"

"It's one of the last photos of all them together. Would you look at Howard . . ." Gladys tapped his photo.

"He doesn't look too happy." He was older and wider now, and objectively much better looking in his younger years. But the look on his face in the photo was definitely that of an unhappy man. Even a mean one. Isn't that what Benji had said? That Joseph came home one day and accused Howard of being mean? The older man who introduced himself to her today did not have that same edge. Perhaps time had mellowed him.

Gladys huffed. "Some things never change."

"You're saying he's always been unhappy?"

"He's always embroiled in a new scheme. The get-rich-quick sort. Only nothing ever pans out, so he's perpetually browned off."

Interesting. "I don't recognize this pub," Siobhán said.

"That is the pub where they were going to start a snooker club. It closed down shortly after Tommy disappeared." She swallowed. "Shortly after he was *murdered.* I'm not used to saying that."

Siobhán studied the photo. *Mulligan's.* "They were going to turn Mulligan's into a snooker club?"

"There's an old warehouse on the property. It

used to make butter. They were going to buy out the warehouse and expand."

Siobhán knew the old butter warehouse. It too had been abandoned for ages. Some unknown brand that couldn't compete with Kerrygold Irish butter. It was then that she realized there was a fourth man in the photo, standing in the open doorway to the pub. He was smiling, but unlike Tommy's infectious grin, his looked uneasy and staged for the camera. "Who is this?"

"That's Benji." Gladys gave a soft laugh. "The two loves of my life in one photo." She pointed out a leather satchel in the photo, at the base of Howard's feet. "That's the missing money. This photo was taken the day they raised the thirty thousand quid." Money was in euro now, but back in the day it was the British pound. Siobhán peered at the satchel, which indeed looked stuffed to the brim with cash.

"Raised it?"

"Won some of it in snooker tournaments, others on the horses, and finished it up with a fundraiser."

"I can imagine they were excited." They still had that moment of joy; thank heavens they had no idea how the future would turn out. This was why it was the little moments in life that counted the most.

"They were quite proud of themselves. You can see the grins on them."

"Except for Howard."

Gladys laughed. "Believe me, that's as close to smiling as I've ever seen him."

Siobhán pointed to the child. "Is that Joseph?" He was a scrawny thing, no hint of the muscular man he would grow up to be. Or was that why he'd grown up that way? Had he been fighting his whole life to shed the scrawny little boy inside? "How old is he here?"

"Goodness. I wouldn't know." She shrugged. "You'll have to ask Benji or Rose." She shook her head. "Lad was only with them a week at this stage, and he's in the dirt in front of a pub."

"He looks happy out. Wonder what's in his hand?"

"Heavens, your eyesight is better than mine."

"You and Benji never had children of your own?"

The kettle shrieked, making Siobhán jump. Gladys sighed, handed the photo and album back to Siobhán, and headed to make the tea. Siobhán sprang up.

"You sit. I'll wet the tea."

Gladys didn't argue as she retook her seat, groaning with the effort. "We tried, but no, we never conceived."

Siobhán set a cup of tea in front of her, then rooted around the fridge until she found the milk. Sugar was already on the table.

"It's a family curse," Gladys said. "None of us O'Learys had children of our own."

Siobhán didn't pursue the line of questioning. She had too many conflicting thoughts about herself and Macdara having children. On one hand, it was impossible to imagine having a baby. On the other hand, it was impossible to imagine not having a baby. *Someday.* Was her clock ticking? She wanted it to stop. There were so many things she wanted to do. "Do you mind if I hang on to the entire album for a bit?"

Gladys looked stricken. "They're my only photos of Tommy."

"I swear to ya, I won't let it out of my sight."

"Do you really think it will help?"

"It can't hurt."

"You may borrow it, then. No sticky fingers."

Siobhán didn't know if she meant it literally or figuratively, but she intended on avoiding both definitions, so she agreed. She wet her own tea and sat, watching Gladys stir spoonfuls of sugar into hers. Siobhán found that when subjects had something to keep their hands busy, they had less time to keep track of their lies.

"When did you last see your brother?" Siobhán asked.

"Last night," Gladys said, staring at the steam curling up from her tea. "He went up to the guest room at half ten."

"He was staying with you?" Siobhán asked.

"He lives here," Gladys said. "*Lived,*" she corrected glumly. "Linda does as well. We're like you."

"Like me?"

"You live with your siblings, don't ya?"

"Yes," she said. "Most of them."

"There's nothing more important than family."

"You call his room the guest room?"

Gladys nodded. "He moved out at one stage, then moved back in by degrees. Said he was just going to stay a few days. Ended up being the rest of his life."

She thought about her siblings. They probably wouldn't live with each other forever. But she would be happy out if they did. Would Macdara? Or did he imagine them living in that stone house all by their lonesome? She couldn't imagine such a thing. All that quiet. How would she be able to think?

"And that's the last time you saw him? When he went up to bed last night at half ten?"

"Yes." Gladys pursed her lips.

Siobhán didn't know if she disapproved of Alan's bedtime or her questioning. "How are you so confident about the time?"

Gladys pointed to a large round clock on the opposite wall. "I was in here and glanced at it when he said he was turning in." She folded her arms. *Take that.*

"Before he turned in, what did you talk about?"

"What do you think?" She stared at Siobhán, as if actually waiting for an answer. Siobhán kept silent. "We talked about Tommy."

"Did you confront him about the note?"

"Note?"

" 'Sorry. Goodbye.' "

Gladys smacked her lips together. "I did."

"And?"

"He said he didn't remember." She looked away. Siobhán got the distinct feeling there was more to the conversation. Had Gladys's last conversation with her brother been an argument? Was it shame she saw on the old woman's face or guilt?

"Have you located this note?"

Gladys shook her head. "I don't think I saved it. Why would I want to save it? Maybe I burned it."

"Maybe? One wouldn't forget burning a note, would one?"

"It was a long time ago."

True, but it was a traumatic event. Either she burned the note or she didn't. But if the note simply said sorry and goodbye, then perhaps it didn't matter after all. "Was that the end of the discussion? You asked him about the note, and he said he didn't remember?"

Tears came to Gladys's eyes. "He lied," she said. "He looked me straight in the eyes and lied."

"Why do you think he was lying?"

"Because I knew me brother. He was a gentle man except when he was lying. Then he would get defensive. He never did learn to control his face. Gave him away every time."

"And he was defensive when you asked him about the note?"

"Very. Didn't even try to remember. Immediately barked at me that he knew nothing about a note." She pushed her tea away. "I have to live with it now. The last thing I ever said to my brother. I called him a liar."

Siobhán reached across the table and placed her hand on Gladys's shoulder. "You couldn't have known what would happen to him, luv." *Unless you're his killer.* "I think you should finish your tea and change out of your dress." It was possible that Gladys was suffering from a mental breakdown. She needed to rest. And as much as Siobhán wanted answers, she was afraid to push the frail woman too far. There was another possibility, that Gladys was cunning and wanted everyone to think she was suffering from a mental breakdown. But Siobhán wanted to err on the side of caution.

"Ask your questions first," Gladys said. "I want to help."

Siobhán would proceed gently and stop if Gladys

showed further distress. "Did you see Alan this morning?"

Gladys shook her head. "No."

"Take me through your morning."

Gladys lifted her head, and a gleam came into her eyes. "I watched the sun rise. It's a sight to behold, watching it crest over these hills. You'll see what I mean soon enough."

That did sound nice, even though she equally enjoyed the sun rising over the abbey on her morning runs. "Lovely," she said. "And you did not see Alan while you were watching the sun rise?"

"I did not see my brother come down, nor did I see him out in the fields."

"Is he usually an early riser?"

"Heavens, no. That's what I can't work out. Most of the time he didn't rise until half nine. Linda and I always tease him about it."

"But you have no idea when he actually awoke?"

Gladys shook her head. "How could I? I told you I hadn't seen him since half ten last night." She frowned. "But given I was awake early and didn't wander far from the house, I'm assuming he must have gotten up in the middle of the night. Why on earth would he get up in the middle of the night and go into that dairy barn?"

That was exactly what they needed to figure out. Siobhán flipped through her notebook. "Take me through finding the note in your dressing room the morning of the wedding."

Gladys scrunched her forehead. She mimed pointing at something. "It was tucked into the corner of the mirror in the church dressing room.

There was no telling how long it had been there. I didn't notice it until Alan pointed it out." She ran a trembling finger along the tabletop. "If I only I had seen the note when I first arrived. I would have spared meself the humiliation. Standing at the end of the aisle in me wedding gown. Staring up at a blank spot where my husband-to-be should have been standing." She frowned again. "At least that's what I thought at the time. But if Tommy didn't leave that note, then who did? And *when* did they tuck it into the mirror? It could have been after I left to walk up the aisle."

"Why would you leave to walk up the aisle?"

"Pardon?"

"Surely someone would have mentioned the groom hadn't arrived."

Gladys blinked. "It was humiliating nonetheless! People had to see me leaving the church in me wedding gown."

"I'm so sorry." Siobhán squeezed her hand and gave her a moment. When she tried to pull her hand away, Gladys gripped it, crushing it with her hand. Siobhán cried out, and Gladys finally released her.

"I know you feel my pain, chicken. You know *exactly* how I feel, don't you?" She peered at Siobhán as if she was trying to see through to her soul.

"How do you mean?"

"Your wedding was canceled too. We're birds of a feather. Jilted brides."

Jilted brides. Had Gladys purposefully interrupted Siobhán's wedding? "No," Siobhán said. Earlier, she'd felt the strength of the old woman's grip, she'd had to yank to remove her hand. She was older, but

she was strong. "Our wedding is just postponed."
She didn't like the direction in which Gladys seemed
to be steering their little chat. Perhaps she wasn't a
woman to be pitied. Perhaps she was a cold-blooded
killer. "How could you be sure the note was from
Tommy? Did you recognize the handwriting?"

"I never saw much of Tommy's handwriting. He
wasn't Shakespeare, nor was he Cupid, and he
kept his to-do lists in his head."

"But you still didn't question whether or not he
wrote the note?"

"Alan found it in the church dressing room
right before my wedding. The groom didn't show.
Who else would I think it's from?"

"I see." It made sense, but Siobhán bristled at
Gladys's tone. "Given that we now know Tommy
was murdered and thus did not write the note, I'll
suggest it was the killer."

Gladys stood and walked over to the window
above the kitchen sink, where she stared out at the
fields. "It's still so hard to wrap my head around.
The fact that Tommy did not write that note."

"Dead men can't write," Siobhán said.

"Alan swore it wasn't him." Gladys whirled around.
"If not Tommy, and not Alan, then who? Who wrote
the note? Is it the killer?"

"That's one of the things we're going to find
out," Siobhán said, standing to take her leave.
"And by 'we,' I mean the guards. You're not to in-
terfere anymore. I know you meant well." Siobhán
gestured to her wedding dress. "But you must not
take any more matters into your own hands, and if
I ever catch you in an active crime scene again, I
won't hesitate to arrest you. Do you understand?"

Gladys bit her lip and nodded. Siobhán's heart squeezed for her. There was something likable about Gladys, even if she was a killer.

"I promise you we'll do everything we can to get justice for Tommy and Alan."

Was it one killer or two? They really didn't know yet. Her gut said it was one killer, but fifty years was a long time in between. Yes, they would do everything they could to find the killer or killers. It seemed to comfort Gladys, but that was only because Siobhán had kept the rest of the repeating thought to herself: *Even if it's you.*

Chapter 8

When Siobhán exited the Burnses' house, she found Rose alone on the porch, whistling to herself. Perhaps the constant whistling was due to being around all those birds; maybe she was speaking their language. She fell silent when Siobhán appeared, and smiled, although there was something soft and sad about it. "Is it my turn, then?"

Siobhán nodded. "Why not? Would you mind if we have a stroll? I need to stretch me legs."

"That's music to me ears. I hate standing still." Rose was an outdoorsy woman. Her comfort zone was being active. And Siobhán did want to stretch her legs, not to mention explore the property. They were only a few steps into the field when Rose spoke.

"I heard Gladys and Alan arguing last night. I'm not saying Gladys had anything to do with this. A tiny woman like that murdering two men. Can you imagine?"

"I don't think our killer would have needed strength," Siobhán posited. Not if both victims were pushed from behind. *Just quiet feet and the element of surprise.* And Gladys, as Siobhán had just discovered, *did* have strength, at least a very firm grip. "Where were Gladys and Alan when they had this argument?"

"The kitchen."

That fact matched what Gladys had reported. It was always a win when you could corroborate details, no matter how small. Maybe especially when they were small. *The devil is in the details.* . . . "Where were you when you overheard this argument?"

"I was coming in to use the jax before going back to my tent."

"Tent?"

Rose pointed across the field. Sure enough, there was a red tent propped up in the distance.

"You sleep in a tent on their property?" It struck Siobhán that that was something Ciarán and Ann might like to do. Their back garden at the bistro wasn't large enough for a tent. Here they would have plenty of room to roam and sleep beneath the stars. But not by themselves. Was she willing to stay out with them? She'd ask one of the lads to do it. She really didn't think sleeping on the ground was her thing. Maybe she'd try it once and see. "And you enjoy that, do you? Sleeping outside with a killer on the loose?" Siobhán hadn't meant to say that and immediately worried it would harden the dynamic between them, but Rose just laughed.

"It's not a regular thing. We all spent the night

last night—and I brought my tent because I'd rather sleep out here." She wrapped her arms around herself. "I didn't think about the fact that there was a killer on the loose. You're quite right. It wasn't a smart thing to do, and I shall not do it again. Not until you catch him."

"Or her."

Rose lifted an eyebrow. "I suppose. But aren't killers usually men?"

"Anyone is capable of killing under the right circumstances."

"This is why I deal with birds."

"Birds of prey. Killers."

"Your job forces you to see the cynical side of everything, I suppose."

Siobhán froze. Just as Aretta had said. She'd never thought of herself as a negative person. Was she? She forced the thought out of her mind; it wouldn't help her solve the case. Besides, she would rather think of herself as committed and focused. "Why was everyone spending the night?"

"We'd gathered to mourn Tommy, of course, but also to try to figure out who did this and how it happened."

Siobhán wanted to remind her that that was *her* job, but she also wanted to hear more. "I'd like to hear your theories in a moment," she said. "But let's continue with the argument. You came in from the tent . . . ?"

"I came in and heard voices raised in the kitchen. Gladys and Alan. The only thing I heard clearly was Alan saying, 'How could you say such a thing?'"

How could you say such a thing? Had Gladys accused him of murdering Tommy? Or lying about the note? The former would probably induce a stronger reaction. "Can you describe his tone in terms of how strongly he was reacting? Was it a little reprimand, or did he sound appalled?"

Rose thought about it for a minute. "I would say he sounded appalled."

Gladys had accused him of murdering Tommy. . . . "And then?"

"And then they stopped arguing, because I walked in. I kept me head down and said, 'Don't mind me,' and I passed through the kitchen. They clammed up. By the time I came out of the restroom, they were still here, both of them red-faced, but they didn't let me hear another word."

"Did any of you enter the dairy barn?"

"We all did when Gladys screamed."

"Before that?"

"Obviously, Alan must have." She stopped. "Do you think he was killed elsewhere and his body was laid in that pit?"

"All options are on the table." *And we will not be discussing them with you.* "Leaving Alan aside, do you know of anyone entering the dairy barn after it was cordoned off?"

"No." Rose was chewing on her lip. Was she telling the truth? Had they all been trampling all over the crime scene all night long?

"Did you hear or see anything else last night or this morning?"

"My son and I worked with a falcon this morning. He's a young one but shows great promise. We were in the field with him when we heard the scream. Before that, I watched the sun rise."

"With Gladys?"

Rose frowned. "No. I was out here by myself."

"Gladys said she watched the sun rise this morning from her porch."

"Mystery solved. I watched it from back here, so I wouldn't have seen her."

"But you would have been able to see the back of the barn, where Alan supposedly snuck in . . ." Siobhán had been thinking about it, and it was the only thing that made sense. If Alan had entered from the front, he would have run into the guards. If only they'd posted a guard at the back door.

"Oh," Rose said. Her head darted to the dairy barn in the distance, proving Siobhán's point that she would have had a clear sight line. "I didn't see him."

Alan was a big man. He should have been visible even from this distance. Perhaps he had snuck in while everyone was still asleep. What on earth would have prompted him to do that? "Why don't you tell me what theories people have been floating around."

"I'll do you one better than that," Rose said. "I'll tell you who the killer is."

"Okay." Siobhán did not want to give Rose the impression that she was going to automatically believe any such declaration. Especially given they'd found a falconer's glove in the slurry pit with two dead men. That put Rose square in the deep end of the suspect pool. Then again, the glove seemed to have been recently dropped into the pit. By Alan? Had he purposefully invaded the crime scene to anonymously leave a clue as to who he thought the killer was before ending up the next victim?

Siobhán had no intention of mentioning the glove or asking Rose about the fact that Joseph claimed his glove was missing. Only the guards and the killer knew that a falconer's glove was in the slurry pit, and they had to hold on to that advantage as long as they could.

"First, I want to show you the best hill," Rose said. "You'll want to be climbing it every morning and night just to see the sun rise and set."

Climbing hills. That might be a nice change from her morning runs. Siobhán followed Rose, noting that the woman was able to keep pace at a bright clip. "It must have been such a difficult time for you," Siobhán said. "You had just adopted a son, and then your husband left you for another woman." Siobhán wasn't trying to be unkind, but pushing buttons was part of her job. It was all in service of a greater goal, catching a killer.

Rose stopped at the apex of the hill, her face toward the horizon, her chin up. "Yes," she said. "It was. But I was only a lass eighteen years of age, so to be honest, I was finding everything difficult back then, especially my marriage."

Siobhán took a moment at the top of the hill to catch her breath. The view was stunning. From here she could see undulating green waves and a stretched horizon. She could see Saint Mary's steeple and the original stone walls that encased her medieval town. Siobhán knew she was treading on a sensitive topic with Rose, but she couldn't help but explore it. Granted, fifty years was a long time, and Rose had only been eighteen years of age. But it seemed odd to Siobhán that they behaved as if they were now one big happy extended family, and the fact that two others were dead proved that not everyone had been able to forgive and forget the sins of the past.

"It seems a little unusual to adopt a baby when you were so young," Siobhán said gently.

Rose nodded. "I have a medical condition. I knew I couldn't conceive on me own."

"But adopting an older boy. Was that the plan?"

Rose shook her head. "He came to our attention through Howard Dunn."

"Through Howard?" Siobhán tried to reconcile the photo of the angry man with a man who would recommend a child to adopt.

"He put in a pool table at the boys' home. Joseph took an interest. Next thing you know, he's encouraging Benji and me to adopt him."

"How did you feel about that?"

"I was resistant at first. But we met him, and that was that. I loved Joseph at first sight."

"He was very lucky."

Rose smiled. "I'm proud of the man he is today."

"It must have been a shock when Benji left you," Siobhán said once more. "Especially so soon after adopting Joseph."

"I may have told a little white lie," Rose said. "Not to you. I'd never lie to a garda. But at the time. There is something I didn't tell Gladys."

Here we go . . . "I'm listening."

"I've always been better with birds than people. Especially birds of prey. I know that must sound strange."

"I must admit it was quite something to see one up close," Siobhán said. "There's something awe-inspiring about them. I can see the attraction."

"You can?"

Siobhán nodded. "I'm going to have to make a point to bring my younger siblings to the wildlife center."

"You must! You need to feel one land on your fist. It's something you'll never forget."

Ciarán and Ann would be over the moon. She would make a point of it. The wedding had been all-consuming, and now with the new house and two unsolved murders . . . she had to carve out time for Ciarán and Ann, or she would never forgive herself. Her only saving grace was that it was summer and both of them had plenty of friends and outside interests. Still. She would arrange a visit to the center as soon as she could.

"It must feel very special to work with them."

Rose nodded. "You said it must have been a very difficult time. And it was. That part was true. But not for the reasons you think. Don't for one second let Gladys fool you. She did not have a fairy-tale romance with Tommy. He was not the love of her life." Rose's tone abruptly shifted from sweet and friendly to dripping with resentment. There it was, finally. The tone one would expect when a woman was talking about the other woman.

"Doesn't Gladys get to decide who the love of her life is?"

Rose squinted; she didn't like the comment. "She's been married to Benji for fifty years. Fifty years! And Tommy is the love of her life?"

"I see your point." Siobhán had thought the same thing herself. Rose wasn't finished.

"Is she free to delude herself? Of course. But we all knew Tommy. Think about it. We didn't even look for him. That's how much we all knew that taking off on his bride was a pure Tommy thing to do."

"What was the little white lie?"

"I grew up with Tommy. I was closer to him than any of them."

"I didn't realize that." Rose was avoiding the question, dangling this little white lie but never handing it over.

"Tommy wasn't himself the day before the wedding. At first, I thought it was a case of the jitters. He even snapped at Joseph—which he never did."

"Did you find out why he was so upset?"

Rose nodded. "He'd told Gladys he couldn't have children." She took a deep breath. "He was in the same predicament I was. It's such a strange feeling, being young and of reproductive age, yet knowing you'd never have biological children. And despite the fact that we did it, adoption wasn't as mainstream then as it is for couples today. I must say it brought Tommy and me closer together." She sighed. "To be honest, I don't know whether Tommy couldn't have children or just didn't want to have children. Then again, he was quite sweet to Joseph."

"Okay . . ." Siobhán was having a hard time predicting where this conversation was leading. Gladys had mentioned how none of her siblings had biological children either. Were all these folks barren, or was that just an easier explanation than saying they didn't *want* children? It wasn't a popular viewpoint, especially back in the day. Life was considered not worth living if you didn't have children. All animals were genetically predisposed to carry on their genes. Joseph must have been the center of attention when he arrived. "I'm not quite sure what you're getting at. You're saying Gladys was upset that Tommy couldn't—or didn't want—to have children?" Even though Gladys had told her she and Benji couldn't conceive, she had said they had wanted to and they had tried.

Rose laughed. "You didn't know Gladys's parents. Mr. and Mrs. O'Leary." She swept her hands over the landscape. "At one point the O'Learys owned all of this."

"Yes, I've heard that." The O'Leary family had reigned as dairy farmers long before subdividing the land and selling off parcels, including the one that Macdara had purchased.

"This used to be a family empire. But did you know that when the youngest of their children reached twenty-five years of age, they intended on leaving the property to the one who had the most children?"

Siobhán frowned. "No."

"They were desperate for grandchildren. Dreamed that the grandchildren were the only way their dairy farm would live on. Turns out they were right about that. As in it certainly hasn't lived on."

"But none of them had children," Siobhán said. "Yet Gladys and Benji seem to be the primary owners of the house, am I right?"

Rose let out a snort. "Is that what she told you? You're aware that Alan and Linda live there too?" She stopped. "Or *lived*, I suppose I should say, at least when it comes to Alan."

"Yes. I thought . . . Gladys and Benji were being generous, allowing her siblings to live with them."

"Generous! That's brilliant." Rose enjoyed the thought, laughing to herself. "The three of them have been like vipers their entire lives. All of them sticking to this place like glue, refusing to give up their piece. Gladys owns the property only because she found a loophole and then her siblings never did have children of their own. She lets them stay with her because she knows she doesn't deserve it—because she knows what she did to get it." Rose headed back down the hill without warning. "And I think Alan must have found out. I think he put it all together when Tommy's remains were found, and confronted her."

Siobhán had to run after Rose to keep up. "I don't quite see what that has to do with Tommy."

Rose came to a sudden stop and whirled around, so close Siobhán could smell the leather in the thick bracelet wrapped around her wrist. "It has everything to do with Tommy. *He* couldn't have children. He didn't want to adopt, like we did. They had a horrific argument about it in the days leading up to the wedding."

"You're saying Gladys killed Tommy because he wouldn't give her children?"

"I'm saying that Gladys killed Tommy so that a certain someone who, let's face it, had always been in love with her—and she knew it—would step in and marry her. Oh! And he came with a son. As long as none of her siblings had children of their own, he came with an inheritance."

"Joseph," Siobhán said.

"Joseph," Rose said, picking up the pace. "Apparently, by that point, her parents were so desperate for an heir that they were willing to consider stepchildren if none of them had any biological offspring. Was it just dumb luck that neither Alan nor Linda had children? You'll have to ask them. Or Linda. I keep forgetting Alan is dead. And now that I know how dangerous she is—how diabolical—I beg you not to tell her what I've been saying. You'll be putting me squarely in danger."

"Moments ago, you stated that a little old lady like Gladys couldn't be a killer."

Rose nodded. "I wanted to see your reaction."

"That's not how these interviews are supposed to go."

"I'm solving the case for you, don't you see? Mark my words. Gladys didn't want my husband because they fell in love. She wanted my husband so she could use my son to cheat her siblings out of the family farm."

Chapter 9

After her conversation with Rose, Siobhán needed time to think. She began walking the length of the farm, and soon the rhythm of her steps soothed her into the perfect mindset to ruminate on what she'd just learned. Family. The group of people that knew you best, whether you liked it or not. All your faults and quirks and mistakes and sensitivities and passions. They should be your soft cushion, your rock in a storm, your wolf pack that surrounded and protected you. But there was no greater pain than when they turned on you. And nothing set family against each other like inheritances. And parents who stoked that competition and instilled panic within their children? *Diabolical.*

It was another reminder of how lucky the O'Sullivan Six were to be raised by Naomi and Liam O'Sullivan, even if their lives were taken way too soon. Siobhán felt them with her nearly every day of her life, and often spoke to them, especially when she was in need of a little comfort. After her conversation with Rose, Siobhán was shaken. Gladys had inherited the family farm by cheating? Was it possible? And if so, could she also be a cold-blooded killer? Or was it Linda? Had she been carrying resentment so long it finally came bursting out? What if Alan had discovered that Linda murdered Tommy and had decided to confront her that morning? Not only would Linda have murdered her brother to protect her secret, but what if she wasn't finished? What if she wanted the murder to be pinned on Gladys? That would leave her the sole winner of the farm.

Winners. Losers. And in the end, it was all for nothing. What good was a family farm without a family? Siobhán would live in a cardboard box to protect her brood. But not everyone had their priorities straight. But elders? Weren't they supposed to be wise? She could not discount the elderly sisters, but she would keep the options open. It was dangerous to think you had a case solved this quickly; such a mindset could allow a true killer to slip away.

Except this killer wasn't really the slipping-away type; this was the circling and hovering type of killer, who had stayed and visited the crime scene over and over. Who had added a second victim to the same scene—assuming they were looking at one killer, and Siobhán could not shake the feeling that they were. After her walk she headed back to the squad car, where she found Aretta and Macdara finishing up a conversation with Gladys and Benji in the front yard.

"We'll be calling you both in for formal interviews at the garda station," Macdara said. "But it will have to wait until our state pathologist has done her job. If I hear of anyone even looking at our property while that crime scene tape is still up, well . . ." He cleared his throat. "Neighbors or not, you're going to see a side of me that you won't soon forget."

"I swear to ye, we won't go near it," Benji said.

"When can we bury them?" Gladys asked.

"As soon as Dr. Jeanie Brady has done her work. Believe me, if you want answers, we don't want to rush it."

"I suppose we've already waited fifty years," Benji said. "We can wait a bit longer."

Gladys turned to Benji, determination in her eyes. "Tell me you didn't do it."

A pained look came over the old man's face. "Me?"

"You're the one who profited off of Tommy's death."

Siobhán's antenna twitched.

Benji asked the question everyone else was thinking. "How on earth did I profit off me best friend's death?"

"You got me, didn't you?"

The laugher that erupted from the old man was genuine. "That's rich. Coming from you." His tone took on a sinister bite.

Gladys's face went scarlet. She pointed at her husband. "If Tommy was going to run off with something, it would have been me." She looked up at the sky. "Forgive me, Tommy. I let them convince me that you had run away. Will you ever forgive me?"

"Let the guards do their job, luv, and find out what really happened." Benji's tone immediately shifted to a softer gear. "It could have been a terrible accident." Benji put his arm around his wife.

She shoved him off. "Accident? How did that go down? He took a dive into a slurry pit to avoid marrying me?"

"He could have been tipping the bottle to calm the nerves or having a smoke and tripped over a piece of farm machinery. How do I know?" Benji said.

"My Tommy did not smoke," Gladys said.

"He smoked," Benji said. "Just not in front of you." He looked at Siobhán. "All husbands hide things from their wives," he said. "Every single one of them." He had turned and stared at Macdara when he said it, then at Siobhán.

Siobhán was starting to feel itchy. Was she coming down with something? Was she allergic to something? Was she allergic to farm life? What if she was allergic to farm life?

Macdara leaned in and whispered, "I couldn't hide anything from you if I tried."

"And what are *you* hiding?" Gladys asked Benji. This seemed to shut him up. "You're saying it's all my fault." She sank down on one of the porch chairs.

"Fifty years of this," Benji said. "Tommy should be thanking me. Begging my forgiveness. It's not too late to change your mind." The last bit was directed to Siobhán and Macdara.

"Never," Macdara said.

When Siobhán didn't answer, she felt an elbow in her side. "Right," Siobhán said. "What he said."

Gladys jabbed her finger at her husband. "They've been the best years of your life, better than that bird woman and your odd—" She stopped, then shook her head, as if admonishing herself, then mimed zipping her lips shut and throwing away the key.

"My odd what?" Benji said, anger vibrating his vocal chords. "Son? Is that what you wanted to say?"

Gladys bit her lip. "He is odd. And that's nothing to do with me."

Benji sighed. "There's nothing wrong with Joseph. He may beat his own drum, but he's solid."

Siobhán was glued to every word. Gladys certainly didn't sound as if Joseph had been the answer to her inheritance. Was Rose Burns a liar? Had she purposefully tried to throw Siobhán onto a new scent? And even though they had just discovered her brother in the slurry pit, Gladys Burns was focused only on Tommy. Was she Alan's killer? Was her rage all about trying to justify it?

"Don't forget, we'll be contacting you to come into the station," Macdara said.

They had heard enough. As they headed for the car, Gladys called after them.

"You're going to have your work cut out for you. Asking all us blue hairs to remember events from fifty years ago? Benji can't even remember what we had for supper yesterday."

"Bean soup and brown bread," Benji said. He crossed his arms. "Satisfied?"

"We had bacon and cabbage."

"Oh." He shrugged. "Let's hope they don't ask me what I had for dinner fifty years ago and it will be grand."

Macdara gave a nod, and they piled into the car. Siobhán eased her window down. As they pulled out, she heard Gladys yell, "You better hurry up with that wedding. Take it from a dairy farmer, you don't want to be giving away the milk for free."

Macdara snorted, his hands shaking on the steering wheel, as he tried not to laugh.

"Just say it," Siobhán said, throwing an apologetic glance to Aretta through the rearview mirror.

"It's a good thing I'm not lactose intolerant," Macdara said with delighted glee.

"Good to know," Siobhán said.

"I'll take all the milk I can get."

"You're going to spill it and start crying in a minute if you don't shut your gob."

"Slurry pit and bad marriages," Macdara said. "You don't get muckier than that."

"Is it a bad marriage?" Aretta asked. "Or a typical marriage?"

The group fell silent. Siobhán opened her mouth to assure her it wasn't a typical marriage, but how did she know? What if it was? Would that be them many years from now?

"I'll tell you this," Macdara said. "I hereby give you permission to take me out to pasture and put me out of your misery if we ever start bickering like those yokes."

"Did you hear that, Aretta?" Siobhán asked.

Aretta nodded. "I certainly did."

Siobhán grinned. "I have a witness."

"Not even married and already thinking about putting me out to pasture."

"And that," Siobhán said, "is why you never buy someone a dairy farm."

The next morning the O'Sullivans sat at the breakfast table as a family. Eoin had gone all out with the spread, full-on bells and whistles. He had surprised Siobhán by convincing Gráinne and James to come home, and he'd made a feed fit for a queen. Given the bistro was still closed to the public the rest of the week, they had it to themselves. Music in the background, delectable scents wafting from the table, the clatter of plates, the scream of the kettle, and the comfort of laughter. For the first time in a long while, they were able to enjoy just being together. Ann and Ciarán seemed happy to let Siobhán cuddle them, even though they were getting so grown up.

Soon breakfast was finished, and they were just lounging. Siobhán had the day off, which made her feel itchy. Macdara had convinced her that there wasn't much they could do with the case until Jeanie Brady arrived, and even after that, they would be waiting on the forensic investigator for any information on the old bones. Two murder inquiries at once. Macdara had emergency meetings with Dublin this morning; no doubt headquarters would want to make sure they were up to the task, and there was a chance they would send in their own men. Siobhán worried that this would just complicate things, and she hoped Macdara could convince them to let them give it a go.

"Do you like the house?" Ann asked Siobhán when there was a lull in the gossip about the case. Siobhán, of course, had not divulged anything, but it was natural for her siblings to talk about it. The entire town was abuzz.

"I like the outside of the house," Siobhán said. "I haven't seen the inside yet."

Ciarán piped up. "Why not? Can we go now?"

Siobhán laughed. "I absolutely want all of you to see it. But Macdara meant it as a happy surprise, and so we've decided to wait until this case has been solved."

"Is it?" Ann said. "A happy surprise?" She was getting so grown up. Her pretty blond hair framed her face nicely, and both she and Ciarán were nearly as tall as the rest of them. Gráinne, it seemed, would be the shortest in the family at five feet six. Eoin and James were just at six feet, and Ciarán was quickly closing on them.

"It's not for sure that we'll live there," Siobhán said. "We'll look at the house and decide as a family."

Ann chewed on her lip and nodded. "Would we have to change schools?"

"Of course not. It's only a few streets away."

"Will I get to drive a tractor?" Ciarán asked.

"No," Siobhán said.

James laughed. "Why not?" he said. "I'll teach him."

Gráinne lowered the fashion magazine in her hand and stared at James. "You know how to drive a tractor?"

He shrugged. "Sure. Lookit, how hard can it be?"

The outside buzzer sounded, startling all of them.

"What now?" Siobhán said out loud.

"I'll get it." Eoin popped into the hall, and soon they heard voices at the front door. Seconds later Eoin returned. "Father Kearney is here to see you."

"Me?" Siobhán felt like she was back in school and Sister Margaret Healy was hauling her out of the classroom with a lethal grip. A familiar flush started at her neck and spread up to her cheeks.

Eoin leaned in until he was an inch from her face. "I dunno. Are you Siobhán O'Sullivan?"

She laughed and shoved him away. "Bring him in." Her siblings scrambled to sit up straight.

"I'll get an extra plate," James said. He headed for the kitchen.

"I'll put the kettle on," Gráinne said.

Eoin ushered Father Kearney into the room, and they gave him the coveted seat by the window overlooking Sarsfield Street. A few folks were out and about, doing their messages, and the sun was just starting to peek out from beneath a patch of gray clouds.

Father Kearney leaned back in his chair and rested his hands on his ample belly. He was moving slower than in the past, and his hair had gone completely white. He had a calming presence and a soothing voice, essential qualities for a parish priest. "I apologize for the surprise visit. I didn't realize the bistro was closed."

"It's never closed to you, Father." Except a little notice would have been nice, Siobhán thought.

"My job entails many things, pleasant and un-pleasant," he began.

That didn't sound good.

"We're lucky to have you," Siobhán said. It was always wise to stay friendly with the parish priest. Gráinne arrived with tea and brown bread.

"Thank you, petal," Father Kearney said, flashing a smile.

"The lads will be along with your breakfast," she said, patting him on the shoulder like he was a child. He grinned and placed his own wrinkled hand on top of hers before she parted.

"You may already know that I have a close relationship with the owner of this building," Father Kearney said.

Siobhán nodded. Her father had leased the building under a contract that allowed for them to stay and rent for life as long as they were all paid up. The building had changed hands a few times in the past few years, but the new landlord had no choice but to abide by the original contract. Unless, of course, he wanted to pursue legal avenues, which he was likely to lose.

"Does the landlord have a complaint?" This was the last thing she needed to deal with, but given the fact that Father Kearney was here in person to deal with it, she would have to be polite and listen.

"No, no, nothing like that." Father Kearney cleared his throat. "But he was wondering, now that you're getting married and moving into a new home—"

"Possibly . . ."

Father Kearney remained silent and stared at

her, mouth open as if in shock. It took her a minute to realize why he was gaping at her.

"Definitely getting married, *possibly* moving into
a new home. We haven't decided about that aspect
yet."

Father Kearney's gaze swiveled around the bistro.
"This place isn't big enough for a married couple
and all your siblings."

Siobhán composed herself. Telling off a priest
wasn't on her agenda this morning, even if he was
nosing into territory that was none of his business.
"What is it that you're here to tell me, Father?"

"He was hoping you planned on vacating the
building."

"Excuse me?"

Eoin arrived on with a full Irish breakfast and
set it in front of Father Kearney.

"You shouldn't have done that," the priest said
while arranging his napkin and picking up his
fork. "But since you've gone to the trouble, I must
say this looks like it will hit the spot."

Siobhán made eye contact with Eoin to see if
he'd overheard the bit about the landlord. It was
obvious he had. He lingered nearby to listen.

"Why on earth would he want us to vacate the
building? We're all paid up." She glanced at Eoin
to confirm this. He nodded.

"He wants to open a bistro of his own."

"You're joking me!" Siobhán didn't realize she'd
shouted it until she saw the priest flinch.

"His wife died last year, and supposedly, he took
up a little hobby. Cooking."

"Cooking as a hobby hardly qualifies one to

open a bistro. And given we've made a success of this one, he can't just swoop in here and take over." Siobhán could feel her blood pressure ticking up, and she had to remind herself not to lose her temper.

"I'm just the messenger," Father Kearney said between bites. "But if I were you, I'd do a little negotiating. You might fetch a nice price for the business." When she didn't reply, he continued. "And don't you have a new farmhouse to restore?"

She sighed. Despite knowing that life was a series of changes, she felt like they were all happening at once, threatening to sweep her out to sea. Why couldn't things stay the same for just a little while longer? Why couldn't she keep everything frozen in time? If she had her way, her siblings wouldn't grow up, she wouldn't move, and the bistro wouldn't change hands. And as long as she was controlling the world, murderers wouldn't get away with their crimes.

"Even if Macdara and the young ones and I move into the farmhouse, Eoin runs the bistro now, and he and Gráinne would continue to live here. Possibly with James."

"I see." Father Kearney looked disappointed. "I'm afraid there is a part two."

Chapter 10

Siobhán tensed as Father Kearney delivered the statement. *I'm afraid there is a part two . . . There is always a part two.* "And that is?"

"If you're going to stay, he's going to have to raise the rent considerably."

Siobhán shook her head. "We have a contract."

"His solicitor has found some issues with the contract."

"Issues?" Siobhán said.

"Loopholes," Eoin offered.

Father Kearney nodded. "I do believe he intends to pursue all avenues. That's why I volunteered to have a word with you first." He cleared his throat. "I wouldn't want to see you lose out on what could be a healthy buyout payment."

"I see. Well, thank you for keeping me abreast of the situation." Siobhán felt like bursting into tears. She didn't want to spend money on solicitors and fight a grieving man over the property, while trying to solve two murders and reschedule a wedding. "Now that you're here, I do have a few questions for you, if you don't mind."

"If this is about rescheduling the wedding, I'm afraid I don't have my calendar book with me."

"It's not about rescheduling the wedding . . . yet, but it is about your calendar book."

Father Kearney had not been expecting this, and he looked somewhat amused. "If you're going to say I need one of those electronic organizer yokes or to somehow have me calendar on a phone or a pad or a laptop, forget it. I can't be bothered. Me calendar book and Biro works well for me, thanks very much."

Siobhán laughed. "I'm a bit of a Luddite myself. It's not that. I was wondering if you remember that when we originally tried to schedule our wedding, we picked an earlier Saturday in June, but when you consulted your calendar, it was only June sixteen that you could squeeze us in."

"I'll take your word for it. I schedule many events. I can't keep them all straight."

"Not a bother. Does anyone else ever write in your calendar book?"

"How do you mean?"

"Do any of your assistants write in your calendar?"

"When it comes to my appointment book, only two people write in it, and that's me and Sister Helen."

"I would like to look at the entries for June, and I'll need to know who made them—you or Sister Helen or unknown."

"Unknown? What on earth is this all about?"

"I can only assure you that it's garda business."

"My calendar book? Garda business?" From his outraged tone, she was going to have to give him something.

"As you know, we're investigating a very serious case. A possible double murder inquiry."

"I am aware." He shook his head. "Tommy Caffrey was always a wild one. But I was sorry to hear what became of him."

"Did you know him well?"

"We were about the same age, but we ran in very different circles. He was always in pubs, playing billiards." Father Kearney paused to sip his tea, then clinked it back to the plate. "Quite good at billiards. He could have gone professional."

"Snooker, apparently."

"I'm afraid I couldn't tell you the difference," Father Kearney said.

"Snooker uses more balls," Gráinne said from the corner of the room. "Twenty-two, including a white ball called the striker. Billiards uses only three balls, one each of white, yellow, and red, and both the white and yellow act as the striker ball. And snooker always uses a pocketed table."

They turned and gave her a questioning look.

"I dated a snooker player once," Gráinne said.

"Of course you did," Siobhán said.

"He said it's all about the angles."

"Excellent," Father Kearney said, bobbing his head in agreement, when Siobhán had no reply.

Men were like accessories to her beautiful sister. She had a variety of them and didn't seem interested in hanging on to just one. She'd never brought a boyfriend home for them to meet. In some ways it was a relief. Siobhán turned back to Father Kearney. "What else do you know about Tommy Caffrey?"

"It's been so long, nothing comes to mind."

"What about Howard Dunn or Gladys and Benjamin Burns or Linda O'Leary?"

Father Kearney shifted in his seat, then turned his gaze out the window. "I don't think my personal opinions will be very helpful to your case. We're all sinners in one way or another, but no more so than anyone else."

It was a bit of an odd statement. Which one in particular was he thinking of as a sinner, and why? "Were you supposed to officiate over the marriage of Gladys and Tommy fifty years ago?"

Father Kearney lifted his head and stroked his chin. "As a matter of fact, it was to be my first wedding. I was very excited. And then, of course, there was no wedding. I'll never forget the look of anguish on Gladys's face. She was so young and in love. Tommy was a bit wild, but I'll give him credit. I made them take marriage counseling with me, I made sure he was attending Mass regularly, and he complied with all of it. And then when he didn't show . . . to see the pain he caused." Father Kearney shuddered at the memory. "I feel terrible that I didn't raise an alarm at his disappearance. But Tommy was the type to do something like that. I hope he forgives me." He lifted his head and made the sign of the cross. It was jarring to hear a priest ask for forgiveness. It reminded her that he was all too human.

"Do you realize," Siobhán said, "that their wedding was also scheduled for June sixteen?"

"It was?"

"Yes."

"That's . . . a coincidence."

"It certainly is."

"And you think . . . it's . . . not a coincidence?"

"I would very much like to look at your calendar book for the month of June, and I would like to know who made each and every notation, and if it wasn't you, then I would like to speak with Sister Helen."

He nodded. "I'll check with Sister Helen and have it ready for you by tomorrow afternoon. Will that do?"

"Yes. And please, I have to ask you to keep this to yourself."

He laughed. "I'm a priest, my dear. I keep everything to myself." He patted his stomach. "That's why I'm a bit plumper than the rest of ye. I'm keeping too much inside."

Eoin passed by again, and Father Kearney held up his empty mug and plate. "Would you like a refill?" Eoin asked, taking them.

"I wouldn't want to put you to any trouble."

"No trouble at all. More tea?"

"Did you mean just a refill on the tea?"

"No, no," Eoin said, quickly copping on. "Another Irish brekkie as well. Something needs to keep all those secrets company." Eoin winked.

Father Kearney grinned. "If you insist."

"Do you think you'll be wanting seconds if yer one takes over the bistro and forces everyone to eat his little hobby?" Siobhán asked.

"Why do you think I'm enjoying it while I can?" Father Kearney said.

Chapter 11

"I have updates," Aretta said the minute Siobhán walked into the garda station the next morning.

After a restless night of worrying about the bistro, Siobhán had been up for ages, had already had her run, and was jittery from multiple cappuccinos. "Grand," Siobhán said. "Can you walk and talk?"

"I can, so," Aretta said.

"Off we go, then." Siobhán headed to her office, with Aretta following close behind.

"The coroner has issued the certificate, and Dr. Brady has been officially summoned."

"Perfect."

"She's bringing the forensic pathologist with her." Excitement rang in Aretta's voice.

Siobhán couldn't blame her. Ireland had only a few forensic pathologists, and it would be exciting to meet one. Siobhán glanced around her tiny of-

fice and found her favorite mug: I CAN ONLY PLEASE
ONE PERSON A DAY. TODAY IS NOT YOUR DAY. She
picked it up and continued to the kitchen. "Do
you want one yourself?" Siobhán asked, holding
up the mug.

"No, thank you. I'm sorted," Aretta said.

"What else?"

"Detective Sergeant Flannery will not be able to
accompany Dr. Brady. He's due at a department
meeting."

"That's not a bother. I can handle it." Siobhán
saw a spark of hope in Aretta's eyes, and she knew
what question was coming next. She would have
done the same.

"I was wondering, if you don't mind, if it wouldn't
be too much of a bother, if I could . . ."

"Why don't you accompany me?" Siobhán said.
"You can take notes."

Aretta's face broke out in a beautiful smile.
"Thank you."

"Not a bother. Now." Siobhán looked around
the cramped kitchen. "Where are the tins of biscuits? Tip number one. Jeanie Brady likes her
treats."

Dr. Jeanie Brady pulled up to the farmhouse
bang on time. When she emerged from the driv-
er's side, Siobhán almost mistook her for the forensic pathologist. She looked as if she'd lost half a
stone. Her once plump figure had smoothed out,
and her once full face was sporting cheekbones.

"You're looking well," Siobhán said.

Jeanie nodded. "I better be. I haven't eaten a

morsel of sweets or bread or nuts in three months."
Jeanie Brady's eyes landed on the tin of biscuits in
Siobhán's hands. Siobhán pawned them off on
Aretta, who stared at them for a moment before
stashing them in the garda car.

"Well done you," Siobhán said. Inwardly she
groaned. Would Jeanie Brady still have her cheerful disposition? Depriving oneself of sweets and
breads sounded like complete torture, something
she hoped she'd never have to endure. She had a
theory that her height was what allowed her to in-
dulge without putting on weight, along with her
daily jogs. She knew if she had to deny herself, it
would only make her want it more. But Jeanie
Brady did have a healthy glow about her.

Siobhán was still adjusting to the change when
the passenger door opened, and an older man
emerged. This must be the forensic pathologist.
He had thick black hair but a gray beard and thick
glasses.

"May I introduce our esteemed forensic pathologist Dr. Rory Doyle."

Siobhán wasn't sure how to greet an esteemed
forensic pathologist, and she nearly bowed before
sticking her hand out. "I'm Garda O'Sullivan, and
this is Garda Dabiri. We've been looking forward
to your arrival."

Rory Doyle limply shook Siobhán's hand, then
Aretta's. He grabbed a case out of the car and
suited up.

"My least favorite part," Jeanie Brady said as she
too pulled on her protective gear. Siobhán and
Aretta were already in theirs.

Soon an ambulance arrived, on the ready to

transport Alan's remains to the morgue at Cork
University Hospital. Most likely, the bones would
be transferred to Dublin. Siobhán knew they would
not learn much of anything today, but she was
eager for the process to begin. Additional techni-
cians emerged from the ambulance; they would
wait behind until Jeanie Brady summoned them.

Siobhán glanced at the feet of the doctors, pleased
they had received the message to wear their Wellies. They would don paper booties before entering the dairy barn. A soft rain was falling as they
headed across the field, as if the heavens were crying for the victims.

"I look forward to your upcoming nuptials,"
Jeanie Brady said.

Siobhán almost asked, *Whose upcoming nuptials?*
when she realized Jeanie Brady was waiting for *her*
to say something. "Yes," she said. "I am looking forward to it as well. And you will be our guest of
honor. I don't see how we can proceed unless we
get these murders sorted first."

"Then there's not a single moment to waste,"
Jeanie Brady said.

They stood around the slurry pit as the overhead bulb swung from its chain, sending patches
of light bouncing through the slatted shed. The
forensic pathologist took more photos before they
called in the men to remove Alan's body. Siobhán
pointed out the pile of branches James had removed from the slurry pit.

"We've both seen the photos you took before
the recent victim was found in the slurry pit,"

Jeanie said, walking the circumference of the scene as she spoke. "It must have been quite a shock to see a fresh one lying on top."

"It's not something you encounter every day," Siobhán agreed. She pointed out the blood at the corner of the slurry pit. "The blood is recent as well—it wasn't there when we found the skeleton. You're likely to find a corresponding wound on poor Alan's head."

Dr. Doyle knelt next to the pit and stared down at the skeleton. "There you are," he said, as if talking to a dear friend. "Been here for a long time, haven't you, lad?"

His voice was so congenial Siobhán found herself staring at the skull and bones, as if expecting it to answer.

"What is your working theory?" Jeanie Brady said. "Did they both happen to take a tumble, or was something more sinister at play?"

"I believe they were pushed from behind," Siobhán said. "Alan hit his head on the left-hand corner of the pit, which suggests he was standing on the right-hand front side, just below that swinging lightbulb." She pointed to the right-hand corner of the pit as she spoke. "There's more than enough room for someone to have come in from behind. One shove and he would have toppled into the pit. I believe the blow to the temple as he fell in is what killed him. That's my hunch."

"Hunch?" the forensic pathologist said, as if Siobhán had just offended him. "Well, you're lucky we're here to discover the *facts*."

" 'Tis only a fool who would ignore the hunches of Garda O'Sullivan," Jeanie Brady said.

Siobhán felt a flash of heat up her neck at the compliment, and she gave her favorite state pathologist a nod of thanks.

Jeanie Brady was not deterred by the forensic pathologist's brusque manner. "What else have you been thinking?" she asked Siobhán.

Siobhán pointed to the pile of branches. "These were lying on top of the skeleton," she said. "Whereas it's plausible that Tommy simply took a tumble, I think we can agree that a pile of branches did not march in on their own and cover him up." She looked at the forensic pathologist to see if he agreed, but he did not make eye contact.

"You're missing the obvious," Rory Doyle said. "Yer man there could have died any number of ways, and then someone could have tossed the body in this pit."

"Of course," Siobhán said. "You'll want to examine his skull and compare it to Alan's to rule out that both these men hit their head on the edge, thus causing a wound to their temple and their death."

He did make eye contact now, and she saw a flash of anger behind his eyes. "I must, must I?"

"I . . . I just meant I assume you will."

"Perhaps you should wait outside while we finish our work," he said.

"Don't mind him," Jeanie Brady said. "He'll warm up to ye. It will take only about twenty years."

The forensic pathologist narrowed his eyes and then gave a shrug, as if conceding. "My apologies," he said, not sounding at all sorry. "If Dr. Brady trusts your instincts, then who am I to say otherwise?" He stood and stepped back from the slurry pit. "We'll need to take a close look at the angles. All the positions someone could have been standing in, in order for him to be pushed from behind and hit his head in such a way that it causes his death. I'll take some measurements, but if he was killed in such a manner, then the killer just got plain lucky."

"How so?" Aretta asked.

"I could push someone into this pit a hundred times over and not kill them," he replied. "In order to succeed, the victim would have had to be standing about here." He stood in front of the pit, pointing to the corner. "Dr. Brady, would you come up behind me and pretend to shove me?" Jeanie Brady stepped up to his left side. "As Garda O'Sullivan has stated, the victim would have to have been standing at this front right corner in order for me to fall and hit my head in that corner."

"Right, so," Jeanie said. "I'm a little rusty at pushing pathologists into pits." She threw her head back and laughed. She may have slimmed down, but her laugh was as full as ever. She moved to his right side.

"You'll need to come at me from the side and push—"

Jeanie Brady gave him a sudden shove, and he let out a yelp as he nearly toppled into the pit. Siobhán grabbed him just in time and yanked him back from the edge. He swallowed hard.

"I am so sorry," Jeanie said. "I don't know me own strength. Lucky for you, O'Sullivan here has mad reflexes."

Another laugh erupted, this time from Aretta.

"Let's finish with our photos and begin the

process of removing the bones," the forensic pathologist said. "It's going to take some time."

Jeanie sidled over to Siobhán and spoke under
her breath. "Pity," she said. "I was hoping to get in
another shove."

Siobhán and Aretta gave the pathologists space
to work. First, they returned to the garda station
and had an hour to catch up on emails and paper-
work. When it was time for lunch, they decided to
return to the farm and picnic in the field. Siobhán
led them up the same hill where Rose had dropped
the tidbit about the O'Leary parents demanding
grandchildren. She spread out a blanket, and they
sat down to eat.

"The view is gorgeous," Aretta said.

Siobhán felt a flush of pride. Maybe she could
get used to this farm. "It is something to behold,"
she agreed.

Aretta had a small salad and soup, barely a cup
full, and although Siobhán didn't get too nosy, it
appeared to be only broth. For a second Siobhán
looked down at her ham and cheese toastie and
large packet of crisps and wondered what Aretta
thought of her diet. Then she thought of the
bistro changing hands and wondered what she
and Macdara would do if they didn't have Eoin
making delicious meals all day long. Was Macdara
expecting *her* to cook? She'd make her brown
bread, of course, but it was always the lads who
cooked at the bistro. But Eoin and James would
not be living with them, so she and Dara were
going to have to start cooking. She couldn't get ex-

cited over the idea, since it sounded like one more thing to add to an already full to-do list. But eating from the chipper daily wasn't a healthy habit to get into. Siobhán was so lost in thought, it was Aretta who noticed Jeanie Brady waving at them from across the field. They packed up what remained of their lunch and headed back. Once they arrived at the dairy barn, the forensic pathologist said his curt goodbyes and headed out. Jeanie Brady would remain with Siobhán and Aretta to process the pit.

"Why don't you have a lunch break while we get a start on it," Siobhán said.

"I brought a sad sack of greens," Jeanie Brady said morosely. "But your picnic looked lovely. Perhaps I will take a few minutes while the sun is shining down on us."

"We'll be here," Siobhán said. She turned to Aretta. "Are you ready?"

"As I'll ever be," Aretta said.

Siobhán had finally spoken to a slurry pit manufacturer, and he had assured her that after all this time they wouldn't be inhaling poisonous gases unless they began mixing the dried muck with water. But if they wanted additional protection, he had suggested they be well suited up and wear face masks. A forensic team was standing by, and Jeanie Brady would want to examine everything they uncovered, but Siobhán wanted first crack at it. She readied her evidence bags, and she and Aretta quickly slipped on new protective suits and masks. Siobhán had also brought along rakes, picks, and small shovels. They stood over the pit, contemplating the tasks ahead.

"It's like an archeological dig," Aretta said, her eyes twinkling with excitement.

First, they sorted through the pile of branches off to the side. The first fifteen minutes yielded nothing but leaves and bits of bark for their effort. Then Aretta called out, "Found something." Siobhán heard a chiming sound and looked to see Aretta holding a small silver bell. "From a child's bicycle maybe?" Aretta said. She placed it in an evidence bag and handed it to Siobhán. "There's nothing else in the branches."

"Good call," Siobhán said. "It does look like it's from a child's bicycle." There was plenty of rust on the bell, suggesting it had been here a long time. "Joseph must have had a bicycle, don't you think?"

"I imagine there were plenty of lads on bikes around here back in the day," Aretta said.

"You're right. But only one of them lived next door."

"Perhaps Joseph saw something as a child? Do you think he'd even remember?"

"It's definitely tricky with someone who was so young at the time. Our memories aren't always reliable. However, if he saw something traumatic and violent, I would say the memories are still there somewhere." And although she certainly hated the idea of children with traumatic memories, it would be helpful if Joseph had witnessed something back then, something that could help them catch the killer.

"Shall we begin?" Aretta asked.

Siobhán nodded as they stared into the pit. "If you don't want to climb down with me, it's okay," Siobhán said. "I can hand items up to you."

"Are you joking me?" Aretta took a small shovel from Siobhán and without hesitation climbed the ladder welded to the side of the slurry pit. Siobhán followed suit.

Siobhán gestured. "I'll take this half, and you take that half."

Aretta nodded and within seconds was methodically going through her half. Siobhán began lightly scraping the bottom of the pit, dividing it into further sections so she wouldn't miss any spots.

"Is everything to be placed in a separate bag?" Aretta said. "Each individual cigarette butt or scrap of anything?"

"Yes," Siobhán said. "Don't worry. We brought plenty of bags."

Siobhán turned back and noticed a flash of mustard yellow. She peered closer, then picked it up. It was a shard of pottery. There was hardly any dirt, and it didn't appear as if it had been buried here for fifty years. Did it fall in at the same time as the falconer's glove? Or was it *placed* in? The falconer's glove was obviously an object that related to Rose, and this pottery shard suggested a connection to Joseph. Was the killer or even a witness trying to send a message?

"Look," Siobhán said after she slipped the shard of pottery into an evidence bag.

Aretta's head popped up, and she squinted at the evidence bag. "What is that?"

"I believe it's a piece of broken pottery. But there's hardly any dirt on it, so I'm guessing it was tossed in recently."

"And one of our suspects is a potter," Aretta

said. "Who may or may not have also lost the bell to his bicycle."

"And another one of our suspects is a falconer," Siobhán said.

"I found something." Aretta's voice was high with excitement. She held up something round, shiny, and gold. "It's a coin."

"Woah," Siobhán said. "May I see that?"

Aretta handed it to her, and Siobhán took a closer look. She recognized it immediately. It was one of the tokens from the arcade that used to be in town. Like the shard of pottery, the large gold token was relatively free of mud. "We used to have an arcade on Sarsfield Street," Siobhán explained. "This is one of the tokens."

"An arcade?"

Siobhán nodded. "It had video games and rolly-ball games and table soccer." Even James still had a pile of tokens somewhere in the bistro. It would be rare to find a household without them.

"Oh," Aretta said, sounding disappointed. "I thought it might be valuable."

"It may not be valuable in that sense," Siobhán said. "But every scrap in here is priceless as long as it leads to our killer."

"Did many people frequent the arcade?"

Siobhán nodded. "You used to see these tokens everywhere. Even me brother has a handful of them somewhere. I'm afraid it doesn't help us nail down our killer." The O'Sullivans used to go to the arcade at least once a week. Siobhán loved the one where you tossed a ball up a ramp, trying to get it into the top hole. James had been fierce good at it, and she still had some of the plush teddies he'd won for her.

"I think I found another one!" Aretta held up an object blackened with muck. She wiped it with a cloth, revealing a second gold arcade token. One recent, one old. That was odd.

"The arcade used to have a snooker table," Siobhán said. "Those could have come from Tommy's pocket."

"Why is one covered in muck and the other isn't?"

"Maybe one stayed protected in one of his pockets until they moved the body and the other fell out as soon as he fell in?"

"I'd say that is an excellent hunch," Aretta said. "Jeanie Brady is right. You have good instincts."

"Thank you," Siobhán said. "You do as well."

Aretta held up a cigarette butt. Siobhán groaned. She could only imagine how many useless bits they'd find down here, tossed in by lads over the years who had no clue that someday she'd be on her hands and knees, sifting through this dried muck, grasping on to whatever dirty yoke they could find. "I hope archeological digs are more exciting," Siobhán said.

"They unearth lost civilizations," Aretta said. "But we get to unearth a killer."

"Good woman, I like your style." They treated each other to a rare smile and got back to the muck.

Chapter 12

It was late afternoon when Siobhán returned from the pit, showered, and changed. Macdara arrived at the bistro, and Siobhán filled him in on the adventures in the dairy barn while her cappuccino machine whirred alongside her.

"He's an odd one, that forensic investigator, but on the bright side, the word about town is he's good at his job."

"The odd ones always are."

"He missed the branches, though. That was my catch."

"Still impressive, even though it's the third time you told me."

Since her hands were full with her favorite machine, she gave him a kick.

"Our killer likes to sit and visit," he mused. "Given many of our suspects are in their golden years, that isn't too surprising."

Siobhán finished making her cup of salvation and grabbed a lemon tart from the bakery case. She took her goods to the chairs near the fireplace as Eoin brought out Macdara's Irish breakfast and mug of tea.

"Will Aretta be joining you?" Eoin asked, glancing out the window with anticipation.

"She's on her way," Macdara said, failing to hide a grin. "Time to break out the cologne."

"I just wanted to prepare her tea," Eoin said. He wrinkled his nose. "Do I need cologne?"

Macdara chuckled. "Never hurts."

"Believe me, it can hurt," Siobhán said. "We don't need him overpowering the scent of breakfast."

Eoin gave her a look, and she stuck out her tongue, then laughed as he turned red. "You're sweet on her, she's sweet on you, and we're all thrilled for ye as long as you don't get in the way of her training. There's a lot to learn in the beginning, and she doesn't need distractions."

"Siobhán O'Sullivan, are you trying to squash love?" Macdara said, laughing at the gesture Eoin flashed her before heading back to the kitchen.

"Squash it?" she said. "Have you been in the same room with the pair of them? You practically need a fire hose. I'm just trying to help slow it down, so they don't burn themselves to the ground."

Macdara chuckled again, and then they turned to their list of suspects. They'd decided to hold the first round of interviews at the bistro, in a more informal approach. The interview rooms at the garda station were being painted. Everyone had figured with the wedding, it was a good time to do it. Life was definitely what happened when you were making other plans, and Siobhán loathed when cliches came true. But there was an added benefit here: people often talked freely when they thought they were simply *helping* an investigation rather than being afraid they were targets of it.

"Falconer's glove, a shard of pottery, and two arcade tokens." One by one, Siobhán laid photocopies of the evidence photos out on the table in front of them. "Otherwise we found cigarette butts and a few food wrappers, most too faded to identify. All that we saw in the branches was a bell, like that from a child's bicycle."

"Joseph's?"

"Most likely, although over the years I'm sure other children played in the dairy barn."

Macdara nodded. "We'd have better luck figuring out what neighborhood children hadn't played in that dairy barn. Especially since it's been abandoned, it must be like a beacon to the young ones."

"True, but there's also a lot of rust on it, suggesting the bell has been there awhile. I believe the falconer's glove and the shard of pottery fell in recently," Siobhán said. "Or more likely were placed in recently." Macdara raised an eyebrow. "They would have been buried in muck, but they were pristine. Just like one of the arcade tokens."

"I haven't seen an arcade token around for ages," Macdara said. "But I probably have a jar full of them at home."

"I think everyone in town does," Siobhán said. "My guess is that these tokens were in Tommy's pocket when he went into the pit. I believe one fell out when he fell in, and that's why it's covered in muck. But the other remained in one of his pockets until they removed his remains, and that's why it looks shiny and new."

"Given the arcade has been closed down for the past decade, I say that's a safe conclusion." He looked at her photos of the falconer's glove and the shard of pottery. "This is very interesting. Did our killer place these here to misdirect, or did our killer place these here hoping we would think he or she was trying to misdirect when it was a blatant confession?"

"Given the objects each point to a different killer, I don't think we can call them a confession," Siobhán said. "Whoever dropped them in had to know we'd be processing the pit."

"We'll have to verify that this glove belongs to Rose and then see if she remembers the last time she saw it." Macdara sighed, then stroked his chin. "Unless she's the killer, and then, of course, she'll lie."

Siobhán nodded. That was always the problem with a murder inquiry. *Liars.* She wished Aretta was here to see that Siobhán wasn't being pessimistic—just realistic. She glanced at the preliminary suspect list they had prepared for the first set of interviews. Howard Dunn was their first subject of the day. Outside, the skies had suddenly gone gray. Just like her mood.

"Gladys O'Leary threatened to kill our second victim," Macdara said. "And shortly after, he did indeed turn up dead."

"She doesn't strike me as senile," Siobhán said. "Why would she threaten to kill him in front of so many witnesses if she was serious?"

"Sometimes murder cases aren't very compli-cated," Macdara said. "Sometimes you find the killer right away."

"People use that expression all the time, and you know it."

"True. But if someone uses it and then the person he or she used it against does indeed turn up dead, one simply cannot ignore it."

"I'm not suggesting we ignore it, but I don't think we should jump to conclusions."

"Sometimes the most logical explanation is the right explanation."

"And you think it's logical that she would threaten to kill him in front of all us guards and then go and kill him?"

Macdara grabbed a poker stick and jabbed at logs in the fire, even though it wasn't lit. They were talking in circles. "I'm only speaking my mind."

"What about Benjamin?"

"What about him?"

"Why do you think it's *her* over him?"

"Go on." Macdara set the fire poker back in its stand and leaned back to listen.

"Benji Burns also lives next door. He was Tommy's best friend, and he coveted his wife-to-be. Perhaps he's been pulling up a chair for fifty years to chat with his best pal."

"Perhaps," Macdara agreed. "But why would he kill Alan?"

"Maybe Alan figured out that Benji was the killer and confronted him."

"What if Alan himself was the killer? Maybe the guilt got to be too much."

"Even if he wanted to take his own life, I hardly

doubt he hurled himself into the slurry pit and somehow managed to conk his head on the side and thus guarantee his own death."

"Howard and Alan could have been in it together," Macdara mused.

"Talk me through that."

"We only have Howard's word for it that his thirty thousand quid was stolen. What if he did something else with the money and Tommy found out?"

"Interesting," Siobhán said. The exact opposite of the story that had been told. It was possible. "And how does Alan fit in?"

"Maybe Alan figured out that Howard lost the money, Tommy confronted him, and he pushed Tommy into the pit."

"But don't forget Benji," Siobhán said.

"Go on, so," Macdara said, although he sounded reluctant to hear anything negative about Benji.

"Benji was in love with Gladys. He wanted his best friend's wife-to-be. Together, Howard and Benji's problem was Tommy."

"I'm on board with looking at all angles of a case, but all we know for sure is that Alan entered the dairy barn the other morning and was either pushed or fell into that pit. We do not know for sure that he was meeting anyone or accusing anyone of anything."

"And in several of our scenarios, it requires our suspects to keep each other's secret for fifty years," Siobhán said. *Not likely.* "If they'd managed to keep the secret for fifty years, why would anyone confess now?"

"Because we found Tommy's remains."

"And?"

"And either the guilt was too much when his bones were unearthed or maybe we'll discover Alan had an underlying illness. You know how people get when they're facing their demise. They want to confess."

"It will be interesting to see if the autopsy reveals any signs of a life-threatening illness. But even if it does, that doesn't draw a straight line from Alan to any of our suspects."

"It also doesn't exclude the possibility of any of our suspects keeping a dark secret with Alan." Macdara wrote the name Gladys in his notebook and then tapped the name with his Biro, as if somehow in doing so, all would be revealed. "Let's say her act is to be believed and Benji is our killer. I don't see Gladys letting Benjamin get away with killing her one true love, do you?"

"But you don't believe her act," Siobhán said. "Otherwise she wouldn't be your top suspect."

She'd interrupted his thoughts with that one, she could tell. He'd even stopped eating, something he was usually fully capable of doing whilst doing almost anything else at the same time. "Perhaps I am holding on to a bias," he said. "Gladys and Benji have been married for fifty years, and he's not the love of her life?"

"If you died right now and I remarried, you'd still be the love of my life," Siobhán agreed.

"That's either the most romantic thing you've ever said to me or the most horrifying," Macdara said. He let his fork clink to the plate and pushed it away. "I've lost me appetite."

"I do think we can solidly conclude that whoever killed Tommy is someone from his past, and if the killer isn't Gladys or Benjamin, it's still someone in their orbit, who visits them regularly enough that he or she could easily walk in and out of that dairy barn without raising an eyebrow."

"The barn hasn't been in use for fifty years," Macdara said.

"But one could walk around the property and not draw attention or alarm unless one is a complete stranger."

"We'll have to ask them about the workmen they've had over the years." He rubbed his chin. "I suppose if one were really motivated, it would be easy enough to sneak onto the property. But there have been cattle using the land to graze for just as long, so to your point, there have been eyes on the place."

"And either the eyes haven't been sharp enough or they've seen nothing to draw alarm."

The bell dinged, and a few moments later Aretta appeared. She was loaded down with notebooks and recording equipment.

"Good morning."

"Good morning," Macdara and Siobhán said in stereo.

The kitchen door swung open, and Eoin emerged, tea on a tray, whistling. "Perfect timing," he said. "Good morning, Garda Dabiri. Here is your tea."

Aretta smiled and thanked him, and Eoin cleared a space for all her gear. "Can I make you a boiled egg and toast?"

"No thank you," she said.

"Lemon tart?" Eoin suggested. "Or perhaps a fruit salad?"

"I'm all sorted," Aretta said. She arranged a few tables for their interviews. "Howard Dunn will be here in an hour," she said, glancing at Eoin, who was hovering nearby, with full-moon eyes and a silly grin on his face.

"Let's put him off for a few hours," Macdara said. "I want to go back to the garda station and gather everyone in the main room."

"Now?" Eoin said. "She hasn't even had a sip of her tea!"

Aretta picked up the tea, took a sip, put it down, then smiled at Eoin. "Lovely."

Macdara gestured to the photos in front of him. "We need to present these findings to the team. I have a feeling this one is going to require all hands on deck."

Chapter 13

The large screen in the training room at the Kilbane Garda Station was pulled down, and chairs had been set up for the meeting. A photograph of the slurry pit rose on the screen, the light of the single bulb swaying above it.

"This is how most horror films begin," someone cracked.

The next photograph was a close-up of the falconer's glove and shard of pottery. "We believe these items either were in victim number two, Alan O'Leary's pockets or someone threw them in with the body," Macdara began.

Alan's pockets had been processed, and nothing had been found in them, bar a handkerchief. He was dressed in brown trousers and a white shirt and Wellies. Gladys and Linda had stated that the white shirt was an undershirt, which Alan would often be seen in, in the mornings, as well as the trousers. The Wellies, however, suggested he had entered the dairy barn on his own volition. The question was why. His usual morning attire suggested this may have been a last-minute decision, something impulsive. Had he been summoned? Had he seen something alarming that he wanted to check out? Or, as Siobhán was starting to wonder, did he have anything *stashed* in the dairy barn? Something he hadn't wanted the guards to find? Or perhaps he had simply wanted to know whether or not they had already found it. What could that something be? Drugs? Money? Howard's stolen cash?

Who would steal cash and then squirrel it away for fifty years? Cash seemed the least likely, in Siobhán's opinion. But at the moment that was all any of the theories were: possibilities. . . .

All their suspects had been expressly warned to stay away from the crime scene, and yet despite those warnings and crime scene tape and guards posted at the front of the barn, Alan had taken the risk and entered. Something, or someone, had drawn him out there.

The slides clicked, and the golden arcade tokens appeared on-screen. Someone made an exclamation of glee.

"Don't get too excited," Siobhán warned. "These look fancy, but they're actually tokens from an old arcade. You'll notice the coin on the right is shinier than the one on the left?" Heads nodded all around. "We believe one of the coins stayed protected in one of Tommy's pockets and the other fell out when he went into the pit. Then when the remains were removed, the other fell out."

"Could it be some sort of calling card?" Aretta asked.

"Say more about that," Macdara said.

"Something the killer throws in with his victims?"

"What year did the arcade close down?" Macdara asked.

"Two thousand five, was it?" someone said. "Plenty of folks have the old arcade tokens lying around. I believe there are some floating around my house as well."

"Fingerprints?" someone else asked.

"Not with years of muck," someone answered. "We'd find either no prints or too many."

Siobhán looked at the clock on the wall. It was time to meet Howard Dunn at the bistro. "Aretta, are you up for accompanying us to the bistro for her meeting with Howard Dunn and taking notes?" Macdara asked.

"Absolutely."

"If we hurry, we can get a bite to eat ourselves before he's due to arrive," Siobhán said as they headed out of the station.

"No thank you," Aretta said. "I'm grand."

"I'll have her share as well as mine, then," Macdara said.

By the time they were fed and back at the bistro, not only had the skies darkened, but they were leaking as well. The rain was coming in sideways, drumming against the windows. "When Mr. Dunn arrives, let's not mention the arcade tokens just yet," Macdara said. "I don't want any of our suspects to know what we found in the slurry pit."

As if he had heard his name and had been magically summoned, the little bell above the door to the bistro jingled and Howard Dunn stepped into the hall. Siobhán headed out to greet him. Howard had the door propped open and was standing half in and half out, violently shaking a large black umbrella. "The heavens are weeping," he said.

"I'm sorry you had to go out in this," Siobhán said.

"Not a bother. I'm a bit of a night owl anyway."

Siobhán gestured to the umbrella holder near the door. Howard tossed his umbrella in, then looked down at his shoes. "A good wipe on the rug and you'll be grand."

Howard nodded and dried the bottom of his shoes as best he could.

"Mug of tea and brown bread to warm ya?"

"I wouldn't say no to that now."

"Come on in."

"I'm afraid I'm still a sopping mess," he said, glancing down at himself.

A head appeared at the top of the stairwell. Gráinne stood, hand on hip, looking down on them. "I'll fetch him a towel."

"Thanks, petal. My sister will bring you a towel." Siobhán glanced into the bistro and saw James tossing logs into the fireplace. "My brother is lighting a fire as we speak. We'll have you warmed up in no time."

Siobhán headed into the dining room and signaled Eoin to put the kettle on. Ann and Ciarán were upstairs, probably huddled over the iPad. She wished this case were finished and they were simply having a night in, keeping cozy from the rain. The image of the farm with the stone house rose to mind, the table filled with laughter and noise, then spilling out onto the fields after, perhaps establishing a routine of after-dinner walks.

"It doesn't feel like summer," Aretta said as she stood near the front windows, watching the rain come down.

"We have two seasons in Kilbane," Siobhán said. "Raining and not raining."

"Don't forget the wind," Macdara said. "Windy or not windy, that makes it all four seasons." He chuckled to himself.

Howard finally entered and stood awkwardly with the towel now draped around his neck. Siobhán pointed to the chair, and he lowered himself into it with a grimace.

"Are you alright?" she asked.

"Would you happen to have a pillow for me back?"

"Of course." She threw a look to Gráinne, who rolled her eyes but nodded before she flew up the stairs to fetch a pillow. "Have you always had back pain?"

He grunted in response, then shrugged. Had he thrown his back out recently? Bending down to fetch something out of a slurry pit? Wrestling with someone? Someone like Alan O'Leary?

Eoin sorted out the tea and brown bread with butter and jam, and although it took several minutes, soon Howard was dry, whetted with tea, and fed. It was time to begin. Siobhán opened with asking Howard to tell them everything about his relationship with Tommy, up until the last time he saw or spoke to him.

"And before you do that," Macdara interjected, "I'm able to tell you that we did not find a satchel stuffed with cash in the slurry pit."

"We didn't even find an empty one," Siobhán said.

Howard nodded. "I suppose I wasn't holding out much hope. It's making me question the entire narrative, the grudge I've been holding on to for fifty years."

"Question it how?" Siobhán asked.

"I blamed Tommy for everything," Howard said. "I called him a thief. It appears I was wrong to do so." He stared at the crackling fire and shook his head. Thunder rumbled outside. "When I think of him lying there for the past fifty years . . ." He shook his head. "No one deserved that."

"Take us back to the beginning," Siobhán said. "Your partnership with Tommy."

Howard raised an eyebrow but then seemed to settle in to tell a story. "Tommy and I grew up together. We were in the same classes. Truth be told, we didn't like each other much. He was a bit of a hooligan. I minded my parents. He skipped school. I excelled. But when me father died and I was thinking of taking over the family pub, it was Tommy's idea to revive business by turning it into a snooker club. Tournaments were becoming popular, where lads were traveling all over Ireland, competing, and Tommy had this whole plan that he swore we could accomplish with thirty thousand quid. If may not sound like much these days, but it was back then."

"It's not a sum of money I'd want to be losing even today," Macdara said. "Where did the money come from?"

"Me father had an insurance policy. It was all the money from that and his estate, with the extra bob from betting on the horses, and even a fundraiser for the snooker club. It was everything I had." His fists curled up at the memory as he stared into the fire.

"Why did you need it all in cash?" Aretta asked.

"Tommy said he had contractors willing to do the whole pub and supply the snooker tables at cost, but they needed it in cash. I had it in a satchel that belonged to my uncle who used to be a book-maker. The renovations were scheduled to start a week after the wedding." He shook his head. "All these years later and I still don't know how Tommy figured out me hiding space. That's the one question that bothered me all these years."

"Hiding place?" Macdara asked.

Howard nodded. "You don't leave thirty thousand quid out in the open."

"Where was your hiding place?" Aretta asked.

Howard shifted, as if he didn't want to give it up even now. "In the ceiling of me kitchen," he said. "There was a little hidey space. I thought I was careful, but obviously, someone was watching. And the only one hanging around me those days was Tommy."

"Wait," Siobhán said. "You still suspect Tommy of stealing your money?"

Howard nodded. "There's no one else it could have been. But maybe someone forced him to do it. Maybe he was in some kind of trouble. And now that he's dead and the money isn't with him . . . I have to face that I've been wrong about his motives for fifty years. But if Tommy didn't take the money, who did?" He looked at them as if he expected them to answer. "I swear, he was the only one who could have sussed out me hiding place."

"You hid it in your ceiling," Siobhán said. "Instead of a proper safe?"

It took Howard a few seconds to collect himself before he spoke. "I thought I was so clever, not needing a proper safe. A proper safe is like an advertisement that you've got something to steal. I had to stand on a ladder and push in the ceiling tile to reach me hiding place. I suppose it wasn't all that original. But all the same, I thought it was the safest place for it."

"But people knew about this arrangement you had with Tommy."

"Everyone knew. I should have waited, but it wasn't easy getting all that money in cash in the first place. I wasn't going to hand it over to a bank only to go through the rigmarole to get the cash again in a week."

"When did you realize the satchel was gone?"

"I checked the minute I came back from the wedding that never was."

"Directly after the canceled wedding?" Macdara asked.

"Yes, right after," Howard said. "Well. Not right after. First, we drank all the alcohol and ate the food. Couldn't let a wedding feast go to waste."

Siobhán and Macdara exchanged a glance as images of the food and drink from their disrupted wedding floated through her head.

"And then you checked on your satchel of money," Macdara suggested. Siobhán could imagine a tipsy Howard climbing the ladder to his ceiling.

"Yes, right after we ate and drank. Well. Not right after. After we ate and drank, we did a bit of a drive around, looking for the runaway groom. When all that was said and done—I checked on me money."

"That same day."

"Yes. Well, no. Because we did all those other things, you know? The eating and the drinking and the driving. Which led to a bit more drinking. Turned into a bit of a session, alright. I'd say it was about three days later that I went to fetch me money. I'd decided to put it in the bank. I wasn't going to go through with the snooker club. Tommy was the expert and the one with all the contacts. The big plans. But then I pushed open that ceiling tile and pawed around. No satchel. I almost fell off the ladder. I nearly tore me whole ceiling apart looking for it. That's when I knew. He'd swindled me. Tommy took me thirty thousand and ran." Howard exhaled, as if trying to get rid of fifty years of anger. Tears came to his eyes. "I've hated him for fifty years. I need to know. Did he do it or not?"

"Until we find the satchel, all possibilities are on the table," Macdara said. "If we find it at all. But I will tell you it's not in that slurry pit, and dead men can't spend money."

"What about Alan O'Leary?" Siobhán asked. "When was the last time you saw or spoke to him?"

Howard rubbed his chin. "The night we all gathered at their house," he said.

"Was there anything about his demeanor that struck you as out of the ordinary?"

"How do you mean?"

"Did he seem overly upset or frightened?"

Howard shook his head. "We were all upset. I didn't notice anything apart from that."

"Did he say anything to you about . . . anything?" Siobhán was reaching. Alan was like a tantalizing thread that somehow fit into the tapestry. She couldn't help but pull on it.

"Not that I can recall." Howard appeared to think on it some more and then shook his head.

"Do you know if Alan was looking into buying a snooker table?"

"Alan?" Howard raised an eyebrow.

"Yes. Shortly before he died, Benji overheard him talking to someone on the phone about a snooker table. He thought maybe he planned on buying one as a memorial to Tommy."

"I see," Howard said. "Where was he going to put it?"

"I don't know," Siobhán said. "But he never mentioned it to you?"

"Not a word," Howard said. "And I should have been the first person he called. I can get them at cost."

Siobhán turned to Macdara. "We need to find out who Alan called that morning."

"Benji may have been lying."

"About a phone call?"

"I'll put in a request for the records. As you know, that could take considerable time."

Siobhán nodded. Everything was a waiting game.

"Let's get back to Tommy," Macdara said. "You've stated that you believed that Tommy had done a runner?"

Howard nodded. "I suppose I should have realized that something was very wrong. I thought maybe Tommy went far away. Every now and again he'd talk about jetting off to Australia. Said he had a cousin down under. I always assumed that's where he went."

"Tell us about the last time you saw or heard from Tommy," Siobhán said. "Take your time."

"I don't need to take my time. I've been doing nothing but replaying it since you found the poor lad. The last time I saw Tommy Caffrey was two days before the wedding. We went to the pub. And that night he told me a secret that I thought I'd be taking to me grave." He paused for dramatic effect.

The three of them leaned in.

"Not only will I tell ye the secret," Howard said, "but I believe it will also reveal his killer."

Chapter 14

The wildlife center just outside of Kilbane teemed with the sounds of birdcalls. Gorgeous green fields rolled out as far as the eye could see, topped off by windmills churning in the distance, just beneath the curves of the Ballyhoura Mountains. Aretta walked quickly behind Macdara and Siobhán as they headed for the information center, the falconer's glove they found in the slurry pit tucked in an evidence bag and stowed underneath Macdara's armpit. Siobhán wanted to tell him that there was something about his habit of using his armpit as a pseudo–carrying case that she'd been irked by lately. But she equally recognized it wasn't that big of a deal, and the closer they came to marrying, the more she was worried about turning into one of those wives who pecked, pecked, pecked. Perhaps it wasn't a great idea to be surrounded by all these birds in this moment, and who really cared if Macdara liked to carry things in that manner? Files, books, a newspaper, once his car keys . . . Should she get him a briefcase? A man bag? A satchel? It reminded her of the satchel full of cash that Howard insisted was missing. He had come across as sincere during his interview, but killers were often excellent liars.

As they progressed across the field, Aretta periodically flinched and ducked keeping an eye on the trees above, as if every branch was filled with untold danger. The third time Aretta reacted as if she was under imminent attack, Siobhán whirled around.

"Are you afraid of birds?"

"Where is this coming from?" Macdara said. "Of course she's not afraid of birds."

"I don't mean just any bird," Siobhán said. "Birds of prey. Eagles, hawks, falcons—"

"What on earth gives you the idea that she's afraid of birds?" Macdara asked.

Suddenly an enormous falcon swooped overhead with a loud cry. Aretta shrieked and dropped to the ground. Seconds later she was curled up in a fetal position, with her hands covering her head.

"Just a hunch," Siobhán said, staring down at the top of Aretta's head.

"Is it gone?" Aretta asked.

Siobhán and Macdara glanced at the sky, then across the field, where a figure stood, leather-gloved arm outstretched, a bird of prey perched atop it.

"Coast is clear," Macdara said.

Aretta did not move.

"Perhaps you'd like to check out the visitors' center?" Siobhán suggested.

Macdara knelt next to Aretta. "Why didn't you mention you disliked birds?"

"It's much stronger than a dislike," Siobhán said. "I believe she has a phobia."

Aretta looked around as if to make sure no one else was listening. "Ornithophobia," she squeaked.

"Ornithophobia?" Macdara repeated.

"It's an intense fear of birds," Aretta said. "At times it's unreasonable, and I am aware of that, and yet my body takes over and just . . . reacts." Between her spread fingers, her eyes were wide, and a drip of sweat trickled out from underneath her garda cap.

"How can we help?" Siobhán said. "Will you be able to continue?"

Aretta looked as if she wanted to answer yes, and she spread her fingers so she could see, but first, she tried to swallow and found it difficult. "I need to focus on my breath," she said, then began taking a deep breath. "I'm sorry. I know it's irrational."

"Most phobias are irrational," Siobhán said. "But that doesn't make them less real." Siobhán held her hand out to Aretta, who accepted it, and Siobhán helped her to her feet.

Aretta gave a nervous laugh but kept her gaze away from the sky and the trees. "I'm fine with the little chirpy ones. It's the big cawing ones with beaks and talons that shred that terrify me."

Caw, caw, caw. Siobhán could see that. "Yes, I suppose knowing they're descendants of dinosaurs doesn't help either?" She thought about the leather glove and imagined how sharp their talons must be. And that wingspan. Something to behold. Perhaps this fear was very rational indeed. Should she be afraid of them? Could a hawk or a falcon kill a man?

"As you know, we need to speak with Rose Burns," Siobhán said. "You could pop into the visitors' center and ask for her work attendance records." Siobhán pointed out the building in the distance. They probably wouldn't learn a great deal from her work attendance, and for all she knew, the center didn't even keep those records, but she wanted to give Aretta a way out.

"I can do that," Aretta said, the relief evident in her voice. She seemed to be clocking the distance from where she stood to the building. "Is it bad to run? Do they come after you if you run?"

"I think that's bears," Siobhán said. "And there are no bears in Ireland."

"However," Macdara said, "I saw a show on telly once that gave some great advice. If you happen to travel somewhere with a population of bears and you run into one, you're supposed to stand your ground, make yourself appear as large as you can by standing on your tiptoes, raise your hands, and then . . . This is the good part. Are ye listening?" He grinned and waited until he had their rapt attention. "You're supposed to sing," Macdara said. "Bears will stop and reassess you. They won't know what you are."

"It must work," Siobhán said. "Because I'm stopping and reassessing you as you speak." A little smile formed at the corner of Macdara's lips, and he shook his head.

"Seriously," Siobhán said. "What are you?"

In an uncharacteristic public display of affection, Macdara wrapped his arm around Siobhán's waist and pulled her into him. "I'm the man who will stand between you and a bear."

"And I'm the woman who will be hauling her arse as fast as she can away from both of ye," Siobhán said, playfully shoving him off. "As the old joke goes, I don't need to outrun the bear. I just need to outrun youse."

"Woman of my dreams," Macdara said. He turned to Aretta. "Nightmares, that is," he said with a wink.

"What are you supposed to sing?" Aretta asked. " 'Danny Boy'?"

Macdara nodded. " 'Danny Boy' is always an excellent choice."

Siobhán could hear Aretta attempting to hum "Danny Boy" softly.

"You have a nice voice, but it's totally unhelpful in this situation," Siobhán said. "Just head over to the center. You'll be grand."

"What about seeing birds on telly?" Macdara asked. "Would that frighten you?"

"Yes," Aretta said. "If they're big."

"The birds or the telly?" Macdara asked.

"Falcons, eagles, hawks," Aretta said. "But the reaction is much stronger in person."

"I bet you're glad all the pterodactyls are extinct," Macdara said.

"What about bats?" Siobhán said. "I suppose I have a phobia of bats. The thought of them nesting in me head." She shuddered and felt a wave of empathy for Aretta. Some people were crippled by their phobias. It was just a matter of degrees. Even one degree could tip the balance between managing a fear and losing the plot altogether.

Murder probes were like that too. You thought you knew a case, and then the tiniest clue could shift it in a new direction. . . .

"I hear hypnosis can do wonders with phobias," Siobhán said.

"Do you have any phobias?" Aretta sounded hopeful.

Did she? She was afraid of men getting away with murder, but that didn't seem like a true phobia.

"I'll stick with bats nesting in me head," Siobhán said. She turned to Macdara. "Your turn."

He frowned, then shrugged. "I can't think of a single one."

"I'm sure there must be something. Spiders?"

"Not at all," Macdara said. "I'm fascinated by their webs."

"Snakes? Heights?"

"Snakes wouldn't be high on me list, but Saint Patrick has taken care of that for Ireland," Macdara said with a grin. "And I'd climb the highest mountain for you."

Siobhán was relieved to see Aretta was already headed for the center.

"I'm not saying I'm perfect," Macdara said as they headed across the field to the woman with the falcon.

"Don't worry," Siobhán said. "Nobody would ever think that."

* * *

"Welcome to the ancient field sport of falconry." Rose's voice hummed with excitement. "This is my heaven." She gestured to the endless fields and the nearby babbling river, the falcon or hawk alert and majestic on her gloved fist. What must it feel like to fly? Soar above Ireland's rolling green hills without a care in the world? "If you'd like, I can show you around the grounds." Rose lifted her arm, and the large bird took off, the tiny bells attached to one foot chiming as it soared. "We'll head over to their pens. Charlie will do a loop and find me."

"That was Charlie?" Siobhán said. "I didn't recognize him." Macdara gave her a look. "I must admit I can't tell the difference between a falcon and a hawk."

"We should get a couple of bells like that for you," Macdara said, leaning into Siobhán and lowering his voice. "This way you can't sneak up on me when we're at the farm."

She gave him a gentle shove. *Sneak up on me when we're at the farm* . . . She couldn't help thinking that someone had snuck up to their victims while they stood over the slurry pit. But why would not just one but two men approach a slurry pit and just stare down into it? It was hardly plausible. They would have to wait for the official cause of death before getting too attached to theories. If only that stopped them from swimming around her poor head.

"Do you know much about falconry?" Rose asked as they strode across the fields.

"Pretend we know nothing at all," Siobhán said.

"Because we know nothing at all," Macdara added.

"It's thought to have originated in Korea in two thousand BC," Rose began.

Siobhán wasn't sure they needed to go back that far, but there could be drawbacks to interrupting a subject too early, especially when the atmosphere was friendly. As if on command, Siobhán heard the flap of wings, and Rose held her gloved arm out straight. Charlie lowered himself onto it with the grace of a dancer, then spread his wings massive as she gave him a treat. The power evident in this prehistoric bird was remarkable. Rose jostled her arm. "Home." Charlie took flight once again, his massive wings stretching and gliding, giving Siobhán a light-headed feeling. She suddenly wished she was wearing a falconer's glove so she could feel it land on her fist.

Rose was still watching Charlie fly. "I wish I was one of the first falconers," Rose said. "What an amazing thing, to use those majestic birds to help hunt quarry in their natural habitat."

Natural habitat. Slurry. That was the habitat someone had left Tommy in. Then had visited him periodically over a fifty-year period. Was Rose Burns that "someone"?

"Falconry spread to China and Japan, Persia, and the Arab world with the Mongol hordes of Genghis Khan," Rose was saying, excitement in her voice. "And then with the returning crusaders, it became a social sport in the hub of medieval Europe. It was all the rage until the invention of firearms. Specifically, the fowling piece."

"The fowling piece?" Siobhán asked.

"The long barrel of rifles," Macdara said proudly. "Once it was invented, they could shoot fowl out of the sky instead of using the hawks and falcons."

"Thank you, Mr. Wikipedia," Siobhán said. His laughter filled her.

"He's not wrong," Rose said. "Very good, Detective Sergeant Flannery." She treated Macdara to a smile that made his cheeks flash red. Complimenting her long black hair streaked with white, Rose Burns had prominent cheekbones and big brown eyes with flecks of yellow—very much like a falcon. She was tall and busty, with thin legs and the glow of a woman who had spent most of her life outdoors. She had, as they say, sex appeal. She was a beautiful older woman. The sound of wings flapping drew near as Charlie returned once more with a cry to rest on Rose's fist.

"Charlie is the one my brother saw flying over the dairy barn the morning Tommy was found in the slurry pit?" Siobhán asked.

Rose bit her lip and threw a glance at the main visitors' office in the distance. "Yes, it was Charlie," she said. "But I'd prefer it if you don't mention that to anyone here. I wasn't supposed to take him out without permission."

"Why did you?" Macdara asked.

For a moment she looked stunned by the question. It took her a long time to answer. When she did, there was a forced cheer to her voice. "Because I love this big guy. And as wonderful as this center is, he likes a change of scenery now and again. And since that property is abandoned . . . *was* abandoned . . . we've made a few trips just to shake things up."

Her excuse definitely sounded forced. *Rehearsed?* Why did Siobhán get the feeling Rose was lying? She thought back to that morning. Hadn't Rose said that Charlie had escaped? Now she was claiming she'd brought him there? Which statement was the truth, and which was a lie? "Change of scenery?" Siobhán said. "Isn't all scenery the same to a falcon?"

"Charlie isn't a falcon. He's a Harris hawk."

Rose still hadn't answered her question about the difference between a falcon and a hawk. It had nothing to do with the case, but Siobhán really wanted to know. "It's still called falconry if you're working with a hawk?" she asked.

Rose laughed. "Yes, luv, it's still called falconry."

"Would you mind explaining the difference between a falcon and a hawk?"

"About two letters," Macdara said. "One's *o-n* at the end, and the other isn't."

Rose laughed at his joke, but Siobhán groaned.

"If you keep interrupting, I'm never going to hear the answer," Siobhán said.

Rose laughed. "Hawks are usually larger than falcons, and they're often flying slower—gliding through the sky. The tips of a hawk's wings look like little fingers, whereas a falcon has slender and pointed wing tips. Hawks use their talons to catch and kill their prey. Falcons use their powerful beaks to break their prey's necks."

"Would a hawk ever attack a human?" Macdara asked.

"Under the right circumstances," Rose said. "If they were trapped in a small space, and they felt threatened. But those situations aren't common."

Siobhán was suddenly glad Aretta wasn't here for the discussion.

"What happened that morning?" Macdara asked. "We were told that Charlie appeared to be in distress."

Rose bit her lip. "Something spooked him." She held him a little higher, and a glint of sun shone off his brown and white feathers. "He could have even picked up on your brother's fear. Perhaps he sensed the chaos that was about to unfold."

"Seriously?" Siobhán said. She was open to expanding her mind during murder inquiries, learning new things, but weren't psychic hawks a bridge too far? Then again, animals did have the ability to sense dangers before humans. Earthquakes, floods, all kinds of storms . . . But what about murderers? Could they sense the dark energy of a murderer? If so, perhaps they ought to think about adding a few hawks to the garda station.

"I think Charlie sensed the spirit of Tommy that day," Rose said. "Perhaps Tommy himself was hanging around, waiting for us to discover his remains."

Or he witnessed the murderer hanging around. If Rose was the murderer, would Charlie have behaved the same way?

"Charlie," Siobhán said out loud. The bird's head swiveled, and he regarded her.

"Careful," Rose said. "You'll need a glove, or his talons will slash your hand to bits."

Talons. Not feet. Talons. The word *shredded* came to mind. Her empathy for Aretta was ticking up by the second.

They reached an outdoor enclosure of large

pens arranged in a square with open space in the middle. Charlie immediately flew to a post, where he stretched his wings with a satisfied caw.

"He's well trained," Macdara said, admiration in his voice.

"Charlie is the oldest here, and I've trained him since he was a baby," Rose said.

"That's a very special relationship," Siobhán said sincerely. It was magical, the connections one could make in life. Talk about a special relationship. But there was another relationship she wanted to know even more about. The secret Howard Dunn did *not* end up taking to his grave. "Speaking of special relationships . . . how close were you and Tommy?"

Rose headed for a hose. "I hope you don't mind if I work while we talk?"

"Not at all," Macdara said.

Rose turned on the water and headed for the nearest pen, where she emptied and refreshed a bowl of water. "I knew Tommy well," she said. "We all grew up together."

"Good friends, then?" Siobhán said. "Like brother and sister?"

Rose shut off the water as she moved on to the next enclosure, the hose trailing her like a snake. Charlie ruffled his feathers from the post. "Do you know what I like about these birds of prey?" Rose said. "Charlie doesn't pretend to be something he's not. He doesn't play games. You know when they're hungry. And they're usually hungry. You know when they want to be left alone. And you respect their power. Their immense power." She stopped as the hose seemed to catch on something, and she yanked it forward with such ferocity that Siobhán took an involuntary step back. "When we were younger, I guess you could say he was like a brother," Rose said, hosing down the next pen.

"Charlie?" Macdara asked, his voice thick with confusion.

Rose stared at him a moment, hose in hand; then she tilted her head back and roared with laughter. "I meant Tommy," she said. "Charlie is more like my baby."

Macdara cleared his throat. "Only messing."

Siobhán gave him a look—he so wasn't. "When you were younger, Tommy was like your brother, you say?" Siobhán said. "And then?"

Rose let out a long breath, which meant she'd been holding it in. "I can tell from the way you're asking the question that someone has already said something to you about Tommy and me. And I would just caution you not to believe everything you hear." Resentment leaked out of her voice, and the water pressure increased.

"We never believe everything we hear," Macdara said. "But we always ask."

She shut off the water and nodded. "I understand. I'm sorry if I sound angry." She whirled around. "How could we not know that he was there all that time? How could I not know?" Sudden tears came to her eyes, and she allowed them to spill down her cheeks before wiping them away. It was as she was blinking and clearing her throat that she noticed the evidence bag underneath Macdara's arm. She pointed. "Is that a falconer's glove?" Her face was very still; her voice thick.

Macdara nodded and removed the bag, then

held it up so she could see. Rose took a step forward and stared at it for a moment. She stumbled back, shaking her head, then came close once more as if she wasn't quite believing her eyes and she needed to double-check.

"It has some unique beading and tassels," Macdara said.

"I know it does," Rose said. "I certainly know my own glove."

Chapter 15

❧

"You're saying this is your falconer's glove?" Macdara asked, dangling the evidence bag in front of her.

Rose nodded, never taking her eyes off it. "It was always my glove, but the added adornments were a present from Benji many years ago."

"When is the last time you saw this particular glove?" Macdara asked.

Rose frowned. "It's been a long time. I just can't believe you're even holding it."

"We'll need you to be more specific," Siobhán said. "Please try to remember an exact time when you last saw this particular glove."

"It was when I was still married to Benji—one of his last gifts to me as my husband—so it had to be around the time of Gladys and Tommy's wedding. Yes. The week before. I was very distraught when I couldn't find it. I was afraid Benji would be hurt.

He was so proud of the little adornments to my glove. Later I thought maybe it was a sign."

"A sign?"

Rose nodded. "As if losing the glove was a sign that my marriage was lost too."

Siobhán reached into the inside pocket of her uniform and brought out the second evidence bag. It contained the chunk of pottery with a mustard-yellow sheen that they had found in the slurry pit. She presented it to Rose. "Is this from your son's shop?"

"I wouldn't be able to tell you that," Rose said, glancing at it. "Unlike falconer's gloves with special tassels and beads added just for me, pottery is ubiquitous." She swallowed. "Why are you showing me these? Where did you find them?"

"Do you know what this could have been? A bowl, a cup, or a plate?" Siobhán asked, turning the piece of pottery around. She wasn't sure if she believed Rose's nonchalance about the shard of pottery, so she was throwing wet noodles at the ceiling, trying to see which bits might stick.

"I have no idea. Not only does Joseph sell a good deal of his work, but he's also very generous, and we all have many instances of his pottery." She frowned. "You didn't answer my question. Where did you find these?"

Siobhán simply stared, hoping her look conveyed the answer: *We don't have to answer your questions.*

"At the crime scene," Macdara said. "In the slurry pit."

Rose went slack-jawed and simply stared. Macdara had obviously decided that telling her and witnessing her reaction was worth the risk of her spreading the gossip around. She certainly did seem shocked.

"Odd, isn't it?" Siobhán asked.

"Are you saying Tommy had these items on him?" Rose continued to stare at the evidence bags, as if mesmerized.

"No," Siobhán said. "That's not the only option."

"I don't understand." Rose's voice wavered. Whatever she was expecting, it was obvious that this had thrown her.

"The killer could have tossed these items into the pit," Macdara clarified.

"But . . . *why*?" Rose asked.

"Getting rid of evidence," Siobhán said. "Before we discovered Tommy's remains."

"How is a shard of pottery and a falconer's glove evidence of a murder?" Rose asked.

"They were both found in the pit," Macdara said. "Where two murders occurred."

Rose shook her head. "I know nothing about it." She crossed her arms and stared Siobhán down. "Are you accusing me of something? Benji? My son? Because Joseph was only a wee lad when Tommy went missing."

"We're simply asking questions," Macdara said.

"If you found these in the slurry pit, then someone is trying to frame us."

Macdara tugged on the collar of his uniform as if to loosen it and took off his hat to wipe off the sweat. It was punishing under the sun.

Siobhán returned her attention to the glove. "You claim this glove went missing a few days before Gladys and Tommy's wedding."

"I didn't *claim* it. It's a fact."

"Where was the glove before it went missing?"

"My house," Rose said. "It was stolen from my house. In Charlesville."

Charlesville was a neighboring town with quaint shops and restaurants. Siobhán wondered if she would stay in a house after going through a divorce. Wouldn't there be too many memories of your ex? Then again, it wasn't practical to pick up and move, especially when a child was involved.

"Why do you say it was stolen, as opposed to being lost?" Macdara asked.

"Because that was my grandfather's glove. The anniversary of his death was coming up, and Benji dressed up the tassels as a gift to commemorate him. We were going to have a remembrance at the wildlife center, which my grandfather helped start. One day the glove was on me worktable, and the next it was gone. We turned the house upside down. It was nowhere. We didn't lock our doors back then, and in those days, we had people in and out of our house all day long. Someone took that glove."

And then dropped it in a slurry pit with a dead body. Unless Tommy was the thief. But the glove was rather large. Siobhán very much doubted that on the morning of his wedding, Tommy had a falconer's glove hidden in his tuxedo.

"Do you think Joseph might have taken it?" Siobhán asked.

Rose narrowed her eyes. "Why do you ask?"

Siobhán shrugged. "You'd had Joseph only a year back then, is that right?"

"That's right," Rose said.

"Kids take things sometimes, just for the mischief," Macdara added.

"We're back to Joseph again? Are you two off your heads?" Rose put her hands on her hips, as if awaiting an actual answer. She'd roused the mother bear in Rose. Perhaps they should make themselves appear large and break out in "Danny Boy."

"Detective Sergeant Flannery was simply wondering why you said 'stolen,' as opposed to 'lost.' Kids play with things and then lose them," Siobhán said.

"And then lie about it," Macdara added.

"It's possible one of the lads Joseph played with could have nicked it from the house, but both Benjamin and Joseph knew that was me grandfather's glove. It's of no worth to anyone but me. And when you're done with it, I expect it to be returned." Rose's fingers flexed, as if she physically wanted to snatch the glove out of Macdara's hand.

Siobhán wouldn't have wanted it returned. Not after being in that slurry pit with not just one but two murder victims. Then again, it wasn't blackened to the degree other items in the pit were. Siobhán had been mulling over the possibility that someone had tossed it in recently. Was that why Alan had gone into the dairy barn? Had he stashed the falconer's glove in there? Whatever for? Had he suspected Rose of being the killer?

"It will be returned when the case is closed," Macdara said. "We reserve the right to hold all evidence until after a trial."

"Are you saying the glove has been in the slurry pit for fifty years?"

"We've neither confirmed nor denied that," Siobhán said.

Rose folded her arms across her chest. "What if it was Tommy himself who stole it?"

"Say more," Macdara said.

"Tommy could have stolen the glove, couldn't he?"

"Anything is possible," Siobhán said. *Just not probable . . .*

"Joseph certainly wasn't making pottery at five years of age, so I can't help you with that bit."

Five years of age. It did seem reasonable to cross Joseph off the suspect list for Tommy's murder. But he was fair game for Alan's. Were they looking at one killer or two? Siobhán returned her attention back to Rose's original statement. "Why would Tommy steal the glove?"

Rose turned away from them. She checked that all the pens were securely locked, then began to stride toward the visitors' center. Siobhán and Macdara had no choice but to follow.

"He was in love with me. Is that what you're waiting for me to confess?"

Exactly what Howard had said. He'd seen them together outside the snooker club. Standing close and arguing like lovers. And then he'd seen them kiss. A week before the wedding. They were keeping this under their caps for now, waiting to see what Rose would divulge on her own.

"And nothing says love like stealing your falconer's glove?" Siobhán asked.

This stopped Rose in her tracks. "I rejected him," she said, her voice thick, her back to them.

"When?"

"The day before he was supposed to marry Gladys. A few hours later my favorite glove was missing." She turned around. "Tommy was brilliant. Charming. Full of life. But he could also be vindictive. I'm sure no one has admitted that, because you're not supposed to speak ill of the dead. But Tommy was far from perfect."

"Back up," Siobhán said. "What exactly did you reject? What did he want?"

Rose sighed. "He was having a meltdown over the wedding. He said he and Gladys had had a horrible fight. I told you this already," Rose said to Siobhán. "How Gladys wanted children, and before the wedding Tommy dropped the bomb that he couldn't have them. Frankly, I don't believe that part. I think he just didn't want them. Either way. Gladys had a freak-out over the news, and he said it was a sign."

"A sign not to marry her?"

Rose nodded. "Please don't misunderstand. There was never anything untoward between Tommy and me. At least . . . nothing we ever acted on."

"We have a witness who says otherwise," Siobhán said. Sometimes you had to play the card; this was one of those times.

Rose looked as if she wanted to take flight like one of her falcons. "Who is it?" she said. "And what did he or she say?"

"Do you want to try answering the question again?" Macdara asked. "If not, we can make this more official."

"I have no idea what you heard. I swear I never indulged any of Tommy's flirtations. We had always had a strong attraction. Tommy had charisma. He exuded it. There were times when he looked at me that I felt like an electric current was shooting through me. He was attractive, and believe it or not, I was too back then." She stopped to run a hand down a length of her hair. She was still beautiful, but only she knew what she had felt like in her glory. They'd all been in their shining twenties then. "I suppose it's Howard, is it? He saw Tommy kiss me outside the pub, is that it?"

"Is that your definition of 'nothing untoward going on'?" Siobhán asked. She turned to Macdara. "Would you be fine with me shifting other men?"

"Let me be extremely clear," Macdara said. "I would not."

"Me neither," Siobhán said.

Rose stomped her foot, startling Siobhán. "He kissed me. I don't care what it looked like. I put a stop to it."

"Let's return to the day before the wedding," Macdara said. "What exactly did Tommy ask you?"

Rose sighed, then nodded, as if she knew the question was coming and there was no way of avoiding it. "Let me put it this way. When Tommy didn't show up to the wedding, I was neither alarmed nor surprised. If you must know—he asked me if I would run away with him."

Chapter 16

After Rose's admission, Siobhán and Macdara said their goodbyes and met up with Aretta at the visitors' center before heading back to the squad car.

"I learned something interesting," Aretta said on the drive back to the station. "I don't think Rose had permission to take Charlie out of the center."

"We heard that as well," Siobhán said. "She asked us not to mention it to the staff."

"They already know," Aretta said. "And they weren't happy about it."

"Did you learn anything more?" Macdara asked. "When did she sneak him out? Why did she sneak him out? According to her, she's been doing it for ages."

"The woman I spoke with said that Rose considers Charlie to be her hawk, but that he belongs to the center."

"I wonder if it's just coincidence that she took him to our farm that morning," Siobhán said.

"If it helps, the employee seemed annoyed about it rather than alarmed," Aretta said.

"Who wants to pop into the chipper?" Macdara asked.

"Me," Siobhán said.

"I had planned on lunch at home," Aretta said.

Macdara offered to drop her off and added that she should take the rest of the day off. She didn't argue, a signal that her brush with fear had taken its toll on her for the day.

After seeing her safely home, Siobhán and Macdara burrowed into a booth at the chipper to discuss the day. Had Rose been telling the truth? Was this Tommy/Gladys love story from long ago not really a love story? Was it a saving grace that Gladys hadn't married Tommy?

Siobhán gazed at the heavenly baskets of curried chips in front of them. "Hear me out on this," Macdara said. Had he purposefully waited until Siobhán's gob was full? "Let's assume for a moment that Rose, and Howard, for that matter, are telling the truth. Tommy and Gladys had a big fight over the fact that Tommy couldn't or wouldn't have children. He's getting cold feet about the wedding. He kisses Rose. Then he tries to get Rose to run away with him." He stopped and waited.

"And?" Siobhán said.

"You know what the Irish grapevine is like. What are the chances it *didn't* get back to Gladys?"

"Slim to none," Siobhán said.

Macdara pounded the table in glee, making her jump. "Don't you think that kind of news might incite a nearly bride into a murderous rage?"

"It's possible," Siobhán said. "But doesn't that also apply to the best friend slash best man?"

"Go on."

"What if Benji got word that Tommy was pursuing his wife—and by wife, this time I mean Rose. Or what if he saw something? Or maybe Joseph saw something and told his new father? Thus equally inciting a murderous rage in Benji." She paused and then slammed the table with her fist in imitation of Dara. A little flush of pleasure ran through her when he jumped.

After he recovered, he held up a finger. He'd been waiting for this bit. "Yes. I see your point. However . . . let's look at our second victim. Gladys's brother."

"Alan," Siobhán said.

"Think about it. Who would be more likely to kill Alan? A sibling or a brother-in-law?"

"I don't think it matters."

Macdara raised an eyebrow. "How could it not matter? Don't you think we're looking at one killer?"

"Most likely," Siobhán said. "But no matter who our killer is, his or her motivation for killing Alan is the same."

Macdara picked up the thread. "You think Alan figured out who the killer was."

"That," Siobhán said, stealing one of Macdara's chips because his were bigger, "is exactly what I think."

"I can see that." Macdara nodded. "I suppose it

could go either way. But would you agree it's either Gladys or Benji?"

"I think it's too early to eliminate the rest. And don't forget Benji is the one who had access to the falconer's glove. He's the one who added the special tassels and beads for Rose. It was in his house at the time. But Howard supposedly had money stolen—that's a big motive. Rose would be my number one suspect if Gladys or Benji had been killed . . ."

"She seems to have made peace with the past," Macdara said. "If it's an act, it's a very good one."

"If you left me right now for another woman, I would never make peace with it," Siobhán said.

"I would hope for no less," Macdara replied. "Not that I would ever leave the best thing that has ever happened to me."

"Are you calling me a thing?"

He laughed. "You *are* a pessimist."

"Perhaps I am." She consoled herself by finishing the rest of the heavenly curried chips. Then she leaned back and exhaled. Her adrenaline had been on high ever since her nearly wedding, and she could almost curl up on this hard seater and fall asleep.

"Someone needs to be put to bed," Macdara teased.

"We picked the wrong profession if we wanted to sleep," Siobhán said.

They stood, threw away their containers, and headed out. There was a break from the rain, and the sun was peeking through. Macdara leaned in and kissed her like he didn't care who was watching. She let the helium rise to her head. He'd been very affectionate this week, and her heart gave a squeeze.

"I could have gone through with our ceremony," she said. "I don't want you to think I didn't want to marry you."

The wind blew a strand of her hair into her eyes, and Macdara gently moved it away. "There was no way we could have had the kind of ceremony we deserve with that interruption," Macdara said.

"James didn't realize we'd already begun the service, or he never would have entered the church."

"I know that." He took her hand, and they began to walk back to the station. Siobhán took a moment to imagine their wedding had gone through and the body had never been discovered. Would they be going back to the farmhouse now to make love and dream about moving into their new home? Would they have spent a week in wedded bliss and curried chips?

"Tomorrow I'm going to have Aretta give Rose a bell," Macdara said. "I want to know if Rose told anyone else about Tommy's supposed visit the day before the wedding. I can't believe we forgot to ask her. I think the falcons distracted me."

"Hawks," Siobhán corrected. "At least Charlie is a Harris hawk."

"They use their talons to rip prey to shreds, while hawks use their powerful beaks," Macdara added. "Or is it the other way around?"

Siobhán shrugged. She was probably never going to know the differences. The little details known by experts. Just like the killer did not know all the little details. All the little mistakes they made that could lead authorities straight to them.

Even fifty years later. "I agree that we should have Aretta follow up with Rose. But let's not send her back to the wildlife center. That's just cruel."

"I wouldn't dream of it," Macdara said. "We'll have her call Rose into the station, set her up in an interview room. Let Aretta handle the questioning, with a more experienced garda backing her up."

They stopped just outside the station, and Siobhán took a few deep breaths. She would rather spend all day outside than stuffed in a tiny office with artificial light. At least her job afforded her plenty of time to have a walkabout.

They headed inside, and Macdara motioned for Siobhán to follow him to his office. Once there, he began jotting next steps on his whiteboard. *Aretta— Interview Rose in IR-1.* "That brings me to our next subjects. Father and son. Where do we start?"

Siobhán was ready for this. "According to a bit of gossip I've picked up, Gladys has a regular bingo game and ladies' lunch in town tomorrow. It's our opportunity to catch Benji alone." It was nearly impossible to interview a couple married that long at the same time. One would always be interrupting, finishing the other's sentences. Could they write it into their vows that no matter how many years rolled by, Siobhán wanted to finish her own sentences?

"Sounds like a plan." He reached into a drawer, pulled out a key, and held it up. It swayed in front of her like a hypnotist's pendulum.

"What is that?"

"The key to the farmhouse." He handed it to

her. "I know we're going to wait. But I had that made for ya."

It came with a key ring. A claddagh symbol with the heart in red. Tears threatened to spill from her eyes, and she had to bite the side of her lip. "Thank you." She tucked it in her pocket. "I'm saving these until we can go in together."

He took a step toward her. "I've been thinking about that. I think you should go in the first time without me."

"What?"

"You don't want me breathing down your neck, hoping you fall in love with it—you need the freedom to explore your own reactions. If it's going to be your house too, you need to feel it. Fair is fair. The time after that, we'll go in together."

She stared at the key.

"When the time is right," Macdara said. "No pressure."

She nodded. "I'll think about it." Just having the key gave her a trill of excitement.

Macdara had one small window in his office, and in the distance, you could see the steeple of Saint Mary's. The bells began to chime. It made her think of Father Kearney and his appointment book. Why hadn't he followed through with his promise to look into it? Time was of the essence. As a garda, she was prepared for just about anything, but she was going to need serious therapy if she found out the local parish priest was keeping deadly secrets. The receptionist stopped her on her way out.

"Father Kearney left a message. He won't be

able to speak with you today, but he said he'll give you a bell tomorrow morning and set something up."

Siobhán sighed. Was he avoiding her? "Thank you." He had better call. Otherwise she was going to have to pay him a visit in the morning. She certainly felt a confession coming on.

Chapter 17

Built in 1879, the collegiate church never failed to awe Siobhán. Its spiral steeple rising proudly above the town, ten gorgeous stained-glass windows, bright colors intersecting into a five-light arch, and the interior ceilings, with Victorian-era mosaics and intricate leaves and flowers painted on the original wood beams, made for a delightful and inspiring experience.

The next morning Siobhán headed for the church after her run. She would not have time to stop and admire the ceiling today, apart from an appreciative glance. One of the nuns was in the garden at the side of the building, surrounded by colorful pots and flowers, so intent in her work she did not look up as Siobhán headed inside. At the bistro they had a small garden out back, and Eoin kept up with planting fresh herbs and the girls and Ciarán tended the flowers. At the farm they'd have the ability to grow vegetables if they liked, and the gardening possibilities were slightly dizzying. Siobhán's thumb wasn't at all green, so she'd have to leave it to her brood. But the thought of having all that land and not using it set her nerves on edge. She could see them living there, one big group, with room to roam. But she doubted gardening would give her the same joy as was on the nun's face as she worked away, oblivious to anyone else around her.

She found Father Kearney hurrying down the aisle toward his office. "Hello," she called. He stopped, his back still to her, as if he were afraid to turn around. He took a moment. Then when he did turn and greet her, she knew by his expression that she was not imagining things: he did not look thrilled to see her. "Sorry to pop in unannounced, but you were supposed to call me about your appointment book."

"Right," he said. "Of course." He gave a resigned smile and motioned for her to follow him. "I'm afraid I forgot all about it, but now that you're here, I'll have a look."

She followed him down the hall and into his office. It was cluttered but in a somewhat orderly manner, with stacks everywhere you looked, books, papers, newspapers. His desk was clear except for the large leather appointment book. He gestured to a seat across from his desk as he eased himself into his chair.

"You are here to reschedule your wedding date, is that it?"

"Not yet," Siobhán said. "We're waiting until this case is solved."

He frowned but did not comment.

"I'm actually here on official business."

He glanced at his appointment book. It seemed he did remember her request, or at least she had jogged his memory. He drew it close. "I meant to give you a bell, but you're here now." He adjusted the appointment book and waited.

"I'd like you to check your book for our original wedding date. You penciled us in but then called to say something else had been booked." She gave him the date.

He nodded as he thumbed through the pages. "That rings a faint bell, so it does." He reached a page and stopped. He lifted the book and brought it closer to his eyes, then lowered it. "Someone erased my original entry and in Biro wrote 'baptism' on top of it—" He stopped and rubbed his chin.

"Something wrong?"

"It is odd. When my secretary—Sister Helen—went to confirm the baptism, they said there must have been a mistake." He leaned back and rubbed his eyes.

"May I see?"

He looked as if he didn't want her to see, but in the end he slid the appointment book across the desk.

Siobhán took in the penmanship: *Granger Baptism.* "How did you know what number to call to confirm the baptism?"

"We know only one Granger family—that was the other mystery—and neither of us could remember taking the appointment. Sister Helen said this was not her notation, but we're the only two who touch this appointment book. To be honest, I'm a bit relieved."

"How so?"

"I was worried one of us was having memory issues. I know I didn't write this—she says she didn't either. I write all my entries in pencil, and she confirms them with the Biro."

"What would your notation have said for our wedding?"

"D.S. Flannery wedding," Father Kearney said without hesitation.

Now was not the time to inquire why it was only Dara's name on the appointment book. She had bigger things to think through. "Is your appointment book always on your desk?"

"I think you know the answer to that."

She nodded. "And your door is often open?"

"It is." He sighed. "If anything, you'd think a simple appointment book in a priest's office would be safe!"

"I agree, Father, and I am sorry to trouble you. But I'm afraid I'm going to have to take this in as evidence."

"You think someone deliberately snuck in here, leafed through the book to find your wedding date, and exchanged it for a baptism so you'd be forced to change the date?" He looked as if he didn't know whether to laugh or cry.

"I do."

He tapped the book with his index finger, then scanned the days after it. "All the rest of these notations appear to be in Sister Helen's penmanship. What do you think you can gain? Are you going to hire a handwriting expert? Ask all your subjects to write something down for you?"

"I really haven't gotten that far. It's simply a part of a larger picture," Siobhán said. They would have neither the funds nor the time to chase down handwriting experts, but she knew either the killer was behind the date changes or he or she had influenced someone else to make the changes. If gossip took its natural course through town and the killer got word that Siobhán had retrieved the appointment book, it may lead him or her to take action. And, in doing so, hopefully make a mistake.

"Did you see Sister Helen in the garden when you came in?" Father Kearney asked.

"I did. She looked happy out amongst the flowers."

"I'm going to need her to photocopy my appointment book before we release it to you. I hope you will allow it."

"Of course." She stood. "If you could have someone drop it off at the station, I'd appreciate it very much."

He stood. "It will be done today."

"And you might want to consider locking your office door."

He shook his head. "I won't, petal. This is God's house, and my door will always be open."

She nodded; she had expected as much. "Until we catch this killer, just . . . be careful."

"Would you mind asking Sister Helen to come in on your way out?"

"Sure thing."

Siobhán made her way back outside to the garden. This time Sister Helen was standing, a mustard-yellow pot gripped in her hand. A little bell in Siobhán's mind dinged.

"Good morning, Sister Helen," Siobhán said.

Sister Helen nodded. "Hello to you, Garda O'Sullivan. It's a fine day, is it not?"

"A lovely day," Siobhán said. "Father Kearney asked me to speak to you on my way out. We need a little help with his appointment book."

She nodded. "He mentioned as much. When he didn't remember scheduling that baptism, I was seriously concerned. He never writes in Biro in his appointment book, not once in fifty years. And I know I didn't write it."

Siobhán nodded. "Do you remember seeing anyone go into his office that shouldn't have been there?"

"You know what this town is like. Folks stroll into his office all the time."

"Anyone in particular around that day?"

Sister Helen shook her head. "I'll have to think on it."

"I appreciate it." Siobhán's gaze fell to the garden. "It's lovely."

Sister Helen grinned and held up the pot. "It's my joy."

"Did Joseph O'Leary make that for you by any chance?"

"He did indeed. You recognize his work?"

"I was only guessing. I've heard he does great work—I don't know of any other potters in town."

"He gives me one every year." She gestured to a row of colorful pots lining the garden.

"That's very sweet."

"He had a hard start in life, that lad. But the good Lord made sure he found him a new home. And he's a grateful man for it."

Siobhán's mind flashed to Joseph standing with his shirt off, giving her the side-eye. Let Sister Helen have this innocent impression of him. He was, it appeared, an excellent potter, and it was sweet of him to give her a pot every year. Another thought struck her, absurd perhaps, but she had to ask. "Have you any broken pieces around?"

"Broken pieces?"

"I have a friend who collects broken pieces of pottery to make mosaics." Her stomach twisted in a familiar knot. She'd just lied to a nun. Years of schoolgirl guilt flooded her at once. Some white lies seemed kinder than the truth. The truth that in Siobhán's world everyone was guilty until proven innocent.

"I'll keep that in mind, but they're always put out with the recycling."

Put out with the recycling. Which meant any of their suspects could have come upon the pottery shards and scooped one up. But why? Was the killer throwing everything at the wall, hoping to obfuscate his or her identity? *The smoke-screen method of getting away with murder* . . . Or was he or she bent on specifically targeting Joseph and Rose? Who would have been angry with the pair of them?

"I see. Thanks anyway."

Sister Helen nodded; then she said goodbye and headed inside. Siobhán stared at the colorful pots. She was going to have to pay Joseph a visit and maybe purchase a few pots of her own from his studio. She could imagine one on each side of the door to their new stone home. She could see them bursting with flowers. She could imagine planting and tending them. A little smile escaped her lips; perhaps she had an inner gardener after all. Siobhán had nearly left the property when she heard someone call her name. She turned to see Father Kearney running up to her. She had never seen him run before. She hoped never to see it again.

"I'm glad I caught you." He was wheezing from the run and stopped to wipe moisture off his brow with a handkerchief.

"Is something wrong?"

"I just now thought of something. It might be nothing."

"Go on, so."

"A long time ago, someone popped into the confessional with a strange message. It was my first week taking confession, so it would have been around the time Tommy disappeared."

"Okay."

"And it was just before Tommy and Gladys's wedding."

Siobhán knew he wasn't about to reveal what a parishioner had said in confession, so she waited to see where he was going with this.

"Have you popped into the bookshop lately?" he asked.

Siobhán frowned. "Not lately, Father. Why do you ask?"

"I hear they've expanded their offerings," Father Kearney said. "You may want to ask Padraig or Oran for a recommendation."

She stared at him. He stared back. "I see. I will indeed, Father. Thank you."

"You're most welcome. Will you be doing that right now?"

"I believe I will."

He nodded. "Good. Good. I don't know if it will be of any help, and I'm afraid that's all I can say."

Siobhán was thrilled to have an excuse to enter the bookshop during a workday. She loved all the woodwork, from the floors to the shelves and the crown molding. She loved the smell of books and the colorful spines just waiting to be slid out of their spots on the shelf. She even loved the old bathtubs Oran and Padraig had set up in the middle of the floor and filled with bargain books. She headed for the counter, where Oran sat hunched over a book, a cup of tea in hand.

"Good morning," she called.

Oran looked up and smiled before returning to his book. She stood in front of him and waited. From here she was staring at his curls, watching his glasses slide down his nose. A few seconds later, the door opened, and Padraig walked in, whistling and carrying a pastry bag.

"Good morning, Garda O'Sullivan," he said. "Oran? Would you ever look up from your book? You have a customer."

Oran looked up and forced his lips into a smile. "Pardon me, Garda. I just needed to finish the page. How may I help you?"

"I spoke with Father Kearney this morning, and

he mentioned you might have a book recommendation for me."

"Ah, right, so." Oran rose from his seat, removed his glasses, and headed over to a back shelf. He removed a book and handed it to her. She was surprised to find herself looking at a book on Irish wildlife.

"Are you sure this is the right book?"

"He said you'd find page eighteen very interesting. I do not normally allow patrons to underline passages in our books, especially before they're paid for, but I suppose if you can't bend the rules for the parish priest, who can you bend them for?"

"Thank you."

"I can settle the bill at the counter."

She paid for the book and looked longingly at the shelves as she headed out. She'd carve out some time soon with Ciarán and Ann, and they'd spend a proper few hours in the shop. Padraig followed her out.

"Sorry about Oran," he said. "He's an introvert."

"It's okay." She didn't mind Oran's ways, and he'd actually grown friendlier over the past few months.

"It's not," Padraig said. "But it's hard to teach an old dog new tricks. Here." He held out the pastry bag.

"I couldn't."

"I insist. Think of it as a wedding present."

Siobhán accepted the bag from Padraig and glanced in it to find two chocolate eclairs. They smelled heavenly. "Thank you." The first wedding present she could open. She'd eat one and save the other for Macdara.

She headed across the square to the garda station. Once outside the station, she thumbed through the book, looking for page eighteen, as she bit into an eclair. She took a moment to enjoy the pastry. Outstanding. It had to be one of the best eclairs she'd ever tasted. Soft and chocolaty, with sweet cream in the middle. It was fab. What Macdara didn't know wouldn't hurt him. She finished the first eclair, then plucked the second from the bag and got rid of the evidence before turning her attention to the book again. It was a section dedicated to owls. Her eyes landed on the bit Father Kearney had underlined:

An old superstition still holds weight amongst believers:

If you hear an owl hoot three times, heed this warning:

someone you love may be about to die.

Chapter 18

At the garda station, Siobhán jotted the superstition about the owl on the whiteboard. Macdara stared at the note for a long time.

"What are we supposed to do with this?"

"We could play a recording of an owl crying three times and see which one of our suspects react," Siobhán said, half joking, half considering it. "What I believe Father Kearney is telling us is that a few days before the wedding, someone slipped into the confessional and uttered this superstition."

"I'll say it again," Macdara said. "What are we supposed to do with that?"

"It had to be Rose," Siobhán said. "She's the one who works with owls and hawks and falcons." Siobhán glanced at Aretta.

"I'm fine talking about them," Aretta said. "What

if this confession came from our second victim, Alan O'Leary?"

"What makes you say that?" Macdara asked.

"I find it hard to believe Father Kearney would divulge anything about a confession from one of his living parishioners," Aretta said. "However, if the person was deceased and he believes the confession may help solve a murder or two . . ."

Macdara jabbed a marker at her. "That makes sense to me." Underneath the quote he wrote *Alan. . . .*

"If that's the case," Siobhán said, "it changes things."

"How so?" Macdara asked.

"Right now we're working on the assumption that Alan *recently* figured out who the killer was, and that's why he was the next victim. But what if it turns out he'd known all this time . . . ?"

"Then something else happened recently," Aretta said. "Perhaps Mr. O'Leary and the killer had some kind of agreement—and recently somehow that agreement was broken?"

Macdara picked up the thread. "Perhaps when Tommy's remains were found, Alan was worried the killer would try to drag him in as an accomplice?"

"Perhaps he *was* an accomplice," Aretta said.

"They're all possible," Siobhán said.

"One thing is for sure," Macdara said. "Whoever slipped into the confessional to utter that phrase a few days before Tommy disappeared knew that Tommy was about to die. Do you think I'm reading that right?"

Siobhán and Aretta nodded.

"Which means it was either the killer or an eye-witness," Siobhán said.

"Did Father Kearney say if this person was a male or female?" Aretta asked.

"He did not," Siobhán said. "And I don't think we'll get any further by pressing him."

"Why make a confession?" Macdara continued. "Why would anyone risk it?"

"Perhaps one of the locals actually did hear an owl cry three times and was worried about it, then decided to leave that worry with the parish priest," Aretta said. "People are superstitious, are they not?"

"They are," Siobhán said. "But given the timing of the confession, I think it's more sinister."

"This was fifty years ago," Aretta said. "Was Rose even working with birds of prey back then?"

"She was," Siobhán said. "Benji gifted her our missing falconer's glove fifty years ago."

"This feels like someone is trying to set her up," Aretta said.

"I was thinking the same thing," Siobhán said. "There may come a time soon when we have to warn her. Maybe she knows who it is. Maybe if she knew the killer was pointing a fingerlike wing at her, maybe Rose would have no choice but to tell us who she thinks this person might be."

"Given we've just spoken to her, let's keep this on the back burner, see what else we learn as we talk to the rest of our suspects, and we'll circle back to it," Macdara said.

"Circle," Siobhán said. "Like Charlie." She tapped

Joseph's photograph on the wall. "Maybe the son can shed some light on it. Maybe if he knew someone was targeting his mother, he'd be willing to share anything he knows."

"He was around Howard, Tommy, and Benji in those days," Macdara said. "Who knows what he may have seen, what he may have heard. He may not even know what he knows."

Siobhán nodded. "Exactly. And I'm in the mood for a little pottery shopping. How about ye?"

The Potter's Shed was just a short drive outside of town, situated near the roadway, with nothing but lush green fields surrounding it. Large colorful pots like the ones Sister Helen had collected were displayed in the small garden out front. When the trio of guards entered, a bell dinged. Through an open doorway in the far back of the shop, they could see Joseph sitting in front of a pottery wheel, working on a mound of clay. He had his shirt off but wore a large white apron and goggles. His biceps flexed as the machinery spun, and he rhythmically worked the wheel with his foot.

"Does he ever wear his shirt?" Macdara said under his breath.

Gleaming bowls, vases, plates, and mugs took up the shelves in the small front room, and earrings and necklaces made from pottery had been placed on handmade stands by the register. They nosed around until he noticed them. Moments later the wheel stopped, and he emerged, grinning and wiping his hands on a towel.

"Hello, hello. Welcome," he said brightly, despite how it must feel to see them in front of him in their garda uniforms.

"How ya?" Siobhán said. "Your shop is lovely."

"Thank you." He beamed.

Macdara picked up a mug. "How long does it take you to make something like this?"

"Several days. A prep day, a day on the wheel, and then time to bake, cool, and glaze."

Bake. That was why it was so hot in here.

"This is my favorite," Aretta said, pointing to a large green vase that had the curves of a woman.

"You have a good eye," Joseph said. "That's one of my best pieces. That one took over a month."

"How did you get into this?" Siobhán asked. It never hurt to flatter a suspect, but in this case, she was also genuinely interested.

"You mean with a mammy who was into birds, and a father—" He stopped abruptly.

Macdara stepped forward. "A father who . . . ?"

Joseph shrugged. "I just didn't know what to say. He's had a number of jobs over the years. Handyman, I guess you'd call him. That should come in handy for you, given you'll be living next door. That is . . . are you still planning on moving in? I wouldn't blame you if you weren't."

"We are," Siobhán said. Mostly because he seemed as if he was trying to goad them into something, and she, for one, did not like to be goaded. She noticed a flush of pleasure infuse Macdara's cheeks.

"I didn't get into pottery until I was supposed to go to uni. I knew schooling wasn't for me. I agreed to go for a year. Best decision I ever made."

"You did not finish university?" Macdara asked.

"I did not. But I discovered pottery. And it's sustained me ever since. There's something so cathartic about the wheel—and not the kind of nonsense they portrayed in that American film where yer one was a ghost and all over Demi Moore. What was the name of that film?"

"*Ghost*," Siobhán said.

"That's right. I said it was a ghost. Now, what was the name of that film?"

"*Ghost*," the three guards said in stereo.

Joseph looked disappointed. "Right, so. *Ghost*." He shuddered. "I've seen enough of those in me life."

"You've seen ghosts?" Aretta asked. "As in more than one ghost?"

"I have," Joseph said. He pointed at Siobhán and Macdara. "There's been one hanging around your place for fifty years, and now I know who it was."

"Tommy," Siobhán said.

Joseph nodded. "It makes sense now."

"What kinds of things did you experience on our haunted farmland?" Siobhán asked. Why was he so against them moving in? It was as if he was trying everything under the sun to discourage them.

Macdara picked up a mug and held it up to the light.

"If it breaks, you break my heart, and if you break my heart, you have to break out yer billfold," Joseph said with a grin.

"If you've seen strange happenings on our land,

we'd like to know about it," Macdara said, carefully placing the mug back on the shelf. "There may be logical explanations."

Such as a killer visiting his or her crime scene.

"Things would go missing all the time. Like my red bicycle."

Kids misplaced bicycles in Ireland all the time, and other kids ran off with bicycles all the time, and there was probably a field somewhere chock-full of kids' bicycles and socks from the dryer. But it brought to mind the bicycle bell found in the pile of branches.

"That's your ghost story?" Macdara asked. "A missing bicycle?"

Joseph shook his head. "It's hard to explain. A lot of things went missing, then turned up in a different spot. It was just the feeling I'd get whenever I was near that dairy barn."

"Do you have any items in mustard yellow?" Siobhán asked, making sure not to look in the direction of Macdara's armpit. He had the evidence bag tucked in there. She definitely needed to buy him some type of man bag.

Joseph frowned. "It's funny you say that. I had a mustard-yellow plate." He moved to the front of the store, where a display case flashed objects to those passing by the window. Given the shop was set outside of town and there was nothing but farmland nearby, she doubted he attracted many window-shoppers. He pointed to a stand in the middle. "The plate was right there. A few days ago, I came into the shop . . ." He stopped and headed for the door. He was going to reenact his movements. Siobhán felt as if he was putting on a performance of his own, and she found herself wishing for hot, buttery popcorn. He went out the door.

Macdara looked at his watch; Aretta continued examining the pottery. Soon the door opened. Joseph took a few steps in, then stopped and stared at a spot on the floor. "Smashed!" he said. "Right there." He continued to point, staring at the floor, as if in doing so, broken pieces of pottery would materialize. His head popped up, as if he'd just thought of something. He took a few steps forward. "How did you know?"

"When was this?" Siobhán asked, taking out her Biro and her notebook.

"I don't remember exactly," he said. "It was after you found Tommy, but before Alan was . . ." He swallowed. "I don't know how Alan died. Do you think it was murder or just . . . a macabre coincidence?"

"We don't have that information at this time," Siobhán said.

He held up his hands. "I understand."

"What did you do with the broken pieces?" Siobhán asked.

"I kept them," Joseph said. "They can be used to make mosaics."

"I said that meself just a bit ago to Sister Helen," Siobhán exclaimed. "She loves your pots, by the way."

He grinned. "I've always had a soft spot for nuns. They get a bad rap, but there were a few that were good to me at the boys' home."

"We'd like all the pieces of your broken plate," Siobhán said.

"You're joking me," Joseph said.

"I assure you we are not," Macdara said.

"Whatever for?"

They did not answer.

"Fingerprints?"

"Perhaps we'll make a mosaic," Aretta said, flashing a grin.

Macdara finally produced the evidence bag. "We need to see if it matches this."

"May I?" Joseph gestured to the bag.

Macdara nodded and held it closer. Joseph removed a pair of eyeglasses from his shirt pocket and peered closely. He then headed for the back of his shop. They heard him rummaging around, and when he returned, he was holding a piece that, although it was in the yellow family, was much darker than the shade of the shard they had found in the slurry pit.

Joseph held it up. "It's not from my plate."

"Might we have a look through all your broken pieces?" Siobhán asked.

Joseph shrugged. "I suppose." Macdara nodded to Aretta, who moved to the back of the shop. "You'll see a blue container filled with chipped bits." She nodded, and he turned back to Siobhán and Macdara. "Won't you tell me what this is all about?"

"It's evidence from a crime scene," Macdara said. "And it will be analyzed thoroughly."

"You found my pottery in a crime scene? Do you mean the slurry pit?"

"Do you recall having anything that resembles the piece in our evidence bag?" Macdara jiggled the bag.

"People don't just steal bicycles," Siobhán said. "They steal everything."

"If it's one of mine, it's not a recent piece," Joseph said. "But have I ever made anything that shade? I'm sure I have. I've been making pottery for thirty years now. I've given gifts to nearly everyone in town. If you found that at a crime scene, it may be from my shop, but it has nothing to do with me." He stopped, as if waiting for them to assure him he wasn't a suspect.

Siobhán was chewing on something he had said. It was true that anyone could have dropped the broken piece of pottery into the slurry pit. But why? Had they found an entire smashed mug, they might have surmised Tommy or Alan had entered the dairy barn with a mug of tea. Not that she would drink a mug of tea near a pit of muck, but a man might. But they hadn't found an entire mug; they'd found a piece. Just like the falconer's glove. Someone was directing them to investigate the mother and son. And she, for one, did not believe it was a ghost.

He wiped sweat from his brow. "Do you mind if we step outside? I need a bit of air."

"Right there with you," Macdara said, turning and heading outside. Siobhán and Aretta followed suit.

Once there, Joseph reached into the pocket of his apron and pulled out an electronic cigarette. He inhaled and waited for them to continue.

"Did you like Tommy?" Siobhán asked.

Joseph nodded. "I'd been living with my mother and father only a year when I met Tommy, and everyone else. I must admit I was very drawn to Tommy. He had that edge—like me from the boys' home. I suppose you could say we bonded. Or I bonded with him, and he didn't shove me away. He taught me to play snooker. He said I had real potential."

"Did you ever play in the dairy barn?"

Joseph shook his head. "No. I didn't like the barn. Tommy told me there were bats in the rafters, and that was enough to keep me out of there."

"Bats?" Siobhán said, resisting the urge to pat her head.

"Looking back on it, I think he was probably just messing with me. Or was he trying to keep me out of the barn? He was always going in there with Howard and Alan. No doubt planning that snooker club of theirs and smoking cigarettes or some such thing."

Siobhán's ears perked up. "They used to do that around you in the pubs, didn't they?"

Joseph nodded. "You're right." He took a drag on the electronic cigarette and blew out vapors. "I never thought about that. I don't know why they didn't want me in that dairy barn. Perhaps they were worried I'd fall into the slurry pit."

"It wasn't a functioning dairy barn back then, was it?" Macdara asked.

Joseph opened his mouth. Then closed it. "You're right. It wasn't. I didn't put that together until just now."

"Put what together, exactly?" Macdara asked.

"Why they lied." He frowned as he appeared to think it through. "Tommy used to go on about how the three of them took turns stirring the slurry for money. I believed them. What lad in short trousers wouldn't?"

"Why are you just mentioning this now?" Macdara asked.

Joseph crossed his arms. "I just told you. I never thought about it until I heard meself say it. They all behaved as if that slurry pit was still in use. Me father complained about it all the time. How those pits were dangerous. But now . . . now I'm wondering the same thing you are."

"Which is what exactly?" Macdara asked.

"Why they lied. Why they didn't want me in the dairy barn."

"But you went in anyway, didn't ya?" Siobhán asked.

Joseph shook his head emphatically. "I went in only if I was with an elder, and we certainly didn't go near the slurry pit."

"What was your relationship like with Howard Dunn back in the day?" Siobhán asked.

"I wouldn't say we had a relationship. Tommy used to take me around the pubs, and I tagged along when they were scouting locations for the snooker club. I got the impression Howard didn't like lads in short trousers. I kept me distance."

"Were you ever at his house?" Siobhán continued.

Joseph frowned. "Not that I recall."

Siobhán wanted to get as many questions in as she could think of while he was talking. "Can you think of anything else you can tell us about Tommy? Anything around the time of the wedding that struck you as odd?"

Joseph inhaled on his contraption again and

took his time exhaling. "Not off the top of me head."

"We know Tommy and your father were close," Siobhán said. "Was he also close with your mam?"

"Tommy and my mam?" Joseph asked. He sounded amused.

"Would you say they were good friends?" Siobhán asked. Had he ever seen Tommy flirting with his mother?

He frowned and stuck the electronic cigarette into the pocket of his apron. "Is there something I should know about Tommy and me mam?"

"No," Macdara said. Joseph patted the pocket, as if he suddenly wanted the cigarette again. "How long since you quit smoking real cigarettes?"

Joseph lowered his head. "It's been ages. I smoked as a lad. Gave it up when I started lifting weights and eating healthy. Around twenty years of age."

"I think that's all for now," Siobhán said.

"Don't leave town," Macdara said.

Joseph treated Macdara to a puzzled look. "I never leave town."

"Good," he said. "Don't start now."

Aretta popped back into the shop, then returned and held up a baby blue mug. "How much for this?"

"It's on the house."

Aretta shook her head. "I cannot accept that. I'll come back when I'm not on duty."

"I could give you a two-for-one deal, if there's another interested party." He gestured to the door to the shop.

"Deal," Siobhán said, then headed back into the

shop, where she picked up a lovely green mug with stripes of blue. It made her happy. She could imagine standing in front of her new stone house, drinking a cappuccino out of this mug every morning. Macdara would have to get his own. As if he had read her mind, Macdara entered, took a step back to avoid crashing into Siobhán, only to send a bowl crashing to the floor. "Make it three."

"I'm feeling a wee bit heartbroken," Joseph said. "That'll be a hundred euro."

Chapter 19

"**W**ell done you," Siobhán said to Macdara once they were outside with three extra bags. A bag for Aretta's mug, a bag for Siobhán's mug, and a bag holding Macdara's broken bowl.

"I don't know why you insisted on retaining the broken pieces," Macdara said. "Don't tell me you're going to make a mosaic."

"I was thinking of a swan for the wedding, with champagne coming out of its gullet," Siobhán said. Macdara tried, and failed, not to laugh. "I thought maybe someone could examine the broken pieces and see if they can then tell if the one from the slurry pit is from the same . . . I don't know . . . pottery formula or batch, or anything to prove it's from Joseph's shop."

"That's another movie moment for ya," Macdara said. "If you haven't noticed, we don't exactly have quick turnaround when we send items out to our forensic labs, and I highly doubt the experts are going to think it worthwhile to go down the rabbit hole for a piece of broken pottery."

"Then I'll work on the swan," Siobhán said. "Do you think there's anything to his story about being kept out of the dairy barn?"

"Do we really see Joseph Burns as a suspect?" Aretta said. "A lad so young at the time?"

"He's old enough to murder now," Siobhán said. "We could be looking at a pair of killers."

"The two murders must be linked somehow," Aretta said. "At least that's what my logical mind says."

"We don't even know if either of them was murdered," Macdara said. "We can safely assume and proceed, but there's a possibility that both men simply found themselves in the same place at the same time that their heavenly number was called."

"Remind me never to play bingo with you," Siobhán said. Macdara was technically right, given they'd yet to receive the official causes of death, but not a single one of them believed either man had landed in that slurry pit by accident. They were looking at cold-blooded murder.

"What's next on the agenda?" Aretta asked.

"Speaking of bingo," Siobhán said, "doesn't Gladys play tomorrow afternoon?"

Aretta leafed through her notebook. "Right as rain."

"We want to catch Benji at home without Gladys," Macdara said, turning to Aretta. "Will you interview Linda, the sister, at the station around the same time?"

"Of course," Aretta said. "By myself?"

"We'll have a more senior garda observe you, but you can take the lead," Macdara said. "We have Interview Room One set for tomorrow. Cancel Rose Burns for now. Let's make her wait and worry. Schedule Linda O'Leary instead. Then you can debrief afterward with Siobhán and me."

"On it," Aretta said. "As long as I never have to return to that wildlife center ever again."

"Or the dairy barn," Siobhán said, patting her head. "Don't forget the bats."

Siobhán was relieved when the workday was finally over. Macdara had to drive his mam home, and Siobhán contacted her siblings to request a family supper. When she arrived at the bistro, she was thrilled to find music turned up and her brood splayed out in the dining room, the smell of chicken curry wafting from the kitchen. Siobhán squeezed Ciarán, then Ann, then Gráinne until each let up a squeal of protest; then she hurried upstairs to change before treating herself to a nip of whiskey and an attack cuddle on Eoin and James.

The two elder O'Sullivan lads were in the kitchen, making each other laugh. They fell silent when she entered, then started up again as she joined them. Before long they had pushed several tables together in the dining room so they could all eat near the windows. James finally filled them in on his goings-on. He was working on another old stone house with a team of more experienced builders, and he seemed rather upbeat. Siobhán couldn't remember if this was the longest he'd been without Elise. The pair had broken up more than once these past few years. Siobhán tried to keep her advice to a minimum and often repeated the old adage that many had said to her over the years: *What's for you won't pass you.*

Ciarán and Ann were enjoying the first few weeks of summer freedom and the lightness that came with it. Soon the conversation turned to the new farm.

"Will I have me own room?" Ann asked, a tinge of excitement coming into her voice.

"You will, so, luv." Siobhán grinned and stuck her tongue out at Ann, who laughed and then stuck hers out in response.

"Do I get me own room too?" Ciarán said.

"Eejit," Ann said. "If I get me own room, that means you get your own room. There's only the two of us, like."

"There are *six* of us," Ciaran said.

"Your older siblings aren't moving in with us," Siobhán said. "But I'm sure they'll be over all the time."

Ciaran chewed on his lip, then thrust his index finger up as an idea struck him. "Can I take your scooter to school?"

"No."

"What about a horse?" Ann asked. "Can we ride horses to school?"

"The farm isn't really a farm anymore," Siobhán said. "There are no horses."

"We could get horses," Ann said.

"Or scooters," Ciarán said. "Do I get the biggest room?"

"We haven't decided on rooms yet, petal," Siobhán said. "And no one is riding my scooter but me."

"That's a maybe on getting horses, then," Ann said.

"That is a very creative interpretation," Siobhán said.

"If there are three bedrooms, then we each get our own room," Ciarán said, counting with his fingers. "It's Eoin and James and Gráinne who won't have their own room."

"We'll just stay here," Gráinne said.

Eoin and Siobhán exchanged a look.

Gráinne let her fork clink to her plate. "What?"

"Apparently, the landlord wants this space back," Siobhán said.

"To open a bistro of his own, like," Eoin said.

"He can't do that," Gráinne said, her voice filled with outrage.

"He might be able to wear us down," Siobhán said. "I don't know if we feel like fighting him in court."

"I had a few other ideas," Eoin said. "I'm just waiting for the right time to present them." He flicked a glance at Siobhán.

"We're here now," Siobhán said. "Let's hear them."

Eoin shook his head. "Not just yet."

Siobhán wanted to push the subject, but Eoin was as thickheaded as the rest of them, so she let it drop.

"You haven't been inside the house at all?" James said.

"I'm dying to see the inside," Siobhán said. "We've just been busy with the case."

"Maybe you should see it without Dara," James said. "After all, he saw it without you, didn't he?"

James had a point there. And Macdara had given her a key.

"I want to see it," Ciarán said.

"Everyone will get to see it," Siobhán said. "There's no need to panic."

"I want to see the falcon," Ciarán added.

"He's a Harris hawk," Siobhán said. "And I'm glad to hear that, because the next time I go to the wildlife center, I was thinking of taking you and Ann."

"We've all been on school trips," Ann said. "But I'll go again."

"Me too," Ciarán said. "The falcons are class."

"Who's ready for dessert?" Eoin said as he and James started to clear plates. "We've got apple tarts and ice cream."

Siobhán rose to help, but Gráinne gently shoved her back down and joined them. "We'll tend to ya, missus," Gráinne said. "Just don't get too used to it."

Whether it was talk of her pink scooter, which she hadn't ridden in ages, or the heavy meal and dessert keeping Siobhán awake, or James reminding her that Macdara had seen the house without her, or perhaps the shiny new key dangling from her claddagh key ring, in any case, long after supper was over, Siobhán O'Sullivan found herself throwing together a quick overnight bag, including sheets and a pillow, and hopping on her scooter before she could talk herself out it. Although the roads were dry and clear, she was careful, given it was nighttime and you never knew when a lad or lass was coming toward you at high speed or taking a curved road too fast. The night air was crisp, and the hum of the machine kept all her senses engaged as the world around her went by in a dark blur; and before she knew it, she was pulling up to the farmhouse, the scooter shaking on the uneven driveway leading to the house.

Once there she took off her helmet, shook out her hair, and then gazed at the partial moon suspended over the dairy barn, casting it in a bone-white glow. All was quiet except for the sound of her own footsteps, the jangle of her keys, and the hoot of a nearby owl. This was the first time she'd been to the property at night, and she paused to hear if the owl would hoot two more times. When it didn't, she let out her breath and approached the large stone house. Soon she had the key in the lock and the door pushed open with a low groan. She reached in to feel for a light switch, and just then she heard a distinct sound from within the house, like an object hitting the floor.

"Hello?" Siobhán willed her heart to settle down, for it was beating so loud in her chest, it was making it difficult to hear.

Floorboards creaked from within the house, once, twice, and then stilled.

"Hello?" Siobhán called again. "Is someone here?" She spoke loudly and with more confidence than she felt. Now that she was here, she realized how foolish she'd been. Her adrenaline had been running so high since the wedding and discovering the skeleton that she hadn't been thinking straight.

She gripped the house keys so tight, they bit into her skin as she fumbled for her mobile phone. "I'm a garda, and I'm going to call for backup if you don't speak up right now." Foolish or not, there was another streak in her—a stubborn one. Whoever was inside was an unwelcome intruder, and she was not going to be run off of her own property.

Siobhán stepped inside and allowed her eyes to adjust to the dark. Soon she could make out cabinets, a sink, the fridge, and a table in the center of the room. Beyond the kitchen, an open doorway was visible, with a dark room beyond, most likely the sitting room. It was there that she saw a figure inching his or her way along the back wall. "Stop moving," she said in a loud voice. "This is Garda O'Sullivan, and you're in my home."

"I'm sorry, I'm sorry," a female voice called out. "It's only Linda from next door." A light popped on from the sitting room, and there stood Linda, huddled up in a large blanket, with a pillow at her feet. Siobhán stepped in, angry that her private tour of her future home had been interrupted, but knowing there was nothing to be done about it now.

"You're sleeping here?" Siobhán said, staring at the pillow and what appeared to be nice wooden floors. They could use a bit of shine, but she liked the wide planks against the stone walls. It had a fireplace at one end and several windows overlooking the field.

"I swear I haven't been sleeping here long," Linda said. "But things are tense at home right now. You know yourself."

Siobhán's home life was perfectly content at the moment, but she did not wish to open up her personal life for scrutiny, so she let the comment go.

No matter where you went in life, there would always be the begrudgers. "How did you get in?"

Linda pulled the blanket tight around her. "Heavens, we all have keys next door. We've looked after the place all these years, kept it from falling to ruins. I suppose you'll be wanting to change the locks."

Indeed. "You mentioned things were tense at home?" As much as Siobhán wanted to scold her and then toss her out, she couldn't pass up the opportunity to question her. Especially when she was standing right in front of her, red-faced and apologetic. She tried not to get distracted by the beams in the ceiling, which she quite liked, or the large windows overlooking the field, or the room to the left of the sitting room, or the curved stairwell leading upstairs. *Well done, Dara.* She loved it. It startled her how much it instantly felt like home, and her mind was already racing to decorate and fill the space with those she loved.

"Benji and Gladys are fighting. Gladys is beside herself. And I'm waiting until you find out what happened to me brother, so we can bury him." She pointed to a small stool in the center of the room. "If you'd like to sit down for a spell." With that, Linda sank to the floor. "I suppose you'd like me to go back home." She did not look as if she intended on making a move anytime soon.

"Is it really that bad?"

Linda held up a bottle. Golden liquid sloshed. "Whiskey?"

"Why not?" It had been a long day, and she was not on duty. Linda was a sneak, and possibly a murderer, but Siobhán did not feel under any undue threat. Still, it never hurt to fortify one's position. She held up her mobile. "I'm texting Detective Sergeant Macdara Flannery to let him know the situation." She had no intention of texting Macdara, but she felt better once she had made the assertion and pretended to text him.

"Are you going to arrest me?" Linda's voice was filled with concern.

Good.

"No. I'm going to protect myself in case you were thinking of murdering me."

Linda began to cough. She slapped her hand over her mouth. "Murder you? Me?"

"You broke into my home at night at a time when there's a murderer on the loose," Siobhán said. *And a moon that spells trouble. And bats in the barn. And an owl that may have simply forgotten to hoot twice more.* She left those bits out.

"You're right, you're right. I had no idea you'd be coming by."

"It is my house."

"I should leave."

"Let's have that drink first."

"There's a glass in the cupboards," Linda said, gesturing to the kitchen. It was odd, this neighbor knowing her new home so intimately.

Siobhán found the light switch this time and was soon staring at a kitchen that needed work—the cabinets and appliances replaced—but it was roomy, and it had good bones. Not a kitchen fit to feed a village—but this one didn't need to be. She should sit down with Eoin and have a long talk about his thoughts on the bistro. She rummaged through the old cupboards and soon found two empty glasses. She switched off the light as she left the kitchen, slid the stool next to Linda, and sat as she waited for the pour of whiskey. When it came, she simply drank and took in the sitting room.

It was large enough that someone could be sitting and reading or watching telly, while others could be playing cards or a game, and yet even others could be doing their homework. The ceilings were higher than she imagined they'd be, and the wooden beams were a delight. Siobhán could see future celebrations—the far corner, where a Christmas tree would shine; the big windows, where they would watch the seasons change around them; the fireplace, which no doubt would be on night and day to combat the chill of the stones. Siobhán sat and thought and sipped her whiskey.

"I hear you weren't a fan of Tommy Caffrey," Siobhán said when the silence had stretched long enough.

"I always knew Tommy was trouble," Linda said with a vigorous nod. "But my sister is a stubborn woman. She thought she was in love. I take no pleasure in being right."

"But you weren't necessarily right, were you?"

"Pardon?" Linda's eyes were large and attentive.

Siobhán took another sip of whiskey, allowing Linda to squirm with anticipation. "I said you weren't necessarily right. Because Tommy Caffrey didn't do a runner after all, now did he?"

Chapter 20

Linda chewed on her lip as she considered Siobhán's statement. "I suppose you're right. But I can't help but think he brought it on himself."

"I see." Linda was victim blaming. Siobhán was hoping she'd bring the blame a little bit closer to home, to the living, to the killer. "And what of your brother? Did he bring it on himself?"

"How dare you!"

"How dare I? I might remind you that you are the one who broke into me house without permission—the house a detective sergeant recently purchased, I might add—and I am simply asking you a question."

"I'm sorry. But me brother was a good man. And no. He didn't deserve to die in a slurry pit with those ghastly bones of Tommy Caffrey!"

Tommy was a sore button for Linda, and Siobhán could not lose this opportunity. She poured

Linda another glass of whiskey. "I'm very sorry you lost your brother," Siobhán said, lifting her own glass. "To his memory."

"To his memory," Linda repeated, and they drank, and they crossed themselves.

"I have three brothers of me own, so I know what it's like. Were the three of you close growing up?"

"I was the older sister, but it was Alan whom Gladys listened to. And for some reason, Alan always gave Tommy a pass."

If that were true, it brought up a lot more questions. Did Tommy have something over Alan? Had Tommy been blackmailing him? If Alan was Tommy's killer, who killed Alan? Only one name echoed in Siobhán's poor head, and she didn't want to hear it. *Gladys.* What if Alan finally confessed what he'd done after Tommy's remains were found? The guilt could have tipped him over the edge. In that case, it wasn't difficult to imagine Gladys reacting, lashing out and pushing her brother into the pit. . . .

But where did the falconer's glove and shard of pottery fit in? Nowhere. Because Gladys wasn't the killer. This killer wasn't impulsive. He or she had meticulously planned every step.

"What did your parents think of Tommy?" Siobhán wanted to keep the conversation on the O'Leary family dynamics and suss out if anything Rose had suggested about this family was true.

"My parents?" Linda drained her glass. "What about them?"

"Did they like Tommy?"

Linda frowned, and they both listened as the fire crackled. "As a matter of fact, they didn't like

Tommy. They even threatened to cut Gladys out of the will. That's when I knew she loved him. She didn't even blink."

Siobhán found herself returning yet again to her conversation with Rose. How Gladys had married Benji so that she could have a ready-made family. A stepson. What if she *had* blinked? What if she had blinked very, very hard and had gotten away with it for fifty years? Was Macdara right? Was Gladys their killer? And was Siobhán just being stubborn, because it was his gut feeling that Gladys was the killer and not hers? Would this competitive drive in her weaken their marriage?

"Do you remember anything out of place, odd, or alarming in the days leading up to the wedding?" Siobhán asked.

"Isn't my official interview tomorrow morning at the garda station?"

"It is."

"If I talk to you now, can I skip it?"

"I'm afraid not. I'll stop chatting if you'd like."

Linda fidgeted, appearing not to like the answer. "Nobody wants to repeat themselves," she said.

"I completely understand. Even if it's good practice."

"Good practice?"

"If we do a bit of practice, it might calm you down a bit. You'll appear less nervous."

Linda rubbed her hands together. She tried to pour more whiskey in her glass, but the bottle was empty. She'd obviously been tipping it for a while. "I remember how happy Gladys was about her wedding," she said. "I was older, yet she was going to be the first to be married. She always thrived whenever she was the center of attention. My sister has to be the bride at all the weddings and the corpse at every funeral. Oh. Oh! I must sound so heartless! I'm sorry, Alan. I'm sorry!"

"Grief brings up a lot of emotions," Siobhán said. "Don't be so hard on yourself." *Unless you're a cold-blooded killer . . .*

"I did tell her. I told Gladys exactly what I thought of Tommy. And when he didn't show up at the church, I told her it was good riddance! I was trying to make her feel better. She didn't speak to me for five years. Five whole years. Even though *he* was the one who ran away. Or so we all thought." She stopped to gaze longingly at the empty whiskey bottle. "Gladys watched Joseph the night of her wedding, and because of it, Tommy didn't spend the night, even though he had planned on it—they had no interest in tradition. I told her it was bad luck to see him before the wedding, and then when Benji and Rose had their little emergency, they asked us to take Joseph for the night. Gladys may not have been superstitious, but it's best to be cautious if you ask me."

Superstitious . . . Was Linda the one who heard an owl cry three times? "What little emergency?"

"Pardon?"

"You said Benji and Rose left Joseph with you because they had 'their little emergency.' "

Linda chewed on her lip for a moment. "Heavens. I don't know. I don't think they even told us at the time. They just suddenly had somewhere very urgent to be and pleaded with us to watch Joseph.

They'd only just adopted him, and to be honest, none of us knew what to make of him. He was very quiet—my heart squeezed for him—as he'd spent most of his life in a home for boys, and I think he was afraid of doing or saying anything that would make his new parents reject him. Oh, it does break one's heart. They would never have given up on him. Even after they gave up on their marriage, Benji stepped up and was a father to him, even after he divorced Rose. Say what you want, I don't believe in divorce, and they shouldn't have done it, but they did right by that lad, and look what a nice man he's grown into."

If she knew Gladys had a more sinister plot— i.e., instant family equaled instant inheritance—either Linda was a very good actress or time had allowed a heavy curtain to fall down on those suspicions, smothering them.

"Did you ever hear Gladys talk about wanting to have children with Tommy?"

"My word, did I ever. Yes. It was the only thing she could say to my parents that would make them rally behind the idea of her marrying Tommy. They did so want grandchildren." Check mark for Rose.

"And none of you ever had children of your own?" Siobhán already knew the answer, and she wanted to be as kind as possible, in case it was a sensitive topic, but she also knew this was an important piece of the puzzle. Three siblings fighting over a family farm. Winner takes all, as long as the winner produced an offspring.

"The curse of the O'Leary family. All of us seemingly barren. We've never been tested, mind you, but we all wanted children and none of us had them, so draw what conclusions you will. What a shock and disappointment to our parents. I suppose there are options today that we didn't have back then. I always thought it was God's plan and that was that. But my parents were heartbroken. They eventually treated Joseph as their grandson."

"And Gladys alone inherited the farm . . ."

"How did you know that?" Linda's voice turned icy cold. If this were a neighborly chat, Siobhán would be treading into mind-your-business territory.

"I can wait and ask you at the station if you'd like."

Linda blinked. When she spoke again, there was a clip to her voice. *A hostile witness.* "Technically, Gladys inherited the farm. What does that matter? Alan and I have been living here as well. It's big enough for all of us. We didn't care whose name was on the deed." She stared into the unlit hearth. "Had Gladys sold the farm and moved away, leaving us homeless, now that would have been a different matter. But she didn't, did she?"

That was true. Whatever issues had arisen with the inheritance appeared to have been worked out long ago. But what if that was just an act?

"You didn't resent it at all?"

"Why should I?"

Siobhán was going to have to find out exactly what this little emergency was that Benji and Rose had had the night before the wedding—something else that Rose had conveniently omitted.

Linda could be lying, but that seemed like an odd story to make up all these years later. "Do you have any idea where Tommy spent the night before the wedding?"

"No. I assume with one of the lads."

"One of the lads?"

"Howard or any one of his pub lads. I believe he was bedding down in the snooker club they were going to build. It might not seem like it now, but that was a big deal back then. Howard poured his soul and every pound he had into it. What a mistake getting involved with Tommy. He had the ability to wind everyone up around him and then walk away whistling when they spun out of control . . ."

Except he didn't walk away. He'd been stuck here for fifty years, waiting for the slowly churning wheels of justice. . . .

Linda suddenly stood and gathered her blanket and pillow from the floor. "I'm going to sneak back into my room next door. They must be done arguing by now."

Siobhán's curiosity pinged. "What were they arguing about?"

"If I had wanted to know, I would have stayed to listen," Linda said. Her tone was clipped; she was not going to reveal anything more.

"I know these are difficult times, but sometimes even the most innocent piece of news can change an investigation . . ."

Linda headed for the door, then hesitated. "There is something I need to tell you and the detective sergeant. But I want to say it only once, and I want to say it in a formal setting. Then accept my punishment, whatever it may be."

"Punishment?" The tips of Siobhán's fingertips tingled, and her palms took a flash of heat.

"No one can punish me more than I'm punishing myself. I've made my mistakes, and believe me, I'm going to own up to them. If I had said something earlier, maybe my brother would still be alive." Linda stepped onto the porch, dragging her blanket on the ground.

"I would like you to tell me now."

"No. I need to tell Gladys first. I'll tell you during my official interview. Like you said."

"Wait," Siobhán said. "Whatever this is, I'd rather you not say anything to Gladys. Not just now."

Linda whirled around, her eyes wide, her mouth slack. As she stood and swayed, it confirmed Siobhán's suspicions that Linda had had a lot more to drink than she'd first realized. Whatever brought Linda here, whatever was on her mind, had needed massive amounts of alcohol to drown out. No one ever found solutions to their problems at the bottom of a bottle, but she'd save the lecture for another day.

Linda raised the whiskey bottle and jabbed it in Siobhán's direction. "First, you accuse me of being a murderer, and now you accuse me sister?"

"Anyone who was close to the victim is a suspect. That's not me being cruel. It's just part of the job."

Linda clamped her lips shut, as if struggling not to reply.

"We'll have a much better chance of catching a

killer if you just tell us what you know, no matter how inconsequential you think it is. Please. Let us do our jobs."

But Linda was on the move, and when Siobhán stepped out the front door, she could see her hurrying across the field, her back illuminated by the moon, before she faded into the darkness and the night swallowed her whole.

Chapter 21

"Morning." Siobhán opened one eye to find Macdara looming over her. He had a large mug in one hand, and the other hand was hidden behind his back. The heavenly scent of a cappuccino roused her.

"Is that for me?" She reached for it.

"Do you deserve it?" He lifted his other hand and jiggled a familiar pastry bag. "Oran and Padraig said they hoped we liked our wedding eclairs. And seeing as how I didn't even know such a thing existed, I had to find out for meself." He shoved his face into the bag and gave a moan of pleasure.

She laughed. "Guilty as charged, Detective Sergeant."

He pulled up the stool as she sat up, and then he handed her the cappuccino. "Well?" He looked eager for a report.

"How did you know?"

He winked. "You can't spend the night alone in a new house and not have it get back to your husband-to-be."

After Linda returned home, Siobhán had wandered the rest of the house. Three bedrooms and a bonus room downstairs. Two bathrooms. Room to roam. Room to grow. She loved it, and it terrified her. "Despite an intruder, I loved it."

He immediately stood. "An intruder?"

She filled him in on her visit and run-in with Linda.

"What do you think she wants to confess?" he asked.

"I don't know, but she was definitely on edge."

"We'll get the locks changed."

"Pronto."

"Gladys is off to her knitting circle, and Linda is on her way to the station, so what do you say we catch Benji alone?" he asked. "And after, let's pop into the house together."

"That's the best idea I've heard all day." She reached for the pastry bag. He held it away from her. "One bite?"

Macdara continued to eat the pastry slowly until there was only one bite left. Eye contact was maintained. His lopsided grin appeared. In the end, he handed it over.

Benji Burns was whistling when he greeted them at the door. This time his overalls were blue, and his shirt was white. But it was the grin on his face that made him a stranger, and now she could see he had nice white teeth, somewhat unusual for a farmer of a certain generation. Perhaps they were dentures. Whatever it was, they suited him. Was he a happier man without Gladys around? She'd known couples like this. Where one was usurped by the other, like a dominant tree using its root system to drain life and resources out of a neighboring tree. Was that dynamic there from the start with some couples, or was it something that happened the longer folks were together? Was it because Gladys had never really loved Benji? Had she married him only for selfish reasons? The first chance she got, Siobhán was buying Macdara a dozen eclairs.

"My turn in the hot seat, is it?" Benji said enthusiastically as he led them to the kitchen. The aroma of an Irish breakfast filled the room as eggs and rashers, sausages, black and white pudding, and beans sizzled on the grill, while toast and tomatoes waited on plates. "Gladys isn't much of an eater, but I still like to cook," he said. "Hungry?"

Siobhán was debating whether or not to accept when Macdara pulled out a chair and slid into it. "Don't mind if I do."

"Good man."

Siobhán sighed and pulled out the chair opposite him. If she had a big feed, she was going to need a nap. She eyed Macdara's thin physique. Where did he put it? "Just a piece of toast and an egg for me," she said. "After all, I had one whole bite of an eclair."

"And don't forget two whole eclairs yesterday

all to yourself," Macdara said. Was this the start of watching Macdara shovel massive amounts of food into his gob while she switched to counting every bite? Once they married, would they just continue to widen until they were one of those couples toddling down the street and arguing over who was going to get up and find the remote to the telly? *Never.* She shivered at the thought.

"I'll give you a bit of everything, but don't worry. What you don't eat, I'll give to the dogs," Benji said.

"The dogs?" Her head swiveled, and she took in the kitchen, wondering if she'd missed something.

Benji laughed. "I'm only messing. I have always wanted dogs, but Gladys is not a fan." He thunked plates in front of them, with enough to feed a small village. Siobhán could only stare at her plate.

"We have a small dog, Trigger," Siobhán said. "You'd be welcome to treat him as your own."

Benji began cleaning up.

"You're not eating?" Siobhán said.

"I've been up for hours," Benji said. "There's something about living out here that rouses one before the sun. You'll see for yourself soon enough. How was your night in the house?"

Siobhán grabbed her napkin, as the comment had caught her mid-bite and she'd begun to cough. Before she could even reach for her water, Benji was behind her, putting his arms around her waist and squeezing. She sputtered and slapped at his hands. "I'm fine, I'm fine!"

He let go of her and stumbled back. "Sorry. I thought you were choking."

Macdara watched it all while continuing to shovel down his breakfast. Siobhán gave him a look that made him stop eating. "Alright?" he asked.

"Fine," she said, hoping he'd pick up on her tone.

Benji was strong for an old man, she'd give him that. He also had lightning quick reflexes. She couldn't help but imagine him shoving unsuspecting victims into the slurry pit. Had he fed them first too? Was this supposed to be their last meal? She was feeling too hot. She pushed her plate away, wishing there was a dog. Not that a dog needed all this cholesterol. She couldn't wait to introduce Trigger to the farm. When was the last day she took time off and just cuddled with her pooch?

"Did Linda mention she was at my house?" Siobhán asked once she could speak without coughing.

"I saw her, alright, but we haven't spoken. She left early this morning, probably getting in her messages before her interview at the station."

The food and veg market was the only shop open, along with Liam's hardware shop and the chemist, not to mention their bistro, but as long as she showed up for her interview, Siobhán wasn't fussed about Linda's early morning errands. "Does she break into our house often?" Siobhán continued.

Benji smacked his lips. She wanted him to sit down. He'd gained the upper hand: Macdara was thoroughly ensconced in his brekkie, and Benji was standing over them.

"Do sit," Siobhán said. Macdara pushed his plate

away with a satisfied sigh, then eyed Siobhán's. She gave him another look, and he refrained from a second helping. "Linda said things were tense here last night," Siobhán continued. "Were you and Gladys arguing?"

Benji glanced at Macdara, as if asking for a bailout. Macdara folded his arms across his chest and stared. A free meal only got you so far.

"This business of finding Tommy's skeleton has put my wife on edge," Benji said. "She thinks she's a suspect. Will you do me a favor and tell her she's wrong?"

"We can't do that," Macdara said. "Why don't you tell us what we need to know?" Macdara loved this form of questioning. He sounded as if they all knew perfectly well what Benji needed to tell them, a trick that often dredged up surprising answers.

Benji removed their plates and poured himself a mug of tea before taking his seat. "I do regret gathering everyone together after you found Tommy. We were so shocked, and I thought we should all be there to deal with it."

"How did that work out for you?" Siobhán couldn't help but ask.

Benji dropped his head. "I always thought Tommy was off on a tropical island somewhere, cozying up to the women and swindling the men." He rubbed his face, then slowly made eye contact. "Do you think it's my fault Alan's dead?"

The abrupt switch from Tommy to Alan took Siobhán by surprise. "Did you push him into the slurry pit?" Siobhán asked. If only he would say yes. *Yes, I pushed Tommy into the slurry pit, and yes, I pushed Alan into the slurry pit, and this case is closed. Go back to your wedding, your honeymoon, your new house, your new farm.*

"No, I wasn't confessing to murder, Garda O'Sullivan. I was only expressing regret that I brought everyone together and one of those visitors might have been a murderer."

"Which one would you say?" Macdara said. "If you had to guess."

If Benji heard Macdara's question, he didn't answer it. "We just didn't want to deal with the horrible news alone, and we have this big house, so we wanted to fill it. You'll see yourselves."

"You have enough room for everyone?" Siobhán asked.

Benji shook his head. "Rose pitched a tent in the yard. She loves sleeping outside in the summer."

"Rose," Siobhán said. "The wife and mother you dropped like a hot potato the minute Gladys was left at the altar."

Macdara's mouth dropped open, but he didn't interrupt. She hadn't planned on a snarky approach, but now that she'd taken it, she was curious to see how he would react. To her surprise, tears came to his eyes.

"I know what you must be thinking about me. I loved my wife."

"Which one?" Siobhán asked.

He frowned, showing the first signs of anger. "Both of them. I loved both of them. But only one needed me."

Siobhán sincerely wished Ciarán was here to play his violin. "Gladys needed you, but your wife, Rose, a new mother, did not?"

"In the beginning my only intention was to offer comfort to Gladys. I had no intentions of falling in love. I suppose one never truly does. It just happens." Now he stuck his chin up and looked directly at Siobhán. "Men can fall out of love as quickly as they fall in it. Don't ever forget that."

She felt her fists clench as his words made her heartbeat tick up.

"Not this man," Macdara said. "There's only one woman for me for the rest of my life." He paused and grinned. "A life sentence."

Benji gave a soft smile. "I wish the two of ye the best."

"The night before Tommy and Gladys's wedding, you left Joseph here with Gladys," Siobhán said. "And I presume Alan and Linda were living here at the time as well."

Benji frowned. "Did I?"

"You and Rose had some kind of emergency." Siobhán leaned forward. "I'd like to know what that emergency was."

"Where did you hear that?" Benji's defenses were up; Mr. Cheerful was turning away from the sun.

"Answer the question," Macdara said. He was taking a while coming around, but he was finally seeing through Benji's hospitality act.

"It's been a long time," Benji said. He stroked the gray fuzz on his chin. "What did Rose say?"

"Don't tell me you've forgotten," Siobhán said.

"I honestly can't remember. Give me a minute." He looked to the ceiling, as if the answers were there in the form of a puzzle he had to put together.

Had Linda been lying? Benji appeared stressed

and flummoxed. Siobhán eased up on her tone. "Do you even remember whether or not you dropped Joseph off to spend the night?"

Benji began bobbing his head. "That sounds familiar." He suddenly stopped and snapped his fingers. "It was Gladys. She asked if she could have Joseph."

"The night before her wedding?" Macdara asked. "Why would she do that?"

"Tradition," Benji said. "She was afraid Tommy was going to sneak and try to spend the night with her. She thought that was bad luck. She decided if she had the lad, he wouldn't be able to sweet-talk her into letting him in." He leaned back, satisfied. "There's your emergency," he said.

"That's not an emergency," Siobhán said.

"I agree," Benji said. "If Linda thinks it was an emergency, she's got the wrong end of the stick."

One or both of them were lying. Siobhán would have to approach Rose with the same question, but for now she let it drop. "You and Gladys weren't fighting last night?"

His eyes slid to the clock on the wall before turning back to them, as if he was wondering how long he would have to endure this torture. "We may have raised our voices. But I was only trying to calm Gladys down and assure her that no one in this village thinks she's a murderer!"

"We've never called you that," Macdara said. "We're just doing our jobs."

"We're too old to be murderers. Don't you know that?"

"As long as you have breath left in ya, you're capable of taking someone else's," Macdara said.

Benji frowned, crossed his arms against his chest, and slumped into his seat. He was too polite to walk away from a pair of guards, but his desire to do so was palpable.

"What is your relationship like with your sister-in-law?" Siobhán asked.

"Linda?" This caused Benji to straighten up. "Between you and me? She's the one you need to look at. Maybe breaking into houses isn't her only criminal activity, you know? Tommy drove a big wedge between herself and Gladys. I wonder, did Linda kill Tommy to spare her sister a lifetime of misery married to that man?"

"Wasn't he your best friend?" Macdara asked.

"We were lads who grew up together, but we weren't thick as thieves. Tommy was trouble, but as long as he was someone else's trouble, we were right as rain." He scratched his chin. "I hate speaking ill of the dead, but . . ."

"Yes?" Siobhán asked the question, but this time both she and Macdara leaned in.

"I did fight with Gladys last night. But not for the reasons you think." He hesitated.

"You'll be doing yourself a favor if you tell us everything," Macdara said. "Everyone eventually talks, and you don't want to be the last horse out of the gate."

Benji walked to the kitchen sink and unlatched the window directly above it. He reached into a drawer and pulled out a pack of cigarettes. He lit one over the sink and blew the smoke out the window. "I used to go to the dairy barn but now . . ." He shrugged. "It's my house too. I'll smoke if I want to smoke."

"Smoke 'em if you got 'em," Macdara said. Although they both detested cigarette smoke, they also knew that suspects opened up more if they were at ease.

"Shortly after Tommy disappeared, Alan and Linda came up with the money they needed to save this farm," Benji said, flicking an ash into the sink.

"Save it?" Macdara asked.

"Nobody could ever accuse me of marrying Gladys for the family farm. The O'Learys were in terrible debt. Close to losing their land altogether. They'd been turned down for every loan in the book. Sure, lookit. That's nothing new. It was the amount that nibbled at me. Been nibbling at me all these years. Thirty thousand quid. Shortly after Tommy and the satchel of thirty thousand disappear, Alan comes up with the money to pay off their debts. Close to twenty thousand. And then he buys a new tractor and a few other bits and bobs, and that gets you close to the thirty."

"Did you ask him about it?" Macdara said.

Benji shook his head. "Not at the time. I wouldn't have stuck my nose into their business. I asked Gladys about it last night. That's what started the fight."

"Did she have an answer?" Siobhán prodded.

"No," he said. "Alan told her he'd worked it out, and that was all she needed to know. And I believe her. But there's someone else I'd have my eye on if I were youse. Do you want to know what Linda did when she heard me asking how Alan got the money to save the family farm?"

Siobhán nodded, but she already knew. She ran.

"She didn't leave the house because we were fighting. She left the house because she knows where Alan got that money—I'd stake me life on it. I don't know if she had anything to do with it or she was simply a witness to the theft. And I'm not a betting man. But if I was . . . I'd say Alan got his hands on a satchel full of money, and they've been keeping it secret ever since."

Chapter 22

"One of them is lying," Siobhán said once they were outside in the fresh air.

"They could both be lying," Macdara said.

"Linda was breaking and entering. We could use that to our advantage."

"Indeed. We'll also get to see what she says to Aretta during the interview today."

"Agreed. She said she had something to confess, so let's not bring the big stick out too soon."

"Am I the big stick?" Macdara stood up straight, as if wanting to live up to his role.

"No."

Macdara laughed and took her hand. "Shall I give you the official tour of the house now that you've seen it on your own?"

Siobhán glanced at her watch. They had some time. "I would love that."

* * *

When Siobhán and Macdara returned to the garda station, they saw Linda hurrying away from the front entrance. They immediately read through the transcript from Linda's interview. Siobhán had to scour it twice to believe what she was seeing. No wonder Linda was running out of the station like her arse was on fire. There was no confession. She admitted she never liked Tommy but that Gladys was stubborn and there was never anything you could do to sway her. After she and Macdara read through the transcript twice, they called Aretta into the interview room.

Siobhán lifted the report. "There's no mention of a confession or financial trouble with the farm."

Aretta's eyes widened. "I didn't know to ask."

"Have a seat, luv. I'm not pointing fingers at you." Siobhán filled Aretta in on her run-in with Linda the previous night.

"Should we call her back right away?" Aretta asked.

Macdara shook his head. "Let her stew and worry for a spell. Benji tried hard to shove us in her direction. If he thinks we're going easy on her, and he's guilty, he may get worried as well."

"Sometimes, no matter how hard you want to chase after them, you have to turn the heat up on suspects and let them come to a boil on their own," Siobhán added.

"I did learn one interesting tidbit," Aretta said. "I know where Linda and Gladys will be this evening."

"Where is that?" Siobhán asked.

"Their knitting circle is having a fundraiser tonight at the Kilbane Castle." Located a few miles outside town, the eighteenth-century structure was originally a tavern. Expansive views of the Ballyhoura Hills and the Golden Vale made it a special outing. Now family owned, it was a restaurant and an event site. It was a lovely place for a night out.

"Knitting circles need fundraisers?" Macdara asked.

Aretta laughed. It was a lovely sound, and Siobhán found herself laughing along with her. "I believe they raise money for charity," Aretta said.

"They do," Siobhán said. "The knitting circle is always very generous to local causes."

"I think I'll leave that little shindig to you two," Macdara said.

"Why, Detective Sergeant Flannery, that's mighty sexist of you," Siobhán said.

"Aren't you due for a little night out with your friends?" Macdara asked.

Siobhán looked to Aretta. "It does sound nice. I can ask Maria and Aisling. Are you in?"

Aretta frowned. "Is this . . . official?"

"We won't go in uniform, and no one will know it's official, but of course, you never know what we might overhear."

"Unofficially official," Macdara said.

"Then I'm in," Aretta said.

Siobhán grinned. She hoped one day Aretta would be in whether it was official garda business or not, but this would do for now.

It had been ages since Siobhán had properly spent time with her two best friends, Maria and

Aisling. They'd known each other since they were in nappies. Aisling had gone away to Trinity College after getting her leaving certificate, but now she was back and happily married to a local lad. Maria was a bit like Gráinne when it came to boyfriends, mercurial and constantly dissatisfied, and was at the moment in between them. She had been so thrilled when Siobhán suggested a night out with their new garda that Siobhán had felt a tug of guilt that they would be doing double duty. Siobhán stepped into O'Rourke's Pub, where Maria was finishing up her shift. She paused to smile at the Laurel and Hardy memorabilia showcased in the window. Declan O'Rourke, the owner and longtime publican, was a big fan of American movies and television. Inside, the walls were peppered with black-and-white posters of John Wayne. She looked around for Declan, but the larger-than-life man with the big laugh was nowhere in sight.

Maria's eyes lit up when Siobhán approached. "Yes," she said, throwing down the rag she had been using to wipe down the counter. "Finally! A proper hen night." Maria was short, with dark hair and a booming voice.

"Not a proper hen night," Siobhán said. "I have work in the morning. This is just us attending a little event."

Maria squinted and crossed her arms. "We'll see about that. Where are we going?" She rattled off the names of pubs in Cork City, excitement growing with each option. "Or would you rather go into Limerick?"

Siobhán swallowed. "There's a local event with

food and drink and the craic," Siobhán said. "I think there's even a live band."

"I haven't heard of this local event," Maria said. "And I hear everything first."

The bell dinged and Aretta entered. She was still in her garda uniform. "Are you coming to the knitting circle fundraiser?" she asked Maria. Aretta stopped to take in Siobhán's little black dress. She looked down at her uniform. "I forgot I was supposed to change."

"Knitting circle?" Maria's voice was loud on a good day, this level was going to give Siobhán tinnitus.

"Don't worry," Siobhán said. "There's going to be drinking and gambling."

"Tea and bingo," Aretta said.

"And the band?" Maria could not be more outraged.

"I believe it's a waltz, wasn't it?" Aretta said. Her tone was innocent, and at first Siobhán thought she had no idea what she was stepping in, but now she was starting to think that Aretta was rather enjoying this.

"Tea, bingo, knitting, and waltzing?" Maria grabbed a bottle of whiskey, then snatched three shot glasses, and poured. She slid two of them toward Aretta and Siobhán. "Shot," she said, hoisting hers up. "Shot, or I'm not going anywhere with ye."

Siobhán swallowed hard. Aretta took a step back. "You don't have to," Siobhán started to say to Aretta.

Aretta grabbed the shot and hoisted it. "Down the hatch!" She was finished with her shot before Siobhán and Maria brought theirs up to their lips.

Maria laughed. "There's hope for this night after all." She did her shot, and then the pair stared at Siobhán. "Horse it into ya," Maria said.

Why not? She had been working nonstop, and she'd missed her own wedding. Even Macdara had encouraged a night out with the girls.

Siobhán lifted the shot glass. "Here goes nothing." When she finished the shot, Aretta and Maria cheered. Maybe this night was going to be fun after all.

"Is this about the murder?" Maria asked. She flicked a glance at Aretta. "Are you wearing that?"

"No?" Aretta said, as if she was completely out of her depths.

"Correct answer!" Maria said. "You'll be changing into something fit for a night out." Maria turned to Siobhán. "I should have known better than to think me best friend wanted to celebrate with me."

Siobhán grabbed Maria's hands and squeezed. "I do want to celebrate with you. I miss you fiercely. I want to show you my new house too. I want to go to Ibiza and sit on the beach and drink cocktails. But you know what my life is like."

Maria sighed and picked up the bottle of whiskey. "I'm bringing reinforcements. Let them drink tea. We're going to be on the whiskey."

Siobhán knew a bad idea when she heard one. She also knew it was futile to argue. She turned to Aretta. "We'll fetch Aisling and meet you at the castle."

Chapter 23

Aisling Griffin was a tall and slim young woman with pale blond hair and a wide grin. She believed in regularly whitening her teeth, and under the streetlamps of Sarsfield Street, they glowed. She was in a short dress that showed off her long legs and heels. Siobhán was starting to get the impression the girls were up for an epic session. When they found out she had no intention of being hungover the next day, it would create another little groove in their friendship. They chatted excitedly as they waited for their taxi.

"Don't let Siobhán fool you," Maria said. "She's on duty."

Aisling eyed Siobhán's black dress and cute boots. "Are ya now?"

Siobhán grinned and looped an arm around each girlfriend. "I'm mostly *not* on duty."

"That's what I like to hear," Aisling said. "Barry

and I have been married only a year, and we're already one of those boring couples arguing about what to watch on telly."

The taxi pulled up, and the girls piled in. Once in the back Aisling brought out a flask, took a drink, and passed it to Siobhán. She took it and passed it to Maria, who shoved it right back at her.

"How often do we do this?" Maria demanded.

Siobhán was opening her mouth to say that it wasn't that unusual when she realized she couldn't remember the last time. She took a tiny sip, hoping that would do the trick.

"Useless," Aisling said.

"We'll work on it," Maria said.

The castle was nestled up to the footpath, and the outside reminded Siobhán exactly of its original purpose, an old stone tavern. Folks were queued up when they arrived, and from the walkers, wheelchairs and canes, it was impossible to keep up the pretense of a girls' night out any longer.

"Do we have the wrong night?" Aisling asked.

"I told you," Maria said. "Work."

Aisling's eyes narrowed. "An hour tops," she said. "And then we're going to the pubs."

"I have to work tomorrow," Siobhán said with less gusto than she'd planned.

"I don't care," Aisling said. "You're not wasting your hen night."

This wasn't a proper hen night, with a clutch of young women dressed up and celebrating a bride-to-be, waving plastic pink phalluses decked out with glitter, but it was the only chance Siobhán was going to have to come close to something resembling a hen night. She'd been too busy in the days leading up to the (first) wedding to have one. That alone had put her on her back foot with Aisling and Maria. Maybe she could let loose for one night. She would mind how much she drank, then would make sure she replenished with a lot of water before bed, or maybe she'd stay up all night, and by the time she was ready to crash, the workday would be over. She took the flask from Maria and took another sip, a real one this time. She deserved to have a little fun.

Maria whooped. "This is going to be good craic.'

Aretta was waiting by the entrance, looking absolutely stunning in a yellow dress. She even had on red lipstick and was wearing ruby earrings and matching heels.

"You're absolutely gorgeous," Aisling said, wrapping her arms around Aretta and squeezing. When she pulled back, Siobhán introduced them.

Aretta, who had probably never been bear-hugged by a stranger, stumbled back a bit and politely muttered a thank-you.

"You do," Siobhán said. "You look gorgeous."

"Absolute class," Maria said. "We're definitely not wasting tonight here."

"We're not?" Aretta said.

Siobhán tried to convey through eye contact not to mind them. "We might go to one pub after,' Siobhán said.

"By the time we're done, we'll be so ossified we'll think it was one pub," Aisling shrieked. She grabbed

Maria's hand and then Aretta's and headed for the entrance.

Aretta looked back at Siobhán with a look of alarm, but Siobhán could only shrug. She could catch murderers, but when it came to her girl-friends, she was completely out of her depth.

The function was held in a large ballroom of the castle. With towering stone walls and a wood-beamed ceiling, from which grand crystal chande-liers hung, along with historical tapestries and even a knight in shining armor standing guard by a roaring fire, the atmosphere was Gothic and lively. The band was indeed playing a waltz. Food and beverage were served, but not the alcoholic kind. And when the rowdy bingo game began, Siobhán could see why. Even without alcohol, the group was humming.

When Aisling returned from a restroom break, her cheeks were flushed as she stared down at her right calf. "I was poked with a cane, and it wasn't an accident."

"Did you try to cut in line?"

Aisling shook her head. "I was only going up to the mirror."

A man dressed in a tux approached. "Ladies, there are card games at the back table. Would any-one care for a game of twenty-five?"

Siobhán's mam loved twenty-five, and she had been wicked good at it. James was too. Siobhán could hold her own, but it had been ages since she played.

"No thank you," Maria said.

Siobhán perused the tables set up along the perimeter, each selling goods to raise money for a charity. At a table in the middle, she recognized the look of a large ceramic vase. It was green, with a Celtic cross. She glanced at the informational sign. SAINT JOSEPH HOME FOR BOYS. A kindly older nun stood behind the table.

"It's the work of one of our lads from long ago," she said.

"Joseph Burns," Siobhán said with a nod. "I'm familiar with his work."

The nun clasped her hands and smiled. "He's come a long way."

"Have you known Joseph long?" Siobhán asked.

"All me life," the nun said. "He's a shining example of how a family can turn a life around."

"Turn it around," Siobhán said. "Sister, can you tell me what Joseph was like back then?"

"He was a bit wild," the nun said. "One of the troublemakers."

"Could you be a little bit more specific?" Siobhán asked as she added her name and an amount to the silent auction for the vase. It was up to a hundred euro.

"Here." The nun handed her a brochure for the boys' home. "It was a long time ago. Suffice it to say that boy had angels looking out for him. Not all of them were so lucky."

Siobhán thanked her and slipped the brochure into her handbag. "How did he get so lucky, do you think?"

"Pardon?" The nun was starting to dislike the

conversation. It was only a matter of seconds before she shut down.

"My heart squeezes for all those young lads. Competing to get adopted," Siobhán said.

The nun nodded. "I suppose it was a bond over birds," the nun said. "We took them on a trip to the wildlife center, and Joseph was the only one who stepped up to allow one of those hawks to land on his fist."

"I didn't realize that's how they met," Siobhán said. It was Rose who had first fallen in love with Joseph. Hadn't one of their other suspects suggested Howard had made the introduction? Did that change the story Rose had tried to tell about the fighting siblings? Siobhán felt a squeeze on her arm and turned around to find Maria staring up at her.

"Tick, tock," she said. "An hour tops. Go do your snooping, and then we're hitting the pubs."

"There," Siobhán said when she and Aretta were alone, trying to spot Gladys and Linda. The sisters had just finished a bingo game, and they were headed toward the back of the cavernous room. Siobhán and Aretta kept their eye on them while still maintaining a distance that wouldn't raise any alarm. Soon Gladys and Linda exited onto a back patio.

"They'll see us," Aretta said as they looked out toward the sisters. The pair looked as if they were arguing.

"Upstairs," Siobhán said. "There's a balcony directly above them."

"Quickly," Aretta said.

Siobhán hurried toward the side exit. She was almost to the door when Father Kearney popped in front of her.

"Siobhán, how lovely to see you," he said. "It does the heart good to know you can enjoy yourself now and again." He turned to Aretta. "And you as well, Garda Dabiri." He nodded toward Siobhán. "Does she know your secret?"

"Secret?" Siobhán said, torn between the seconds they were wasting and whatever this secret was.

"I don't believe I have any secrets," Aretta said.

"Have you heard her sing?" Father Kearney asked Siobhán.

"No," Siobhán said, with a glance to Aretta.

"We're trying hard to get her to join the church choir. Work on that for me, will ya?"

"You bet, Father," Siobhán said. She headed for the exit.

"If you're looking for the ladies', it's the other exit," Father Kearney said, pointing across the room.

"Yes, yes," she said. "I'm just giving Aretta the tour."

"Wonderful," he said. "May I join you?"

"Of course," Siobhán said. "The apple tarts are probably gone by now anyway."

"Apple tarts?" Father Kearney lifted his head, and his eyes landed on the table across the way.

"I swear, they get better every year, and Bridie's absolutely outdone herself this time."

"I'll catch the next tour," Father Kearney said before hurrying away.

Siobhán picked up her speed, exiting the ballroom and heading for the winding stairs to the right. Aretta was right behind her.

"Are there really apple tarts?"

"There are always apple tarts," Siobhán said.

They crept onto the upstairs balcony. The grounds were dark save for a string of patio lights. From above, it was difficult to tell which one was Gladys and which one was Linda. The sisters were similar in height, and it was nearly impossible to tell them apart from the tops of their heads.

"Have you told anyone else?" one said to the other.

"I swear on me life, I haven't told a soul."

"What about Alan?"

"What about him?"

"Did he tell anyone?"

"I would have said no, but . . ."

"But?"

"Someone pushed him into that pit. What if it was Howard?"

Aretta and Siobhán exchanged a look. *Howard.*

"You swear to me it wasn't you."

Siobhán had finally identified who was who. The last statement came from Gladys.

"Me?" Linda said. "I could ask you the same thing."

"Why would I push our brother into the pit when I didn't know about your little secret until just now?"

"I have only your word that he didn't tell you, don't I?" Linda said.

"Calm down. We can't turn on each other. Not with guards moving in next door."

"That's another reason you need to change the will," Linda said.

"Don't start with that again."

"You can't do this to me. I'm the only family you have left."

"I have Benji."

"Benji," Linda spat. "He's the one who prevented me from telling the guards the truth."

Siobhán clenched her fists. Was that true? Was that why Linda had denied she had a confession?

"This is getting us nowhere," Gladys said. "We need to keep our mouths shut before that O'Sullivan girl gets wind of this."

Siobhán had an urge to jump off the balcony and land on Gladys's back. *That O'Sullivan girl.* This was one of the problems growing up in a small village. You could grow up. You could become the guardian of your four siblings and do a reasonably good job minding them. You could graduate top of your class at The Garda College in Templemore. You could return to your hometown with the title of garda. You could get married, buy a farm. Have children of your own. And you'd still always be *that O'Sullivan girl.*

"Siobhán?" Aretta touched her arm. Others were piling onto the patio now, and Linda and Gladys moved back inside. "What do you think they were on about?"

"I don't know," Siobhán said. "But it fits in with Linda admitting she had something to confess."

"Something to do with her brother Alan?"

"I'd say that's a good guess." Benji might have been telling the truth when he brought up Alan and the mysterious amount of money he seemed to have had just after Tommy disappeared.

Someone cleared their throat. Siobhán whirled

around to find Maria and Aisling fortified in the doorway.

"That's it," Maria said. "An hour is up. It's officially your hen night." She lifted a fresh bottle of Jameson.

"Where did you get that?" Siobhán asked.

"I brought it with me. What do you think?" Maria grinned. "The workday is over, and your hen night has officially begun."

If Siobhán O'Sullivan wanted to defend herself, the rationale would go something like this: She didn't do it very often. Every pendulum eventually swung to the opposite end of the spectrum. She wanted to be a good friend, and they wanted to celebrate her hen night. She wasn't going to be young forever, and did she really want to look back on her life and have zero stories of the crazy sessions she had with her best friends? But the simplest excuse was the one she would stick with. Maria and Aisling made her do it. . . .

It started with one pub. A few pints in and Siobhán was feeling relaxed. Even Aretta was lively and smiling, although at some point, she switched to pints of water. The second pub had a live rock band, and they danced in between pints. Shots were called, and by this point, Siobhán's hair was already down, and she was flying it. Aretta bowed out before the third pub, and Siobhán was slightly aware of clomping down the street, with Maria and Aisling each grabbing an arm, stumbling, and loudly singing the refrain "I'm Getting Married in the Morning." After the third pub (or possibly the fifth), they took the dancing to the streets again, and that was when Siobhán had a brilliant idea.

"Do you want to see my new house?"

"Yes!" Maria said, pointing to the off-license. "It's still open. I'll get another bottle of Jameson. We simply must have a drink in the new house to celebrate!"

When you must, you must. And in that floaty state she was in, where everything still felt good, where her head was like a helium balloon and her lungs were full of song, it sounded like the best idea Siobhán O'Sullivan had ever heard in her entire life.

Chapter 24

They traipsed from room to room, filling each with laughter as they downed more shots. The kitchen with the wood-burning stove, the sitting room with the wood beams and larger fireplace, each of the four bedrooms, and even the two bathrooms.

"It's ginormous!" Maria said, twirling around the sitting room with the half-empty bottle of Jameson.

"Ann and Ciarán will each get their own room, and then we'll have a room for the others to cycle through," Siobhán said. "And guests."

"To guests!" They drank.

At some stumbling, babbling point, Aisling ran outside, and Siobhán and Maria followed. In the distance the dairy barn had been reduced to something shadowy and formidable.

"Is it still a crime scene?" Aisling said.

"Technically, no," Siobhán said. "But . . ."

"I want to see it," Aisling said before Siobhán could figure out what to say to dissuade her. She was already skipping toward the building, her pale hair illuminated by yet another bright moon.

"Wait."

"We need a torch," Maria called after her.

Aisling stopped and held up her mobile phone. They both saw it light up. "We're sorted."

"I'm not going in there," Maria said. "Bad things happen in there."

"We'll go in another time," Siobhán said. "When the moon goes to bed."

Maria found this funny and howled with laughter, which started Siobhán howling with laughter. Maria switched to howling at the moon, and Siobhán joined in.

"If you were an owl, how many times would you hoot?" Siobhán asked.

Maria gave three hoots.

"No," Siobhán said. "That's bad."

"Let me try again." Maria was louder this time, but the number was still three.

"It's an omen. Three toots of an owl is a bad omen." *Death.*

"Toots!" Maria said. "You said 'toots'! That's gas. *Literally.*" She dissolved into a fresh fit of laughter as they stumbled after Aisling.

Siobhán yelled for Aisling to stop, but their friend continued her stride across the field to the dairy barn. Siobhán wanted to leave her on her own, absolve herself of the responsibility, but even in her drunken state, she knew this was not going to be possible.

"Just a quick look. She'll see there's nothing but

empty stalls and an old slurry pit," Maria said, picking up speed and tugging Siobhán along.

In the distance an owl hooted.

Siobhán stopped. "Did you hear that?"

"It's an owl," Maria said. "Don't mess with me."

"How many times did it call out?"

"Hoot," Maria said. "The word you're looking for is 'hoot.'"

"How many hoots?"

"How many hoots!" Maria laughed. "You're a hoot!" She hooted in imitation. *Three times.*

"That's what I thought," Siobhán said, dread rising in her as she and Maria stumbled after Aisling. "That's what I thought."

The cavernous dairy barn felt like a living, breathing thing, but its exhalations were icy cold. Aisling had the doors thrown open and stood a few feet from the entrance, shining the light of her mobile phone into long-abandoned stalls.

"Spooky," she said, drawing out the word and causing goose bumps to form on Siobhán's flesh.

"Let's get out of here," Maria said.

"I want to see the slurry pit." Aisling swung around, accidentally shining the light directly into their eyes.

Siobhán and Maria yelped in unison as colorful spots danced in front of Siobhán's eyes. She was drunk but was beginning to realize what an eejit she'd been, was already admonishing herself for the price she was going to pay in the morning. And she didn't know if it was the owl or the bright moon juxtaposed with the dark shadows in the dairy barn, but her little voice was insisting this was a very bad idea.

"Are the bodies still in it?" Maria squawked.

"No, of course not," Siobhán said. "Not a trace of anything left."

"Then let's go," Aisling said, but this time instead of tromping ahead, she was rooted to the spot.

"It's dangerous," Siobhán said. "If you fall in and conk your head . . ."

"We'll walk slow," Aisling said. "You lead the way."

Aisling's eyes were alight with alcohol and mischief, and Siobhán knew the quickest way out of this would be to go through it.

"We'll walk slow. There's a light above the slurry pit. I'll need to find the string. One quick look and we're out. Agreed?"

"Agreed," Aisling said, holding up two fingers.

"I'm going to wait outside," Maria said. She turned to go. Siobhán caught her arm.

"I don't think you should." There was still a killer on the loose, and she couldn't get the owl out of her mind, hooting three times, a warning of death. "Please. We have to stay together." Their footsteps echoed in the large space.

"It's freezing," Maria said, clinging to Siobhán's arm, as they proceeded toward the slurry pit.

"Do you think the ghosts of Tommy Caffrey and Alan O'Leary are here?" Aisling called out.

"No," Siobhán said.

"I don't like this," Maria said.

"We're so sorry you were murdered," Aisling called, her voice rising with her confidence. "But Siobhán O'Sullivan is going to find your killer."

"We should have never gone to the fourth pub," Maria said.

"Was it four?" Siobhán said. "I thought three."

"Six pubs in all," Aisling called out in front of them as nervous laughter bubbled from her. "We should give the ghosts a shot." Aisling hoisted the whiskey bottle, and the dredges sloshed when she stumbled. "To the cows who lived here, and the ghosts who haunt!" She began to moo, her voice echoing throughout the structure.

"We definitely should have stopped at three pubs," Maria said.

"We're almost to the slurry pit," Siobhán said. "Slow down, and don't go through that doorway in the back."

At least the slatted shed had somewhat of a separate entrance. It reminded Siobhán that none of their victims had found themselves in front of the pit by accident. Entering the slatted shed was a purposeful action. But how was it that both men had stood at the exact same corner? And why? Was there something so compelling about a cement pit that one couldn't help but stand at the edge and stare into it? Given that was exactly what Aisling wanted to do, maybe there was simply something about human nature that compelled one to stare into the abyss.

They were nearly at the entrance to the shed when a loud clank sounded behind them. Siobhán froze and felt Aisling and Maria stop short behind her. "Did you hear that?"

"Yes," they said in unison. They stilled themselves to listen.

Next came a squeak and a groan. It was the sound of the main barn doors being closed.

"Someone is shutting us in here," Maria said.

Siobhán's heart was beating so loud, it sounded like a drum in her skull. Maria's fingernails dug into Siobhán's arm.

"Who is that?" Aisling said, facing the back of the barn, as if she was afraid to turn around. Fear had brought with it a sobering awareness, stronger than any hair of the dog or strong cup of coffee.

"Stay calm," Siobhán said.

They heard another sound, and Siobhán knew the doors were being latched into place. Locked. Maria had been correct. Someone was locking them in. Siobhán had to fight against waves of panic welling up inside her. Without her uniform or backup or a clear head, she was at a major disadvantage.

"Are you doing this?" Aisling said. "Is this a joke?"

"I need you to slowly move toward me and give me your phone," Siobhán said in a quiet, calm voice. Inside, she felt like screaming. "And take off your shoes."

"Our shoes?" Aisling sounded terrified now.

"Quickly. We don't want to give away our position."

For all their stubbornness, this time her friends listened, and the three girls removed their shoes. Maria and Aisling held theirs awkwardly.

"We'll come back for them," Siobhán said. "Leave them here. In case we need to run." Heels and boots dropped to the floor. Siobhán prayed none of them would step on anything sharp, but she also knew this killer thrived on the element of surprise. They needed every advantage *they* could get.

"There's no reception in here," Aisling said. "I don't have a signal."

"I still need it," Siobhán said. "For the light." Aisling shoved her phone into Siobhán's hands. "I need the pair of ye to stay quiet and stay behind me."

"I don't want to die," Maria said. "I don't want to die."

"We're not going to die," Siobhán said. "But I need you to get behind me." Aisling moved quickly, huddling with Maria behind her.

"Now what?" Maria said.

The back entrance, the door Gladys liked to sneak in and out of, was closer to them than the front barn doors, but presumably, the person who had locked them in knew about this door as well. Would he or she expect them to run for the back entrance? Or was this person headed there this very second? The back door did not have a board to slide across, but Siobhán had never examined the door closely, and there could be a way to lock it that she had yet to learn.

"What are we doing?" Maria whispered, panic evident in her voice.

Siobhán shut off the light of the phone, making her friends squeal. *Mistake.* "Quiet," Siobhán said. "Darkness is our friend."

"I don't like the dark," Aisling whispered.

"This was your idea," Maria scolded Aisling.

"Whoever it is, is probably running away," Siobhán said.

"Probably?" Maria said.

"I need you two to stay here. I'm going to check out an exit door."

"We're going where you're going," Maria said. "You said yourself."

"Stay behind me," Siobhán repeated. She hated the thought of using the phone light, in case it was somehow visible from the outside, which sounded crazy. But they were near the slurry pit, and its walls were slatted. The light from the moon and their own torch made them visible, and if the intruder was standing near the slats, he or she would know exactly where to find them. But standing still was not an option. Anger coursed through Siobhán. If only she had her wits about her. Was this the killer or someone else? Perhaps the killer's habit of visiting his or her crime scene hadn't stopped with the removal of the bones. Habits were hard to break.

Siobhán checked the signal on the phone. A single bar indicated low reception. There were probably spots in the barn that had better reception than others, but discovering one of them could waste valuable time. Her first priority was keeping them safe, and if someone meant them immediate harm, there was no way the guards could get there in time. They were on their own, and every second counted.

"Who has the whiskey?" Siobhán asked.

"Now?" Maria said.

"It's a weapon."

"Here." Aisling shoved the bottle at her.

Siobhán felt better just holding it. She shone

the light of the phone on the floor, trying her best to angle it away from the slurry shed. They inched their way to the back door. When they reached it, Siobhán stopped and tried to listen for any sound behind it.

"I'm going to slowly open it and shine the light," Siobhán said. "If anyone is there, I'm hitting them over the head with the bottle. That's when you run."

"Where?" Maria asked.

"Run for the Burns house," Siobhán said. "Have them call the guards."

Just as Siobhán reached for the door, they heard another sound. A click and a pop. Suddenly a light blared on. They shrieked and whirled around. The lightbulb above the slurry pit was on, swinging violently back and forth. Below it, the concrete tomb came into view, as if welcoming them into its depths. Maria threw herself at the door.

"Wait." Siobhán grabbed her. "Don't." The phone slipped out of her hand and hit the cement floor.

"I didn't mean it about the ghosts," Aisling said. "This is all my fault."

Siobhán readied the bottle of Jameson, and with her other hand, she found the knob and pushed on the door. It didn't budge. The light continued to swing.

"I can't do ghosts," Maria said. "I can't do ghosts."

"It's not a ghost," Siobhán said. It was much worse. Someone had reached the light string through the slats in the shed. That was the only explanation. It meant whoever it was, he or she was circling them on the outside. "Maybe someone is just trying to stall us so he or she can get away," Siobhán said, not believing it for a second.

"What's that smell?" Aisling said, sending another wave of shivers up Siobhán's spine.

"Petrol," Maria said. "Does anyone else smell petrol?"

Chapter 25

As the smell of petrol permeated the space, instinct kicked in and Siobhán's fear was replaced with white-hot rage. She dropped to the ground and pawed around until she found the phone. It was cracked but still working. She shoved it at Maria. "You two move around the barn until you find a signal and then call nine-nine-nine."

This time Maria and Aisling didn't hesitate and took off. Siobhán kicked the back door. Pain roared through her foot. She'd been hasty removing her boots. "Hey," she yelled. She didn't know if the person could hear her, but she was going to give it her all. "I'm Garda Siobhán O'Sullivan, and the rest of the guards are on their way. Stop what you're doing right now." She heard a swish, as if more petrol was being tossed onto the building. "Maria. Aisling. Run to the front doors."

"I haven't found a signal," Maria called back.

They were no longer trying to be quiet. The goal had urgently morphed into one of escape.

"Front doors. Run." The three of them took off at a crouch for the front of the barn.

She could hear their frantic breaths and pounding footsteps, and soon she heard a crackling noise from behind them. It wasn't long before she smelled the unmistakable odor of smoke. She'd given away their location, and whoever was on the outside had started the fire at the back door. How long before it reached the front? If anyone was awake in the Burns house, they would see the flames. She could only pray someone was awake. They reached the front barn doors, and although Siobhán knew it would probably be useless, the three of them used their bodies as battering rams and hit the doors as hard as they could with their shoulders and hips. The doors bounced slightly but did not give.

Siobhán tried to remember everything she knew about the barn. Were there any weak points? "The slatted shed," she said out loud. If there was a single board loose, they could create an opening and at least lift Maria or Aisling through it. But the slatted shed was near the back entrance, where now fire was licking along the wall, the red and orange flames hazy behind clouds of rolling smoke. More often than not, it was smoke inhalation that killed victims of fire.

Siobhán remembered seeing a shovel in one of the stalls on a previous visit. "Listen to me carefully," she said. "Remove any loose piece of clothing and wrap it around your nose and mouth, even if it's your dress. When we get closer to the fire, drop to the ground and crawl. We need to find the shovel in one of these stalls to the right, and we need to get into the slurry shed."

"What?" Maria said. "It's on fire."

"Not yet. Listen. The shed is slatted. We're going to need to break through one of the boards. Maria, you're the smallest. I can give you a shove through."

"Great," Maria said, her voice dripping with panic and sarcasm.

"I'll keep looking for a signal," Aisling said.

"It's too late," Siobhán said. "We need the light of the phone. Don't think. Just focus." Aisling handed her the phone. Aisling had a scarf to wrap around her face, Maria had a vest, and Siobhán was forced to take off her dress.

"A hen night that ends with your dress off is one to remember," Maria said. Siobhán was grateful she still had her sense of humor.

They hustled and found the shovel in the third stall. They were on the opposite end of the barn from the fire, but it was spreading fast. It had yet to reach the slatted shed, but it was only a matter of minutes.

"Run to the back wall on the left side," Siobhán said, shining the light. Pumped by adrenaline, the girls ran. They reached the slatted shed and entered. Smoke was starting to billow in. Siobhán maneuvered the shovel and began jabbing at boards.

"Feel around and see if any are loose," she said.

It felt like forever as Siobhán jabbed the shovel at each opening and the girls shook the slats to see if any were loose. Smoke curled around them, making them cough.

"Here," Aisling said from the right back corner. "It's loose."

It was the worst option, as this slat was so close to the fire, but if they could tear it loose, maybe the one next to it would loosen. Siobhán didn't waste any time. "Move back," she called. She swung the shovel, focusing all her rage into it. On the third try, she heard a crack, and the light of the moon poured in. In the distance, they heard sirens. Someone had called the volunteer fire department. *Heroes.* But they still had to get out themselves before it was too late.

"Maria, here," Siobhán called. Maria was already there. Siobhán laced her fingers together to make a step, and Maria wasted no time placing her foot into Siobhán's upturned palm. Using strength she didn't know she had, Siobhán lifted, and soon Maria was halfway out of the shed. Siobhán's arms and legs shook as she held the position. "On the next heave, jump and roll," Siobhán said. "Then run to the front doors."

"Jump and roll," Maria repeated, fear in her voice. "Jump and roll."

Siobhán lifted once more, summoning every ounce of strength she could, and when Maria was hoisted high enough, she jumped. Siobhán closed her eyes as Aisling prayed beside her. Soon they heard a thud.

"I'm okay," Maria yelled. "I'll run to the front."

"Good woman," Siobhán called. Then she and Aisling crouched down and ran back into the dairy barn. A full half of the barn was now on fire, the flames growing more confident and enraged by the second. They could no longer see in front of them, and Siobhán no longer had the phone. "Drop and crawl," Siobhán said. "Get to the front doors."

"Worse hen night ever," Aisling said as they crawled as fast as they could toward the barn doors.

"Or the best," Siobhán said, hoping to keep them distracted.

The sirens drew closer. Siobhán heard Maria sliding the board away from the front doors when her internal alarm bells rang.

"Maria," she yelled.

"I almost have it," Maria said.

"Don't shove it open all at once. We're in danger." A rush of oxygen could fan the flames and overwhelm them.

"What should I do?"

"How close are the fire trucks?"

"I don't see them yet."

"Count to three, then open the doors just far enough for us to squeeze out, and run."

Aisling was still praying behind her. "When we get an opening, run as fast as you can," Siobhán said. "As fast as you can."

Aisling nodded, her lips still moving in prayer, her eyes wide with terror.

"Ready?" Maria said. "One, two, three." She slid the doors open, slow and steady, and just the width of a person.

Siobhán and Aisling bolted out, and then the three of them ran for their lives.

"You could have been killed."

They were back from hospital, where all three

women had been checked out and released. Thankfully, due to covering their noses and mouths and getting out before the entire dairy barn was engulfed in flames, none of them, bar the dairy barn and their shoes, had suffered any serious damage. Siobhán was laid up at the bistro, on the comfy chair near the unlit fireplace. It was way too soon to see flames of any type. Macdara alternated between pacing and hovering over her, driving her a bit mental. She was on forced leave and finding it difficult to relax, and her throbbing head and queasy stomach were of no help. She was itching to get back out there. Someone had tried to kill her and her two best friends. This was personal now.

"That's the nature of the job," she said, trying to sound as if she was completely fine.

"It was supposed to be a girls' night out!"

He had a point there. "Would you please stop pacing?"

Macdara sighed and threw himself into the chair across from her. "It's not like you to take friends to a crime scene."

"Apparently, it's like me when I'm full to the gills with alcohol."

"Speaking of which, how's the head?"

Siobhán groaned. "About what I deserve."

"You saved your friends' lives. I think you should lighten up on yourself," James said, coming into the dining room from the kitchen. He sat a large Irish breakfast on the small table in front of her.

She gently pushed it away. "I can't look at food."

"It will help your hangover," Macdara said.

She doubted it. She couldn't even drink her cappuccino. "Enough stalling. What did you find at the scene?"

"Nothing," Macdara said. "Not even an empty petrol can."

"Who called nine-nine-nine?"

"Linda O'Leary. Apparently, she got up in the middle of the night to use the restroom and saw the flames."

Siobhán nodded. "The call came from the house?"

"From her mobile."

"Which means she's not excluded as a suspect."

"Correct. Her mobile would have pinged off the same mobile towers whether she was in her house or on our property."

"Nothing on the ground where the dairy barn used to be?"

"They're still sifting through it, but nothing so far."

"I guess that's one thing off our to-do list," Siobhán said. "We didn't need a gigantic dairy barn anyway."

"The slurry pit is still there."

"Lovely." She sighed. Although perhaps she should be glad. Had the slurry pit not been there, there wouldn't have been a slatted shed, and thus escape may have been impossible.

"The killer keeps returning to the dairy barn," Siobhán said. "He or she either planned on burning it that night, and we just happened to be in it . . ."

"Or the killer was following you," Macdara finished.

She nodded. "We did see Gladys and Linda at the charity event, but I don't think they saw us."

"You don't think. But they may have."

"We didn't go straight home."

"I know," Macdara said. "Six pubs, was it?"

Siobhán gave him a look.

He held up his hands. "I'm not judging. You, of all people, deserve to let loose once in a while."

"I believe I've made up for lost time," she said.

"You're my hero." This came from Gráinne, who lowered her fashion magazine long enough for Siobhán to see the smirk. "But seriously, I'd die if you died, so just . . . *don't.*"

"Noted," Siobhán said. "I'll do me best."

The sound of multiple footsteps trudging downstairs stole their attention right before Ciarán and Ann entered the room and barreled toward Siobhán. They threw themselves on her like they used to when they were much smaller and lighter than they were now. And even though she could barely breathe, she engaged in the group hug.

"Where's Eoin?" she said when they finally peeled off her.

"He left early, dressed in a suit," Gráinne said. "He's up to something."

"Listen," Macdara said, "I want you to know the barn was insured. We'll be able to add a little to our nest egg. We could use it to do any remodeling you want with the house."

Siobhán took Macdara's hands. "Maybe a little sprucing, a little paint, shine up the floors, and a new kitchen. But the bones are charming."

Macdara grinned. "I agree."

"In fact, I'd love to go there right now."

Macdara looked at James. James sighed, removed his wallet, and handed Macdara twenty euro. "No," Macdara said, pocketing the money. "You're to keep your arse in the bistro all day and all night, and maybe even tomorrow and the rest of the year."

"Not a chance," she said. She too looked at James. "I'm surprised you don't know me better."

"I do," James said with a grin. "I just wanted to keep Macdara from losing the plot. Distracted him with a little bet. He was nearly jumping out of his skin when we heard what had happened to you. We all were."

It felt odd to be the one who was the center of concern. Usually, she was the one mothering all of them. "I'm okay. If you take anything from this, it's that I can take care of myself."

"We know that," Macdara said. "But no one is invincible. When I think how close you came . . ." His voice thickened, and he covered it with a cough.

"We're dealing with someone very dangerous," Siobhán said. "Whoever was out there, he or she knew we were inside. They slid a board across the doors. And they had no problem letting the three of us perish." *Burned alive.* This wasn't an ordinary killer. This was a psychopath.

"I want to lock all our suspects up until we figure this out," Macdara said. "If only I had the power to do it."

"We need to work up a profile," Siobhán said. "This isn't an ordinary killer. Do any of them have a history of arson?"

"Garda Dabiri is looking into that as we speak," Macdara said, rising from his seat. "And speaking of which, I have to get back to work."

"She must be slightly hungover too."

"She's not," Macdara said. "She drank moderately unlike some people."

"Is that so?"

Macdara nodded. "At least one out of the four of ye used the sense that God gave ye."

Siobhán groaned. "I'll take me cap off to her when I'm well enough to put it back on again. I'm a right eejit."

"I'll say," Gráinne said.

Chapter 26

The next day at the garda station, Macdara popped his head in the door of Siobhán's office. He'd tried to get her to stay home one more day, but she was having none of it. "If you've sufficiently recovered from your hen night, Jeanie Brady would like us to meet her at what's left of the dairy barn."

Siobhán nodded and slipped a few more headache tablets into her gob. She washed them down with water, and they were off. By the time Siobhán and Macdara were standing in the spot where the dairy barn used to be, Siobhán thought she was doing a remarkable job of holding it together. Charred wood and earth spread out in front of them, and it hit Siobhán hard. How easily they could have been part of this wreckage, how lucky they were to have escaped unharmed.

"You took a fright," Jeanie Brady said the second she laid eyes on her.

Siobhán bit back tears and nodded.

Before she knew what was happening, Jeanie Brady had her arms wrapped around her. When she pulled away, she cleared her throat. "Thank heavens you're alright," Jeanie said.

"Yes," Siobhán squeaked. She couldn't help but think she had a few angels on the other side who had looked out for them that night.

Jeanie hoisted up a bag at her side and pulled out a skull. "He's plastic," she said. She moved his jaw up and down. "Are we clear to walk to the slurry pit?"

"Yes," Macdara said. "The entire scene has been combed through. We'll hear their findings as soon as they're available."

"The skeleton has formally been identified as that of Tommy Caffrey," Jeanie said. "We were lucky we had an idea of who he was. The dental records were a match."

They moved toward the slurry pit, and as they did, flashbacks of the smell of smoke and petrol, and running for their lives, invaded Siobhán's memory. Was she now too damaged to continue investigating? She'd never felt this vulnerable. But she didn't want anyone to know, for Macdara would remove her from the case immediately. As it was, he barely let her out of his sight. When they reached the slurry pit, Jeanie held up the plastic skull once again. In her other hand, she held a red marker.

"They had lethal injuries on roughly the same spot." She circled the left temple with the red marker. "A blow here." She looked down at the slurry pit.

Already blackened from fifty years of muck, it didn't appear any different than it had before the fire. "From the bloodstains and the positioning of the blow to the left temple, we've done some calculations." She put a red chip on the right-hand corner of the slurry pit. "Both victims would have been standing about here." She backed up. "The killer would have approached at a sideways angle and pushed . . ." She mimed pushing someone, then took the plastic skull and hurried to the back left corner. "Taken off guard, they would have tumbled quickly in this direction, thus hitting their head on this corner."

Siobhán and Macdara stared. *Playing the angles.* "One of our suspects, Howard, was going to open a snooker club with the first victim," Macdara said.

"And that is the exact spot where there was a hanging bulb," Siobhán said, pointing to the spot above the slurry pit where the light used to hang. "Maybe they happened to stand there because that's where there was the most light." Or was that still too random, too coincidental? "Howard Dunn is also the man who claimed he had thirty thousand quid stolen by Tommy Caffrey. What if that part was true? If Tommy stole Howard's money and was caught red-handed . . . that's a powerful motive for murder."

Macdara picked up on the thread. "Then Howard takes back his satchel of cash and claims Tommy ran away with it. He never started a snooker club, so in this scenario, what did he do with the money?"

"Perhaps he gave it to Alan O'Leary," Siobhán said. "To save the farm."

"Why would he do that?" Macdara asked.

"I don't know," Siobhán said. "Maybe Alan saw something. Maybe Alan blackmailed Howard."

"If that's the case, why would Howard kill Alan after all this time?" Macdara asked.

"Perhaps when Tommy's remains were found, Alan, in his old age, wanted to repent. *Confess.*"

"It is fascinating to listen to the pair of ye," Jeanie Brady said. "But we'll need more evidence to support these theories."

"What are the chances that two men would stand in the exact same spot?" Macdara asked.

"I've been puzzling that out myself," Jeanie said. "And all I can tell you is I don't think it was a coincidence. Perhaps Siobhán is onto something about the light. However, in my mind, that's still a stretch."

"Did you find a measuring tape in Alan's pockets?" Siobhán asked.

Jeanie shook her head. "No."

They hadn't found one in the pit either. Benji had mentioned hearing Alan on the phone, talking about a snooker table, and then he walked out of the house with a measuring tape. If that was the case, where was it? Siobhán stared at the red chip Jeanie had placed at the corner of the pit.

"The gold arcade tokens," she exclaimed. "Two tokens. Two victims."

"And unlike that red chip, the gold tokens, when placed under the lightbulb, would have been bright and shiny," Macdara added. "That has to be it."

"Imagine seeing a gold coin at the edge of a slurry pit? It would have been impossible not to approach it."

"I knew you would work it out." Jeanie grinned.

"You already figured the same," Siobhán said.

Jeanie nodded. "That's why I brought the red chip. See if it would nudge you in the same direction."

"Were you able to tell if one coin has been in the slurry pit longer than the other?" Siobhán asked.

"It's not scientific," Jeanie said. "But yes, one had many more layers of dried slurry on it than the other."

"Do you think one was squirreled away in Tommy's pocket?" Siobhán said.

"No," Jeanie said. "I think both were placed at the edge of the slurry pit. Fifty years apart."

"The same killer," Siobhán said.

"Most likely," Jeanie agreed.

They had just moved from possible to probable. It wasn't perfect, but it was progress.

"I can't wait to get rid of this pit," Macdara said. "I'm calling the removal company today."

"Don't birds of prey like nice shiny things?" The soft voice came from behind. Aretta stood at a polite distance.

"What are you thinking?" Siobhán asked.

"Maybe Rose Burns thought it up," Aretta said. "It's in her wheelhouse."

Macdara nodded. "At least we can now go back to our suspects and use this knowledge to our advantage. But we have to make sure we don't mention this to anyone. This is something only the killer knows. And I want to keep that advantage as long as possible."

Siobhán began to pace. It struck her how lucky she was that she had an entire field in which to do this. Nothing helped her think through a case like walking it out. "Give me a minute," she said as she wandered away from the group. She started from the beginning. The morning of the wedding. Tommy was in his tux. He spent the night supposedly in his room at the pub. *The morning of the wedding he wakes up* . . . Wouldn't he be getting dressed at the church? Did something bring him from the church to the dairy barn? *Someone?* Or did he get dressed for the wedding in his room, then come to the dairy barn?

A common thread about Tommy circled back to her like a boomerang. Tommy was a rebel. Not a rule follower. Definitely not a rule follower. She hurried back to the group. "I don't think Joseph spending the night with Gladys deterred Tommy from spending the night."

"Pardon?" Macdara stepped forward.

"I think Tommy broke the rules and spent the night with Gladys, despite her having Joseph for the night."

Macdara rubbed his chin. "Did any of us think to ask her?"

"No, but she didn't volunteer it either, and we did ask for her movements the day before," Aretta said.

"Caught in a lie," Macdara said.

"She's not the only suspect who is lying," Siobhán said.

"Where are you going with this?" Macdara asked. "He spends the night and then what? He decides to wander around an old dairy barn in his tux?"

"This means it's morning. He wouldn't have worn his tux to bed." Siobhán began circling the slurry pit as she tried to imagine it. "Benji said Tommy smoked, but he was hiding his bad habit from Gladys."

"If you're saying the killer followed Tommy to the barn, doesn't that leave us with either Benji or Gladys?" Macdara asked.

"Perhaps," Siobhán said. "Or perhaps someone had agreed to meet Tommy early that morning or had been summoned."

"Summoned," Macdara said, scratching his chin. "Take me through it."

"Tommy rises early that morning, changes into his tux, and comes out to sneak in a smoke." She stared at the red chip at the corner of the pit. "Did we find any trace of mints or gum in Tommy's clothing?"

Aretta took out the station iPad and scrolled. "There were fragments of gum wrappers found among the remains."

"It could have been any of the lads who worked the barn," Macdara said.

"They were entwined with the clothing fragments," Jeanie said.

"Not conclusive but close," Macdara said.

Siobhán nodded. It was close enough for her, as it fit the theory that was emerging. "He came out to smoke, and Gladys, if we believe her earlier statement, did not know that Tommy smoked."

"The killer knew about his habit," Macdara said, catching on. "He or she had pre-placed the token at the corner of the pit."

"In fact, Gladys was insistent that Tommy didn't smoke," Siobhán said. "I felt she was sincere."

"Or she doth protest too much?" Jeanie Brady suggested.

"I remember the exchange," Macdara said. "I would concur that she seemed very reactive to Benji's suggestion that Tommy smoked."

"Tommy smoked," Jeanie Brady said. "Believe me. I've seen his lungs."

"I don't know how he could hide cigarette smoke from her," Aretta said. "The smell is so strong."

"People believe what they want to believe," Siobhán said. "The smell of smoke could easily be blamed on another lad. And if he took care to use gum or mints, it's possible he deceived her."

"What exactly are you saying?" Jeanie Brady asked.

"Setting aside that Gladys could be deceiving us, if she did not know that he smoked, then Gladys isn't our killer."

Jeanie frowned. "I don't follow."

"The killer was aware of Tommy's habits, and my guess is Tommy regularly snuck into the dairy barn to have a smoke."

"Ah," Jeanie Brady said. "And I didn't even tie one on the other night."

Siobhán laughed, then touched her poor head. "Rose and Benji would have returned the next morning to pick up Joseph before the wedding."

"And Benji knew that Tommy smoked," Macdara said. "Which meant he probably knew when he smoked and where he smoked."

"And Rose is familiar with how irresistible shiny objects are," Aretta stated once again. "Like crows attracted to shiny things."

"As the crow flies," Jeanie said.

"And don't forget Howard," Siobhán said. "He would have known Tommy smoked, he would have tons of arcade tokens from the pub where he worked, and he believed Tommy had stolen his bag of cash."

"Linda O'Leary," Aretta said. "We overheard her telling Gladys she wants back in the family will."

"For a second there, I thought we were getting somewhere," Macdara said. "But any one of them could have done it. Several could be in on it together."

"I feel like we're right back to the beginning," Siobhán said.

"Circling," Aretta agreed. "Like hawks."

Jeanie Brady sighed and cradled her plastic skulls. "People feel sorry for me, having to work with the dead," she said. "But it's so much easier than dealing with the living."

Chapter 27

❧

Siobhán entered Interview Room #1 prepared for battle. Linda O'Leary was not leaving this room until she spilled her secret. Aretta was already seated, with her Biro poised over her notebook. "Linda will be here soon, and as the Americans like to say, we need to play hardball," Siobhán said.

"Hardball." Aretta's tongue stuck out of the corner of her mouth as she wrote the word down. "And how do I do this?" Siobhán was going to let Aretta take the lead. First, Siobhán was too raw from the trauma of nearly being burned alive with her besties, and second, she figured her best approach would be to sit and glare.

"It's all in the attitude," Siobhán said. "Your attitude must convey that you know beyond a shadow of a doubt that Linda is a cold-blooded killer."

Laughter spilled from Aretta, and she slapped her hand over her mouth to stop it.

Siobhán raised an eyebrow. "Something the matter?"

"It is hard to imagine someone with the name Linda O'Leary being a cold-blooded killer. Her initials are LOL." Aretta laughed again, then tried to bring herself under control. "Hardball."

"Let's go over what we know. According to Rose, the O'Leary family owed a loan to the bank and their entire farm was on the line."

"Do we have any of these old records?"

Siobhán sighed. "The bank in question is no longer in operation. I've assigned a garda to try to track down what happened to the bank records, or if we can locate an employee. But until we have that information in hand, you just have to behave as if we do."

"Got it."

"You could even suggest that we have it."

Aretta nodded. "Hardball."

"Rose and Benji, for that matter, suggested that shortly after Tommy did a runner, the loan was satisfied by an extra payment of what today would be known as twenty thousand euro."

Aretta whistled. "Close to the amount in the missing satchel."

"In addition, Benji said that the family bought a new tractor and some bits, suggesting they had come into some money."

"Siobhán O'Sullivan does not like coincidences," Aretta said matter-of-factly.

Siobhán laughed. "Cheeky. But correct."

"Could it have been Alan who stole the money and paid off the loan without his sisters' knowledge?"

"It could have been any one of the O'Learys, or it could have been all of them in it together, but if we are somehow able to get ahold of the records and either Gladys or Linda cannot account for this payment, it's not going to look good for them."

"And if we don't get proof of this transaction?"

"I think we should suggest that we either have the records or are very close to getting them."

"Just to be clear. You want me to lie," Aretta said.

"Bank records don't just disappear, and we're in a race against a killer here."

"I don't mind lying, I just want us to be clear." Aretta jotted down a note.

"If we appear *confident* about the records, that should do the trick." There was another possibility that had been churning in Siobhán's mind, and it complicated matters, and that was the theory that the money was a bribe. What if Alan had found the killer with the satchel of money, and in order to keep him quiet, the killer had let Alan keep the money to save the family farm? This was why they needed to play hardball: one of their suspects was going to have to turn on the others. Family bonds were strong, but when it came to spending the rest of one's life in jail for a crime he or she didn't commit, those bonds could be severed.

"I think you're a natural at hardball," Aretta said. "Is there a reason you want me to conduct the second interview?"

"Because I am going to sit beside you and simply glare at Linda," Siobhán said. "I'm hoping to rattle this confession out of her."

"Is it wrong to say I am looking forward to this?"

"No. It means you're going to be good at your job."

A knock sounded at the door.

"Come in," Siobhán said. The door opened, and a young clerk poked in his head.

"Linda O'Leary is here."

"Give us twenty minutes and send her in," Siobhán said.

He nodded and closed the door.

"Twenty minutes?" Aretta said.

"I want her anxious," Siobhán said, and Aretta made a note of it.

"Confession?" Linda said, throwing a glance at Siobhán before her eyes returned to Aretta. "I think you misheard me, Garda O'Sullivan. I don't have anything to confess. Ask Father Kearney." She gave a little laugh, which neither Aretta nor Siobhán returned. "Perhaps you need your hearing checked?" she ventured. "Did you know that people have lost their hearing because they had bugs crawl into their ears at night?"

"No," Aretta said. "Are you exaggerating for comical affect?"

Linda frowned. "Am I what now?"

"Are you trying to deflect your guilt by using humor?" Aretta asked with a straight face.

Linda shook her head. "No. It's a real thing. If you don't believe me, look it up. I always check for bugs underneath me pillows at night." She threw a glance to Siobhán. "You'll be doing the same once you live out at the farm, so you will."

"I'll be sure to keep an eye out for homeless bugs at night," Siobhán said. *And murderers hiding near slurry pits . . .*

Linda shifted nervously in her seat, licked her lips, and glanced to the door, then the clock on the wall. It was obvious she wanted to be anywhere but here. "I believe you misunderstood me when I said I had something to confess," Linda said. "Guards make me nervous. I might have misspoken."

Aretta turned to Siobhán and lowered her head, as if what she was about to say was between them. "I'm making great progress on retrieving the records from the bank."

"Really?" Siobhán said. "Even though they've been closed for over a decade?"

"Records last forever," Aretta said with a laugh and a shake of the head. "Records will outlast us all."

"Imagine that," Siobhán said. "And I'm sure way back when, if a loan was suddenly paid off in cash—say twenty thousand quid to save a family farm—and a few days prior that exact amount was stolen from a murder victim . . ."

"He wasn't a murder victim at the time," Linda blurted out.

They stopped and stared at Linda. Sweat trickled from her brow, but she clamped her lips shut. "He was," Siobhán said. "He was lying dead in a slurry pit."

"We didn't know that," Linda said under her breath.

"The killer knew," Aretta said as she opened a

thick file in front of her. In it were all the takeaway menus for the local eateries. "Shortly after Tommy went missing with an alleged satchel filled with thirty thousand quid, or euro, as we know the currency today, the O'Leary family paid off a bank loan in the amount of twenty thousand quid."

"Isn't that something," Siobhán said. "They also bought a tractor and some bits. Coincidence?"

"Now you're just repeating yourselves," Linda said. "Coincidences happen every day."

"I suppose it would be a coincidence if the payment had a traceable source. But if that payment was made with sudden cash . . . well, I don't believe that would be a coincidence, do you?" The pitch of Aretta's voice was the perfect balance of confidence and swagger.

Linda squirmed in her seat.

"That is a stretch of the imagination," Siobhán agreed.

"I had nothing to do with it," Linda said. "Nothing."

Siobhán noted she said 'I', not 'we.' "Did Alan have anything to do with it?"

Linda frowned and crossed herself. "Leave my brother's memory at peace, will ye?"

"Who paid the twenty thousand?" Aretta asked.

Linda shrugged. "I suppose it was me father. Do you really think he let his daughters into the personal finances when it came to the farm?" She shook her head, as if she thought they were out of their minds.

"What about his son?" Siobhán asked. "Is it possible your brother Alan might have paid off this loan?" *With money from a stolen satchel?*

Linda wouldn't make eye contact. "My brother is dead. I will not let you sully his name."

"Even if telling the truth would help us catch his killer?" Aretta said.

"I can find a reason to keep you here for a while," Siobhán said. "If you intend on being stubborn."

"What reason?" Linda's face was now a deep shade of red, the same color as Gladys's fabricated cherry tarts. *The family that lies together . . .* "I'm the one who called nine-nine-nine and saved your life," she said, with a stern look directed at Siobhán.

A flash of anger rose in Siobhán. "We saved our own lives, but yes, I do appreciate you calling nine-nine-nine. Are you usually up so late, spying on my farm?"

Linda pounded the table. "I want to make a phone call. I want a solicitor."

"A solicitor," Aretta said. She looked at Siobhán. "I guess you were right about her, and I was wrong."

"What do you mean?" Linda sputtered, her eyes pinging between them.

Siobhán sighed and gave her head a pitying shake. "I told her you'd tell us anything we needed to know because, of course, you want to catch a killer. Especially one who nearly burned three young women alive."

Linda's mouth dropped open. "You can't possibly think I would do such a thing." She hid her face in her hands. Siobhán felt a squeeze of pity, one she must not give in to. Catching a killer had to take priority. This wasn't a job for the faint of heart. If Linda turned out to be innocent, Siobhán would smooth things over after justice had been served.

"Before this meeting I would have agreed that it was impossible," Aretta said. "But this is a serious interview on a serious matter, and here you are playing games with us and, quite frankly, lying." Aretta crossed her arms. "I do not like liars."

"I'm not a liar." Tears came to Linda's eyes; she fumbled through her handbag for a tissue. "From my recollection a distant family member living in London came through with the money."

"I thought you said it was your father," Siobhán said.

"Me father received the money from a distant relative."

"I'm afraid that doesn't match the bank records," Siobhán said, glancing at the takeaway menu for Jade's, the Chinese restaurant near the garda station. She had a yearning for some dumplings. "It had to be yourself or one of your siblings who paid off the loan."

"Heavens." Sweat rolled down Linda's face on both sides, and her tissue was nearly dissolved.

"Do you need a break?" Aretta asked. "Because we've got a lot more to cover with you." She slid a box of tissues nearer to Linda. Linda took one out and dabbed her face, then held the scrunched tissue in a clenched fist.

"Go on, so. You think I have all the answers. I do not. If that money came from Tommy's missing satchel, I swear to ye I had nothing to do with it, I had no knowledge of it, and I did not murder anyone to get it."

"When Garda O'Sullivan caught you breaking and entering her home, she says you stated that you had something to confess—"

Once again, Linda's gaze fell to the wall, then her fingernails, then the floor. "I must have misspoken."

"Do not interrupt me. I am not finished," Aretta said. Linda swallowed and waited. "I know you're lying. I can see it in your face. Garda O'Sullivan knows you're lying. Heretofore she has not decided whether or not to charge you with breaking and entering, but I can do that right now if you please."

A sob escaped from Linda. She hunched over and cried. Aretta held up a finger and looked as if she was going to continue to spear Linda with threats. Siobhán gently laid a hand on her shoulder and nodded. *Good work*, she mouthed. Aretta took a deep breath and sat back in her chair, crossed her arms, and waited. Interrogations were a fine dance. You had to keep the right amount of pressure on but also know exactly when to pull back and wait. Instinctually, it was tempting to keep poking, to ramp up the accusations, but that could backfire. Linda was on the edge; it was best to let her recognize it and ask for help getting down. They waited.

"Alright. Alright." Linda wiped her face with her hands and let the crumpled tissue fall to the floor. "We wrote the note. That's my big confession."

Siobhán frowned. "The note?"

"The banknote?" Aretta asked.

Linda shook her head. " 'Sorry. Goodbye.' "

"Sorry. Goodbye?" Aretta said. "We're not even close to finished."

"She's talking about the note that Tommy supposedly left Gladys," Siobhán said. The reason they all gave for believing he'd done a runner. *Sorry. Goodbye.* What was it someone had said? Tommy wasn't a scribbler; he was a man of few words.

Linda nodded. "Yes. That note. Alan wrote it, and I left it in my sister's dressing room before the wedding."

Siobhán was truly taken aback. "You knew Tommy was dead?"

"No, no," Linda said.

"You knew he wasn't going to show up for the wedding?" Siobhán lightened the tone of her voice, wanting Linda to keep talking.

"It was Alan's idea. When it had been a good thirty minutes and Tommy hadn't shown up, we all knew he had done a runner. Howard arrived on and told us the satchel of money was missing."

"So why write the note?" Aretta asked.

"Because we knew Gladys. We knew she would never believe he'd just up and leave her without a word."

"So you wrote two words," Siobhán said.

"Neither of us knew anything about Tommy's handwriting, so we wanted to keep it short. We wrote it in block letters, as if he was in a hurry."

"And she believed it?"

"Howard had come armed with the contract he and Tommy signed with the snooker club. We tore a section from it to write the note. It was somewhat convincing, and after all, he wasn't there, was he?"

"I don't suppose it was much comfort," Siobhán mused.

Aretta leaned forward. "Does Gladys know the two of ye wrote the note?"

Linda buried her face in her hands and shrugged. When she took them away, she took a deep breath. "When Tommy's remains were found, Alan was besieged with guilt. He said he was going to tell her. I begged him not to. I begged him. What good would it do fifty years later? But once Gladys realized that Tommy couldn't have written that note, she was on a warpath to find out who did. She was accusing everyone, even Benji. That man is the true love of her life, and she has always treated him like he was second best. I finally agreed that we needed to tell her. But we never got the chance."

"Because Alan was murdered," Siobhán said.

Linda nodded.

"Are you positive that Alan didn't tell her before he died?" Siobhán asked.

"I cannot be positive," Linda said. "And it's something I do not like thinking about."

"Why is that?" Aretta asked.

Siobhán stiffened. Macdara was in the other room, watching the interview. She knew what he was thinking in this moment. "Because maybe Alan did tell Gladys," Siobhán said. "Maybe they met in the dairy barn, and he confessed while standing in front of the slurry pit. And maybe it enraged your sister," she added.

Linda stared at Siobhán without speaking.

"And maybe it metaphorically pushed her over the edge, so she literally pushed back."

Chapter 28

Siobhán and Aretta remained in the interview room after Linda was released. Macdara, a folder in hand, entered promptly. He sat across from Siobhán and studied her.

"What?" she said.

"I promise to look under your pillow every night for homeless bugs in search of prime ear condos," he said with a wink.

Aretta sputtered as she tried to suppress a laugh.

"Will you put that in the vows?" Siobhán asked.

"Finally, something I can scribble down."

"How romantic. But it won't be necessary. With a pair of mansions next to me"—she pointed at Macdara's prominent ears—"why would bugs want to move into my tiny little flats?"

"I believe she has a point," Aretta said.

"Hardball applies only to the suspects," Macdara said. He opened his folder, glancing through the suspect sheets. "Now. What do we think? Was Linda telling the truth?"

"I'm afraid so," Siobhán said.

"I thought we'd eliminated Gladys," Macdara said.

"I thought so too. But she could easily have been lying about not knowing Tommy smoked."

"Or Linda could be lying."

"If we arrested Gladys for murder, wouldn't Linda inherit the farm?" Aretta asked.

Siobhán shook her head. "I believe it's Benji. That's why Linda was trying to convince Gladys to change the will."

Macdara chimed in. "Without Alan to back up Linda's story, we'll need to circle back to Gladys. But let me point out that Gladys has never indicated that she knew Alan and Linda wrote that note. If she doesn't know about it, the news is certainly going to cause problems between the sisters." Macdara closed his folder and stood. "Let's schedule an interview with Gladys tomorrow."

"Tomorrow?" Siobhán said. "Why not today?"

"Because I'm taking you to the chipper, and then I'm putting you to bed. You're still not recovered from the incident." Ever since the dairy barn, Macdara had been hovering over her with worry. She opened her mouth to protest, but then imagined a heavenly curried chip going into it and afterward herself sinking into her warm bed.

"Okay," she said. "But I'm equally craving a dumpling."

"Jade's it is, then," Macdara said.

"Okay," Siobhán said.

"Okay?" Macdara and Aretta said in unison.

"I'm not doing this for you," Siobhán said. "I'm doing this for dumplings."

"You see that?" Macdara said. "Miracles do exist."

"I'm shocked," Aretta said. "You didn't even need to play hardball."

The next morning, Siobhán awoke feeling much better, and she was ready to get back into her routine. She dressed in her tracksuit and put on her runners. She was nearly out the door when a groggy Macdara called out, "A jog? You want to go for a jog right now?"

"Yes." She waited. Sometimes he joined her. A few seconds later she heard gentle snoring. She laughed and headed out for her run.

Outside, the shock of fresh air helped shake off the last traces of sleep. She fell into a rhythm and cast her eyes on the rising sun reflecting off the row of pastel-colored shops and homes that lined the street. The early birds were out. Mike Granger was sweeping the footpath of his fruit and veg market, Liam Collins was stocking shelves in the hardware shop, and Eoin was just opening the kitchen to their bistro. It reminded her she still needed to speak with the landlord, but first, she was going to have to have a sit down with Eoin and find out what he truly wanted to do. If he wanted to continue to run the bistro in this location, she would fight the landlord with all they had. If he wanted to take a different path, perhaps art courses or university, or whatever he wanted to do, she would let him know in no uncertain terms that his decision would be fully supported.

When Siobhán reached the town square, she decided to head left instead of her usual right toward
the abbey. Soon she was running past Saint Mary's
Church. There she saw a woman hurrying out of
the church with a yellow silk scarf wrapped over
her head. Siobhán glanced at the sky to confirm
there wasn't a drop of rain on the horizon. The
woman dashed for a car parked across the street. It
wasn't until the car screeched away that Siobhán
saw the bumper sticker. KILBANE WILDLIFE CENTER.
Was that Rose? Siobhán glanced at the church.
Had she been there to see Father Kearney? He
didn't take confessions this early, but perhaps she
was volunteering for this or that. Siobhán knew
that unless she had a good reason, Father Kearney
was not going to divulge the nature of this early
morning meeting. Where was she off to in such a
hurry?

By the time Siobhán finished her run and was
making her first cup of heavenly cappuccino, she
decided she was picking the kids up early from
school and they were going on a field trip.

Rose (sans a yellow scarf on her head) seemed
thrilled to see Ann and Ciarán at the wildlife center, and for the first hour of the visit, Siobhán put
murder out of her mind as she watched them in-
teract with these stunning creatures up close. Ann
was smitten with a white owl named Norman that
toddled after her, squawking for treats; and Ciarán
was over the moon about the hawks, especially Charlie. He was good at keeping his arm out straight
and his fist curled, and she could see the joy in his

eyes every time the Harris hawk landed on his fist. When a young assistant asked if the pair wanted to help with the afternoon feeding, Siobhán took the opportunity to corner Rose in front of the visitors' center.

"I had a few questions, if you don't mind," Siobhán said.

"Not at all," Rose said. "I love talking about my birds."

"Actually, it's about the case."

"Have you learned anything new?"

As if Siobhán would tell her if she did. "I just wanted to double-check with you—I think you mentioned it, but I forgot to write it down. What was the emergency the evening you and Benji left Joseph with Gladys?"

Rose chewed on her bottom lip. "Did you ask Benji?"

"If I did, I must have misplaced his answer." Rose wanted to make sure they were coordinating their stories. Siobhán was not going to let up.

"I suppose we talked about Tommy. And the fact that he asked me to run away with him."

"You suppose?"

She sighed. "I didn't know what to do. Gladys was marrying him in the morning. I felt I had an obligation to say something."

"Did Benji agree?"

"Let's get one thing straight. My ex-husband is not a killer."

It was interesting how protective she still was of her ex-husband. Especially given he'd left her for another woman. "How did he react to the news?"

"He brushed it off, if you must know. He said

Tommy must have been drunk. He bet me Tommy wouldn't even remember it in the morning."

"Where did you spend the night that evening?"

"We rented a room at the Kilbane Inn." It was the Twins' Inn now, but most folks in town still called it the Kilbane Inn.

"Was Benji with you all night?"

Rose turned, her eyes narrowing. "What a question!"

"Was he?"

"Yes, he was with me all night."

"What about the morning?"

Rose began to walk toward the cages. "Pardon?" It wasn't her answers Siobhán found revealing but her pauses. She was stalling before answering, as if giving herself time to carefully think through every word. Guilty people tended to do that more than innocent people.

Siobhán kept pace with her and didn't stop. "Was Benji with you when you woke up in the morning?"

"Of course," she said. "We woke up early. He went to pick up Joseph, and I headed home to get ready for the wedding."

That put Benji squarely at the crime scene around the time of the murder. It took only seconds to push someone into the pit, especially if they were already standing at the edge, wondering what that gold coin was all about. . . . She was dying to ask Rose about birds of prey and how they were attracted to shiny objects, but she didn't want to give away the arcade tokens yet.

"You decided not to tell Gladys about Tommy asking you to run away?" Siobhán asked instead.

"If Benji said it was nothing more than a drunken mistake, who was I to break up a wedding?" She had feelings for Tommy. It was clear as the twinge of pain in her voice.

"And what about all these years later?"

Rose stopped. Turned. Waited.

"When Tommy's remains were found, did you think about telling Gladys what was going on with you and Tommy?"

Rose put her hand on her heart. "You make it sound like I was an equal participant."

"Were you in love with Tommy?"

"I loved Tommy. But no. I wasn't going to fall for his act. Tommy would have made a terrible partner to anyone he ended up with. It was just in his nature to cause trouble." She crossed herself, then looked to the heavens. "Forgive me, Tommy, but you know it's the truth."

"I saw you this morning."

The abrupt change of topic seemed to throw Rose off-kilter. "Oh?"

"I went for an early morning jog past Saint Mary's, and I saw you dash out of the church. You must have been late for work?" Siobhán's voice carried more confidence than she felt. If it wasn't Rose she saw, there'd be no harm done.

Instead, Rose nodded, as if she had expected the question. "A friend of mine has a rabbit that just birthed a litter. You should bring your ones to see them. They're adorable. On the way back, I was dropping off entrance passes to Sister Helen. The center auctioned off a special visit at the knitting circle charity event. The boys' home had the winning bid, and Sister Helen will be bringing them." She stopped and waited to see if Siobhán wanted to dig any further.

"Lovely," she said. "The lads will be thrilled."

Rose nodded. "Will that be all? I have to finish the evening rounds."

"Not a bother. Thank you for your time."

It was almost closing time. Siobhán needed to use a restroom before heading back, and she could hear Ann and Ciarán's excited chattering and wanted to give them a few more minutes to enjoy the center. She headed for the visitors' center, entered, and was making a beeline for the jax when a young girl at the reception desk motioned for her to come over.

"I'm just using the restroom," Siobhán said.

"You're a garda, right?"

"Yes."

"And everything I say to you would be confidential?"

"No, that's a priest, luv, or a solicitor."

"Oh." Her big eyes seemed to be pleading with Siobhán.

"Hold that thought." Siobhán hurried to the restroom and was relieved the girl was still there when she came back out. "I'll make you a promise. Unless you have information that puts someone in immediate danger, I'll do me best to keep whatever you'd like to say confidential."

The girl swallowed, then glanced at the door.

"Are you in some kind of trouble, pet?"

The girl shook her head. "You're working on that murder case, aren't you? Where that skeleton was found in a slurry pit?"

"Yes."

"We had a hawk go missing that morning."

"Charlie."

The girl brightened up. "Yes," she said. "You already know."

"Why do you say he was missing?" Siobhán said. "I thought Rose Burns took Charlie out that morning. She said she likes to give him new places to exercise."

The girl looked down. "Oh."

Siobhán nudged in closer. "Do you recall something else happening?"

"It was her son that took him, and he did not have permission. Mrs. Burns was nearly fired over it."

"Joseph Burns?"

The girl nodded.

"Did he do that often?"

"He used to do it all the time until me supervisors cracked down on it. That's why I'm telling you. I was supposed to be watching and reporting. The birds are not to go off the property. They're a liability. I guess some people aren't good at following the rules."

"I'd say," Siobhán said. "Did you report this to anyone?"

The girl shook her head as a guilty look came over her pretty face. "He brought Charlie back unharmed, so I don't know what the fuss was about."

"The fuss?"

She nodded, then leaned in. "Rose and Joseph had a huge row over it. And then Rose told me if anyone asked that I should tell them that *she* was the one who took Charlie."

"I see." Siobhán shrugged, as if it were a trivial matter. "I wonder why?"

"If Rose was the one who took Charlie out, she would have been fired. But I think she was worried if it was Joseph, they would press charges."

"Just to be clear, you're saying Rose specifically asked you not to tell anyone that Joseph took Charlie out that morning?"

The girl nodded. "She wanted the whole thing swept under the rug, but of course, once you found that skeleton, everyone knew that Charlie had been taken from the center, so it was then that she instructed me what to say in case anyone asked."

"Did Rose get in any trouble when she claimed to be the one who took Charlie out that morning?"

The girl had been waiting for that question. She nodded enthusiastically. "She's on probation. If she's so much as a minute late, she could be sacked."

"Thank you for sharing that with me. I'll keep it to myself."

The girl exhaled and placed her hand on her heart. "Thank you."

Siobhán headed back outside and lingered by the center for a moment to mull this over. The ultimatum from work explained Rose's mad dash for the car this morning, but what, if any, difference did it make whether it was Joseph or Rose who took Charlie out that morning? Siobhán thought of the scratch on Joseph's arm that morning. The blood on the rolling pin. Gladys sticking it in her mouth. Was Gladys protecting Joseph? There was no way a child five years of age had murdered a grown man. What was the real secret they were trying to cover up? It wasn't until Siobhán was headed to reunite with Ciarán and Ann that it hit her.

Joseph must have seen something that morning. Or someone. Did he witness the killer visiting the slurry pit? Trying to remove the bones? Did this incident startle Charlie, resulting in a nasty scratch to Joseph's arm? And who was Joseph protecting? Somehow Siobhán didn't think he'd go to such lengths to protect Gladys. But what about Rose? Or Benji? Had he seen his mother or father go into the dairy barn either recently or that long-ago morning? Was it Joseph himself who intended on removing the bones that morning to protect one or the other of his parents? *Or both . . .* What if Benji and Rose were in cahoots? Might that explain why they had only glowing words for each other?

They'd rescued Joseph from a boys' home, given him a family. Granted, it hadn't lasted long as far as Benji and Rose staying married, but Joseph had continued to have a home. Two homes. Three parents. Perhaps he would protect Gladys as well. Siobhán felt like the Harris hawks, flying out but always returning to the same fists. Benji. Rose. Gladys.

What of Linda or Howard? Joseph had been spending quite a bit of time with Tommy, who had spent quite a bit of time with Howard at the pubs and snooker games. He could equally have witnessed something sinister between the two men. The only logical explanation was that Joseph had seen *something*. He might not even have realized it, but the killer could be worried that Joseph's memory would be triggered. . . . She had to find out why he took the bird out that morning. Perhaps it was time Joseph felt the squeeze of suspicion.

It was easy to be loyal if it didn't cost one anything. But if Joseph thought they were suspicious of him, then perhaps he would spill his secrets. Perhaps it was time to nose around this boys' school where he'd spent his first five years. If Sister Helen was active in both the boys' home and socializing with her potter friend, then it wouldn't take long for word of Siobhán's visit to the boys' home to get back to Joseph and perhaps rattle him.

Simultaneously, she wanted to turn the heat up on Benji and Howard. Benji most of all. He was the common denominator. Husband. Ex-husband. Father. Best man/best friend. Macdara might not like it, but Siobhán's instincts might have been spot on from the start. It was time to shake all their suspects up, as if the village of Kilbane was a snow globe, and see where all the little pieces settled.

Chapter 29

Siobhán found Benji Burns waiting for her out-side of Naomi's Bistro, his hand shaking as he stubbed out a cigarette, then flicked the remains to the ground. Siobhán stared down at it, then back up at him. It took him a moment to realize he'd just littered the footpath that was in front of her family business. When it finally dawned on him, he picked up the discarded butt and stood holding it, his awkwardness growing by the sec-ond. Siobhán pointed out a nearby rubbish bin. He nodded to the kids, then stole a glance her way before hurrying over and discarding the cigarette.

Siobhán turned to the young ones. "Eoin has supper ready," she said. "Wash your hands, and I'll be in soon." They clambered inside in a manner so carefree Siobhán felt a pang of longing deep in-side, even though she couldn't quite put her fin-ger on what exactly was out of reach. Perhaps just the days where nothing but sunshine was on the mind. But given the mercurial weather in Ireland, most sunshine dreams were never realized. They were having an unusually warm start to the summer this year, and she was going to try to enjoy every second of it, even while investigating a murder.

As soon as Ann and Ciarán disappeared indoors, Benji didn't even wait for her to say hello. "Why are you harassing Rose?"

"Pardon?"

Had Rose immediately phoned Benji? The answer was obvious from the frown on his face, his Adam's apple jutting out, his hands clenched at his sides.

"Watch yourself, Mr. Burns," Siobhán said. "I'm doing my job, and I do not have to answer to you."

He licked his lips and stared at the footpath. "I suppose you're wondering why I didn't tell you meself."

"What are you on about?" She could hear the false notes in her tone but doubted he could. If he wanted to apologize for withholding information, he at least had to own up to the information he'd omitted.

"Truly," he said, holding up his right hand, as if she had a Bible behind her back, "I didn't think it mattered. Not at all."

"The night before your best mate's wedding, you find out he asked your wife to run away with him, and you didn't think it mattered?"

His shoulders rolled forward, and his head slumped. "I thought Tommy had tied one on. You could never believe what came gushing out of him when he was tipping the jar. You know yourself."

Was that a reference to her girls' night out gone wrong? Or was he speaking in generalities? He hadn't even asked after her since the fire. What was wrong with people lately? Where had all the decency gone?

"I can think of only one reason you weren't upset that Tommy wanted to run away with Rose." She waited to see if he would fill in the rest.

He crossed his arms and looked over her shoulder. "Go on, so."

"You were already in love with Gladys." His excuse about falling in love with her after Tommy had done a supposed runner was a cover story. He'd probably been pining after his best friend's girl long before that.

He straightened back up. "I'm not here to dig up ancient history."

"I think Tommy Caffrey would want it dug up, don't you think?"

"That's very unfair. Very unfair."

"Murder inquiries aren't always fair, Mr. Burns. We're in pursuit of justice."

He threw open his arms. "I'm here, aren't I? I was his best friend. You think you want to find his killer more than I do?" He moved uncomfortably close to her. "I'm an old man, and I've done a lot of terrible things in me life. But murdering me best friend is not one of them."

It had the ring of truth. She took a step back and waited for him to do the same. "Did you see Tommy that morning?"

"I did not."

"It was fifty years ago, yet you don't even want to take a second to think about it?"

"I would have remembered seeing him, Garda."

"Take me through your movements after you left the Kilbane Inn that morning."

"You're joking me. I haven't a clue."

"You just said you clearly remember *not* seeing Tommy, yet when it comes to what you did see, that's when it suddenly goes blurry?"

He shifted his weight to the other foot, then back again. "I'll do me best to remember."

"Let me help you through it. That morning you left the Kilbane Inn to pick up Joseph. Did you head straight to the farm?"

Just as she was expecting an answer, instead came the sound of glass bottles being jostled, clinking together. And since Benji was openmouthed before her, it took her a moment to realize the sound had come from behind her. She whirled around to find Joseph standing behind a felled recycling bin that had just been put out to the curb.

"Sorry, sorry," he said as he bent to grab bottles rolling out of the gaping mouth of the bin. "The sun was in me eyes, and I wasn't looking where I was going." Benji hurried over to help, and the pair of them managed to get the bin upright and the stray bottles inside. Joseph cocked a thumb at the recycling bin and shook his head, as if it were to blame.

"I thought I told you to stay in the car," Benji said.

"I'm not a child, Da," Joseph said. "And I was

getting bored." He rocked on his heels. "Did you tell her about Linda and Alan?"

Siobhán squinted in Joseph's direction, then stared intently at Benji. "He did not," she said, turning to Benji. "What's the story?"

Benji sighed. "It's probably nothing."

"It's always nothing," Siobhán said. "Until it's something."

Siobhán and Macdara were tucked into the back booth at Butler's Undertaker, Lounge, and Pub. John Butler had served them a cup of tea and biscuits and let them be. At exactly half four, as John Butler had predicted, Dan Maloney wheeled his electric chair into the tiny pub, his enormous stomach obscuring even the side rails. He pulled up to a two-seater in the small seating area behind the counter and waited. Moments later, John Butler emerged from behind the red curtain that separated the pub from the entry room and set a pint in front of him.

"Good man, John," Mr. Maloney said, licking his lips in anticipation.

John nodded, his gaze flicking to Siobhán and Macdara. "It's on the house today, Dan."

"On the house?" Mr. Maloney said. "Are you dying?" John Butler flicked a nervous glance at Siobhán and Macdara. Mr. Maloney was oblivious to it. "If you were dying, you wouldn't have a far commute, if you know what I mean." Mr. Maloney threw his head back and laughed at his own joke, while John trembled with nerves.

"There's a pair of guards waiting to talk to you."

Mr. Maloney's eyes slowly traveled to Siobhán and Macdara. He then eyed his pint, as if debating whether or not it was worth it.

"He'll throw in a ham and cheese toastie on us," Macdara said.

"And chips," Siobhán added.

That seemed to perk Dan Maloney up. "What about another pint?"

"Done," Siobhán said. Before he could work out whether or not that was as good a deal as he was going to get, Siobhán and Macdara swooped in and sat at his table.

Mr. Maloney sighed, held up a sausage finger, and then drained his pint in one go. He set it down with an exhale, wiped his mouth with the back of his hand, and turned to the curtain.

"He's going to be a minute," Macdara said. "You're going to need to talk to us first."

"This is about the O'Leary property, isn't it?"

"I was right about you," Siobhán said. "You're sharp as a tack, bound to remember the details even if it was fifty years ago."

"You worked at the local bank back in the day," Macdara said. "We heard the place wouldn't have run without you."

"I did indeed." The flattery was working: he was puffed up like a peacock.

"Were you the loan officer involved in the O'Leary property?" Siobhán asked. They already knew he was, but it was often a good idea to test whether or not the subject was going to be truthful.

"I was indeed. I surely was." He bobbed his head to a beat no one else could hear.

"We hear they were in quite some debt," Macdara said.

Another nod. "I hated seeing it. A family farm struggling. Parents lording it over their kids' heads, trying to use it to manipulate them."

"How do you know they were doing that?" Siobhán asked.

"Because the father told me. Said once they got the farm back on its feet, they had to decide which of their three children would inherit it. I remember as if it was yesterday. I said, 'Why not all three?' Mr. O'Leary laughed. He said the only way to do it was to make them work for it. And the only way they'd work for it was if there was competition." He shook his head. "I always knew it wouldn't end well. But then, miraculously, it seemed to settle, you know? Gladys was the only one with an heir, even if he was only a stepson, and when she married Benji, they did right by Linda and Alan, as they got to stay on, and as far as I know, the feuding stopped once the parents had both passed."

It appeared that way, but Siobhán knew appearances could be deceptive. And in this case, downright deadly.

Macdara continued with the questioning. "Who paid off the debt?" Siobhán was eager to see if the story would match the one Rose had told her.

"Alan and Linda came in one day with a sack filled with cash."

Linda. What a whopper of a lie. Was there any reason she would lie about it, other than she was the killer? "Wait," Siobhán said. "Do you have an exact date?"

He frowned, then looked to the velvet curtain.

"I promise your pint and toastie will be served as soon as we're finished," Macdara said. "But not a second before."

Dan Maloney laced his fingers together and rested them on his stomach. "I can't give you the exact date, but it was a few weeks after the wedding that never was."

"You seem awfully sure," Macdara said.

"Of course. Tommy doing a runner was all anyone could talk about. Even the betting shops had a go at whether or not he would go through with the wedding. I remember the wedding was a Saturday, because I was invited myself, and I like a good Irish wedding—especially when they don't skimp on the food and drink. You wouldn't know to see me now, but I was quite the dancer in my day." He paused and pointed to his head. "Up here for thinking used to be down there for dancing." He finished by gesturing to his lower half, then sighed. "And now here they come a few weeks later, as if the world was smiling rainbows, and they plunk down a bag of cash—enough money to save the farm, which incidentally was left to Gladys. I remembered thinking about how every cloud did have a silver lining. I never could have imagined they'd murdered him for the money." He shuddered.

"Did you ask how they suddenly had so much money in cash?" Macdara asked.

"Of course I did. They told me everyone pitched in. Some relative in England, and a few locals passing around a hat at the pub. We took care of each other back then, so we did. It was a bit unusual, I'll tell ye that. But we were thrilled for them. Nobody wanted to see them lose the farm."

"And you didn't raise any flags or try to trace the money?" Siobhán asked.

"Am I in any legal jeopardy here?"

"No," Macdara said. "I assure you all we're trying to do is find a killer."

"Like I said, we took care of each other back then. Tommy goes missing, and everyone feels sorry for Gladys. It wasn't unheard of for locals to pass the hat and at least save the family farm. 'Twas as plausible to me back then as it is now." He leaned forward as he poked the tabletop with the tip of his index finger. "I swear to ye, if I had had any idea that money was the same money Howard Dunn had accused Tommy of running off with, I would have called the guards then and there." He punctuated it with another jab of his finger and a nod of his head that sent his jowls wobbling.

"It didn't seem odd to you that it was nearly the exact amount of the money Tommy allegedly stole?" Macdara asked.

"It wasn't in a satchel. It was in one of them sacks from the dairy barn. And I told ye, people felt sorry for Gladys. I thought of it as poetic justice. I assumed they wanted to raise the exact amount he stole."

Macdara nodded, taking a moment before asking his next question. "Did Howard Dunn ever come talk to you about his missing money? Was he suspicious?"

Dan Maloney rubbed his chin, then shook his

head. "He did try to get a loan, but he was convinced that Tommy had run off with his money. Absolutely convinced, there's no two ways about it."

Unless Howard had been putting on an act. It was possible he knew that was his sack of cash. Because he was paying off a couple of blackmailers. Linda and Alan had witnessed something that they were able to leverage to get the cash. . . .

"Did you give him a loan?" Macdara asked.

Mr. Maloney shook his head. "I didn't get a chance. Howard withdrew the application the next day."

"Did he say why?"

"Apparently, Tommy had been more popular than he realized. Once he was gone, several builders and investors pulled out of the snooker club deal."

John arrived on with another pint and his food. Dan stared at it like it was a lover before throwing a glance at the guards. "Is there anything else?"

"No, thank you," Macdara said. "You've been very helpful."

Dan grinned and lifted his pint. "Down the hatch it is."

Chapter 30

Even though it was getting late in the day, they headed back to the garda station and paced the room with the whiteboard, staring at all the suspects on the wall. Aretta joined them, and they took turns going over suspects and the three keys to any murder inquiry: motive, means, and opportunity.

"How do we figure this out?" Siobhán asked. "We still have too many viable suspects."

Macdara's mobile rang, startling all three of them. Siobhán watched him straighten his spine as he listened, heard the change in his tone. He hung up. "Investigators just found a can of petrol on our property. It could be the one the arsonist used on the dairy barn."

"Our killer."

"It's possible we're looking at two different murderers and an arsonist," Macdara said.

"But not probable," Siobhán and Macdara said in unison.

"Why do you sound so excited about a can of petrol?" Aretta asked.

Macdara grinned. "Because we're hoping they bought it from Liam's Hardware."

Liam, as Siobhán knew, kept meticulous records of all purchases at his shop. They might be able to trace the purchaser.

Macdara glanced at the clock on the wall and groaned. It was half five; Liam worked until three, and then younger clerks took over the shop. Liam was the one with the steel-trap mind for purchases, and there was no use trying to get the information from an underling. "Let's get some sleep. We'll pay Liam a visit first thing in the morning."

When Macdara dropped Siobhán off at the bistro, she noticed a light on in the back garden. There she found Eoin on one of the chairs, staring into the herb garden. He'd turned on the white patio lights, which made the outdoor haven sparkle.

"You're up late."

Eoin jumped at the sound of her voice. "You shouldn't sneak up on people like that."

"You must have been deep in thought not to hear the door squeak."

Eoin shrugged, then nodded as she sank into the seat next to him. "Have you spoken to James?"

She could only hope it wasn't more bad news. She shook her head. "What's the story?"

"He wants to collect any materials left from the dairy barn once the investigation is complete."

"Good to know."

"Do you ever think about switching professions?"

"Where's this coming from?"

"When I think of what almost happened to you . . ."

Siobhán reached over and squeezed his shoulder. "I'm fine, luv."

He placed his hand on top of hers. "We can't lose you. We'd never be the same."

"It's a good thing you're stuck with me, then." She made a face, and he laughed. "Have you come to any decisions about the bistro?"

"I have," he said. "But I'd rather discuss it after you close this case."

He was driving her mental with all this dragging it out. "May I ask why?"

He grinned. "Because I need your full attention on what I'm thinking, and we all know you obsess on a case until it's over."

"Fair enough." She rose, kissed Eoin on the cheek, and headed inside.

She'd forgotten to ask Macdara where exactly they had found this can of petrol. Whoever had set the barn on fire had had plenty of time and the cover of darkness to escape. How could he or she have made such a rookie mistake as to leave behind a can of petrol? Especially one that could be traced. Was this the equivalent of tossing a falconer's glove and a shard of broken pottery into the slurry pit? A misdirection? The killer was indeed rattled, but at the same time Siobhán couldn't shake the feeling that he or she liked the game. Thrived on it even. It was an unsettling thought, and even after Siobhán cuddled with Ann and Ciarán and turned off the lights, she knew she was in for a restless night. She calmed herself by counting sheep jumping over their suspects.

Liam Collins was a short and stern man in his seventies, with a recent head of black hair, which, for all Siobhán knew, was a wig. He'd been running this shop for longer than Siobhán had been alive. Framed photos on the wall showed a much younger Liam Collins was actively engaged in the theatre, and Siobhán wondered if he had ever considered trying out for the Kilbane Players, but everyone knew that Liam did not like customers engaging in personal conversation. The weather and his goods were the only two acceptable topics of conversation. The shop sold mostly hardware goods: tools, paints, ladders, torches, batteries, and so on. But one could also find the odd houseplant, kitchen supplies, and toys. A little bit of everything and anything.

The next morning Siobhán and Macdara were the first customers in the door. Liam greeted them with a nod as the bell rang and announced their presence. Macdara approached the counter, holding the can of petrol up in the see-through evidence bag.

"May I?" Liam said.

Macdara nodded. "As long as you don't take it out of the bag."

"Yes, this is from my shop," he said, pointing to the price sticker. "But it's not from this calendar year."

"How can you be so sure?" Siobhán asked.

"Because I made a mistake when ordering the price stickers this year—to be honest, the mistake was on the part of the sticker manufacturer—and they're all orange." He picked up a package of biscuits and showed her the orange stickers. From the sour look on his face, he was not a fan of orange.

"Now all you need is green and white, and you'll have the Irish flag," Siobhán said. Macdara chuckled and Liam frowned.

Macdara spotted a pack of biscuits by the counter with a white sticker tag. "Does this tag mean they're from last year?"

"That's right," Liam said. "You've got it."

Macdara grinned, as if Liam had just patted him on the back. "Are these really still good if they're from last year?"

"Haven't had a complaint yet."

"Because nobody's buying them," Macdara continued.

"If you'd like to buy them, Detective Sergeant, I'll make sure to give your money back if you don't finish every crumb."

Macdara nodded and placed the biscuits on the counter. There was a split second when Siobhán wanted to reprimand Dara. Did he really need another pack of biscuits? The thought itself alarmed her. Was this what marriage was? Nitpicking over what he bought, what he ate, what he wore, what he did? She wasn't that kind of person. Was she? She would not lecture him about the biscuits. Instead, she would wake up every morning, take her run, and eat an apple. Lead by example. Perhaps he'd take notice and follow. Or stay in bed, snoring, then wake up and eat a pack of biscuits. Let his doctor lecture him. She was definitely going to stay out of it.

Siobhán brought their attention back to the petrol can in the evidence bag. "Do you know what year this was purchased?"

"The only thing I can say at a glance is not this calendar year," Liam said.

"Which means even if we trace who purchased it, it doesn't matter. There are too many ways it could have changed hands in the past year." The frustration was evident in Macdara's deep voice.

"Thank you for your time," Siobhán said with a smile and nod to Liam.

"What about a discount?" Macdara said, still eyeing the biscuits. "Half off?"

"No discount," Liam said. "If you don't finish them, I give your money back."

"You don't need a pack of biscuits," Siobhán said before she could stop the words from tumbling out. "We run a bistro," she added. "We have loads of biscuits. I don't mind if you eat biscuits. Eat all the biscuits you want. Here." She paid Liam for the biscuits and handed them to a perplexed Macdara. "Enjoy. I mean it." He tore them open and popped one into his mouth. They turned to go.

"Wait," Liam called after them. "May I see that again?"

Macdara turned and held the package of biscuits to his chest, as if he wasn't going to give them up without a fight.

"The petrol can," Liam said. A look of relief

crossed Macdara's face as he handed Liam the can of petrol. Liam peered at it, then nodded. "Sister Helen," he said confidently.

Siobhán felt the back of her neck tingle. "Sister Helen?" she repeated.

Liam nodded. "I can't say for sure she bought this one, but she's the one who asked me to stock petrol cans in this smaller size. She likes it for her mower. Did you know she does the mowing at the church?"

"We do now," Macdara said.

"Sister Helen," Siobhán said once more. An image rose in Siobhán's mind. Sister Helen standing with colorful ceramic pots. An image of Father Kearney's appointment book replaced it. *Interesting.*

Liam handed the petrol can back to Macdara. "Thanks." Macdara gave a nod of appreciation then took Siobhán's arm and hurried her outside. Once on the footpath, he turned to her. "Don't tell me you suspect a nun of being our killer."

Siobhán snatched one of his biscuits. "We can't rule it out." She took a bite. "Not bad."

"Right? Remarkable shelf life. Hate to think of all the preservatives." He couldn't hate them that much, for he took another. "Why can't we rule out a nun?"

"Sister Helen is the one who had access to Father Kearney's appointment book. She's the only other one who writes in it."

"We're going to need more than that." He rubbed his chin and sighed. "You're not really suspecting a nun of murder, now are you?"

"I'm not *not* suspecting a nun of murder."

"Siobhán!"

"She's still human, isn't she?"

He closed his eyes for a second and shook his head. "If she is, I don't want to know about it."

They headed past shops, walking toward the garda station. They paused by Chris Gordon's comic book shop and took in the colorful posters in the window depicting creatures and monsters and superheroes. If only suspects in real life could be identified as good or bad at a glance. But real life didn't work that way. She looked across the street toward the bookshop. Oran McCarthy stood out, with a mug of tea clutched in his hands. He spotted them and waved; they waved back. Siobhán would have to pop in soon for a nose around. She still felt a little thrill every time she laid eyes on the bookshop; it was a welcome addition to the town. Patrick McCarthy, Oran's husband, stuck his head out, and they went through another round of waving and smiling. They continued on toward the passageway underneath King John's Castle, the entrance to the town square.

"Anyone is capable of murder. I know you know that," Siobhán said.

"I know you know I know that, but a nun wouldn't be high on my list of suspects."

"That appointment book was handled by our killer. Manipulated to interrupt our wedding or take advantage of our wedding to move Tommy's remains. Sister Helen not only had access to the appointment book, but she's also been receiving free garden pots from Joseph. Maybe she dropped the shard into the slurry pit."

"Along with the falconer's glove?"

"I don't have that connection yet."

"Yet." Macdara walked away, then circled back to her. A breeze blew his messy hair back as he stared into her eyes. For a second, she was distracted by how much she loved this man, and felt a twinge of regret they weren't already married. "Why would she kill Tommy?"

"She's the same age as Gladys. Maybe she was in love with Tommy."

"A nun?" He sounded pained.

Siobhán laughed. "Macdara, do not tell me that you think nuns are perfect! They're human. They're women. They have the same desires and foibles as anyone else."

He gripped the can of petrol and nearly smooshed the last of his biscuits as his fists clenched uncomfortably. "I beg you. Never ever again say *nun* and *desire* in the same sentence ever, ever again. It's the only thing I'll ever, ever ask of you."

Siobhán shook her head and grabbed the remaining biscuit from Macdara. "Have you ever thought of starting off your morning with a juicy apple?"

"You think a nun almost set three young women on fire?"

"I'm not saying anything definitively," Siobhán said. "But if we don't follow up just because she's a nun, then we're not doing our jobs."

Macdara sighed, held up the can of petrol. In the distance, the bells of Saint Mary's began to peal. Macdara held the petrol can aloft as if it were a lantern. "It's as if we're being summoned," he muttered. "Let's go pay a visit to Sister Helen. But first, I need to pop back into Liam's."

"You're buying more biscuits, aren't you?"

"Someone ate half of mine," he said, holding up the empty package. "But I tell you what. If they have a juicy apple, I'll make sure and buy it for ya."

Chapter 31

Father Kearney looked on with concern as Sister Helen counted her empty petrol cans. As she turned and seemed to be counting them for the third time, a drop of sweat ran down her left cheek. "I don't understand who would do this," she said. "One is missing."

"I believe it's right here," Siobhán said, holding up the evidence bag.

"Do you lock this shed, Sister Helen?" Macdara asked.

The shed was situated at the very back of the church, away from parishioners, but not completely out of sight. "I lock it at night, but during the day I'm in and out of it too frequently to lock it up each time. Besides, we've never had reason to lock it. But I will be doing so from now on, I can promise ye that."

"I don't suppose there are any CCTV cameras

pointed this direction," Siobhán said, already knowing the answer.

Father Kearney and Sister Helen shook their heads in unison. "I am deeply disturbed," Father Kearney said.

"As am I," Sister Helen said.

"Have you seen any townsfolk near this shed the past week or even month?" Siobhán asked.

Sister Helen considered it. "I don't recall seeing anyone who wasn't supposed to be near it."

"I wonder if our killer stole it the day he or she changed the notation in the appointment book," Siobhán said. "Which means the burning of the dairy barn was planned in advance . . ."

"We can't be certain the arsonist is also our killer," Macdara said.

"You're right," Siobhán said. She knew in her gut they were one and the same, but she did not need to go into this here and now.

"Are you saying the arsonist did or did not know you were inside when he or she started the fire?" Macdara asked.

"The 'arsonist' knew we were inside," Siobhán said. "The three of us were screaming our heads off."

"He or she could be hard of hearing," Macdara said. "Given the average age of our suspect pool."

"Besides keeping the shed locked, how else can we help?" Father Kearney said.

"Let us know if you think of anything else," Macdara said. "That's all we need for now."

"An alibi wouldn't hurt," Siobhán said. "Sister Helen, can you account for your whereabouts the night of the fire?"

Sister Helen fluttered her eyes, and a little tic developed at the corner of her mouth. She was not expecting this. Siobhán could feel Macdara cringing next to her, but she couldn't help that. "I was here, of course," Sister Helen said. "I'm always here." She glanced sideways at Father Kearney, who cleared his throat.

"Of course, of course," he said. "Where else would she be?" He grinned, which was so out of character for him that now Siobhán was cringing too.

"Nature of the job," Siobhán said. "I suppose you were here as well, Father?"

The grin faded from Father Kearney's face.

"He was here," Macdara said before the priest could answer. "They were all here. Sleeping. In God's house." Macdara lifted his pack of biscuits and offered one to Sister Helen. She took the entire package.

"Thank you, Dara." She patted his hand. He nodded glumly, his eyes never leaving the pack.

"Sorry we couldn't be of more help," Father Kearney said. "Our doors are always open."

"Except the shed," Sister Helen said. "From now on we'll be keeping it closed."

A few steps into their exit and Siobhán turned back. "One more thing."

"Seriously?" Macdara looked as if he wanted a shovel so he could dig himself a giant hidey-hole.

"I'm not asking you to give away the reason for her visit, but the other day I was on my run, and I saw Rose Burns leaving the church grounds in quite a hurry. She said she had stopped in to give Sister Helen entrance passes to the wildlife center. I just want to confirm this to be the case."

Sister Helen's face remained passive. "I'll check with the other sisters," she said. "Perhaps they haven't made their way to me yet."

"Is it true that she was supposed to drop off passes and that you are arranging a visit with the boys' home?"

"Yes, that is correct," Sister Helen said. "I've been a supporter of the home my entire life. I'm very close to all the lads."

Rose had told a partial truth. She was supposed to drop off entrance passes. And even if she had indeed dropped off passes—what else might she have been doing? Then again, Siobhán had seen Rose *after* the fire, so maybe she was climbing up the wrong tree. Could Rose have been there to *return* the empty can of petrol? If that were the case, how did it end up back on the farm?

The pottery shard, the falconer's glove, the petrol can . . . Siobhán couldn't shake the feeling that one of their suspects was onto the killer and doing things behind the scenes to help the guards piece it together. Why all the subterfuge? Was it fear of becoming the killer's next victim? Or did this person not want the killer to know that he or she was turning them in? Perhaps this person was wrestling with the decision. Loyalty and love over his or her conscience. It was something to ponder. But wasn't it equally plausible that these were all intended distractions? Red herrings? She would keep to herself until she worked it out.

They returned to the garda station to find Aretta waiting for them, a look of excitement in her eyes.

"We've just confirmed Howard Dunn's alibi for the morning of Alan's murder."

"Do tell," Macdara said.

"He was in Limerick City all day, and that's been confirmed by multiple witnesses, receipts, and even CCTV footage of him in front of a pub."

"Well done," Macdara said.

"Maybe now that he's not under suspicion for Alan's murder, and if we convince him we're convinced the killer is responsible for *both* murders, he'll be a little more open with us," Siobhán said.

"Why don't you have a word with him," Macdara said. "I've got meetings the rest of the day, and Aretta is in training." He glanced around the station. "I can see who's available to accompany you."

"I'd rather go alone," Siobhán said. "I want it to feel informal."

"Are you sure? He's not been cleared for the first murder."

"I'm sure." They were looking at one killer. She knew it. And they were also possibly looking at someone who really wanted them to find this killer and was dropping clues like bread crumbs. Unfortunately, these good intentions were muddying the waters. Could this person be Howard?

She found him in the old warehouse behind his local pub, the one he and Tommy had planned on turning into a snooker club. Instead, the space looked as if it served as a workshop for craftsmen. Howard was engaged in polishing a brand-new snooker table.

"Lovely," Siobhán said, startling Howard.

"Garda," he said, "please tell me you're not here with bad news."

"Quite the opposite. I'm here to inform you that your alibi for Alan's murder has checked out."

He nodded. "What about Tommy's murder?"

"Between you and me, we're looking at one killer, and therefore, you are no longer a person of interest."

He chuckled. "Never thought I'd be so happy to hear that."

She nodded. "But I was hoping you can help me with something, although I need your word that it will stay between us."

He put the rag down and faced her. "I give you my word. There's a Bible in the pub, if you want me to put me hand on it."

"That won't be necessary."

Siobhán took out her mobile and showed him a photo of the arcade token. He took off his glasses and peered at it.

"You'll find heaps of these everywhere," he said. "There's an entire jar of them in the pub." He pointed to the local pub in front of the warehouse.

"Are most of the ones you see shiny or dull from years of use?"

"Most show their age," he said.

"Have you seen any that are shiny?"

"Hold on." He held up a finger, then went to a nearby workstation. He picked up a clean rag and a bottle of Windex. He then headed out, and she followed. They entered the pub. Even at this early hour, men sat at the counter, fresh off night shifts in factories.

"Can I see that jar?" Howard said to the publican. Without asking why, the publican nodded, then plucked the jar of tokens off its shelf and slid it over to Howard. Howard plucked a token out, shined it up with the Windex, and handed it to Siobhán. "Here you are. Good as new." The token gleamed. "Owner of the arcade used to shine them up like that."

This was the kind of statement that made Siobhán pay attention. "He did?"

Howard nodded. "Not personally. He hired young lads to do it."

She stared at it, thinking it through. The token hadn't necessarily slipped out of Tommy's pocket. Instead, the killer had shined it up so that when the bulb above was turned on, the light would make it gleam. Luring his victims to the exact spot he needed them . . .

"Was Joseph one of those young lads?"

"He was, after I caught him stealing."

"Stealing?"

"Joseph used to climb up on this counter when he was a wee lad just to nick a fistful of tokens. Caught him with both pockets stuffed full and jinglejangling." He shook his head and laughed at the memory. "After that I suggested he shine 'em up for the arcade owner and earn his tokens."

"Did Joseph steal often?"

"He was a bit wild when he first came to live with Benji and Rose," Howard said. "I suppose that's to be expected."

"But he was only five years of age when Tommy was murdered," Siobhán said, mostly to herself.

She just could not bring herself to think a five-year-old could commit murder, let alone get away with it for fifty years.

Howard frowned. "Five years of age? Who told you that?"

"I believe it was Joseph himself," she said.

Howard shook his head. "He was a runt. But I think he was older than that."

Now every cell in Siobhán's body was humming. "How old?"

"Ten years of age rings a bell."

"Ten?" That was twice the age he had said he was. Vanity did not seem to be a factor here, so why the lie? Because a lad ten years of age was a horse of a different color. Because a lad ten years of age was capable of sneaking up on a grown man and pushing him into a pit. "Are you sure?"

Howard shook his head. "I'm afraid I can't say for sure. Benji or Rose will know."

But would they tell the truth? "What about the school for boys? They would have to have his records, no?"

"Sure, they'll have the records. But even if he was older, you really don't think a child did this, do you?"

"Thank you for your help, Mr. Dunn. And once again, I have to remind you that everything we talked about today stays between us."

"I give you me word," he said. "I give you me word."

From the outside, Saint Joseph's Home for Boys looked straight out of a Gothic novel. A rectangular stone building set up on a hill, with gnarled trees casting shadows on stone steps leading to an ornate wooden door. Siobhán was relieved when she entered into a bright and clean space. Given the hour, the boys would be in class. She headed for the office, where a white-haired woman sat behind a computer.

"May I help you?" she said, tapping away, with hardly a glance.

"I'm Garda Siobhán O'Sullivan, and I need to ask you about one of your residents from long ago."

"I was wondering when someone was going to arrive," she said.

"You were?"

"Yes," the woman said. "I almost came in on me own. But just because a lad is a hellion in his youth doesn't mean he grew up to be a killer, now does it?"

Siobhán slipped into the empty chair across from the desk, feeling nearly faint with anticipation. "It also doesn't mean he didn't," Siobhán said.

The woman stopped typing and made eye contact with Siobhán. "Exactly," she said. "He may have been a runt, but he was filled with rage, and he was cunning. As cunning a lad as I ever saw."

"A runt," Siobhán said. "I've seen pictures. He appears to be around five years of age when Rose and Benji adopted him."

The woman laughed. "Appearances can be deceiving," she said.

"How old was he?"

"He was *twelve*," she said. Siobhán nearly gasped. "He looked five, but he was twelve years of age. I can't help but think that was one of the reasons for his rage. Well. That and growing up an orphan." She leaned around the computer. "But he was one of the luckiest ones. I can still see him skipping out of here with Mr. and Mrs. Burns. A mam and dad at last. I tell ya, I was spitting mad when Mr. Burns left them for another woman. His best friend's girl, of all people." She tutted and glanced at a mug on her desk stuffed with Biros. On the mug was a familiar, cheeky white owl. Siobhán knew if she twirled the mug around, it would have the logo of the Kilbane Wildlife Center.

"Is there a reason you're looking at that mug?"

"It's odd," she said. "I had one that Joseph made me long ago. But about a month ago, Rose Burns popped in to see me. And . . . well . . . I don't have any proof, mind you, but after she left, the mug was gone. And this was in its place." The woman shook her head. "He's her son. I'm sure she has all the mugs she wants. Why did she have to go and nick mine?"

"Was it yellow?" Siobhán said. "Like mustard?"

"Like mustard," the woman said, with a pleased bob of her head. "How on earth did you know that?"

Chapter 32

Calling Macdara would be futile; he was hours away at a department meeting. The school for boys was surrounded by partial woods, and Siobhán decided to have a walkabout while she mulled things over. The green background and the earth scent mixed with a hint of heather provided the calmness she needed to go through the case. It would be even better to jog, but she would make do walking at a fast clip. Now that she knew who the killer was, the trick would be getting him to admit it. Given the manner of death was a shove from behind at exactly the right angle, the case was circumstantial at best. Joseph Burns had lived a troubled life. Short for his age, he'd probably been mercilessly teased. After he was adopted by Benji and Rose, life was suddenly going Joseph's way. Then Tommy Caffrey waltzed into it.

Siobhán had two working theories on why Joseph killed Tommy. The *means* were obvious to her now. Joseph was an excellent pool player—he understood the angles. He'd placed a shiny gold arcade token at the exact right position on the slurry pit. A shove from that angle and a person would hit their head on the upper left-hand corner of the concrete tomb. Tommy was killed using the angles from his infamous snooker shot. Joseph had been a little diabolical sponge, soaking up the dark side. He'd realized that not only could shiny objects be used to entice birds of prey, but they could work on people as well. In his warped mind, he'd most likely been protecting his family. . . .

Had he overhead Tommy asking Rose to run away with him and panicked? Perhaps he'd thought if his parents' marriage was destroyed, he'd be returned to the boys' home, like an unwanted pet back to an animal shelter. Howard had said he'd caught Joseph stealing. Had he stolen Tommy's satchel of money that morning? What if Tommy had caught him red-handed and chased him out to the dairy barn?

Alan had ended up with the satchel of money. Had he always known Joseph was the original thief, or did he figure it out after Tommy's remains were found? Although questions remained, Siobhán knew Joseph was the one and only killer. But he wasn't the only guilty party. Siobhán suspected that Rose Burns knew her son was a killer. Her behavior, however, had sent mixed messages.

She'd tried to take credit for taking Charlie out of the wildlife center, a fact that indicated she was protecting Joseph. On the other hand, Siobhán was pretty sure it was Rose who had dropped the falconer's glove and the shard of pottery into the pit, and she'd taken an empty petrol can from Sister Helen's shed to drop at the crime scene. Was she conflicted about what to do, and was her warped strategy to both protect and point fingers—then see if the guards could sort it out? Or had they all been attempts to create a smoke screen so that the guards would be so confused, the identity of the killer would remain in perpetual limbo?

Either way, Siobhán knew the only chance she had of getting Joseph to confess was to trick him into it—and in that case Rose might prove to be useful. Joseph thought he was in the clear. He did not yet know that Siobhán had visited the boys' home and learned his real age. But news traveled fast in a small town. How long before Joseph was tipped off and she lost her advantage? Instinct told her she was working with a matter of hours.

She was passing Liam's hardware shop when he called out to her.

"I'm in a hurry," she said. "Is it urgent?"

"I was asked to check my CCTV cameras for any suspicious activity following the discovery of that skeleton," Liam said.

"And?"

"I'm sending the tape over to the garda station. It's the footage from hours after you found the skeleton. Alan O'Leary."

This gave Siobhán pause. "What about Alan O'Leary?"

Liam shook his head. "Video shows him going through my rubbish bins the day before he died. I can't imagine why. Is it important?"

"Did he remove anything?"

"That's the strange bit. He was throwing something away. Hard to tell from the footage exactly what it was. But it was like he was trying to bury it deep in the rubbish."

"Thank you," Siobhán said. She wasn't sure what it meant, but she knew just who she was going to ask.

Like hawks returning again and again to circle over familiar areas, people were creatures of habit. This particular killer especially. He considered the O'Leary farm his home. He'd stayed to visit Tommy's grave because it gave him a thrill. Siobhán phoned Macdara and left a message detailing her theories. She headed back to the station. Even before entering, she knew something was up. Usually, a few guards would be hanging out in front of the building, having a smoke. Just as she was trying to convince herself they'd all given up the bad habit en masse, her mobile started pinging. She entered the station to ringing phones and harried clerks crisscrossing each other in the lobby.

"What's the story?" she said to the young garda at the front desk. He was a new recruit, fresh-faced and dimpled. Normally, she had to battle the urge to pinch his cheeks, but the panicked look on his face stopped that thought in its tracks.

"Garda O'Sullivan, we've been trying to reach you. It's chaos. First, we have the phone records in for Alan O'Leary." He slid a folder over to her. She opened it and looked at the line item detailing his last phone call. It was to a pub. The clerk waited for her to read it. "Garda Dabiri called the number. It was the pub where Tommy first made that special shot. The publican said Alan wanted to know the exact measurements of the angles."

"That's it?"

"Yes."

"Nothing about buying a snooker table?"

The guard shook his head. "Only wanted to know the exact angles—but to a precise degree. He wanted exact measurements."

When Alan finished that call, he left the house with a measuring tape. And went straight to the dairy barn. He'd pieced it together. He was going out to measure the pit for himself. If only he'd called the guards instead.

"What else?" Siobhán said.

"The Kilbane Wildlife Center has had a theft of at least five birds of prey, we've got a farmer saying he's had a litter of prizewinning baby rabbits stolen, and there's been a possible break-in at the arcade." He stopped to blow his curly fringe out of his eyes. "Detective Sergeant Flannery is on his way back from Dublin, and I think we've got it sorted. We've sent guards out to the farmer, and Garda Dabiri is checking on the arcade."

Hawks and baby rabbits. The arcade. Luring guards into it. What on earth was he planning? Somehow, he knew that they were onto him. Siobhán held up a finger and called Aretta's mobile. It went straight to voice mail. She sent a text: **Hide. On my way.** She waited for a reply, but there was none. Aretta may have already been separated from her phone.

"Redirect all gardai back to the station," she instructed. "Get Rose Burns in here now, no matter how you have to bring her in, and any and all trained falconers at the wildlife center. Do we still have that falconer's glove in evidence?"

The clerk's face was one of shock, but he was listening. "Yes. At least no evidence has been returned."

"I'm going to need that glove."

Siobhán had had only that sliver of experience at the wildlife center, and she was no expert, but she also couldn't leave Aretta in there, terrified, all on her own. Was Joseph planning on escaping while they conducted the rescue? That was her guess. Unless he just had to stay and watch the chaos, which was equally likely. Her mobile rang. *Macdara.*

She didn't even let him speak. "We've got a hostage situation at the arcade. Aretta is trapped in there with hawks and baby rabbits. Joseph is either using the time to escape, or he's in there watching what he hopes is a circus."

"What?" the clerk squeaked, even though Siobhán was speaking to Macdara.

"I'm on my way, but . . ." Macdara said, anguish evident in his voice.

"You won't be here in time. I know."

"I'll organize the teams. You go do what you have to do. Be careful."

Joseph had been watching the guards; that was the only explanation. He knew Macdara was in Dublin. He also knew Garda Dabiri would be a logical choice to check out the break-in, and given Siobhán O'Sullivan did not like coincidences, she was convinced he knew that Aretta had a major phobia of these birds. Being locked in a closed space like the arcade, with rabbits loose and hawks trapped inside, was bound to be a terrifying situation.

When the clerk returned with the glove, Siobhán tapped the three guards closest to her. "Does anyone have thick leather? Leather coats, leather bags—anything?"

"I'll check," the young clerk said.

"Good man. Gather all you can and meet us at the arcade. I'm also going to need the lock-picking set and our best lock picker."

Joseph was a planner. He was smart. He would have left an opening for Aretta to enter, but then he would have sealed it up. She pushed the thought of razor-sharp beaks and talons out of her mind as they took off for the arcade.

Chapter 33

The front windows of the old arcade had been completely boarded up. Siobhán had passed the arcade just yesterday, and the windows, dingy as they were, had not been boarded. The front door was impossible to break through, according to the lock picker. "There's definitely a chain on the other side of the door. It's going to take time to get what we need to see if we can break through it or the boards first."

She had a feeling all the other arcade entrances would be chained as well. "Upstairs," she said, suddenly remembering the flat above. "Get me in upstairs, and we're going to need a few materials."

The upstairs flat, just like the downstairs, had been vacant for years. It was easy to break into that door and gain entrance. Joseph was smart and a few steps ahead of them, but no man could be everywhere and think of everything. His kills had been accomplished using the element of surprise. It was a cowardly way to murder someone—from behind. This time he was trying to create the element of surprise. *Force it.* Siobhán could only hope Aretta was keeping her wits about her and that this experience wouldn't scar her further. As they worked on sawing through the floorboards along the edge of the far wall, Siobhán strained to listen for any sounds from below. If birds were flying about, looking for rabbits and feeling trapped themselves, how would the sound of the saw affect the dynamics? If anything, maybe it would startle them into retreat. Fury rose in her. Not only was he victimizing a garda, but he was also victimizing the birds and the rabbits. Nobody would want to feel trapped.

The screeching of the saw ended, and it wasn't long before she could hear the powerful thwack of wings. Siobhán stared into the hole they had just made, large enough for them to fit a ladder through. Once a ladder was in position, Siobhán swallowed and put on the falconer's glove. Experts from the wildlife center were on their way with more gloves and handlers and cages. But first she needed to get Aretta out of there and find out whether or not Joseph was on the premises.

She stared down into the arcade. A black hole stared back. The boarded windows were blocking out all the light. "Torch," she said. Soon a guard handed her a torch. Siobhán tested the ladder, then, gripping her torch, climbed down rung by rung, her legs shaking and her heart thumping in her chest. Five birds of prey had been stolen from the wildlife center, and the sound of panicked wings and screeches made for a terrifying symphony of panic. Nearby Siobhán heard the sound of heavy breathing and the faint tune of someone singing "Danny Boy." She did have a beautiful voice, but now was not the time for compliments.

"Aretta, it's Siobhán. I'm here." She waited, and just as she felt a presence hovering, she shone the light at a giant bird making a dive for her head. She screamed and ducked just in time to see the back of a white tail scamper under an old video game. Behind her, another three guards descended the ladder with torches in hand.

"You're surrounded by guards, Joseph," Siobhán said. "You can't win them all, can you?" She hoped to appeal to his gamesmanship.

"Over here," Aretta croaked.

Siobhán turned to the guards behind her. "Go." They hurried toward Aretta's voice.

Siobhán heard a little squeak and saw a rabbit shivering a few feet away. A familiar *woosh, woosh, woosh* sounded, and Siobhán had to act quick. She shone the torch as best she could on the falconer's glove and held her arm out straight. "Charlie," she said, having no clue which one Charlie was. It was one thing holding out her arm in the middle of a field, with an instructor nearby. It was another in this abandoned arcade center. She felt and heard the creature's approach, and as it drew closer, she could see a baby rabbit struggling in the grips of its powerful beak. "Here," Siobhán said. "Land." It circled, its head tilted, an intense eye on her fist. "Land," she said with more conviction than she felt. She raised her fist a little. "Here." The bird swooped down, and soon she felt its heavy weight descend on her fist, pushing it down, its claws tightening and gripping the glove. She held her breath and felt a surge of adrenaline. The baby rabbit was alive and squealing. Siobhán didn't often pray, especially at work, but she called on the heavens now, first asking that her thumping heart wouldn't burst out of her chest. The bird cocked its head, making the baby rabbit squirm more.

Siobhán hadn't a clue what she was supposed to do. *Think of him as an enormous version of Trigger. With wings. And talons and a sharp beak.* She held out her other hand underneath the baby rabbit, her fingers shaking from fear. "Drop it," she said, mustering up an authoritative tone. She said it once more, louder, and soon she felt a soft body fall into her hand. She cupped it protectively around the rabbit without squeezing too hard.

"The handlers are here," she heard a guard call out.

"Aretta?"

"Safe. We're taking her to the hospital. She may need a sedative."

Siobhán held out the hand with the bunny. "Can someone approach on me right—slowly—and take this wee rabbit out of my hand?"

The guard stepped up and gently removed the bunny. Her arm, still held out with the bird on it, was growing tired and shaking. She took a deep breath, willing herself to stay calm. "Any sign of Joseph?"

"Not so far, but this is a big place."

"Keep looking. But he may already be on the road, so let's think of all his paths out of town and see if we can get guards in neighboring towns to be on the lookout." It was the right call to make, but she couldn't shake the feeling that Joseph was here. Hiding somewhere in the dark, like he'd always done, lying in wait. "Any luck on contacting the electric company?"

"They're working on getting the lights on," another guard said. She could hear the sounds of people descending the ladder.

"Handlers," a guard called out. "And we've got all the kittens safe and sound."

"Kittens?"

The guard chuckled. "Baby rabbits, Garda. They're called kittens."

"I have a bird here," Siobhán said. "There are four more loose, and we need a cage for this big boy." She looked at it. "Or girl." Now that the bird was up close, she could see an unfamiliar white stripe. It wasn't Charlie. She was amazed how well trained they all were.

Siobhán wasn't thrilled with having this many people locked in with a killer, but there was no other recourse. A handler stepped to her left, gloved hand outstretched, and rang a little bell. Calmer now, the bird lifted off Siobhán with ease and moved to the handler's fist. Soon it was caged and being taken out. When it was announced that all the birds of prey were in cages and the handlers were safely out of the arcade, Siobhán called out.

"The scene is safe. The birds are safe. The kittens are safe. Aretta is safe. Do you hear me, Joseph? You won't be able to hide in the dark. There's nowhere you can go now. We're going to find you."

A guard approached. "Your guest is here."

"Bring her down."

Moments later, Rose approached, her face shadowy under the light of a torch. "I didn't know for sure," Rose said, shaking her head.

"You knew," Siobhán said. "You covered for Joseph at the wildlife center. You returned an empty can of petrol to the crime scene. You threw a shard of pottery and the bell from his bicycle at the crime scene. But you also threw in your falconer's glove. Half the things you did pointed to Joseph as the culprit, but what I don't quite understand is why the other half pointed to you." She also made a veiled confession to Father Kearney. But Siobhán would not betray the confidence of the parish priest and kept this to herself.

"I was his mother. What was I supposed to do? I couldn't just turn him in."

"Why throw suspicion onto yourself?"

"I thought it would look odd if all the clues pointed to Joseph. And if you wanted to nab me for it—I was ready to pay the price."

"That's a huge price to pay for two murders you didn't commit."

"That doesn't mean I was innocent. I indulged Tommy's flirtations."

"There must be more to it."

A sob escaped from Rose. "I said yes, okay? I told Tommy I would run away with him. I was supposed to meet him that morning in the dairy barn, and I was going to leave Joseph with Benji."

"But Tommy was wearing his tux that morning."

"And?"

"And that suggests he was indeed going to marry Gladys."

Rose sniffed and straightened her spine. "Because I changed my mind."

"Why?"

"I had just said yes to Tommy when I heard a noise and turned around to see Joseph running away. I knew he'd heard everything—and it snapped me out of the insanity. I knew I couldn't do it. I ran after Joseph. I told him I had changed my mind. I swore to him I'd be his mother. I begged and pleaded until he forgave me. At least I thought he did. I can't believe I even considered abandoning my own son." Tears welled in her eyes, and Rose shook her head. "He was such a wee thing. You should have seen how lads picked on him."

"What we need to do now is make sure this ends peacefully."

"What can I do?"

"Ask him to come out with his hands up, walk slowly toward me."

"Joseph," Rose called into the dark. "Please. You need to come out with your hands up."

"You betrayed me." It was the voice of a bitter man. It came from somewhere nearby. Somewhere above them. "I had it all worked out, Mother."

"No, Joseph, you didn't," Rose said.

"I did! I switched their wedding date to coincide with Gladys and Tommy's. Don't tell me that didn't throw them for a loop. Why look at us when there's a jilted bride and an aggrieved best man to finger for the murder? Then I got that menace James O'Sullivan out of the barn using Charlie. There wasn't time to move the skeleton, because someone decided to cancel her wedding and made it to the barn too soon. But at least I made sure there were plenty of other suspects! The guards believed me when I said I was only five years of age at the time of the murder. It was working. And yet you had to ruin it."

"Because you killed again!" Rose cried out.

Siobhán turned to Rose. "When did you know that Joseph killed Tommy?"

Rose closed her eyes briefly. "A few months after Tommy disappeared. I truly thought he disappeared—I thought when I changed my mind about running off with him that he decided to go it alone."

"You turned him down only because I overheard you!" Joseph's anguished voice ricocheted through the cavernous space.

"You're not wrong." Rose turned to Siobhán. "In the months after Tommy was gone, I noticed Joseph was suddenly going into the dairy barn."

"A place he used to be afraid to enter," Siobhán said.

Rose nodded. "I saw him dragging branches into the barn. I followed. He was throwing them into the pit. I didn't really see the harm in it, but when I questioned him . . . he just came out with it."

"You were supposed to help me!" Joseph yelled.

"I did. I did help you."

"Only to give it all up now? What was the point?" At least Joseph was talking.

Rose ignored him and continued to speak to Siobhán. "He lied. He told me Tommy had chased him into the barn the morning of the wedding. He said he hid and then jumped out to scare him. That Tommy then toppled into the pit, cracking his head on the corner." Rose put her hand over her mouth and shook her head. "It sounded plausible—a terrible, terrible accident. Tommy was a prankster. I could see him chasing Joseph around the barn. And there was nothing I could do for Tommy. It was too late. He was deader than dead."

"Why didn't you call the guards?" Siobhán asked. "If you believed it was an accident?"

"I was worried *they* wouldn't believe him. Joseph was a bit wild. I didn't want him locked away in an institution. Not when he was finally free of one. I thought it was my fault. I'm the one who encouraged Tommy's flirtations. What if the guards heard that I was going to run away with him? What if they thought I pushed him into the pit in a jealous rage? I was paranoid. I was scared. He was dead—there was nothing I could do to bring him back. What was I to do? I became obsessed with the thought that Joseph would be taken away from us. I assumed someone else would find the body. I started bringing the birds out to train, so we could keep an eye on the barn. I was more surprised than anyone that no one else ever discovered his remains." She swallowed. "Until your brother did."

"And just like that you betray me," Joseph said. This time his voice was deep and cold.

"I thought Tommy was an accident. You were only a child. It had to be an accident. But then you killed again. I couldn't cover for you again. I just couldn't. How could you do it again?"

"Alan O'Leary had it coming. When the guards found Tommy's remains, Alan figured out it was me."

"It *was* you!"

"How did Alan figure it out?" Siobhán was genuinely curious. "Was it because of Tommy's snooker shot? Did he go out to the barn to measure the pit?"

The sound of one person clapping loudly jarred Siobhán. "Well done, Garda," he said.

"Did Alan confront you?"

"He suspected all along," Joseph said. "Looked at me sideways the day of the wedding. Asked me what I was doing in the dairy barn. I called him a Peeping Tom. That shut him up. Or maybe it was only the satchel of money that shut him up. I'd stashed it under his bed, because that's where I slept that night. Never intended for him to get his greedy paws on it." Joseph made a guttural noise. "Remember Alan was the one who wrote the note. *Sorry. Goodbye.* I realized it was game over if anyone found me with the money. I decided to leave it under Alan's bed. I half expected him to tell the guards. For a while I dreamed that if the guards found Tommy's bones, they'd think Alan was the killer. He fooled himself all these years that Tommy left that money to Gladys out of guilt. A parting gift. *Save the family farm!*"

"And then what?" Siobhán said. "Did he confront you after Tommy's remains were found?"

"He didn't say a word to my face," Joseph said. "But I heard him on the phone. Talking to someone about Tommy's famous snooker shot. He thought he was so smart, figuring out that the angles I used to kill Tommy were one and the same. After the phone call I saw Alan sneak into the dairy barn with a measuring tape. He was going to be a hero, unmask the killer! What an eejit. I knew he'd visit the barn again. He was that type of man.

Very measured—no pun intended. I waited for him the next morning. Creature of habit. This time I gave him the exact scenario. Placed another shiny gold token at the corner of the pit. He fell for it! People can't help themselves. It's insane. He approached the token and stood in the exact same spot, mesmerized by it. I was hiding in the corner. To be honest, I hadn't quite decided what I was going to do about it. But then, there he was. He didn't even sense me behind him. It was like he was begging me to do it. He wanted to see the angles. I'll tell ye, boyo, he saw them up close and personal!"

"We didn't find a measuring tape on Alan or in the pit," Siobhán said.

"Do you take me for a fool?" Joseph said. "I took it off him."

Rose buried her head in her hands. "Joseph," she wailed. "How could you?" Her shoulders heaved with sobs.

"You're to blame, Mother. You had to throw the falconer's glove and the pottery and the bell into the crime scene? The petrol can? You're not my mother. You never were."

"Surrender is your only option," Siobhán said. "We're not leaving, and this building is surrounded. You need to come out with your hands up."

"Maybe I'll just jump. Roll the dice."

Jump? Siobhán shone her torch upward and swept the area. Soon other torches joined her.

"There," a male guard said, and all lights swiveled in his torch's direction.

Joseph was wrapped around one of the decorative columns. Back in the day the arcade had featured several Greek-style columns around the periphery, a whimsical touch inspired by Las Vegas glitz. Siobhán had never seen anyone climb one before. He was far enough up the column that a tumble could well kill him. Especially if he hit his head on something at the right angle.

"You're very clever, Joseph," Siobhán said.

"Flattery?" he laughed. "Do you take me for a fool, Garda O'Sullivan?"

"Very much the opposite," Siobhán said. "I think you're very smart. I think you almost got away with it, and right now you're trying to distract us while you figure out if you have any options left."

"Is that what I'm doing?" Joseph tried to sound confident, but his voice wobbled.

"You're a grown man climbing a column in an abandoned arcade, while your mammy is pleading with you to turn yourself in," Siobhán said. "I'd call that a bit desperate." He wasn't the only one trying out new techniques. Flattery hadn't worked on him; like it or not, it was time to try humiliation.

"She's not really my mother," Joseph said.

"Joseph," Rose said. "After all I've sacrificed for you?"

"For me? You were going to run away with Tommy!"

A sob broke from Rose. "I didn't do it. I stayed. For you."

"Then betrayed me."

"I changed my mind!"

"For how long?" Joseph said. His voice was bitter.

"What do you mean?" Rose's voice was full of grief.

"You would have run off with him eventually," Joseph said. "I saved you from him. I brought Gladys and Benji together. I saved the O'Leary farm. And now I'm the one being punished?"

I saved the O'Leary farm. "You said Alan figured out you killed Tommy," Siobhán said. "How did he figure it out?" She needed to keep him talking, keep him distracted. "Did you mess up?"

"No! I didn't mess up! He figured it out because I took the satchel of money. I stole it from Howard's ceiling. Eejit didn't even realize I saw everything. That night I had hidden the satchel of money under Alan's bed. That's where I slept the night of the wedding. I hadn't figured out where to hide it, and to be honest, I liked looking at the money. Early the next morning I took the satchel to the dairy barn, thinking I could hide it there. Tommy was out by the barn in his tux. Smoking and pacing. He didn't see me. I had a shined-up arcade token in my pocket. I remembered the angles of the pit. I placed the token at just the right spot. Honestly, I didn't think he'd die. I thought I'd just push him in and run. Tommy saw the light in the slatted shed come on, and the game was on. He saw the shiny coin. Walked right over to it and stood looking at it. Had no clue I was right behind him. Corner pocket. And then I just gave a little shove at the right angle. That was it. I couldn't believe how fast he toppled over." An excited laugh escaped Joseph.

That was what Alan had been doing in Liam's rubbish bins. He must have held on to the satchel and decided he'd better throw it out. If he'd only told the guards about Joseph and the money. If he had only trusted them to do their jobs.

"You're a monster," Rose said softly.

Joseph continued to babble. He'd bottled up his secret for so long, but now the dam was broken, and the water was gushing out. "After I pushed Tommy into the pit, I went back to the bedroom with the satchel. I didn't even know Alan was home. He came in and saw me with the cash. I panicked. I told him Tommy had given it to me with a message. That he was sorry, but he was ditching Gladys and splitting town. I told him Tommy wanted Alan to have the money to save the family farm. As an apology to Gladys, like. Because he felt bad, you know? For leaving Gladys. He believed me! You should have seen his eyes pop out at all that cash. The fool. By the time he had his grubby hands on it, there was nothing I could do. He was convinced Tommy did a runner, and I was smart enough to know letting him keep the money was better than going to prison for the rest of me life for murder."

"I didn't know he had this kind of darkness in him," Rose said. "With Tommy's murder—he was just a child—I blamed myself, convinced myself it was just a horrible, horrible accident. But once Alan was found dead . . ." Rose sobbed again.

"You're the one who said we had to cover up the pit and never tell anyone," Joseph said. "You're an accomplice."

"Indeed," Rose said. "I deserve to be punished." She turned to Siobhán. "I helped cover Tommy up only because it was too late. Don't you see? There was nothing I could do to save him. But I could save my son. Or so I thought."

"Hey!" Joseph yelled. There was now a guard climbing up the column and one descending from above.

"You're not the only one who can play the distraction game," Siobhán said.

An electrical whine sounded, and the lights began to flicker. Soon the space was bright and clear. Joseph stood in handcuffs at the base of the column, a look of rage plastered on his handsome face.

"Joseph Burns, you are being arrested. You do not have to say anything if you do not wish. However, anything you say may be used as evidence against you . . ."

Chapter 34

The second time around, wedding preparations ran smoother. Siobhán had even convinced Gráinne to lighten up on the make-up, and this time her hair flowed down, crowned by the tiara sans the pins. And by the time Siobhán was at the end of the aisle, with James by her side to "give her away," and the wedding march began to play, Siobhán had forgotten to be nervous. Instead, she beamed at everyone as she passed, and they beamed back, even her mother-in-law to be. But once she locked eyes with Macdara, that was where her gaze remained. All through the hymn and Father Kearney's opening prayer, and then it was on to the vows, and before she knew what was happening, she heard Macdara say, "I do," and then she said, "I do," and he was kissing her, and she was kissing him, and there was clapping and cheering, and just like that, they were husband and wife.

Down the aisle they went again, out the doors of the church. Given the recent incident at the arcade, they'd sent all the birdseed they'd planned on folks throwing to the wildlife center, and instead their guests waved happy little sparklers. Soon Himself and Herself were leading a procession of folks through town to the abbey. She walked hand in hand with Macdara. Nearly every shopkeeper who had been unable to attend the second time around was out on their footpaths, waving little sparklers. Siobhán bit back tears of joy as they waved at Oran and Padraig in the bookshop, Chris Gordon standing in front of his comic shop, Liam waving from down at the hardware shop, and Sheila and Pio in front of the beauty shop. There Pio treated them to a few minutes on fiddle, and to everyone's surprise, Ciarán immediately lifted his violin from his case and played along. Everyone clapped. Overhead there was a cry, and Siobhán and Macdara lifted their heads to see a hawk slowly circling above, gliding with his massive wings spread.

"That's good luck," Dara said before planting a kiss on her.

"Only if his droppings fall on you," Siobhán said.

The abbey was even dreamier than usual. White lights and beautiful gauze and perfect white roses adorned the entryways and nooks and crannies of their treasured ruined monastery. A full trad band was set up in the field across from an enormous banquet-style feed. Champagne bottles popped and fizzed as glasses were passed around, and the music began. Macdara disappeared for a moment, and when he returned, he was with her brood. They stood in a semicircle as Macdara cleared his throat.

"I love every one of you, and I'm here to add to this pack, not take Siobhán away from you." His voice wobbled, but before he could continue, he was thrown off-kilter by the hearty laughter of the O'Sullivans.

"We know that, ya big eejit," Gráinne said, landing a punch to his arm.

"You're already part of the pack," Ciarán said.

Ann held up Trigger, who was sporting an emerald bowtie. "Hear that, Trigger? We've got one more mouth to feed."

Trigger yapped and everyone laughed.

"I'm sorry I interrupted your first wedding," James said, lifting a flute of champagne. "But this has been a spectacular day."

"Hear! Hear!" was toasted all around.

"We're all going back to the farm after the reception," Siobhán said. "I want you to see the house."

"Our house," Macdara said. "Everyone's house."

"It will be nice to have a getaway," Gráinne said. "But we have some news too."

"The new bistro owner doesn't want to live in the flat above, so we'll be keeping our rooms," James said. "For now."

Siobhán glanced at Eoin. "Does that include you?"

He smiled. "Depends. We'll talk about it later. At the farm."

Macdara grabbed Siobhán's hand. "Later," Macdara said. "Right now I want to dance with my gorgeous wife."

"And then we'll cut the cake," Siobhán said. It was an exact replica of the first: three white tiers dotted with emerald shamrocks and topped with a porcelain claddagh symbol. *Gorgeous.*

"Cake," Macdara said, taking her hand. "Now you're talking my love language."

The sunset was made for lovers. For the millionth time today, tears welled in Siobhán's eyes as she stood on the hill and looked out over their land. *Their land.* She wanted to say that it didn't feel real, but Gráinne was just to her left, and she didn't need another pinch to the back of the arm. Gift baskets and flowers adorned the front porch. Their neighbors and friends had been more than generous. Siobhán turned to Eoin.

"I can't take it anymore. What is this big idea you want to share?"

Eoin laughed. He cleared his throat. "It's just an idea, and I swear, if you say no, I'll find another spot." He turned to the remains of the dairy barn. "I know you're thinking about taking it down, especially after the fire, but I'd like to rebuild instead."

"You want to be a dairy farmer?" Gráinne said.

"No. I want to run a farm-to-table restaurant," Eoin said. "I want to source all the food from local farmers. I want community-style seating, I want new and changing menus of local and global cuisines, I want artists to fill the space with their works, I want trad bands to play at night, I want the town book clubs to meet in the gardens, and I want—"

"Yes," Siobhán said. "Yes, yes, yes, yes, yes."

"How on earth would you pay for all that?" Gráinne asked.

"The new bistro owner had to settle with us. There's a payout," Eoin said. "I think I can make it work."

"There's also the insurance money from the fire," Macdara said.

"And I can help with the build," James said. "Help you keep the cost down."

Siobhán turned to Ann and Ciarán. "What do you think?"

Ciarán was grinning. "Can I play my fiddle?"

"Absolutely," Siobhán said. "I would be delighted." And she meant it.

"I love it," Ann said.

"Are you sure?" Eoin said. "Because having a restaurant on your property . . . Well, it wouldn't be the quiet farm life you were envisioning."

"I've never been so happy to hear something in my entire life," Siobhán said. "A peaceful life would drive me mad."

Macdara laughed, a low rumble that lasted a long time. "A farm-to-table restaurant it is."

"I want to help," Ann said. "I want to be involved."

"You're all going to be involved," Eoin said. "It's a family venture."

Macdara held up another bottle of champagne, one he'd been saving just for them. He had a glint in his eye. He looked at the bottle. "Shall I?"

"Whatever it is—yes," Siobhán said.

He shook the bottle. "Squeeze in," he said. The

O'Sullivans squeezed in. Macdara popped the cork, and the bottle erupted in a fountain-like spray, little droplets falling on them. "To new and bigger adventures ahead," he said. "To family."

"Are you Mrs. Flannery now?" James asked.

"We're both O'Sullivan-Flannery," Siobhán said, breaking the news.

"I told you I'm part of the pack," Macdara said with a wink.

"But at work I'm still an O'Sullivan."

Glasses were raised as the orange glow of the sky bathed them in its ethereal light. "To family," they chorused.

Siobhán and Macdara wandered a few steps away, and he pulled her in for a deep kiss. He pulled away and gently ran his finger along her jawline.

"Happy five-hour anniversary, wife," he said. "I'm the luckiest man alive."

"Happy five-hour anniversary, husband," she said, pinching his gorgeous cheeks. "You sure are."

EASY-PEASY CHOCOLATE ECLAIRS

Choux Pastry:

4.2 ounces milk
4.2 ounces water
½ cup unsalted butter
1 teaspoon granulated sugar
½ teaspoon salt
1 cup all-purpose flour
3 large eggs

Vanilla Cream:

1 cup cream
1 tablespoon granulated sugar
½ teaspoon vanilla extract
½ cup plain yogurt

Chocolate Glaze:

1 cup chopped dark chocolate
1 cup cream
1½ tablespoons unsalted butter
Pinch of salt

CHOUX PASTRY

Preheat the oven to 180. Line two baking trays with parchment paper.

In a medium saucepan combine the milk, water, butter, sugar, and salt. Cook over medium heat, stirring occasionally, until the butter has melted and the mixture just comes to a boil. Remove from the heat.

Add the flour to the milk mixture and mix it in with a wooden spoon until incorporated. Place the saucepan back on the heat and mix with the wooden spoon until you have a smooth ball that comes away easily from the sides of the saucepan.

Place the dough into the bowl of a stand mixer and, using beater attachments, mix for 2 to 3 minutes, or until the dough cools down.

Add the eggs one at a time and mix thoroughly after each addition. The dough should form a paste.

Place the paste in a piping bag with a plain or a large star nozzle. Holding the piping bag at a 45-degree angle, pipe 4-inch strips of the paste onto the prepared baking trays, leaving 2 inches between each.

Bake at 180 for 10 minutes. Then reduce the heat to 160 and bake for an additional 20 minutes, or until the pastries are golden brown.

Remove the pastries from the oven and prick each with a skewer to release the heat. Cool on a wire rack. Once they have cooled, make two holes in the bottom of each with a piping nozzle.

VANILLA CREAM

Combine the cream, sugar, and vanilla in a medium bowl and beat with a whisk until soft peaks form. Fold in the yogurt. Fill a piping bag with the vanilla cream and place it in the refrigerator to chill.

CHOCOLATE GLAZE

Place the chocolate in a medium bowl.

Combine the cream, butter, and salt in a small saucepan. Bring just to a boil, stirring, over medium heat. Pour the hot cream over the chocolate and whisk until the chocolate has melted completely. Keep the glaze warm and set aside.

ASSEMBLY

Assemble the eclairs by piping vanilla cream into each pastry. Dip the filled eclairs in the chocolate glaze and shake off the excess. Place on a wire rack and allow the glaze to set.

The picturesque village of Kilbane in County Cork, Ireland, is the perfect backdrop for a baking contest—until someone serves up a show-stopping murder that only Garda Siobhán O'Sullivan can solve.

In Kilbane, opinions are plentiful and rarely in alignment. But there's one thing everyone does agree on—the bakery in the old flour mill, just outside town, is the best in County Cork, well worth the short drive and the long lines. No wonder they're about to be featured on a reality baking show.

All six contestants in the show are coming to Kilbane to participate, and the town is simmering with excitement. Aside from munching on free samples, the locals—including Siobhán—get a chance to appear in the opening shots. As for the competitors themselves, not all are as sweet as their confections. There are shenanigans on the first day of filming that put everyone on edge, but that's nothing compared to day two, when the first round ends and the top contestant is found facedown in her signature pie.

The producers decide to continue filming while Siobhán and her husband, Garda Macdara Flannery, sift through the suspects. Was this a case of rivalry turned lethal, or are there other motives hidden in the mix? And can they uncover the truth before another baker is eliminated—permanently . . .

Please turn the page for an exciting sneak peek of

Carlene O'Connor's next Irish Village mystery

MURDER IN AN IRISH BAKERY

coming soon wherever print and e-books are sold!

Chapter 1

❧❦❧

"Stop the show. Sugar kills! Stop the show! Sugar kills!" The thirty-something outraged lad paced in front of *Pie Pie Love*, Kilbane's best bakery housed in a historic flour mill. He was tall and handsome, if you ignored the vitriol pouring out of his gob. In addition to the passion he was bringing to the task, he seemed dressed for the part of a protestor: denims, a t-shirt with the word SUGAR overlaid with a skull and crossbones, and a flannel shirt to protect against a mercurial Spring. The limestone mill was set back in a vibrant field next to the Kilbane River. Unfortunately, no matter how loud the river babbled, the magnificent 9-meter cast iron waterwheel mounted to the side of the building remained immobile, and the river simply meandered around it instead of powering it up. The mill was built between 1850 and 1870 and Garda Siobhán O'Sullivan had read somewhere that the original wheel had been wooden. Despite the switch to cast iron, it hadn't churned for as long as Siobhán had been alive, nearly thirty years, and the bakery sourced its flour elsewhere.

Siobhán didn't know the cost of repairing such a structure, but she knew, the waterwheel notwithstanding, that the family-owned mill was in dire need of basic repairs. The O'Farrell family had operated this flour mill and now-bakery for several generations. Fia O'Farrell was the last living member, and given she was single and past middle-age, many wondered what she envisioned for its future. The back room which used to house events, and the Ground, Middle, and Top Floor of the mill which used to be open for tours, had all been closed to the public for over a decade. But it was still a gorgeous structure, and the bakery, which was housed in the very front portion of the building, was as cheerful inside as it was out. Siobhán took in the outdoor tables with colorful umbrellas, flowers beaming from planters along the front of the building, and the banner above the wooden doors that read: *Welcome Irish Bakers!*

It was going to be a good day for *Pie Pie, Love* not to mention all of Kilbane, and she for one was ready for the festivities to begin.

"Join the health revolution. Sugar is not your friend!" the lad bellowed.

Neither is noise-pollution before coffee, Siobhán thought, but she kept her pie-hole shut. She needed to remain calm which was why she was actively ignoring him while studying the building. Perhaps he would grow tired of screaming into the abyss. Why hadn't he waited until the crowd was allowed in, or was he simply rehearsing for that very moment?

Garda Aretta Dabiri sidled up next to Siobhán, throwing a worried glance at the protestor. "What are you looking at?" she asked. Aretta was the most recent addition to the Kilbane Gardai. She was a petite woman with gorgeous dark skin, a calm presence, and a strong drive to excel. Her family was originally from Nigeria, her father had emigrated to Ireland, and she was born here. She was the first female garda of African descent and a fantastic addition to the team. Siobhán's brother Eoin had a little crush on her, and although Siobhán got the feeling it was mutual, the pair had yet to do anything other than wear out smiles around each other. "You seem fascinated with the wheel," Aretta remarked.

"This was always my favorite place to come as a young one," Siobhán said. "Each time I asked my Da if he could make the wheel turn."

"Did he?"

Siobhán laughed. "He would pretend to blow on it, and meself and James would try to blow on it, and then Da would scratch his head as if he were puzzled and say, 'I thought for sure the pair of ye were filled with hot air'." She laughed at the memory then shook her head. "It's been stuck for ages."

"Nice memories, but it's a pity the wheel is stuck."

Siobhán nodded. "Perhaps the proceeds from the bake-off will change all of that." Historic structures came with historic maintenance which came with historic price tags. Siobhán often thought if

she ever owned a gorgeous flour mill the first thing
she would do was get the wheel churning again.
Siobhán turned to Aretta and grinned. "Because
this week is not about wheels, this week is all about
the *meals*."

Aretta smiled. She had copped-on. "The end of
the meal to be exact?"

"Bang-on," Siobhán said. "Dessert. The part that
everyone *savors* for last." Aretta laughed and shook
her head. Having a sugar addiction was something
that Garda Aretta Dabiri did not suffer from.
Siobhán on the other hand was already drooling.
*Pies, biscuits, trifles, tarts, puddings, cookies, cakes, and
breads. Oh my!* This was shaping up to be the best
work assignment of Siobhán's life. And she and her
giant sweet tooth intended to thoroughly enjoy
every minute of it. The top Irish bakers in all of
Ireland would soon gather here for one week to
show off their massive baking skills. Even the famous Aoife McBride had somehow been coaxed
to compete. Siobhán's late mam had owned every
single cookbook written by Aoife McBride, starting
with *Aoife McBride Takes the Cake* and she went on
from there, also taking the: *Pies, Tarts, Cookies, Puddings, and Breads.* There were at least a dozen of
them. Aoife McBride had been a one-woman-
enterprise going full steam. But the last year, she'd
gone quiet, and rumors swirled about her mental
health. Given she lived all the way up in Donegal,
the northernmost county in the west of Ireland,
Siobhán was cautious to believe anything she'd
been hearing. Gossip distorts as it travels, everyone knows that.

Even so, the story was that Aoife McBride had

unraveled when a fan group of look-alikes descended on Donegal a few months ago to pay her tribute. They dressed in her signature colorful aprons and wigs with thick black hair striped with white, padded their figures, and donned pink-rimmed eyeglasses. Instead of being flattered it was said that Aoife McBride was driven mad by the attention. Apparently she'd accused one of them of stalking her, and for several months no one had seen or heard from her. Her fans breathed a sigh of relief when this bake-off enticed her back into the public eye. Siobhán was very much looking forward to meeting her, and if it wasn't too much trouble, asking her to sign at least one of her mam's books.

Siobhán had no time to bake apart from her famous brown bread. Perhaps this week would inspire her to do more. The bakery needed this, and the town needed this, and she needed this. Only Macdara Flannery, aka her *husband* (Husband!), would have enjoyed it more, but alas work meetings had taken him to Dublin. It was impossible to believe that next month would be their first wedding anniversary.

"Stop the show. Sugar kills!"

The booming voice showed no signs of strain. "The lungs on him," Siobhán said.

"He certainly can project his voice," Aretta agreed.

The man brandished a stalk of celery like a weapon and stared at one spot on the building as if he was speaking to an invisible camera. Somewhere, there was a cameraman around, as well as a director, but Siobhán had yet to meet them.

The door to the bakery opened and Fia O'Farrell emerged without so much as a donut in hand. She was a petite woman with gorgeous silver hair wound up in a tight bun. She wore a cheerful pink top and a cream-colored apron that read: ALL YOU KNEAD IS LOVE. Love was crossed out and above it read: DOUGH.

She put her hands on her hips and glared at the protestor. "You're not supposed to be here. If you don't leave, the guards are going to arrest you." She pointed to Siobhán and Aretta as if their blue suits and navy blue caps with the gold shield had not sufficiently identified them as members of An Garda Siochana. *The Guardians of the Peace.* There was little peace to be found at the moment. Siobhán would have preferred the assignment in plainclothes, but it was eejits like the one in front of them that made that request an impossible one to get approved.

"Do take a rest," Siobhán said to the man. "You'll wear your voice out before your audience arrives."

The comment gave him pause. Perhaps he was capable of listening to reason.

"A rest?" Fia hissed. "Are you joking me?"

"Where is the director and cameraman?" Siobhán asked. It was a two-person crew, which seemed awfully small for a week-long production, but the bake-off was being independently financed by an anonymous benefactor and perhaps a larger crew wasn't in the budget.

"Unloading their equipment," Fia said with a nod to the car park in the back of the building. It would soon be jammers and attendants would be on hand to direct cars to park in the field. The venue could hold a hundred persons in the front section of the bakery, with another hundred outside. The show would be streamed onto screens on the side of the building as well as the interior, and heat lamps had been set up outdoors for those stuck outside when the sun went down. And of course, workers would circulate amongst both crowds with pastries available for purchase, not to mention samples from the guest bakers.

Samples! Siobhán, who had been looking forward to this sweet, sweet assignment, literally hearing eggs crack in her sleep, and dreaming of flour sifting through her hands, was put on her back foot by the protestor. She heard a mechanical squeak and whirled around to see him holding a bullhorn. "Sugar kills," he blasted out.

Brutal. Siobhán approached. "Enough. You are disturbing the peace."

"There's no peace in diabetes now is there?" he replied.

"Everything in moderation," Siobhán said. "Including your temper tantrum."

His eyes narrowed into slits as he dropped the bullhorn to his side. "It's my right to protest."

"Then quietly carry a sign, will ya? Whisper your message to the world."

He frowned as if trying to suss out whether or not she was messing with him. "I don't have a sign."

"Now. There's your trouble. You can't pull off a good protest without a sign, now can you? That would be like me coming to work without me baton." Siobhán patted the large stick attached to her side. He eyed it. "Perhaps you should go make one and come back."

"A stick?"

"A sign."

"Right, so."

"That'll show us you mean business."

"You're just trying to chuck me out."

"If you think you can compete with the smells and sounds of a bakery *without* a colorful sign . . ." Siobhán stopped talking and shook her head. "*Amateur.*"

His mouth dropped open and he began looking around, as if contemplating his next move. To Siobhán's great shock, he began to stride away, taking his bullhorn with him. Before she could completely relax, he lifted it to his mouth once more. "I'll be back with me sign."

Not if she could do anything about it. As she watched him skulk away Siobhán waited for the tension in her body to ease, but she remained on high alert. "Thank heavens," Fia said. "Brilliant, Garda. C'mere to me. Whatever you did there, I applaud you."

"I don't think we've seen the last of him," Siobhán admitted. She needed caffeine, and sugar stat. She'd forgone her morning brekkie, convinced there would be coffee and delectables provided as soon as she arrived. Her husband (Husband!) liked to joke that no one should ever let Siobhán O'Sullivan get hangry. "That's why your initials are SOS," Macdara often said. "When Siobhán O'Sullivan needs to eat it's an SOS!" Technically, she was Siobhán O'Sullivan-Flannery now, but not at work.

At work she would continue to go by O'Sullivan.
And amongst her family and friends. No use getting them all confused when she'd been O'Sullivan for thirty years now was there? And didn't
Siobhán O'Sullivan sound so much nicer than Siobhán Flannery? And despite being on the fence
about the name, at least she loved the husband.
Thinking about Macdara made her wish he was
here, he would have been just as eager for pastries
as she was.

Siobhán leaned closer to Aretta. "She's going to
offer us pastries soon, isn't she?"

"Sugar kills," Aretta said deadpan.

"Then kill me," Siobhán said. "Kill me right now."

Visit our website at
KensingtonBooks.com
to sign up for our newsletters, read
more from your favorite authors, see
books by series, view reading group
guides, and more!

Become a Part of Our
Between the Chapters Book Club
Community and Join the Conversation